"HERE IS AN HONEST-TO-GOODNESS PIECE OF STORYTELLING"*

"There is not one cardboard face [among the characters] and their language and actions during the high-pitched scenes they become involved in always seems reasonable.

Mr. Cunningham has a vivid and intelligent style, and it is unlikely that anyone who starts to read this book will be willing to put it down."

—*The New Yorker**

"IT IS PACKED WITH NIP-AND-TUCK BATTLES on the plains of Montana during the 1880s . . . Mr. Cunningham wrote the story on which *High Noon* was based, and with *WARHORSE* he turns in another robust performance."

—*Saturday Review*

"Cunningham is the only other author I've come across who works within the character's minds as I try to do. Only he does it much better because he reveals the private passion as well as calculation. . . . Cunningham knows that secret power of the novel and uses it beautifully, not only to follow rational thought in characters, but also their private feelings, despair, triumph, indecision."

—Richard S. Wheeler

"Thirty-five years ago I was inspired by John Cunningham's *WARHORSE* and I remember it as one of the best westerns I've ever read. . . . Cunningham is a marvelous storyteller with a voice all his own: a classic stylist who laces his prose with wry humor and makes it fun."

—Elmore Leonard

Tor books by
John Cunningham

The Rainbow Runner
Starfall
Warhorse

WARHORSE

JOHN CUNNINGHAM

A TOM DOHERTY ASSOCIATES BOOK
NEW YORK

This is a work of fiction. All the characters and events portrayed in this book are fictitious, and any resemblance to real people or events is purely coincidental.

WARHORSE

Copyright © 1956, 1984 by John Cunningham

A Tor Book
Published by Tom Doherty Associates, Inc.
175 Fifth Avenue
New York, N.Y. 10010

Tor ® is a registered trademark of Tom Doherty Associates, Inc.

ISBN: 0-812-51360-6
Library of Congress Catalog Card Number: 56-7296

First Tor edition: May 1992

Printed in the United States of America

0 9 8 7 6 5 4 3 2 1

WARHORSE

PART ONE

CHAPTER ONE

The brim of Tucker's hat cut out the sky, a black shield against the immense, pale-blue desolation up above. He sat his horse on the best rise he could find, one knee hooked around the apple. The dry west wind passed his face gently, taking the sweat out of him without pain, cracking his lips and drying out his nose and mouth.

Northward, the pale-gold plains curved, and he could see the remote dust of Long's herd, already twenty miles north of him, a long day's push.

Southward the immense plain died far away into haze. The three thousand head of cattle which he drove, in trust, flowed in a long line down the fold between the low rises, moving fast toward the smell of water. He had been pushing them for a week, making twenty miles a day on this flat country, and the drag strung out half a mile. Those that got sore feet, he let drop behind for somebody else to pick up and bring in; and if he knocked a few pounds off the beef, it didn't matter—they were going on the northern range, not to Chicago. He was four days late now.

Everywhere the plain lay like a great golden ocean, just barely moving up and down, like the breast of a sleeper. It was not flat, there was no real roll, but it moved with a vast motion, obedient to the enormous surges of the wind.

"You got enough men," Tucker said to another rider, sitting before him, a little down the long slope toward the creek. There were five riders behind the fellow with the black mustache. "How come you need so much company, if you're so goddam legal?"

The mustache had a paper in his hands, the long legal kind with a blue back.

"I want you to read it," the mustache said. "I don't want to make any trouble. You just read it."

"What did you say your name was again?" Tucker asked politely.

"Spence," the mustache said. There was a wide, good-looking mouth under the mustache. It grinned, showing a good many wide, good-looking teeth, all natural in color. "Will Spence."

"And who did you say you were working for? This feller that won the suit?"

"Tommy Dickson. San Antonio."

"You don't mean Tommy Dickson the gambler, do you? The Little House feller?"

"That's right," Spence said, smiling patiently. It was a nice smile, guaranteed to work every time, just like an Edison light. You barged in, slammed the door, pulled the string, and there everything was, bright as day.

"Sure, that's where I seen you," Tucker said. "You were dealing faro at Dickson's old house on Yturri Street. Across from the Bull's Head. And now you want all my cows."

Spence nodded and smiled. "Just read the paper, Tucker." He held it out.

Tucker laughed. "Man, don't you know? I can't read. Now my cattle are coming down to the creek, and I got to be moving down there, just to be on hand. So you'll never mind if I move along, won't you?"

Tucker raised his left hand, lifting the reins, and his horse moved forward.

"Just a minute," Spence said. There was no smile, and his tone was just a little sharp and a little cool.

Tucker stopped his horse and said, "That sounds kind of like an order."

Spence said, "This is a court order from the Twenty-Second District Court and it's signed by Judge George H. Noonan."

"I know George Noonan. Him and I used to hunt ducks in the mud puddles over by the San Pedro Acequia. Noonan wouldn't take old Buford's cows. Now don't bother me no more with your damn legal papers, General Spence. George Noonan must be out of his mind—if what you say is true. Good-by."

Tucker turned his horse downhill again. Two of Spence's riders moved out and crossed his path and stopped, blocking him. Tucker pulled up short.

"You better sit and listen," Spence said. "I'll boil it down. The paper empowers me to seize any and all personal property of Buford Allen to satisfy a judgment of $630,000 rendered against him in a civil suit brought by Thomas Dickson in the Twenty-Second District Court, which includes Bexar County."

"Well, I'll be damned."

"I have a signed authority here making me Dickson's agent."

"Well, bless my old soul. Do tell."

Tucker sat still. Down the long slope, down the valley toward the creek, his three thousand head were coming, flowing like some kind of thick, brownish liquid. The soft rumble of hoofs was remote, but he caught the familiar smell. Black, red, buckskin, brindle, every color in cowdom, they streamed down, walking fast, nodding, bellowing, red-eyed, tired and mean.

Tucker's riders were looking up at him. They all sat quiet, letting the cattle go by, except the point riders.

"I never heard of no such of a thing," Tucker said, looking steadily at his men.

First one of the swing pair started up the long rise. Then the others saw him go, and they followed. Tucker sat a little easier in his saddle. The hoofs of the horses made a roll like a drum, and left a trail of dust growing out behind like a fuse smoke running along the ground.

Spence's boys heard the drumming, and the two blocking Tucker moved back, getting out from between. They all wore their customary arms, a Colt apiece and saddle guns, Winchesters or Ballards or Sharps. They sat in a line, now, facing the riders coming up the slope. The two riders down on the herd point were watching, but they didn't leave their posts.

Tucker said, "It's only eighty miles to Ogalalla. Mr. Allen will be there to meet us. Why don't you go on up there and argue with him?"

"I aim to sell these cattle as soon as we hit Ogalalla," Spence said.

Tucker laughed.

Spence's face lost its easy, pleasant look.

Tucker's four riders came up. Their horses fidgeted around, and the men looked from Spence to Tucker, quick and edgy, plainly primed, like a bunch of deer terriers smelling blood on a sack.

"Now, look here," Spence said, easing himself suddenly, "there's no call for hard feelings. Can any of you boys read?" he asked Tucker's riders. "He won't believe what I say about this paper."

One of them laughed.

"None of my boys can read," Tucker said. "They're all too dumb. Like me."

Spence bit nothing once, his jaw muscles twitching.

"Boys," Tucker said calmly to his men, "you better go on back down there and get that herd across. You tell Pete just bull 'em through, the water's fine; I tried it already. No sand, only about a twenty-foot swim. Don't lose no time, now."

His men glanced once at Spence's party, and turned and loped off back down the hill.

"You heard that court order," Spence said. His beautiful smile was gone. The string was broken.

"I heard something," Tucker said. He pulled a sack of bull out of his shirt pocket and began to shake a cigarette together.

"That was a court order," Spence said. He leaned forward in his saddle and his voice rose in proportion. "Don't you know what that means?"

"The Twenty-Second District Court takes in Bexar County, and Gomal and Atacosa, too, as far as that goes. But it don't take in the ass-end of Nebraska, which is where we are now. Ain't you slightly out of your jurisdiction?"

"That order is legal and I can attach Buford Allen's personal property anywhere I can find it."

"You mean, anywhere you're big enough. You got any carpetbagger blood in you, Mr. Spence? You are the most Republican-acting Texan I ever saw in my life."

Spence turned pink.

Tucker folded his cigarette together—it was too dry to roll—and hung it on his lip.

"Where's the next herd?" Spence asked. "Buford Allen started five herds. I've got attachments on all of them."

Tucker sighed.

"He started them out a day apart last spring,"

Spence said. "They ought still to be a day apart. Long told me that much."

"Long is a damn son of a bitch, and I'm going to tell him so in Ogalalla." Tucker fished a match out of his pocket.

"Are you going to force me to take this herd away from you?" Spence asked.

Tucker wiped the match on his pants and held the flare to his cigarette. He puffed and the blue smoke vanished, sucked out of his mouth by the wind. "The old man always did have his neck out," Tucker said. "But I never figured his friends would bankrupt him. But then," he said, inhaling slowly, "this Dickson who's bringing suit ain't a Texan, is he? I believe," he said, calmly recollecting, "the son of a bitch is an Englishman. Ain't he?"

He looked directly at Spence, mildly inquiring. He sucked on the cigarette. It had gone out. So he sucked on the paper.

Down below, the point men were in the water, bullying the old lead ox into the creek, keeping him head on. The others followed, with the swing men shoving the body of the herd up behind the point, crowding them bawling into the water.

They got halfway in and bawled and stalled and stood there protesting as their kindred shoved them deeper, trying to drown them. Then the ones in front gave up and struck out desperately for the far shore, swimming with their eyes bugged and nostrils wide as though the devil had hold of their tails. They only had twenty feet to swim before they stumbled on the bottom again and lunged on out through the shallows. On the far bank they spread up and down the creek, drinking.

Spence's face was set and heavy. "I'm taking this herd over right now," he said. "Don't make any trouble, Tucker. Don't try any shooting. I don't want those cattle scattered from here to Denver. I want you to ride down there and tell your men they are to take my orders from now on."

Tucker fished out another match. He let his hand down calmly to swipe it along the back of his pants, but instead, he dropped the match and pulled his Colt, cocking it as it came up. The rest of them sat there and looked at it.

"I don't want any shooting either," Tucker said, "but if there's going to be any, I'll start it." He smiled at Spence. "Son, you have bit the wrong wolf. I wouldn't give up these cows to the devil himself, much less a half-ass faro dealer and a spare-time pimp out of Yturri Street. You can fight me if you want, but you'll never get these cows. Because my boys will never let you get 'em gathered. Every time you get 'em bunched, we bust 'em hell, west, and crossways."

Spence looked at the solid old Colt, and then up at Tucker's quiet eyes, and then at the cattle, once more stringing out away from the creek on the north side.

"There's a sheriff in Ogalalla," Spence said. "He'll recognize this." He folded his paper. He turned to his men. "Joe, you and Taffy ride on down the trail and keep an eye on Allen's other outfits. They got a B A Bar trail brand like these. Don't let them turn off to Denver or some place. You other two stay and follow this outfit into Ogalalla."

Spence turned and smiled at Tucker, with his same old charm. "I'll be seeing you."

The whole bunch rode off.

Tucker sighed. His dead cigarette came apart in the wind and the tobacco dribbled out. He tore the paper off his lip and picked up his reins.

Down below, as he loped up along the herd, he smiled and called to his boys, "Twenty miles today, twenty miles! Keep 'em moving, boys, keep 'em moving!"

They grinned back through the dust.

"Eighty miles more, boys, eighty miles more!" he called to the swing, and they grinned back, licking their lips.

"Is it true?" one of the point men asked as Tucker came up and shambled down to a walk. "Is the old man broke?"

"He's been broke a thousand times," Tucker said.

"Let's leave that bastard," his top man said. "That fellow with the mustache. Let's point 'em to Cheyenne and sell 'em there."

"Ogalalla," Tucker said, rolling himself another cigarette. "I got my orders in San Antonio, and if Buford wants to change 'em, he can send a rider. Ogalalla it is, and screw the Englishman. If they want to fight, we'll give it to them there."

CHAPTER TWO

Cheyenne, Wyoming
July 8, 1882

Old man Buford Allen stood on the porch of the Elk
Horn Hotel, combing his silky beard with one finger,
scheming how to stall the tall gentleman at his right
elbow. Mike Allen watched his father, and then Morton, and then went and leaned his elbows on the fancy
railing and waited, looking down into Carey Avenue.
The old man had to raise $300,000 by July 15, or lose
an option on a ranch. That was all. Why did the old
man care so hard? There were a thousand other
ranches. But he had his fangs in this one, and he
wouldn't let go, for some reason. Mike shrugged.

"Now, it ain't me," Morton said. "It's mostly my
partners that's getting impatient for delivery, Mr.
Allen."

The old man chuckled comfortably and single-
fingered his beard. "The cows'll be along, they'll be
right along. Tucker—my foreman—knows his business. Just a flood somewhere—held them up."

"Well, now," Morton said, "that wouldn't be my

business, would it? The cause, and all that. My only concern is delivery. They're eight days overdue. I've had my men in camp north of town a week, sir, waiting."

"No need to worry, sir," Buford said, carefully maintaining his expression of calm cheer, of pleasant benignity. "Chicago's still going up. The longer you hold, the longer you wait, the more you'll gain. Take my advice, sir, don't hold these cows for fattening—ship 'em now. Send your men back to work and ship my beef out of Ogalalla, when they come. Let somebody else overstock the range. My advice is, clean up now."

He breathed deeply, with enough vigor to keep it out of the sigh class, carefully denoting *joie de vivre*. "Beautiful weather, beautiful weather," he said, smelling the wind. There was plenty on it besides the prairie grass and wild flowers. Nothing fazed the old boy, Mike thought, listening. He could draw a breath like that in the middle of the K.C. stockyards and sigh, "Beautiful, beautiful," and you'd believe it.

Across the street an old Blackfoot brave in a seam-rotten cutaway threw up in the gutter. Down at the corner of 17th Avenue men were stringing wire for the new electric lights.

"My difficulty," Morton said smoothly, his voice as soft as she-duck's down, "is simple. Our contract—" He paused.

"I appreciate, I appreciate," Buford said with quiet good humor. "But I'll wager they're making twenty miles a day, Mr. Morton. By God, sir, I *am* sorry. If you want to fix a penalty, I'll take your figure, sir. I'll give you a draft for whatever you think fair." The old man smiled, and the Wyoming wind lifted a bit of his white beard and let it fall again. It was a beautiful beard, soft and clean as soap and comb could make it.

Mike sat down and listened absently. Windy old Buford, him and his drafts. The only draft Buford could draw was out of a stein on hotel credit. But Buford was depending on Morton's gentlemanly instincts with all that talk about paying off, and it worked.

Morton's lean face turned ruddy. "Well, now, well, now, that's mighty square of you, but—"

"Of course," Buford said, "some day she'll keep on going up—but she hit $9.32 last May, and I'll bet a dollar that was the peak. I know well enough you could buy cattle any time—I'll let you go."

Morton turned his lean face slowly toward Buford, and his hard mouth curved in a hard smile. "I can't buy cattle in the open market at $55 a head, and you know it. There's nothing down at Ogalalla coming in much less than $60, and you know it. The only thing is, if she slips in Chicago, why, I might get cut down to a fifteen-percent profit before I can unload. You see . . ."

Mike Allen let the voices mumble away. The honey and treacle of his father's old Southern chuckle and the quiet, lipless misering of skinny-butt Morton, trying to hedge a penny this way and that, were just the same old two sides of the same old racket. The honey dripped on, promising delivery, promising this, that, promising good weather, promising higher prices, anything to stall Morton. Morton was cash, quick.

Cash in a hurry, Mike thought. $300,000 to collect in a week, before the old man lost his option. The old man had Morton on the ropes now, spinning daydreams.

But why? What was it about that crummy little ranch up in Montana that Buford wanted? He'd killed himself all spring, starting those five herds on the trail, to make that option—and Montana was full of ranches. But it was Montrose's he wanted.

What was it about Montrose and that ranch that made the old man so secretive? And every time the old man talked about the General, he got mean. The whole thing smelled of revenge—but on the face of it, it was just a simple business deal.

In a minute Buford would buy Morton a deep drink in the hotel bar, and Morton would wander back out to his cow camps north of town, lost in a fog of avarice, and spend the night in a mist of cow-pie smoke, dreaming about ten dollars he had dropped once in a game of Boston, and how he was going to get it back at last.

As far back as Mike could remember, there had been the dripping honey of his old man's voice, the fog and smoke of daydreams, and the glitter of the future. After a few years it made you sick to your stomach.

But the funny thing was, the old man was sincere. He actually believed it all himself—sometimes. Back of all the hot air there was a shrewd mind. There had to be, because old Buford was usually in the money. A man couldn't be a fool and make as much money as Buford. Of course, the fool in Buford that lost the money was easy to see. It was the other person behind the beard, the planner, that Mike in twenty-four years had not yet met.

Mike looked at Morton unobtrusively. A middle-sized wheel in the Cheyenne Club, tall, thin, a little stooped like a lot of tall, thin cowmen. Morton looked mighty dignified astride a horse, with about four hands trotting behind him, like one of the petty feudal barons Mike had read about in St. Mary's in San Antonio. And all he was, was just another back-country Northerner, up to his butt in debt like all of them, and getting deeper.

"By God, sir, but business is dry!" Buford cried out. *Here comes the drinks*, Mike thought. The idea was to get Morton all wound up tight, and then feed him a few fast ones. That would keep him in the right frame of mind—that is, looped—until he dried out tomorrow. Maybe by then the herd would be in. Maybe all of them would be in. They might all come at once. "Now come on in here and wet your whistle, Mr. Morton." "Wet your whistle" was a phrase old Buford would have gagged on privately, but he used it on Morton because of the homey, palsy touch it gave to his malarkey. It might make Morton feel like a boy again. God knew what would happen then.

"I tell you, sir, they have the best damn toddies in this hotel—"

Mike watched them go. He watched his father's big hand hovering at Morton's black-suited elbow, not touching. The old man had too much tact to touch the other. Mike saw him through—tact sticking out like hairs on a caterpillar, sensitive to every little intonation, every little nuance of expression. Buford could feel the touchiness in Morton from eight feet away—the independence, the pride, the stiffness. You might as well pat a coiled-up rattler.

Buford was wheeling Morton into the lounge with his voice alone. He had Morton trained like a cutting horse, after ten days of stalling. No hands, no reins, just a gentle word or two now and then and Morton would climb into the laundry chute and go down smiling.

A kind of pride rose up in Mike's belly, and then, from some other pole in his nature, the soft hurt of shame came up and matched it. He looked away, out over the rail, into Carey Avenue.

A granger's butcher-knife wagon groaned by, and then a three-span Anheuser-Busch outfit. Then came a little surrey, and in it he saw a girl.

A voice said behind him, "Good morning, Mr. Allen." Mike looked at the girl. The surrey pulled up at the hotel porch steps.

"Good morning, Mr. Allen," the voice said again. It was Holt, the manager. It would be about the bill.

"Wait a minute," Mike said in a soft voice, keeping his attention on the girl. She sat below him, and as he looked, Cheyenne seemed to rise from the earth and float away somewhere, and Mike was alone in silence, looking at her as though he'd never seen a woman before.

CHAPTER THREE

Cheyenne
Same Day

Sitting on the Elk Horn porch, Mike watched the girl in the surrey.

A thin-legged man with flat-heeled boots, unspurred, got out of the back, tail-on, so that all Mike could see was the black boots, the gray trousers, and the small-waisted black coat, almost military in cut. There was a colored man driving the single bay mare.

The girl sat there, looking like some kind of prisoner.

"I'm sure it won't take more than a few minutes of your time," the voice said, now at his shoulder. It was just another brand of treacle. "About the bill."

Mike closed his mind to the voice. The girl sat quite still, while the man in the gray pants came up the steps, head down. He was stiff, gray, and thin-shanked, but he moved smartly and neatly as he climbed the steps and went into the lobby.

"I beg your pardon," the voice said, a little louder but with the same cool cheeriness.

"All right," Mike said, looking down at the girl. He knew what was the matter—the girl was hiding from Cheyenne. A man's town, full of men. There were six dozen of them on the hotel porch.

It was not her beauty that touched him, nor her sadness, though she had both. Her mouth was red and wide. Wide, red mouths were supposed to betoken a certain looseness or passion of character, and so most of the good girls in San Antonio spent hours before their plate mirrors practicing primness with properly pinched, though prettily curved, little lips that in later years would look about as beautiful and virtuous as a row of goose gizzards.

It was as though she had been wounded, and did not care, as she sat there in perfect simplicity, thinking of nothing, or perhaps of a wart on the back of the Negro's neck, or maybe remembering a flower at home.

"About the bill," the patient, crisp-apple voice said with a generous hospitality. Mr. Holt's hospitality never wore thin, but the sheriff came knocking nevertheless.

Her hair was dark, and evidently fine, for it made a kind of confusion of shadow rather than a prim cap. On her head there was some kind of scarf, or very light shawl, trying to hold all that gay, dark hair in some order.

The cheek was pale, and its long plane was slightly hollow, although plumpness was all the thing. What Mike wanted to do was reach out and touch the cheek with his finger, to make some gesture, the most delicate, the least offensive, to comfort and protect.

The girl lifted her head slightly and said something, probably to the Negro driver. The driver lifted the two new, light-tan lines and slapped them on the bay mare's rump, and the bay mare took off like a mechanical toy, trotting into the traffic with an action like a cancan girl operating in a Platte River bog.

Mike drew a breath and held it, and half rose from his chair. He watched her go, and one of his hands moved forward. He held the breath until the surrey turned the corner into 17th Avenue.

He turned around. "What about the bill?" he asked the man behind him, trying to suppress a certain sharpness.

A couple of faces turned their way.

Mr. Holt smiled and said softly, "Why not come into my office? It's a little more private."

Mike followed Holt inside. It was a big lobby with an enormous elk head hanging over the dining-room door, directly opposite the main entrance. The lobby was paneled with oak, freighted all the way from Ohio, and the oak columns holding up the ceiling were handsomely carved, by a German firm in Milwaukee, with a highly appropriate motif of oak leaves and acorns. Together with the molded plaster ceiling in cream and gold leaf and the purple-and-gold edgings in stained glass around the main windows, the whole place gave an effect of opulent confusion.

Everywhere there was the soft rumble of men's voices, and to the right, through a carved-oak archway, Mike saw the long, shining mahogany bar fading into the distance toward the billiard tables.

Mr. Holt's office door was made, like the mail-rack at the main desk, of polished cherry.

Mike sat down in a leather chair. "How much is the bill?"

Mr. Holt's smile warmed at his directness. He sat down too, behind his large oaken desk.

"Thirteen hundred and ninety-four dollars."

"It's a good thing it isn't an oyster month," Mike said. "He loves bluepoints and champagne. All his friends do too. How did he manage to run up such a bill without oysters?" Mike looked at the ten-foot ceiling, where plaster cherubs in bas-relief wound ribbons around Donatello fruit baskets.

"I was under the impression your father had considerable resources."

"He has the resources, too, only they're not cash. Not yet. We have five herds on the trail. That's about fifteen thousand head of cattle."

Mr. Holt raised his eyebrows. All of a sudden he seemed to relax. The blood seemed to run a little more freely in the veins on his nose.

Mike watched him.

Mr. Holt thought of something, and seemed to tighten up again.

"Don't worry," Mike said. "I can show you the contracts, if you like. All of them Cheyenne Club. Strictly cash, Mr. Holt. The first herd's overdue now. They may come tomorrow. They may come tonight. Tell me, what's the bar bill? It's only twenty dollars a day for those little rooms we've got, and we've only been here three weeks. That's only four hundred dollars."

Mr. Holt flicked a page over in his mind. "Five hundred and forty-four dollars. A very popular man, your father."

"I hope so."

"You may recall a number of dinners," Mr. Holt said. "Small affairs—modest, really—but still, about $150 a plate. And he never drinks New York wine."

"He's an ex-Confederate officer."

Somebody knocked on the door. One of the sub-clerks sidled in. "Pardon the interruption, Mr. Holt. A telegram. I saw Mr. Allen come in here—"

Mike took it. He pulled a dollar out of his pocket and gave it to the clerk. Mr. Holt's eyes narrowed on the dollar and the clerk backed out fast. The cherry door closed noiselessly, like the sealing of a tomb.

Mike opened the telegram. It read:

> *Ogalalla July 7 1882*
>
> *Mr. Buford Allen   Elkhorn Hotel   Cheyenne*
> *Longs herd is in hes making remarks about*
> *you ran out of Texas to beat your creditors*
> *advise you come down here and protect your*
> *name*
>
> *Streeter*

Mike folded the telegram and put it in the breast pocket of his coat. "Good news," he said. "According to this, a friend of ours just got into Ogalalla. His herd left Texas just a day before our first one. That means our first should be about a day south of Ogalalla. That means we should make delivery tomorrow, maybe."

Mr. Holt looked with not much cheer at the corner of the telegram sticking out of Mike's pocket. "I suppose you'll be going down to Ogalalla, then."

"It's only 160 miles east, Mr. Holt."

"Ah, yes." Mr. Holt looked glum. His two rather tired twinkling eyes watched his cigar go up in smoke.

"I regret our baggage isn't worth more," Mike said. "I'd be glad to leave it till we get back."

"Why don't you assign me one of your contracts as collateral?"

Mike's eyes smiled, but from a distance. "At $55 a head, 3,000 cattle are worth about $165,000. I guess you're joking."

Mr. Holt looked out the plate-glass window. The border of purple-and-yellow glass, leaded around the edges, cast a faintly gruesome gleam across one hand, lying inert on the desk.

He drew a deep breath. "No hard feelings. But I

ought to enter a claim at the justice court this very day."

"Fine. You'll get a judgment, and when we can, we'll pay it. The trouble is, you'll crack our credit in half. Cheyenne Club cattlemen don't like to deal with bankrupts. The mere rumor is enough to ruin my old man." Mike looked at Holt for a moment. "You don't seem to understand how we do business. In Texas, and anywhere on the trail, we take each other's word. We have to. Things move too fast. They always have, and there never have been any courts. If a man breaks his word, Mr. Holt, he's through. For good."

Mr. Holt smiled. "I learned the hotel business in New York. I'll never get used to Wyoming. The way you people trust each other."

"The thing is, back in New York you could sue my old man and it wouldn't mean much. Out here, it would ruin him, because it would mean he had broken his word." Mike sat forward just a little. "That's why a man will kill somebody for calling him a liar, Mr. Holt. Because if he lets it stick, he's ruined. You understand now what I mean when I give you my word I'll pay you my father's bill, if he doesn't?"

Holt looked at the black pupils of Mike's eyes, in the dark-brown irises. It was like looking in an open window. "All right," Holt smiled without a twinkle. He looked like an aging bouncer after a hard night in a new saloon. He stuck out a hand, and Mike shook it.

"Just a minute," Mr. Holt said as Mike turned toward the cherry door. Holt stooped and pulled open a drawer in his roll-top desk. He turned back and held out a small, flat cigar box. "My compliments to your father," he said, his twinkle coming back. "A charming gentleman."

Mike took the box, saying nothing, and, disturbing the cherry door as little as possible, edged out.

He walked slowly over to the big plate-glass window and looked down into Carey Avenue, past the hairy ears and big hats, past the ornate railing. She was gone, really gone, Mike thought. He might have dreamed her. Maybe she had never been there at all.

He turned and walked toward the stairs. In any case, there was another woman in Texas, who had been very real for eight long years.

He forgot the face in the surrey, deliberately.

CHAPTER FOUR

San Antonio, Texas
The Little House
July 8, 1882—4:30 P.M.

The doors of the Little House were open, but hardly anybody was there yet. The dealers loafed in the bar, practicing with various decks of cards of their own brand, and Maybelle, the cashier, who ordinarily sat like a large, buxom bird in her golden cage, smiling sweetly at the suckers, now sat in the ladies' bar with two other ladies, her handsome, pinchable knees spraddled far apart under her luminous yellow silk skirt, her shoes off under the table, and her full upper lip hiding coyly under a handsome white mustache of lager foam.

The other two ladies had large, dark, sad eyes. They looked upon the world of the Little House like lonely children, lost in dreams.

Their names were Eurydice and Amanda. However, they were called Bouncy and Fotts by their friends.

"Listen, Maybelle, for God's sake, can't you lend me anything at all?" This from the Poor Boy, also at the round table. "I only owe Dickson a thousand, and I can't raise it anywhere at all." It was hardly more than a loud whisper. He was so sick.

"Poor boy," Maybelle said. "Why don't you get out of town?"

"What's the use? He'd find me, wouldn't he?"

Maybelle looked with large blue eyes at the poor boy. He was a sweet lad named Hugh, no more than eighteen. His last name, which few people knew, was Buss. He had come down from St. Louis, where his father ran a small leather-skiving plant, to buy cattle hides and he was afraid to go home with neither the hides nor the $1700 he had come with.

"When you got to have it, Hughie?" Maybelle asked. There was a quality about her blue eyes which grew on people. They hardly ever changed. Men died in pools of blood, men lost thousands, men shot off guns at other men, men wept at the dice tables—the blue eyes never changed.

"In half an hour," Hughie said. He looked about a little wildly.

Maybelle shook her head slowly. "Poor boy." She thought, *He should never, never have left his mother*.

Fotts said nothing. Bouncy said nothing. They looked at Hugh with large, dark, sad eyes.

"Not even five dollars?" Maybelle said. "If you gave him five dollars he'd feel better. Tommy would never get mean if he knew you really tried to pay off."

Hughie shook his head slowly. "I lost my last five bucks in the Revolving Light, an hour ago. I've heard—uh—things about Mr. Dickson and—well, welshers. Only I'm not a welsher, Maybelle. I'm truly trying. I'm honestly trying. But is it true? Is it true, the things they say?"

"Of course not, Hughie," Maybelle said. "Those are just lies. Poor boy. Tommy wouldn't hurt a fly." There was a fly in the small puddle of beer on the table. Maybelle put a finger gently on the fly's back and pressed.

"Dear, dear," she said, giggling and wiping her finger delicately on the seat of her pants where it wouldn't show in the cage. "Dear me."

"Dear me what?" somebody said.

They all turned toward the entrance of the ladies' parlor.

"Why, Tommy, darling," Maybelle said, blowing him a kiss with her clean forefinger. "Sweetheart, come in and make us happy. We're all so bored."

Bouncy and Fotts lifted their upper lips slightly. Their teeth showed dully in the dim light, and their eyes shrank timidly.

"Hello, girls," Tommy said, sauntering in swinging his cane. "Not including you, of course, Hughie. What's my boy doing in the ladies' parlor?" He sat down on one of the bent-wire chairs. "Paul!" he shouted through the arched doorway. "Beer! Degen's!"

He sat, smiling, neat as a pin, in light-gray clothes, with a light-gray bowler on his head. There was a diamond in his tie, and another on his hand. He was as clean and cool as the north star, and indeed the whole place reflected Tommy Dickson's coolness, with its gray walls and oyster trim, its white shutters letting in cool, dim light, and the carpeting muffling all hard sounds.

Paul scuttled in. Tommy looked at the girls, and then at Hughie. His long, thin face, so clean and finely boned, was full of pleasant friendliness. "What a lovely party," he said, picking up his beer and smelling it. He put it down again. He spoke with a faint English accent.

"Nice to see you girls out," he said to Fotts. Fotts shrank and smiled at the same time.

"It's their afternoon off," Maybelle said. "Ain't it, girls?"

"Of course it is," Tommy said pleasantly. "My girls know the rules. Don't say 'ain't,' Maybelle. And please don't be sharp. There is a certain innate sharpness in you that sometimes escapes. Like Joanne, it alarms me."

"What's innate?" Maybelle said, swallowing beer. "Anything like naked?"

"Inside one," Tommy said. "Abiding, inherent."

"Like bowels," Bouncy said. She burbled interiorly three or four times, and blushed.

"Please," Tommy said. "Try to be delicate, girls. Delicacy pays. Respect, docility, humble willingness to please. That's your cue. Think of the young ones as your sons. Establish a personal relationship."

"Mr. Dickson," Hughie said, trying to look like somebody's son. There was a peculiar mixture of rank fear and utter adoration in his young face.

"Yes, Hughie?" Dickson said in a kindly voice.

"I tried like everything," Hughie said. "I tried all over town. The bank—"

"You lost your last five in the Revolving Light this afternoon," Dickson said. "You might at least have lost it in here. And I wouldn't go to Colonel Berry for money. Bankers never, never lend money to gamblers who lose. And it doesn't pay, Hughie, it really doesn't pay, to talk about our affairs with people like Colonel Berry. I wish you hadn't."

Hughie looked down, red. "Well, I'm sorry. But honest, Mr. Dickson, I'll get a job. I'll pay you back. Honest. A thousand dollars isn't much; I'll pay it back in a year. Honest."

Dickson looked at him down his long, thin nose. The bridge of Dickson's nose was unusually high, and the aloof, cool pleasantness of Dickson's gray eyes, together with the arch of that nose, had refreshed many a girl's illusions. He was obviously a gentleman, very refined; *he* never sweated.

"You see, Hughie," he said, "it isn't the money. It's the principle of the thing."

He waited. Hughie looked awed.

"You see, Hughie, so many people would take advantage of me, if I were simply to let you go. I wouldn't miss a thousand dollars, Hughie. A man named Buford Allen, for instance, owes me $300,000. I can't afford to have people think they can get away without paying me off on time. As Colonel Berry says, time is of the essence in the matter of negotiable instruments."

"Then what shall I do, sir?" Hughie asked in a kind of desperate, bedraggled squeak.

"We'll find a way," Dickson said, "to make everything right." He tapped the floor with his cane. "Come along, Hughie. Let's go for a walk. I have a couple of matters to attend to, and then we'll go home and think things over—at my house. You've never met my mother, have you? You'll like her."

Two tears came to Hughie's eyes. He stood up, fumbling for his hat on the wall, and knocked it to the floor.

"Well, ta-ta, girls," Tommy said, smiling cheerily and swinging his polished straight cane. "Enjoy yourself, Amanda—Eurydice. What charming names. So classic." They looked up with wooden faces and wooden smiles.

"Ta-ta, Maybelle," Tommy Dickson said.

Maybelle was looking at the fly, squashed in the beer. Her face was remote.

"Maybelle, dear," Tommy said, "you look a perfect bag when you sulk. Brighten up, my girl. Freshen up. That's the girl." He tapped twice on the floor with his cane, sharply, and Maybelle looked up, startled. She looked at his stiff, lean face, and quickly smiled.

"Sure, Tommy. You bet," she said in a quiet little voice. "You said it, Tommy."

She stood up timidly.

Tommy turned, whirling his cane once, and sauntered out the white archway. "Come along, Hughie."

Hughie followed, eyes hopeful and vacant.

"Maybelle," Bouncy said in a whisper, looking all around.

Maybelle looked up slowly.

"Is it true, what Dickson does?"

"I don't know," Maybelle said heavily. "I don't know nothing about his business affairs."

"You sleep with him," Fotts said simply.

"I don't know nothing about it!" Maybelle suddenly yelled, standing up. "Goddamit, so I sleep with him, you think I can read his goddam mind? Don't ask me no questions, you damn dumb tramps! How do I know what he does?" She stood there, her lips shaking.

There was complete silence in the bar, through the arch. After a moment, glasses began to clink again.

"I'm sorry, girls," Maybelle whispered. "I didn't mean what I said. He's such a son of a bitch, is all." She was crying, her lower lip shoving the upper one up toward her nose, squeezing the foam mustache out to the sides. Tears slid into the foam, and she licked it off, weeping.

"That's all right," Fotts said. "We're tramps," she sighed resignedly. She stood up. "Come along, Eurydice." She started sedately for the side door.

"You'll come back next Thursday, won't you, girls?" Maybelle asked, going after them. "I don't know what I'd do without your little visits."

Fotts turned. She said, soberly, close to Maybelle, "Listen, kid, you better get a hold of yourself. You got to keep your head in this business. You remember Joanne, don't you, that used to come with us? The last time Dickson came around at the hotel collecting, she asked him for her money and he wouldn't give it to her—six months' earnings. She cussed him

awful. So he sent her over to the other house across
the creek. With all them stinking Mexicans and all
them rough bush-beaters from the Brazos. She can't
do a thing. If she tries to run, he'll have her throwed
in the can for streetwalking, and then he'll bail her
out and put her back in the house." Fotts's lips tightened.

"It's bad enough at the hotel, with all them fat
German bastards. You watch your tongue, kid, or
you'll be right in there with us."

Maybelle's eyes opened up wide. "He couldn't," she
whispered. "He couldn't."

"Like hell he couldn't," Fotts said, her eyes as
solid as a rock. "He can do anything he darn pleases;
he'll find a way. I made four thousand dollars last
year. The last time I asked him for it, to go home,
he said I should leave it in the bank a while longer.
I ain't got a dime, Maybelle. If I had, I'd go back to
Tennessee. What can I do? If I was pretty enough to
get him in bed once, I'd stab the son of a bitch in the
heart." Her eyes gleamed secretly. "So watch yourself, Maybelle." Fotts smiled stiffly, and went out.

Maybelle blinked and stood staring vacantly after
their dark, sedate, most sober figures, as they turned
back toward the western edge of Irish Flats.

Tommy Dickson and Hughie walked up Yturri past
the Bull's Head, east on Commerce Street to the
main Plaza, on up Soledad past the 101 to Houston
where the mule cars danged along back toward the
Alamo Plaza. Everybody knew Tommy Dickson—he
walked along nodding and smiling with cool civility.

They turned west on Houston Street, four doors,
and went into the little bank. The teller took Tommy's name back, and Tommy waited, talking pleasantly with a bookkeeper.

Colonel Berry sat at his desk in the back, behind
his partition, pondering over a few delinquent notes.

"In a minute," he said to the clerk in a low voice. "Give me two minutes." The clerk went out.

He had a love of paper, commercial paper, any kind of paper—Federal engraving paper, bond paper, it all felt good, like some delicate kind of hide. It almost hurt him when the interest payments ran off the bottom of a note and he had to have the teller pin on a new sheet.

He fingered the notes in his hand, slipping them gently between forefinger and thumb. Then his pet fox bit him again. There was nothing sentimental about an ulcer, and suddenly, as the pain started once more, the paper disgusted him. He picked up the glass of bicarbonate of soda at his elbow, drank, and belched. When he put down the glass, his eyes looked a little brighter, and the lines in his face not quite so deep. The fox was satisfied, for a while.

When the teller knocked again, he said, "All right," and stretched his thin, weak legs.

He did not get up when Dickson sauntered in. He smiled, and made no other move. The notes were in his hand like a full house.

"Good afternoon," Dickson said, waving his cane. He saw a chair, spread his coat tails, and sat down, lean and elegant. "I believe you know my young friend, Hugh Buss," he said, waving a hand in Hughie's direction. Hughie stood by the door, his hat in his hand, a strained, sick smile on his face.

"I do," the Colonel said. "Won't you sit down, Mr. Buss," he said wearily.

Mr. Buss sat down, his knees trembling.

"Mr. Buss and I thought we would drop by," Mr. Dickson said elegantly, "to tell you we have found a way out of his difficulties. His visit to you this morning was a bit impulsive."

The Colonel smiled. "Wonderful," he said. He was tired. The soda would last about half an hour. Then the fox would wake up again.

"Also, I thought you might have something for me," Mr. Dickson said. "A few more notes of Allen's somebody might have been holding. Surely everybody knows by now he won't come back."

"They should," the Colonel said pleasantly. "I have certainly made my opinion of him public enough. At least to knock his credit down to where we want it. Personally, I am beginning to wonder if he really did default on your suit."

"What do you mean?" Dickson said coldly.

"I mean, are you sure the deputy who served that summons up in Cheyenne really did see old Allen? Are you sure old Allen really did refuse to answer the summons to your suit? Judge Noonan is inclined to accept statements in evidence at their face value. Frankly, I am not."

Dickson sat forward slowly. "Are you implying that I bribed the deputy not to serve the summons and to swear that he did serve it? So that I could win the judgment by default? If you are—"

The Colonel laughed gently. "Now, now, Tom, don't get excited. All I am saying is that Allen may be quite slick, and yet not wholly dishonest. He may have a genuine intent to repay—in spite of all the hearsay and the, uh, rumors you and I have put about."

"And his default."

"If it was a default. Whatever one can say, Buford is a Texan. It was most unlike him to fail to pick up a challenge. I know him, after all. In any case, I believe his notes are worth more than fifty cents on the dollar."

"Indeed," Dickson said, sitting back and folding his hands on the top of his cane. "Why the build-up?"

The Colonel picked one of the notes out of his full house. He smiled. "Do you want it? A note for four thousand dollars made by Buford to Keppelbauer—the grocer. Six bits on the dollar."

"Speak English, Colonel."

"Seventy-five cents."

"Fifty cents is all I ever paid you."

"The market has changed. Six bits."

"Well, then," Dickson said, standing up, "keep it yourself and collect your own damn money." He turned toward the door. "Come along, Hughie."

"Now wait, now wait," the Colonel said. "Don't rush off, Tom."

Dickson stopped with his hand on the knob. "We had a strict agreement. I'd buy Allen's notes from you at fifty cents on the dollar, if you could pick them up at thirty-five, just to keep my name out of it until I had them all. Damn it, if you want to haggle like a Liverpool huckster, I'll knock you down to fifteen cents. I know how."

Colonel Berry looked a little bitterly at the notes. "Keppelbauer. Ernst Keppelbauer. Wholesale groceries. He sold Allen all his supplies for his trail crews."

Dickson raised his eyebrows and looked down at the paper. "Four thousand. So you paid him—$1400 for this. That's $1400 cash Keppelbauer's got I didn't know about."

"Is Ernst another of your clients?" the Colonel asked.

"Don't concern yourself with gambling debts, Colonel," Dickson said. "They aren't worth discussing." He picked up the note. "You want cash for this? Or you want me to credit your account at the Little House?"

"Cash," the Colonel said, reddening slightly.

"Very well," Dickson said, and pulled a wallet out of his beautiful gray coat. "You are a greedy man, Colonel. Here is $2000." He laid the money on the desk. "Now, anybody else?"

"Why are you hounding old Allen?" The Colonel asked.

"My dear sir, he has almost a million dollars worth of cattle on the trail. I would hound anybody with a million dollars, if I thought I could get it—especially when he owes me $300,000 in gambling debts which I can't collect legally. It's very simple: he had legal debts amounting to half a million or so. If I could knock his credit down, I could buy them for half their face value, get a judgment, and collect the full value. That gives me my $300,000, roughly." He looked at the Colonel, smiling. "If you want to know how he managed to run up such a bill with me—all I can say is, I don't know. Buford is a lucky old bastard. He's a fool and a plunger, but he's very lucky. And then, too," he said, tucking the notes into his wallet, "I liked him, once. And then, too, he makes money fast—and I want it."

Dickson turned toward the door again. "Come along, Hughie. Good day to you, Colonel. Let me suggest more champagne, and less baking soda." He opened the door.

"Just a minute," the Colonel said in a different voice, leaning forward. He seemed almost a little shy.

Dickson took one look at him and said to Hughie, "Wait outside, dear boy."

With Hughie gone, he shut the door.

"Where is Joanne?" the Colonel asked in a low voice.

Dickson looked blank.

"Joanne," the Colonel said. "You know the one I mean. The little blonde."

"Oh. Joanne. She left town."

The Colonel looked at him sharply. "I don't believe you. I told her last week I would talk to you about setting her up for myself, renting her a little house of her own. Why would she leave town? I was offering her a great deal."

"A very independent girl," Dickson said, some-what absently. "Hot-tempered. All I know is, she is not at the hotel—she left. I don't know where she is. She simply said she was leaving San Antonio. What's the matter with Bouncy and Fotts and the others?"

"Oh, Bouncy and Fotts, Bouncy and Fotts."

"There are some new ones coming up from New Orleans next week."

A look of careful fear came into the Colonel's eyes and he reached for the soda.

"Farewell, *amigo*," Dickson said, putting on his hat. The Colonel didn't answer. Dickson opened the door and went out.

"The son of a bitch," the Colonel whispered. He sat there staring at his notes, lying on the table. He suddenly took a swipe at the papers and got up. He went to a picture on the wall, which showed about thirty officers in Federal uniform, in front of an old army building. They were all young. The uniforms were of ancient style.

He turned away, his face sick. "Joanne," he said. "Joanne."

He banged a bell with his fist, and one of the tellers ran in.

"Get me a man," the Colonel said, "a Mexican, an intelligent one. All I want him to do is follow somebody and see what he does. Any old brush-hunter will do, any old scout. Bring him quick. And bring me a quart of bourbon. The hell with this medical stuff."

The teller hurried out.

The Colonel's lean, sick face sharpened as he thought. It was evident that Dickson was a liar, for Bouncy had said Joanne had not left town, even though she was too scared to tell the truth in full.

He sat and waited, rattling his dry, papery fingers on the shadowy desk.

CHAPTER FIVE

Cheyenne
The Old Man's Bedroom
Same Day

Mike walked up the main staircase of the Elk Horn, carefully sinking his feet into the pile with the feeling that he ought to be stealing something. It was like creeping through a twelfth-century forest, hunting a unicorn. He thought again of Sister Margaret Mary, for some reason—remembering her rather weak, whining voice, the insistent, sickly bee in black and white, boring at the ear through those long, deep, sultry afternoons by the little green river in San Antonio.

Of all those sisters, mostly so bright and cheery, she alone had been sickly and whiney. And yet, looking back, she was the only one, except the Mother Superior, whom he could remember.

Down the upper hallway he could see the old man's door standing open, reflecting light from its warm, cream surface into the dark hall. Bantering laughter. Buford was at it again, teasing some ancient chambermaid.

Mike stopped in the dark hall and listened to the bumbling laughter of his father, and the sniveling titters of the woman. Why did he do it? Maybe there was some kind of a devil in Buford, making him act, always act, in front of people. Mike listened to the bumbling, kindly voice. It was a lie.

He could understand Sister Margaret Mary better than he could understand his own father—she was a simple woman, very good, and what if she was cock-eyed about the San Antonio River? If Mike had told her of the bodies they hauled out of that limpid stream, of the blood that ran down the banks, of the vomit, of the stranglings and the drowning of drunks as well as the unending fornications, she would have said, "Well, that is just sin, isn't it? What do you expect?" And she would have gone on talking about the beauties of the river.

He went toward the door. The chambermaid backed out, giggling.

"And how old is the little darling?" Buford was asking. "As young as you? Ah, you'll see, she'll be a beauty too, one of these days."

The woman saw Mike's feet. She took one look at his black, silver eyes, and scuttled away down the hall.

"And how old is the next?" Buford was saying. Mike stood in the door and watched him, combing his beard in front of the bureau, the French cuffs of his beautiful, full-cut shirt turned back up over his hairy forearms. "Three? Four? Sure, I'll bet she's a beauty, too."

"She's eighty-nine if she's a day," Mike said quietly. "The little one will grow up to look like a horse's butt, just like her grandmother."

"Son," Buford said, "don't be bitter. I think what you need is a good woman, like your mother."

"That reminds me," Mike said, sitting down on

the bed. "I want to make a slight touch on you for $100,000."

"What?"

"I'll get to that later. Right now, here's a nice little box of cigars the manager sent you, with his compliments. It seems you are his dream-guest. Or will be, when I pay your bill."

"Son, now, son, you know these things always get taken care of. I talked to Holt once. I thought I had him taken care of."

"Taken care of. What does that mean? Driven crazy? Anyway, he's loony enough to send you some cigars, so smoke one. You can open the box yourself."

Mike lay back on the bed with his hands under his head. "A piece of news. General Montrose is in town. I heard from that slick-headed clerk on the desk."

Buford stopped combing his beard. "Interesting," he said, and thought for a long moment, his black eyes remote and shrewd. "Of course he's down here on account of money. Nobody ever does anything except for money."

"You mean, you don't."

"I mean, take long journeys, my boy. If they're poor, they go a long way for money; or if they're rich, they go a long way just to throw it away. Montrose ain't rich. Ergo, as my teachers used to say, ergo, he's either come down here to sell cattle or borrow money from a friend. If he's selling cattle, it means he really wants to move back East, and he might extend my option. If he's borrowing money, it means he's going to stick in the game, and he won't extend my option."

"Ergo—" Mike said, looking at the ceiling.

"Ergo," Buford said, looking rapidly around the marble bureau top for something. "I wish he would damn well stay put. I thought I had him taken care of."

"I don't think you've got anything taken care of, Pop. Today is the eighth of July. You've got to take up that option not later than the fifteenth. You've got to collect on all five herds in the next seven days, and not one has even come in sight."

Buford found his nail file. "Damn it, son, you talk like a man with a summons. If you can't be cheerful, kindly get the goddam hell out. I operate on faith." He delicately removed a grain of sand from beneath his left little fingernail.

"Don't think I won't, as soon as I get some of that cow money. Furthermore, how do you pay off?"

"If you mean Montrose, money paid in hand, or on deposit, up in Warhorse, Montana. They've got a stinking little hick bank I was going to wire it to. Run by one of those backwoods Rothschilds." Buford chuckled. "They're so crafty they catch themselves in their own mouse traps."

"You're cutting too fine on that option. You ought to have Montrose to dinner and kiss his butt for a while. Get a week's extension, anyway."

Buford threw down the nail file. "How can I do this with you nagging me? I don't want to see him. I don't want to talk to the stinking bastard. I saw enough of him in 1864."

Mike got up. "Then why do you want his ranch? Why do you go through all this just to get his ranch? There's thousands of others up there."

"That's a private matter, son." Buford picked up the nail file again.

"Like that locked suitcase?"

"I told you what was in that suitcase. Just dirty laundry."

"Then why do you keep it locked? Have you got some special kind of pedigreed flea you don't want to get crossed with these Northern fleas?"

Buford closed his eyes and sighed wearily. "For

the God's sake, son, keep the peace. Some things are private. Do I pry into your affairs?"

Mike kept his mouth shut. The idea of the old man's prying into his affairs, or even showing any interest, was the last thing he would have thought of.

"Damn it," Buford said, digging away, "I suppose I better see him. It would be hell to lose that option by a day, if those damn cows were late. He's such a cold-blooded son of a bitch he wouldn't trust me for part of the money." Under his mustache, his lips twitched. "I could beg him on my knees." He sighed. "I better do it before I have to." He pulled down his white sleeves.

"It's a beautiful place, Mike, that ranch of Montrose's. You ought to see it." The old man smiled. "There's a good big log house, and good big barns, just between the summer and winter range. It's in between two spurs of the Warhorse Mountains up there, and a good creek goes down the valley."

Mike watched him dreaming, his big, rather sad eyes remotely smiling. "You're a Texan. Why would you be going to Montana? You were born in San Antonio."

Buford picked up his emerald cuff links. He folded back his left cuff. "I ain't nothing," he said, the eyes shrunk, wrinkled, and mean. "In the end, a man is just a sack of bones, and all you can hope for is maybe ten years of peace. That's all." He ran the emeralds through the fine broadcloth with big, clever fingers, without looking, unconsciously. "All you got in the end is what you love. That's all is left."

The sun from the window struck one of the emeralds as he moved, and the green light flashed brilliantly across the painted tin ceiling.

"Just tell me one thing, Pop," Mike asked. "Do you want me to bury that suitcase with you?"

Buford frowned. "You find General Montrose and invite him here for cocktails."

"I haven't got your charm. Maybe you'd better invite him."

"You can kiss his butt as well as I. Damn it, convey my compliments. I'll get the son of a bitch drunk and make him write me a new option." Buford grinned and his white beard bristled out. "I'll show him who won the war. August first will give me time to breathe." He shrugged into his coat and picked up his silver comb again.

"I will on one condition," Mike said.

"Imagine that." Buford let the comb fall through his beard.

"Out of this haul you're going to make, I want a hundred thousand dollars so I can go home and marry Nancy Berry."

Buford held the comb in mid-stroke. "Quit dreaming," he said in a voice totally devoid of treacle. "Every cent of this cow money goes into Montrose's ranch. Miss Nancy Berry can marry you for yourself."

Mike pulled out the telegram and looked at it. "Every cent? What about Terman and the others in San Antonio? The ones you owe for the herds. And haven't you any gambling debts any more? What about the Little House? What about that bastard Dickson you were so thick with?"

"For God's sake, don't pin me down! All I meant was, there ain't no money for Nancy Berry." He rapped the comb lightly on the marble top of the bureau. "Why the hell should there be? Her old man damn near owns a bankful of it."

"You're a disgusting, profane old man."

Buford laughed. "Speak up son, I can't hear you."

"I said, you're a lovable old codger."

Buford stopped laughing and looked at himself in the mirror.

"I don't think Nancy Berry will marry me for myself," Mike said. "I mean, only myself. There's plenty of people just as good-looking as I am, in San Antonio, and there's a pack of them out at the Fort that's got uniforms besides."

Buford ran his fingers down through his beard. "All that gold braid must scratch like hell in bed."

"You're a disgusting, evil-minded old codger."

"What you all ought to do is go down to the bathhouse on the Island and let Nancy Berry take her pick by weight. Like cows. What are you trying to do? Buy Nancy Berry?"

"Nancy is just like most other girls. She wants to be taken care of. She's got an eye out for the future, and if she didn't she'd be a damn fool."

"How noble you are—in a cheap way. To your whole philosophy I may say one thing—it stinks." The old man lifted his chin and smoothed his neck hairs.

"Damn it, will you listen to what I say?"

"Don't shout so loud. This is a respectable hotel." Buford picked up the comb again and began parting his beard in the middle.

"All I'm trying to say is I need some of the cow money. I don't give a damn what you do with the rest, or if you pay Terman or not. Let 'em hang you, for all I care. Well, I don't mean that. But I need some of the money. What the hell can I do without money? All I know is riding and shooting. A fat lot you can learn in San Antonio."

"Then why didn't you go to the University of Virginia, like I said? They'd have taught you to drink like a gentleman, if nothing else. God knows I never learned."

Mike sat and kept his mouth shut. Buford was cutting his beard out to the sides in long sweeps. It never tangled, never caught in the comb. It looked, in this light, like white silk, just slightly touched

with blue. Sometimes it looked a little yellow, like
ivory.

"Don't you remember why I didn't go?" Mike
asked.

"All I remember is your balky disposition. And
your desire for a matched set of Remington revolvers. That was in 1875, I believe. Two years after the
panic, and all you could think of for your birthday
was a matched set of Remington revolvers. Cattle
were worthless that year. We drove them north for
the exercise."

"I hate to recall anyone of your dignity to reality.
In 1875 you bought the steamboat. You had given
up cattle. Remember the steamboat?"

Buford stopped sweeping his beard to the sides.

"You didn't have any money, you said. You bought
the steamboat and lost your operating capital to that
fellow from St. Louis who was supposed to bilk the
passengers at monte. Remember that? He was supposed to split the percentage with you. But he didn't
split what he took off you on the way down at Baton
Rouge. Remember that? What I want now is a hundred thousand dollars to start my own damn cow
business. With that, I can talk Nancy Berry into
marrying me, and be a respectable young man in
San Antonio society."

The unhappy look in Buford's eyes suddenly became rocklike, and then a kind of mask of bemused
benignity descended over his face.

"How about it?" Mike asked.

"Son," Buford said.

"Don't say it," Mike interrupted. "Start out some
other way. Every time you call me 'son' in that tone
of voice, I come out screwed."

Buford jerked his neck up. "Goddam it, don't cut
me off like that."

Mike looked into the mirror, into the two hard,
black, fierce eyes.

"All right," Mike said softly to the eyes. "I won't cut you off. Just give me my due and I'll clear out."

"Your due," Buford said, the eyes impenetrably black as cannon bores. "You've lived well with me. You've had plenty of money working with me. You've had your due."

"Like with the steamboat," Mike said.

Buford winced and his eyes dodged. His large fingers delicately tapped the marble bureau top. "What will all this get you?"

Mike slid to the edge of the bed and sat up straight. "I want a clean start of my own. You've got fifteen thousand head of cattle coming. You'll gross damn near nine hundred thousand dollars."

Suddenly the starch went out of Buford's back. He melted. His eyes went down. He opened a white palm toward Mike, and let it fall.

"You're right, son. I know you're right. Forgive me for not thinking about you more." He looked at Mike.

"I owe you plenty, Mike. I get mixed up. I know it. I get mixed up in these big schemes. Mike, don't you know why I keep trying to make a real killing? So I can quit. What I want is to give you a start, and to make a secure home for your mother and me. That's all. I forget sometimes, son, but it ain't because you aren't in my mind—it's just because I get so wrapped up in trying to do what I'm trying to do. Like this summer. Mike, listen—if there's money enough when we're all balanced off, I'll give it to you."

He saw the question of doubt in his son's eyes, and said, "Mike, I can't promise much hope. I can't lie to you now. I've strung you along in the past, but I can't now, because things are coming to a showdown with me. You know that, don't you?"

"No," Mike said quietly. "I didn't know that."

"Well, it's true." Buford was talking quietly, the

lines in his face just normal for once, not blanded out with his second-rate poker face, nor engraved by phony drama. He looked at the Belgian carpet. "This is my last big chance, son. There's too many people in San Antonio got their hooks out for me. Too many people know me. I've fooled away too much of my credit. That damn gambling."

He looked away, beyond the wall, with a bitter half-smile. "After a while they wise up. You can't fool them forever."

He came back to his son, the black eyes familiar, intent, and frank. "Not that I ever tried to cheat anybody, Mike. You know that. It all came of getting too many obligations, trying to beat the son-of-a-bitching game."

Mike said, "That's what you're still trying to do. This summer."

Buford nodded. "Yes, I know. But this time I *can* beat it. This time it's breaking right."

Mike sighed. "You want me to play along with you? Suppose you lose it all again?"

Buford shook his head doggedly. "I can't lose. I haven't touched a card since March."

"Dad, that's a bunch of crap. You can lose. I don't know how. But you can lose it all. It isn't only cards. It's everything you do—it's all just one big damn game of monte."

Buford shook his head, his white beard wagging. "No. I can't lose this time."

Mike saw through him all at once. The old man wouldn't face it. He was shutting his eyes to something, and instinctively Mike knew that somewhere in the old man's figuring there was a wrong turn.

Mike said, "You owe about five hundred and twenty-five thousand for those herds. That's due the shippers."

Buford nodded. "That's right. That will leave me just about four hundred thousand. I can buy Montrose's ranch for three hundred thousand—if I can make the goddam option, that is." He turned suddenly away.

"That leaves me a hundred thousand as working capital. In other words, if you take any, I'm broke. How the hell can I work Montrose's ranch without capital? The damn banks eat you alive.

"Except once." He smiled suddenly. "Just once, I took a bank. Me and my troop, in 1862, on a raid up in Ohio. We hit them before they could run with the money, and we cleaned them out, every damn Yankee cent they had, even the nickels and dimes. I wish you had been with me in the war, boy. We would have been good, Mike.

"Nobody argued about money in the army, Mike. The hell with money. I had the best damned time I ever had in my life in the army, Mike, fighting. And I never chopped a man. I never put a stone to my saber in the whole four years. I never had to." He grinned. "I just whapped the bastards on the head or on the arm, and broke them. But they went home whole—mostly." He looked gloomily at the floor. "I never tried to kill none of those Yankee bastards. They were just a poor, ignorant lot of factory hands that didn't know what they were doing."

He looked up, his black eyes quiet. "It's money is the curse of the world, son. I keep trying to get it. A man's got to have it. How else can a man live? Why ain't there some country near by where we could ride down and take the son-of-a-bitching stuff away from them with a pistol? Like Mexico. Only it's against the law. By God, the law makes a man live like a mule in a field.

"All I do, all I've done for twenty years is scheme after money, the dirtiest, lowest, meanest stuff in the world. And scrabbling for it is the dirtiest, lowest, meanest thing a man can do. A man ought to live by his sword. Why ain't there some army where a man could fight forever? A man ought to live by his sword, and not scheme. A man ought to fight, he should live by his guns, and not be reduced to a goddam peddler, scratching and scritching in the dirt."

He suddenly turned away and stood with his hands on the marble slab with his head bowed. "This modern world is no place for a man, son. It's a goddam store-keeping world, son, and it's a son of a bitch. Don't you ever think it ain't. The one thing I want to do before I leave is to give it the goddamdest screwing it ever got."

He went over and sat wearily on the bed. "So there you are," he said. "I'll be lucky if I get out of this with my skin—much less Nancy Berry."

Mike looked at his father, sitting humped over on the bed. Where his coat stretched tight under the arms, there were small rolls of fat. There he sat, aging, dejected, and as Mike looked at the pulled seam, at the worn evidence of the old man's jovial indulgences, at the modest fat which would be rotted away not too long hence, at the bones which would be helpless, which would lie mute, he understood a little of his mother's long patience.

Buford pulled out a handkerchief and wiped his face. He cleared his throat and spat on the floor. "Well, damn it," he said, "go along and see Montrose."

"I'm sorry to have to bring this up now," Mike said soberly, pulling the telegram out of his pocket. "I just want to tell you, now, that I'll stick with you. We'll get hold of your ranch some way."

He threw the telegram on the bed.

CHAPTER SIX

San Antonio
Dickson's House—Same Day

After they left Colonel Berry's bank, Dickson and Hughie walked on down Houston Street and crossed the river. They turned north on St. Mary's Street and on up away from the crowds of cowmen, hunters, and soldiers from the Fort which boiled in and out of the places on the Plaza around the Cathedral.

The evening set in, cool and quiet in the tree shadows, with the noise becoming more and more remote south toward the plazas. They could almost hear the river, half a block away, running parallel to them on the west. Dickson slowed, and turned in at a walk. His house was simple and dignified, set back from the street and partly screened by trees.

Dickson swung the door open into a dark hall, and Hughie looked all around. It was dusk outside, gentle and luminous, and there was the smell of night jasmine already coming in through the doorway. Before him, down a long hall, parquet shone in the dull light from a distant French door, and beyond that, trees, toward the river.

A tall Negro came down the hall, carrying a three-branched silver candelabrum, the three orange-yellow flames, flowing backward, smoking. He was very tall and thin, his dark face old and sad, and he wore a plain black suit with a white shirt and a black string tie, like a country preacher.

"Get the boat ready, Harris," Dickson said. "I want Mr. Buss to meet my mother, and then perhaps we'll go for a little row on the river. Where is she?"

The Negro bowed his head slightly, as in prayer, and whispered, "The terrace." He bowed a little more and said, a little louder, "Mr. Keppelbauer is here, sir. In the front parlor." He was a West Indies man, and he had a clear, Anglicized accent.

Dickson smiled in the dusk. "Take him some sherry. Have you got anything cold for Mr. Buss? Hughie, you go with Harris here, and have a bite to eat. I am positive you had no lunch. Did you, now?" He smiled and gave Hughie a pat on the shoulder.

Hughie felt like crying. It was like being at home again. He followed Harris down the long, cool hall through the dusk.

Dickson opened the white door to the front parlor, gently clicking the shining brass latch. He went in. A man was sitting in shadow by the big bay window, an empty glass in his hand.

"Ah," Dickson said, shutting the door. "I see Harris has already brought the sherry." He looked out at the hibiscus growing beside the window, almost, now, without color. "Well, Keppelbauer, what good news have you got for me?"

The other stood up, "None, I am afraid," he said, smiling weakly.

"No money at all?" Dickson asked, surprised. He filled Keppelbauer's glass again. Keppelbauer was a staunchly paunched young man with full chin whiskers, placid of eye.

"I have to have something to run the business, Mr. Dickson."

Dickson eyed him through the dusk. "Surely, in a business the size of yours, there must be some profit. I could take a percentage."

Keppelbauer shrugged. "Bad debts. For instance, Buford Allen owed me $4,000."

"Why don't you sue?"

"What can I collect?"

"His hide," Dickson said, quietly and coldly. "Maybe I could take his hide on your account."

"Or mine?" Keppelbauer tried to smile. He set down his empty glass on a little table, with great care.

"I give you until August first. That is over three weeks. You owe me only $4,000. By the way, I heard you were in the Bull last night."

Keppelbauer drew up his chest and took a deep breath. "Is nothing my business?" The dim gray light hid most of his face, all but a dimple in his cheek, which came and went as his mouth worked.

Dickson pulled the note he had bought from Berry out of his pocket and held it in front of the other's nose. "You could have discounted this with me instead of with Berry. I would have given you better than thirty-five cents on the dollar; you could have reduced your debt. Instead, you had to have cash, to throw away in somebody else's house. I give you until the thirty-first of July, exactly at midnight. I advise you to sell your business."

Keppelbauer's fist opened and spread. "I can't sell my business. I don't dare try. If my connections knew the state it's in, they wouldn't give me credit. Nobody knows it but you. I have borrowed all I can, out of town."

Dickson turned toward the door. "Help yourself to

the sherry, Mr. Keppelbauer. Perhaps you can let yourself out—Harris will be busy, I'm afraid. Remember, July thirty-first, midnight."

"Sherry," Keppelbauer said bitterly. "What do I want with your sherry?"

"My dear fellow, suit yourself. I merely offer you ordinary hospitality."

"And tomorrow you will take my hide, as you say."

"Tomorrow is tomorrow, my dear man. Everything in its proper place, in proper proportion. As you say, tomorrow I may take your hide. Tonight you may drink my sherry." He closed the door gently as he went out.

Moving quietly, Dickson went on down the long hall toward the French door at the end. He passed Hughie, eating in a small dining room.

He went out through the French door at the end, onto a terrace of flagstone. At the edge of the terrace a long, smooth lawn began, running down between rows of palm and oleander to a frame of trees at the river edge.

The last light of dusk floated like mist in the air, turning lavender. He could smell the night jasmine from the front, gentle at this distance, and there were two large tubs of heliotrope near the door behind him.

"And how is everything?" a voice said gently from the shadows near the heliotrope.

She was old, full of wrinkles, her sharp black eyes hidden in dark pouches, but she was smiling.

"Well enough, Mother," Dickson said.

He walked slowly back and forth on the terrace, scraping his cane here and there on the flagging. "I had to bring another one home."

"Oh," she said. "Well, if it's necessary, that's all there is to it. There's nothing else to do. It's simply one of the more disgusting aspects of this whole business." She sucked her lower lip. "But no aristocrat ever minded one commoner more or less."

"Aristocrats," he said heavily. "Aristocrats among the bananas. It's all a dream. Why did we ever start it?"

"Everything's a dream, my dear Tommy. If you line up ten corpses, stark-naked, how are you to tell which one is a king and which one is a baker? The only difference between one man and another is life and death—which one is left standing after the fight, which one is dead. You know that."

He stood in silence, looking down the long vista to the river, against the moon, and she sat watching her only child.

She had been a personal maid to the wife of an extremely wealthy landowner in the south of England, at the time of her first and only pregnancy. First and only not because of an otherwise speckless career, but simply because it was the only time she had been pregnant by a millionaire, and the thing had possibilities, so she let it run along for once. She and her son had been very happy for fifteen years, living on the old man's estate at Lamont. Unfortunately, he had died and the legitimate heirs (a wretched clutter of Manchester people involved somehow with yarn) had thrown the poor mother and son out without a penny. If only the old man's passions had been remotely approached by his foresight, all would have been well. But the impulsiveness which gave Thomas his life would hardly have been consistent with the prudence necessary to support it, in anyone. Nevertheless, they had had fifteen very happy years under that great roof, before the old man died. Twice she had been thrown out of that house— once by the mistress, when Thomas was born (the mistress had thought that her personal maid was pregnant by the butler, or perhaps even one of the footmen, until she saw how her husband carried on over the baby). The poor old woman had never been able to bear the old man even a daughter, and this was the whole spring of her hatred, that a mere personal maid should succeed in gestating a male heir—quite as though fertility had something to do with rank. The old mistress had even, after exhausting the resources of the Church of England, taken to local witchcraft, but to no avail. It was the recollection of money spent on witches (they were quite expensive) that enraged the old lady as much as anything else, and if England had not turned so disgustingly liberal in the last century, she would have thrown her maid not so much to the dogs as directly into the kennel. However, Liverpool was almost enough.

Much to everybody's joy, the old lady had died; and the old man, relieved of her morality and vituperation, had brought his little mistress and his beloved son back from the gutters of Liverpool (the old woman had intercepted all the money he had sent them) and they had lived in great happiness and simplicity, until Thomas was seventeen. What to do with a seventeen-year-old bastard? Simple enough—make him legitimate. But the old man had never got around to that.

Therefore, after the second eviction, it had been necessary for Thomas's mother to seduce her first and last true husband—a rather simple civil servant named Dickson. Then something terrible had happened—Dickson had been shipped to Jamaica, where his simplicity could do no harm; and Jamaica had been a nightmare to the mother and the son, a hell wherein England was inverted. There was nothing that she would not have done to escape that place. If she had ever been afraid of hell, she lost the fear with the thought that if the fires of that place of vengeance leaped exceeding high, at least it followed that the relative humidity was exceeding low, and that alone would make it better than Jamaica.

"We've been working only twelve years," she said. "That's not long. I am seventy. When you are seventy, you will be a peer. You have done wonders, Tommy dear. Simply wonders. How many other men have made three million dollars in twelve years?"

"Three million dollars and an English warrant."

"Never mind the warrant. With sufficient money you can turn all that into a signal service to the crown. After all, how would you ever have got a start, if you hadn't killed a man? And what better place could there have been to kill a man than in Jamaica? Nobody cares what happens in Jamaica, except Jamaicans."

The moon lighted her kindly, beaming old face. "Do you remember, when you were a tiny boy, how I used to carry you down into the Liverpool market? How many cabbages I have begged—or not quite begged."

She sucked her lip quietly, thinking.

"Your Aunt Cassie wrote that Lamont is up for sale again. Too remote for modern people. Nobody ever keeps it long."

"That's good," he said. "Let it sit a while. A house like that ought to be deserted. Everything is so damned improved in England nowadays—they even clip the box in some places. Can you imagine? Do you remember the box along the front terrace? Like clouds, and yet at the same time, like marble, so ponderous, and yet with such delicate texture."

"It's come down, too. Sixty thousand pounds was the last. No interest shown, either. How soon can we go back to England, Tommy?"

"Four million is the goal."

"Need it be quite so much?"

"One must have a goal. One must stick to it. Anyway, in another year, Lamont will be cheaper. People aren't interested in the old estates."

Somewhere a night bird called. He smiled. "You

know how I remember it best? In the fall, with the trees all bare, and only the ivy green. Then it was sad, and all our country settled down, locking up tight against the winter—the streams, the ground, the trees. And do you remember how the horse's hoofs used to sound on that ground? By God! That was a world. We'd be so stiff with cold we could barely creak out of the saddles, and our feet would almost break, touching the ground—and we would come bustling in from the horses to the fire, and toddies all would be there. I can smell it, I can smell it now, horse sweat, toddies, fire." He sat silent, his cane in his hand. His mother said nothing.

"You will be like a queen there, Mother. As you should be. England, England, once again."

In the dark she smiled.

A candle gleamed beyond the door. It opened, and Harris came out, holding a silver candlestick. "The boat is ready, sir. Mr. Buss has finished."

Dickson stood up. "Then tell him to come along. And bring the blanket, Harris."

"A miserable business," the old lady said. "The fools. The worst of it is, the danger."

"No danger," Dickson said. "Nobody's dead without a corpse. The story will be that Hughie Buss just ran away from his debts, and evidently he was afraid to face his father—if the old man ever traces him from St. Louis." He sighed. "Anyway, it can't be helped. If I let one of them welsh and get away with it, they all will. I can't collect in court."

He walked restlessly about in the dark. The new moon gave only the faintest light. "Buford Allen is one I keep thinking about. He's due to collect close to a million. I'll squeeze him till he drips."

"They remind me of flies," the old lady said dreamily, "buzzing around a candle. They are so bestially stupid, the whole situation is so inappropriate, I am always heartily delighted when they burn to

death. The fools. People with no brains really should
leave cards alone."

The candle reappeared. Harris and Hughie came
out, and Harris blew out the candle and set it down
on the flags.

"Mother's not here this evening, Hughie," Dickson said in the dark as Hughie blinked at the moon.
"Come along, we'll go for a row. It's almost like England here, Hughie. Such a gentle little river. Ever
been to England? Come along, Harris, bring that
blanket and the shovel."

"Shovel?" Hughie asked. "Are we going to dig
something?"

"Mud bars," Dickson said. "Always need a shovel
on mud bars."

"Oh," Hughie said, and stumbled off the terrace
after Dickson.

Dickson was slashing at the oleanders under the
palms with his cane.

"You know," Hughie said in a faint voice, "all of
a sudden, I don't think I want to go. I think I'd better
go home."

"How's that?" Dickson asked, amused. "It's lovely
on the river at night. You'll see. We'll row down past
Bowen's Island by the Old Mill crossing, and maybe
have a beer at Wolframs. Ever been to Wolfram's
Garden? It's a jolly place. Full of jolly Germans."

"But it's so dark," Hughie said, standing alone in
the middle of the lawn with Harris silent behind him.

"Dark? Oh, that's rubbish. It isn't dark at Wolfram's. Come along, my boy. We'll talk over a job."

Hughie's head lifted at the idea of a job. He started
walking again.

The boat was tied to a small floating pier at the
foot of the lawn. The river slid by, almost invisible,
making a slight murmur against the bank. Across,
willows drooped into the black water, silver in the
moon.

Behind them, Colonel Berry's Mexican brush-hunter came waddling silently out of the oleander hedge and stood helplessly watching them float away down the stream. He started to follow them down the bank, but the garden shrubbery was too thick. They floated on, out of sight. He found a boat locked to a float at the foot of one of the gardens, and spent fifteen minutes getting it loose.

Harris sculled quietly in the stern. Hugh sat on the middle thwart, and Dickson faced him from the forward seat. They drifted in silence down the river, to a stretch under the willows. All around them lay the town, and they could hear the voices of people out in the cool evening. Ahead of them, the Travis Street bridge loomed up.

Under the bridge, Harris shipped his oar and took hold of a rock in the bridge pier, stopping the boat. A carriage rumbled across, overhead. A group of Mexicans went across, singing.

"What are we doing?" Hughie asked nervously. "What are we waiting for?"

"An interlude of silence," Dickson said, laying his cane across his knees.

"Please," Hughie said, looking at Dickson's pale, thin face. "I want to go on shore."

Dickson twisted the handle of his cane and pulled out a long blade. It shone dully in the light reflected into the gloom of the bridge from the water outside. Somewhere up the river, people were singing an old song.

"Why, what's that?" Hughie asked, amazed.

Dickson put the point of the blade on Hughie's coat over his heart, and shoved, lunging forward.

Hughie looked at him for one second with amazed eyes, and fell forward, dead.

Dickson pulled out the blade, cut it through the river water three times, and then carefully wiped it with his handkerchief. He threw the handkerchief away into the river. Harris threw the blanket over the body.

"A disgusting business," Dickson said. "A miserable business. It's much less fussy than shooting, but it's so beastly personal. You miserable little creature," he said to Hughie's body, "why do you force me into situations like this? Why don't you pay up as you ought? You miserable little fools. Row on down the river, Harris, down below Berg's Mill. You can bury him there, with the others."

CHAPTER SEVEN

Cheyenne—Same Night

In the hotel bedroom, Buford picked up the telegram Mike had thrown on the bed.

Long . . . Making remarks about you ran out of Texas to beat your creditors, Buford read. *Advise you come down here and protect your name.*

Buford got to his feet and stood still in the middle of the room, his shoulders slightly raised as though he were afraid of a blow from behind.

"The bastard," Buford whispered.

"Were you?" Mike asked mildly. "Running out?"

"Don't think I haven't dreamed of it," Buford said. "What could Long have heard?"

"He must have heard something on the trail up."

Buford stood there, shoulders up, hands half raised. "Who? Nobody could have passed Long. He drives too fast. Dodge—of course, Dodge. Somebody went up to Dodge on the cars and started the story and Long heard it when he hit Dodge. What son of a bitch left for Dodge after us?"

"Well, for God's sake, how would I know?" Mike said.

"Where's my gun? I'll teach that bastard to play around with my name," Buford said. "What's the world coming to? I'll have to kill the son of a bitch, that's all. I'll have to go down and kill him." He sat down on the bed.

"Why, I haven't killed a man in twenty years, Mike," the old man cried. "Why, the son of a bitch is going to make me kill him in my old age. Damn him, I'll have to stop his mouth, I'll have to make him publicly retract, and if he don't, I'll have to shoot his goddam head off. Do you realize—Do you realize—" His voice died and he sat staring at the carpet.

"What difference does it make what somebody said?" Mike asked quietly. "It's an insult. You can make him take it back. There's no need to get so excited about it."

"They'll be afraid to take my cattle," Buford said dully. "Morton and the rest."

"Why?"

"They'll think maybe there's a lien."

"Don't be silly. There can't be a lien without a judgment. Nobody's suing you. It's just slander, and all Morton cares is if he gets a proper bill of sale. Come on, let's go down to Ogalalla and settle this. If you don't kill him, I will. What will Colonel Berry think?"

Buford stood there hunched. "Get me my hat, son," he said wearily. He was still staring at nothing.

Mike found the old man's big buff hat and handed it to him. Buford took it and stood there, smiling faintly.

"What's the matter with you?" Mike asked sharply.

"I can't kill Long. The trouble is, he's half right."

"Why? You've got the money coming to pay off

your shippers. He'll have to eat every damn word of it."

"There's a couple of things you don't know, Mike."

Mike looked at him for a moment, and then sat down on the bed. "All right. Let's have the truth, for once."

"I've got two private herds on the way north, son. Six thousand. I as good as stole them."

Mike asked, "What do you mean, stole them? When you sell them, you can pay off, and have the profit."

Buford said, "I ain't going to sell them. They're my seed herd, Mike. My one chance. I won't sell 'em, Mike." His eyes lost the dull look and settled down stubborn. "You can call me a liar or anything else you want. That herd goes with the ranch. Six thousand head for seed, son."

"Whose are they?"

"Mine."

"I mean, who trusted you to sell them?"

"They're mine, damn it. I got the bill of sale right here." Buford slapped himself on the breast pocket. "I got it, it's legal, they're mine."

"In a pig's eye they're yours. Who trusted you?"

"Well, Terman. I'll pay him back out of earnings. I'll pay him back double."

"Did he agree to that plan?"

"Hell, no, he didn't. But that's what it is." Buford turned away, putting his hat on, and roamed around like some old bear. "Where's that bottle?"

"Just a minute," Mike said. "That's stealing."

Buford whirled around. "So it's stealing. By God, I had to get out of Texas with something besides my lousy skin. Something to put on Montrose's ranch."

"Something you don't own to put on a ranch you don't own, either. By God, how do you do it? Stealing a man's cows to stock your ranch. By God, I bet you'd rob Montrose if he let you do it!"

"Sonny," Buford said, his eyes shining, "you said one hell of a mouthful. I only wish he was as big a fool as Terman; I'd get his goddam ranch for nothing."

They stood there glaring at each other, and Buford began to laugh, a hearty, warm chuckle. "Man, what a life. Let's have a drink. To a good ranch for your mother."

"Don't drag Mother into it!" Mike said. "She had nothing to do with your stealing your lousy cows."

"Well, by God, she'll have the ranch, and she'll eat the cows. We'll get there, all right."

"Over Terman's dead body," Mike said. "I hope you drown in your damn drink. I tell you one thing, Dad, you can ruin yourself if you want to, but not me. My credit's good and I want it to stay good." He took one step toward the old man, and Buford stopped smiling. "We're going down the trail and sell your damn six thousand as soon as we've delivered on our contracts up here. We'll sell them in Dodge, and we'll pay off Terman. You can buy seed cattle in Montana, anywhere, for cash."

"No," Buford said. "I ain't going back to Texas at all. The ones that get paid, get paid by draft."

"Where are those cattle?"

"I won't tell." The old man's eyes smiled. "They're the last thing I own in the world, and they're moving up the trail right now, headed for home. My last home."

"Who's driving those cows?"

"I won't tell." Buford's black eyes twinkled. He suddenly reminded Mike of a mischievous baby.

Mike erupted. "Six thousand head of cattle heading for a ranch that you got on an option that's about to run out. And you call it a home for Mother. Couldn't you spread it any thinner? Where do you want to spend your last years? In a cell? Dad, don't you know when to quit?"

The old man grinned, his beard bristling. "No. Mike, I'm washed up in Texas. I'll never get back down there. But I can start afresh in Montana. And I'm going to. They can hound me to hell, they can seize every damn cow of mine they can find, and they can seize my horses and my damn boots, but they won't get my seed herd, son. It's lost, right this minute. I lost it on purpose, in the Indian Country, and I told Colby—" He stopped.

"So it's Colby driving them."

"All right, it's Colby. But you'll never find them, and nobody else, because Colby's loyal to me, and I'll see the whole six thousand in hell before I give a one up."

He took a step toward Mike, and Mike backed away.

"And you know why?" The white beard jutted out and the black eyes lit up. " 'Cause they're my one chance, to set up as a man in a new country, with your mother in a decent house of her own. And as for Terman, why, screw Terman. I'd rob the goddam United States Treasury for less excuse than this." He laughed. "Where is that bottle?"

He found it in the bathroom and Mike listened to the gurgle. The old man came back with two glasses.

Mike said, "What you're doing is ruining me. You know that. If you run out on Terman, it's my name too. Why, Dad, you could sell those cattle in Dodge and clear a hundred thousand. You could settle down in San Antonio out of debt and live decent in your own town, instead of getting lost in Montana or some other place."

Buford held out one of the glasses. "Are you with me or against me?"

Mike said nothing.

"You can drink with me, and help me bull this thing through, as I will—or I'll do it alone. I'll go to

Ogalalla alone, and I'll shoot that son of a bitch Long alone, too."

"Go ahead," Mike said. "I'm through."

Buford said, "You'd better come with me, boy. Like you said, if I'm ruined, you're ruined. You'd better take a long chance and play it out with me."

Mike looked at the glass Buford still held out.

"Go away," he said, "I want to think."

"All right," Buford said, and set down the glasses. "I'm going to the station to find out about trains."

Mike looked at him. The beard was warm, white, almost cream in the light from the window. "Why don't you want to go back to San Antonio? There's something behind all this that you're not telling."

"Some things are private, son."

"You were born there, like me. We both love it. What's the reason for Montana? What's the truth?" He waited.

Buford stood there without expression, his face as impassive as the plaster cherubs in Holt's office.

"You're always getting people to go on faith, you're always selling them a line. Why don't you let me in on the whole damn truth, for once?"

The sun struck a wide band across Buford's eyes. "Sometimes you get into something so deep," he said gently, "the only way out has got to be a little crooked. It wouldn't do any good if you knew the whole truth. Trust me, son. I will straighten it out. I swear it, I give you my word of honor. I will straighten everything out, or get killed trying." He smiled. "It's better for us to stick together. Ain't it?"

He opened the door and went out.

Mike sat alone. The odor of whisky faded. A fly buzzed in the bathroom. He thought of Nancy Berry, far off by the little green river. Mike had the sensation of things falling away, dropping out of control. He sat with his head in his hands, trying to think.

The trouble was, a man couldn't join the crowd

against his father. A man was stuck with what God gave him; you had to go along. And then, there was something about Buford, some unnameable quality, that made you love him, after you had got through hating him.

Sons of cheats had to go to other towns, it was always the way. So if the old man went down, he went down too, as far as San Antonio and Nancy were concerned. On the other hand, if, somehow, he could get the old man clear, and safely tucked away on his dream ranch in Montana, then he would have a clear field with Nancy Berry, and his mother could do as she liked.

The only hitch was this seed herd of the old man's, unpaid for, unallowed for, practically stolen. How had Buford got so desperate? What in the name of God could be driving him so hard? The only thing to do was to sell it, lever the bill of sale out of the old man some way.

Mike stood up, got himself a quick drink out of the bottle, and went downstairs. Buford was in the bar, buying toddies for a few compadres.

The headwaiter saw Mike and came over, smiling beautifully.

"I want a dinner," Mike said, "in one of the private rooms. There will be three. See if you can remember the kind of thing Mr. Allen usually eats, and have that."

"Ah, yes, Mr. Buford Allen I know well."

"That's a major delusion with many of us," Mike said and walked toward the front door, past the bar.

CHAPTER EIGHT

Cheyenne
Kuykendahl's—5:00 P.M.

The Negro woman holding the wide oaken door—maid, cook, whatever she was—looked at Mike with a dull, remote hostility.

"Is the General at home?" he asked, standing quietly under her mahogany examination. He handed her his card.

She shut the door in his face.

He looked down at himself. Was there something wrong with his blue lounge suit, or his button shoes? Then he understood. It was his accent. She must be from New Jersey, like the Montroses. He looked up at Kuykendahl's roof. The house was a monstrous English peasant's cottage: long, low, and ranchy-looking, the latest thing in architectural forgery, with a fake thatch roof.

The five-foot oak door swung open again. The old nanny looked at him, and then, with a barely suppressed expression of nausea, got out of his way. She shunted him into a small sitting room and shut the door on him.

He sat in the gloom and waited.

A door opened. He could see the dark figure, in a long gown that whispered, leaning over a table lamp.

A match flared, and he saw her face. It was the same girl he had seen in front of the hotel, and he remembered the old man coming up the steps. That, of course, had been the general.

The girl held the match to the round wick of the lamp and put back the mantle. Her figure had the same quality as her face—the same grave curves, gentleness, and grace. He watched her, entranced, smiling to himself.

She turned and, after a moment, saw him. She said, raising one hand a little, "Oh!"

He stood up slowly and she stood there. "My apologies," he said, trying to look like Lord Nelson. "I was waiting for your father."

"You were?" she asked. "My gracious. How long had you been sitting here in the dark?"

"Three days," he said.

She laughed. It was a nice, plain, warm laugh.

Nancy Berry had a kind of throaty voice, rich and somehow very attractive. Nancy Berry could say things softly, in that unsoft voice, and make them mean twice what anybody else would mean.

"I'll bet you twenty dollars your old nanny never even told the General I was here. She just brought me in here to starve."

"Oh, Herbia." She looked at him. "Who are you?"

"Michael Allen." He drew a deep breath. "My father and your father are—not very good friends."

"You want to buy our ranch."

"Yes."

"Well, kindly do so. I am sick of Montana."

Somebody knocked on the door, and then it opened.

Herbia came in. She saw the girl and then looked quickly at Mike.

"The Genrul," she said. "He says yes."

Herbia looked at the girl with bitter, outraged eyes. How could she have lowered herself to converse with white trash?

The old man was standing in the main parlor in front of the fireplace, of green Italian marble, most suitable to a peasant hut. The General was warming his thin, tightly trousered behind. He looked at Mike with no expression—just a slight upward contortion of the lips, like a plaster smile. He had a high beak of a nose, like a turtle's, and quiet blue eyes.

"Mr. Michael Allen," the General said. Mike couldn't tell whether there was a trace of irony. It should have been pleasant, the voice, to go with the plaster smile. Maybe it was.

"Yes," Michael said in the silence. "It's a pleasure to meet you, sir," he went on, being careful not to let it sound like much of a pleasure. These old turkeys didn't like warmth; they liked respect. "A remarkable house," Michael said, glancing around briefly with a total lack of interest.

"It isn't mine," the General said. "I have not yet had the honor of meeting your father, sir," he said, "since he arrived in Cheyenne. I have been looking forward to a visit."

It was an art, lying in your teeth like that, Mike thought.

"He expressed the same feeling, sir," Mike said, feeling his way down this pitch dark corridor of spoofery. "He sent me to extend an invitation to dinner—dinner tonight, in fact—with his apologies for the late notice. The fact is, we only knew of your presence here this afternoon, and we have to leave Cheyenne this evening—and so we do hope you can find it possible to accept. Would eight o'clock be too early?"

"Please accept my thanks, young man," the General said, "and tender my regrets to your father. Perhaps some other time. It has been a pleasure, sir."

The General's smile increased, which was a signal to depart.

Herbia cleared her throat meekly.

"He will be very sorry, sir," Mike said. "May I ask you a favor?"

The General's eyes opened a little wider, and a look of innocence or incredulity appeared in them.

"My father was hoping to ask you this later on," Mike said. "As that won't be possible, permit me the liberty of bringing up the subject of business now."

How had the General's eyes become so cold, with all that scientific detachment?

"Certainly," the General said.

Mike stood silent. Nothing would come. The General waited with a face like a dead Indian's. He was used to waiting.

The door opened behind Mike; he heard the faint rustle of satin.

The old man's face softened, and the small, habitual smile actually became a smile.

"Mr. Allen is asking me a favor, Clara," the General said.

"Is that so?" the girl asked in a nice voice. "I thought he was praying."

Mike looked at her. "It's simply this," he said. "My father wants an extension on his option." He looked at the General. "He wants a month. Our cattle are coming along in proper order, and he will be able to make his payments. But he wants a little more margin of time. I simply wanted to ask you—don't give it to him."

"What?" the General asked.

"Don't give him an extension."

"Why not?" the General asked. "The odd thing is, I hadn't the slightest intention of doing so. I have obtained money enough to carry on and I don't have to sell, now. I hope your father does miss his date. The only reason I ever sold him an option in the first place was because he talked such immense sums, and I was—well—never mind! I hope he fails absolutely."

"I hope so too," Mike said. "He wouldn't like Montana." He looked at the girl. "Why don't you?"

"So many suitors—all impossible. They're so pitiful, all either like little boys—or drunk." She picked a piece of candy out of a silver dish on a small table by the fireplace. "They idealize women so. Why? Heaven only knows."

"Clara," the General said.

"It's a free country, Father," she said. "I can speak plainly before Mr. Allen. He's a plain-spoken person himself, aren't you—Michael?" She smiled at him and he had a slight attack of vertigo.

"Frankly, I hope your father *does* make his option. I want to go back to New Jersey. Most of the time in Montana, I sew. I embroider horse cloths for Daddy. Don't I, Daddy? Have a piece of chocolate, Mr.—What did you say your name was?"

"Michael Horsecloth."

"What?" the General asked.

"Give Mr. Allen an extension, Daddy," Clara said.

"I won't," the General said. "He has eight days in which to make his first payment."

"Could you tell me one thing, General?" Mike asked.

"What?"

"Why is it that my father wants your ranch?"

"Well, I will say this much. He is pursuing an illusion. I knew your father well at one time. If you will forgive my saying so, he is a man of illusions. For instance, he always thought the Civil War was a personal issue between the two of us. Believe me," he added, "I am not criticizing him. He was a valiant man."

"And this whole Montana venture is another illusion?"

"He has his. I have mine. The pursuit of illusion is a favorite human occupation. No doubt you have yours." He glanced at his daughter with a look of mild malevolence. "Perhaps that the possession of a mere woman will make you happy." He smiled. "That is a very popular illusion."

"Really," Clara said. "Don't mind Father," she said to Mike. "He is just playing with you."

"Not at all," the General said. "I am most serious. We all live in a fog, Mr. Allen. Those who think they have the clearest sight are the most deluded. Only the ones who admit they are lost are wise."

"Rubbish," Clara said. "He's perfectly happy, Mr. Allen."

"My daughter has the characteristically feminine illusion that saying something is so will make it actually exist."

"You've been talking too much with Lydia Kuykendahl," Clara said. "Mrs. Kuykendahl has the unfortunate gift of making Father feel as though he were wise. Have a piece of chocolate, Mr. Allen—I mean, Mr. Horsecloth."

"I wish I could," Mike said. "But really I must get back."

"Why don't you stay to dinner?" Clara asked.

"Yes," the General said. "Why not stay to dinner? Lydia is out gossiping, and old Kuyk is out gambling somewhere, and we will have a nice, private little philosophical discussion. We will call it a seminar in the Pursuit of Illusion, guaranteed by the Constitution of our beloved country."

"I have to go back. My father has a lot of business."

"Duty," the General said. "The only solution. The surrender of the will to the impositions of somebody even more stupid than oneself. We're having some quail. Do stay."

"I wish I could," Mike said, holding out his hand.

"You know," the General said, taking it, "I had the illusion that I would detest any relative of Buford's. And I find myself inviting you to dinner. How we blunder about in our private little fogs! And there's no cure for it, is there? Come," the General said, "I can tell by your face you'd like to stay—surrender, my boy, surrender! Say something, Clara."

"Surrender," Clara said, smiling at him. She was challenging him in a peculiar way. Mike felt a slight giddiness.

"All right," he said. "I surrender." It was a silly kind of thing to say, and do, like stepping off the roof of a three-story building just to prove you weren't a coward; but there was more to it than that—a kind of flash between them, as though she had summed up all their latent and potential hostilities, the little bothersome male-female conflicts that would confuse the issue, and had thrown them in his face, to have it all out at once. That's when he had stepped off the edge, with that faint feeling—when he gave up instead of stringing it out. He wouldn't have done it with anybody else, least of all Nancy Berry—he wouldn't have dared to. And thinking that, he realized with a shock that he simply did not trust his beloved Nancy.

Clara was different. But behind all that nerve, that monstrous affront to the laws of courtship and flirtation, there was something else. She looked like a queen, but on a closer look, he could detect a small girl dressed up in adult clothing. And then he realized that, of course, the old man and his daughter were both lonely. That was why they liked him.

They lived in the wilds of Montana, and he was quite a change with his clean shave, flashing white teeth, and button shoes, plus Southern accent.

He saw a look pass over her face that was the equivalent of a colorless blush—she became more lovely, and yet retreated, smiling just a little, turning her face away from him. She was pleased at her victory, but what was more, he had touched her. More appalling yet, she had touched him. He looked at her half-averted face, feeling peculiarly happy.

"He surrenders," the General said, smiling in his pale Indian way. "Herbia, go tell one of the boys in the stable to ride down to the Elk Horn and tell Mr. Allen, Senior, thanks very much but no, thanks. We have kidnaped his son."

"Yassuh. You ain't going."

"Advise Mr. Allen that his son is staying to dinner."

"Yassuh." Herbia was obviously miserable. She slunk out, kicking her heavy petticoats before her.

"Poor Herbia," Clara said. "She's obsessed with the thought that I can't take care of myself."

"The most deluded of us all," the General said, looking at Mike.

If there was something in the Montroses' status of poor relations, in Kuykendahl's monstrous cottage, the servants didn't show it. The light in the dining room was splendid. The pale candles dripped and fluttered in the chandelier, making the girl's face seem to come and go, like an illusion or a dream. It was extremely difficult at times for Mike not to gawk—but he did his best to maintain a facade of pleasant detachment which allowed him to look at her almost as much as he wanted.

"To subsist, one must be rude," the General said, more or less to himself, and drank off his Chablis. "Fill it up," he said to the footman, who was no laggard anyway. "It is a profound mistake, politically speaking, ever to accept a delicate sentiment or a gentle gesture with anything like courtesy. Must be sure to trample on it in the sight of everybody."

"Dear Daddy," Clara said, picking up a bit of quail with her fork. "Mr. Shoestrap will think you are a cynic."

"So he will," the General said, lifting his wine-glass. "I am overdoing it on purpose, my dear. He is obviously too nice for this poor world, and I am trying to tan him in a vicarious spleen, so to speak, before some woman gets the best of him. He looks as though he'd decay rather easily, don't you think, my dear?"

Clara looked at Mike. Mike's head was beginning to have a rather tight, swollen feeling from the wine, as though he were a good deal more than all there.

"I think he's very nice," Clara said objectively.

"How do you think he would stand up in Montana?" the General asked, pushing his dessert aside. "Can you rope a steer, young man?"

"Without any false modesty," Mike said, looking at Clara, "I can say I am an expert."

"Break a horse?"

"Certainly. The very worst."

"Well, take my advice and stop it," the General said. "You can always hire some fool to get his bones broken for you. Why do it yourself? Dear children, will you excuse me?" he asked, rising. "I feel rather giddy, and I think I will go to bed. Such a delightful evening, Mike, with old Kuyk's wine. I furnished the quail, I'll have you know." He wandered out of the room.

"I have to go too," Mike said quietly. "I'm sorry."

"Do you really?" she asked, rising. How did she do it? At one moment, she was sitting there, erect, swayed forward just a little, and the next, she had risen and was standing, looking at him sadly.

"I wish I didn't," Mike said. "I'd much rather stay here."

"Then why don't you?"

"Such a tangle of business."

"Such a busy young man. I hope you'll make lots of money. Will you?"

"I doubt it," he said, smiling. "Mostly, I'm just working for my father."

"Why?" she asked.

He looked at her blankly for a long moment. It was a simple question. In succession he thought of a lot of answers, none of which was the real one. Then he said, "Because he's more or less helpless, really. And I love him. That's all."

She looked back at him. "I should think, if you love him, he must really be a very nice man. In spite of what Father says. Father must be—prejudiced."

Mike shook his head. "No, he isn't a nice man. He's a headache. Sitting here tonight, I wish I could get out of it—his cockeyed life. It's a terrible thing always trying to get the world by the tail. It's a terrible strain."

"Listen to the wind," she said, and he stopped thinking. The wind was coming over the thatch overhead, from the west.

"I wish I could," he said. "Maybe I can—later."

Then, deliberately, she came up and kissed him, for a moment, and then stood back.

He looked at her in astonishment. "Why did you do that?" He began to blush.

"Because I like you—and I may not see you again. Is that too honest for a woman?"

He watched her, beginning to smile, and the blush died. "No," he said.

"A simple answer from an honest man," she said. "Most men are such fools. As soon as they look at a woman, they start acting. In one way or another."

He looked down at her face, calm and lovely, "Just like a General's daughter." The lightness in his head was gone. "I won't forget you," he said.

They stood looking at each other, and suddenly all his plans, those set and stodgy patterns, divided down the middle and he looked beyond them. What was there, really, to keep him from going to Montana and even from getting a job with the General?

Why should he go back to the hotel? Back to Texas? All that was like some cockeyed nightmare, his father's hallucinations and his own brittle little dreams. Who was Nancy Berry? He could barely recall her face; but then, compunction brought the effort. He was committed there, he had told her he was coming back, and she had said that she would wait. It was practically arranged. Honor was a hard, wooden master in a loose world. He sobered down.

He opened the front door and they stood on Kuykendahl's steps.

How little time there was for anything! Here, on these steps, he was allowed two minutes, when a thousand things hammered at him to be solved. What could he do? He stood there helpless.

"Michael," she said, "you seem to be decaying, right in front of me. Please don't try to solve all the problems tonight."

He looked up at her. She was right, of course. He looked at her eyes plainly, openly. Why think anything? A fat lot of good thought did, or words, or any of the other civilities.

"Good night," he said, looking into her eyes. And then the knowledge of it came up in him, all the way to the top of his head—the simple fact that he was beginning to fall in love with her. He kissed her, a little longer than a friend.

It wasn't much of a kiss, but it said a great deal to both of them. Then it was over, and she was standing there again, as she had been before.

"Michael," she said, "please don't say a word. Go away now, Michael. Please go away."

"I—I—"

"Please, not a single word, Michael—you'll say

something noble. You'll start acting, like all the others, and I don't want you to. Please go away."

"All right," he said. "Good-by."

"Good-by, good-by," she said, and he turned and walked away down the long path to the street. He looked back once. She was gone.

CHAPTER NINE

Cheyenne
A Private Dining Room
at the Elk Horn
Same Day—8:00 P.M.

Buford stood in the ornately paneled room, facing one of Kuykendahl's colored people.

"Yassuh," the boy said. "That's what Mr. Allen he's doing. Eating with the General. The General he sends his regrets."

Buford's hand glided into his pants pocket and came out with a five-dollar gold piece. He tossed it smoothly down the length of the damask-covered table and the boy caught it, ducking expertly and gliding from the room.

The headwaiter stood there with his card under his arm looking like a bandmaster who had just heard that his band had been lost at sea.

"Get out of here," Buford said civilly, not looking at him—looking instead at the four candles on their tall silver sticks in the middle of the table, surrounding the roses. Buford's sensibilities ran along certain obvious, well-established lines. Nothing pleased him as much as red roses, silver candlesticks, and white linen; the picture was standard, inevitable, and unalterable.

"The dinner, sir?" the captain asked, sucking his stomach in, rising slightly on his toes and trying to look menacing.

"Serve it," Buford said, fingering another gold piece in his pocket.

"Here, sir? For one?" It was ludicrous, one old man eating dinner for three in a private dining room. Mr. Allen stood there with his white beard shining genteelly in the candlelight.

"Get the hell out of here," Buford said quietly. "Send me in a bottle of bourbon." He sat down at the table.

"Yes, sir," the captain said, and bowed, and withdrew.

Buford sat eating olives and looking at the wall across the room. The place was like a warm, soft tomb, the ceiling and the paneling dark, gleaming faintly in the light. The candles made no sound, the flames were still as ice.

"Bastard," Buford said, just to hear something.

The door opened. It was another colored boy with the oysters.

"Bring it all in," Buford said quietly. "Then go away somewhere and leave me alone."

"It'll get cold, boss."

"Who cares?" Buford said, skinning the meat off an olive pit. He spat the seed out on the carpet.

"Yassuh," the boy said, his eyes glistening.

They came and went, amiable colored boys of all ages, while Buford looked at nothing. A bottle sat before him. Mr. Holt's pheasants gradually cooled.

What difference does it make? Buford thought, looking about at the waste. He took a stiff drink. Uptown, wherever Mike was, he would be eating with the General and his daughter, enjoying himself, and it was no doubt better. There was no use

feeling offended. Why be offended? He hadn't even
wanted Montrose to come.

No, but he might have liked seeing young Clara
again. A young, immature version of her mother. Or
was that fair? Well, in any case, why expect her to
be like the other Clara?

He took four big swallows from the bottle and ate
two oysters. He sat there looking at nothing, listening to the silence.

Ah, to be young, Buford thought, the whisky tightening in his head. To be a fool again, to see nothing,
to play the fool, to throw it all away. To be young
again, and not to know that everything was dust but
love. Not the sentimental crap that went with the
German valse bands and violins, not the jolly stuff
of housewives, but the disease, hardly recognizable
by the name, that lived like a slow fouling of the
bone, an endless desolation of the heart.

Suppose she weren't dead, after all? Suppose his
Clara had not died at all, as he had been told? What
they said, that she was lying in the ground up there
in Warhorse now, and had been for eleven years,
might not be true. It might be just Montrose's lie, to
put him off. She might have left Montrose for some
reason. She might, she might.

He took another drink. Death was the thing nobody could overcome. That was the end of everything, the unanswerable, senseless eclipse of all one's
reasons, of all the arguments and justifications, of
the self-excusings, the apologies, the pleadings, the
hopings. What had he, Buford, done to her, that could
ever equal death? No drunkenness, no shouting, no
offensiveness; no boastings, no vain accusings, could
have done what death had done to her; all these
things he could have undone; all his stupidities, in
time, could have been paid for, and he could have
got her back, even after she married Montrose. He

could have outlived Montrose, but he could not out-
live death.

He kept seeing her there, or an image of her, vague
and tenuous, sitting across the flowers from him, and
he sat with his fists clenched on the edge of the white
table, feeling the rage which he had felt at the news
of her death rise again in his chest, bottled up and
suffocating. He had heard it in a saloon, and he had
sat in the saloon and after a while the horrible rage
had burst out and he had flung the bottle against
the backbar, smashing what he could, as though the
mirror were death. And always that preposterous
vain rage in his chest, that bursting uncomprehend-
ing sense of affront, of indignation and outrage.
Death was not in it at all. He had planned very well
how to get her back, how to undo all the damage he
had done, to show her again his real love for her,
beneath all the stupidities. And then she had been
taken out by death like a stranger, and all his hope
and rage and grief were useless.

You might really be there, he said in his heart, his
wordless mind making these words to the shape of
her, there across the flowers. *We might be here, old,
yes, through with all that stuff of passion. We could
have had all these years, if I had not been such a fool.*

She sat there smiling at him—not a delusion, for
he knew what he imagined—and the dark room
closed in around them, warm, compact, like a comfortable tomb.

But why worry about that now? she said. *Here we
are, you and I.*

I never knew, he said, *how much I loved you until
I had driven you away. Oh, why was I such a fool,
my dear?*

But it doesn't matter, Buford. We're here, now.

*If I had known what it would be like, all these years
without you—not seeing you, not hearing you, not even*

*knowing where you were—do you think, in my pride,
I would have offended you?*

She sat there, smiling.

*You know I couldn't help it, don't you? That I was
born a fool. God forgive my pride. God forgive me for
hurting you.*

He sat looking at his vision. But it said nothing.
It had nothing to say. He kept her there, so delicately turned out in her white dress, as she had been
one night when they had all gone down to the Palm
Garden and danced, long ago, before the war. She
said nothing, and vaguely smiled.

The image of her vanished and he looked at the
dark wall, clearly. There was no use in illusions, they
were poor stuff, and wore thin. Clara was dead, she
had been dead for years. But what did it matter,
when everything else had died too? Nearly everything he had ever loved was a corpse: his father, the
whole South, and all those towering dreams of his
own capabilities, which he had once believed in as
though he were God. He himself was nothing but a
potential corpse, with barely enough power left to
carry out one more coup, and maybe not that.

In the end, one had to be satisfied with what one
could get, and if that were no more than a woman's
grave, a piece of earth, far off in some God-forgotten
corner of the continent, why, then, a man had to be
content with that, for even a grave was something
real, some relic of what had been, and any solid relic
was better than the rubbish of memories and dreams
that time and age wore down into a finally unrec-
ognizable litter.

And if, there in Warhorse, there was no more of
her than her bones, and those invisible; still, that
much was her, it was not nothing, and he could live
out the last ten years, or whatever was left, at least
possessing that much. How little a man asked, at the
very end.

He got up, his bottle in one hand, and the plate of oysters in the other, and left the private dining room with its banquet, rotting in spotless splendor.

Upstairs he got undressed and brushed and combed his beard and washed and smoothed himself until he felt relaxed and comfortable again, and then, in his beautiful billowing nightshirt, he got his little suitcase and climbed into his big, smooth bed, with his bottle on one side and the oysters on the other.

He opened the little locked suitcase and took a large portrait daguerreotype in a heavy silver frame from a little nest of letters, neatly tied in packets.

He sat and looked at it, and then he looked away.

Outside it was very quiet, and he lay there with a moth beating about the lamp mantle, looking at Clara's face with a faint smile; not thinking, hardly remembering, but simply feeling what he had felt for her long before, and which he still felt.

He put down the picture and picked up a letter.

After she had married Montrose, he had not seen her until 1864, when she had been living in the camp attached to the prison. And after the war, he had not seen her again, only knowing that she was in Montana. But he had forgotten all those years of bitterness and sadness; and as he lay now, alone in the hotel room, he remembered only her—her voice, so sweet; her breath, to which he had listened with such delight; her movements; and he lay now with eyes shut, remembering how he had once sat, with eyes closed, listening to her movements, the small rustle of her dress—blind, yet knowing, foreseeing what she would do, what she would say, as though he had some intuitive gift of understanding her; as though his love actually contained her whole soul.

How was it possible that she could have died, and gone from the earth, and that he would never see her again?

It was not possible. Some day, when he was free of

all the mortal complications of his life, he would see her again in some fashion.

She had gone to Montana. And in that strange, far northern country, she had lived, and each tree, each mountain, had reflected something of her, and something of her—a radiance perhaps—had remained in the stones where she had passed; and in that country, he could follow where she had gone, and the stones and the trees would tell him that she had been there; and perhaps, there, he would find her in some sense. She was there. That was the last place she had been. If he were to find her again in any sense, it would be there, on Montrose's ranch.

And he could do it. Buford closed and locked the suitcase again. He had a million dollars coming up the trail. He was a cinch to make Montrose's option. And from then on he would have peace and a home— a home where all that mattered to him, the little that was left, was waiting for him now.

CHAPTER TEN

The Elk Horn Hotel
Buford's Bedroom—10:00 P.M.

An hour later Mike opened the door and looked at his father. Buford was propped up in bed on four massive white pillows.

Buford smiled with only a slight blear. "I'll keep for days," he said hoarsely, speaking with care. He was at the carefully spoken stage, where he made perfect sense but had to run at reduced speed.

"I hope you got the General's message," Mike said.

"Silly old bastard," Buford said, taking a sip out of his bottle. "I knew he wouldn't come. Have an oyster, my boy. You may take one." He shoved the plate at Mike. Some of the ice-water slopped onto the spread. "Call the maid," Buford said.

"Don't be so finicky," Mike said. "Why did you send me up there for nothing, if you knew he wouldn't come?"

"I wanted you to meet the girl. Clara."

"Oh, you know her?"

"Why, of course I know her. I've known her for

years. When I was in Montrose's prison, she was just
about two years old. Beautiful girl, Mike. I want you
to marry her."

"You're drunk."

"What of it? I can still think circles around you
and that potty old bastard Montrose." He snickered,
snuffling to himself at some private thought. "She
liked you, didn't she?"

"Yes. Why not?"

"If I can't make my option on time, my boy, you're
going to marry her immediately."

"Sure, sure."

"Bed," Buford said. "Beautiful, wonderful bed. Everything good is done in bed. Kings made. Thrones
united. Quarrels settled. Ranches sewed up."

"You're through, Dad. We'd better pack up and go
home."

"Shut up," Buford said with sudden cold sobriety.
"You get Morton—you remember our long-connected
sucker. And McCullough, the second buyer. You start
out tonight and go on down on a cattle train. Make
'em let you off where the line hits the South Platte—
you know where the Lodgepole Creek joins in. You
ride southeast forty miles or so and you hit the trail.
You can pick up Tucker. The way I figure, Tucker is
about eighty miles south of Ogalalla. You cut his
trail before he gets forty miles closer to Ogalalla.
That'll keep you out of Keith County. If Dickson's
agent—" His words died off till he was mumbling to
himself. "Ergo," he burst out again, "he won't have
jurisdiction, in any case. Well, you sell Morton his
cattle and get his money, and then take McCullough
and ride south and sell the second herd. You take it
from there."

"Sounds like you heard something new."

The old man waved a hand at the bureau and took
another drink. "Another wire from Streeter. The
dirty little scut."

Mike picked up the yellow telegram:

*Long says you defaulted a suit by Dickson.
Dickson's agent met Long on trail and has
attachments on all your cattle. In view of this
and various complications I herewith tender
my resignation as your agent but understanding your financial position and appreciating
our past friendship I relinquish all claims to
commissions and fees now outstanding.
Streeter.*

Mike laid the paper on the marble bureau top.
Buford raised the bottle. "No more agent."

"I told you I didn't believe we'd make it." Mike's
voice was shaking. "I told you it was too good to be
true. Another steamboat."

"Don't disturb my peace of mind. Go get Morton
and get started." The old man's speech was beginning to blur.

"What are you going to do? Die in bed?"

"I'm going to Ogalalla to thrash Long and hood-
wink the authorities—if I can."

"My God—more fraud? Why didn't you tell me
about Dickson's suit? And why in God's name did
you default it?"

"He would have won it anyway," the old man said
languidly. "I didn't default it, son. I never got the
summons. Your mother wired me after the judgment. Deputy claimed I refused the summons. Swore
it. I never saw it." He smiled. "Dickson had won by
that time—he had all my notes. Just go on and get
Morton, boy. We'll get something out of the mess
yet. I was just hoping—just hoping I could sell them
cattle before Dickson could attach them."

"You haven't got any conscience at all, have you?
Nothing bothers you, does it?"

"Nothing," Buford said, closing his large handsome eyes, "except starvation. And defeat."

Mike said nothing.

"Get going, sonny."

"Suppose I said I was through?"

His father looked at him. "Would you?" he asked quietly. "You know if you don't take Morton down there and sell that herd, I'm sunk. I'm too old to ride a hundred miles without stopping. Anyway, Dickson won all that money off me by cheating at cards. I know right now, without being told, how Dickson got all my notes. That's why Long is so sore, because he sold my notes for peanuts to Dickson, and now he sees Dickson is going to collect at par. Damn Long anyway, can't a man be a simple business competitor without stabbing me in the back?"

Sudden fury rose in Buford's face, swelling the veins and turning it red. He half rose in bed. Then, without a word, he sank back and lay breathing a little fast.

"I'll kill that Long. That lousy bastard, selling me down the river to that—"

He stopped himself and lay quiet, staring at nothing. He turned suddenly to Mike. "What does it matter to you, stealing what? We're all a pack of thieves, by God! Dickson most of all. What's thievery among thieves? It's past all accounting. And as for you and your priggy little notions, what would you do if you didn't thieve with me? Do you think there is anything honest to do in the world? What else can you do if you're not a preacher or a priest? Why didn't you become a priest, the way your mother wanted you to? Either that or sell fertilizer." He took a long, hard pull at the bottle.

Mike looked at him. All he noticed was the babble, the froth of words coming out of the old man. He was helpless—holed up in bed with a bottle.

"Or are you with the others?" Buford said. "Are you going to sell me down the river too?"

"Hell, no," Mike said. "I don't suppose I can. I suppose you'll drag me right down with you."

"What do you mean, down?" Buford said. "Where I am is up."

"As long as you didn't steal 'em, I'll sell 'em," Mike said.

The old man smiled. "That's the boy. I knew you wouldn't let me down. *Caveat Emptor!* Troop, charge, ho! I'll go to Ogalalla. Oh, God, God help us all."

Mike shut the door and went to his own room for his guns and his boots. Evidently the time had passed for button shoes.

CHAPTER ELEVEN

Ogalalla, Nebraska
July 9—4:00 P.M.

In the evening the foremen and the men from the
herds which were bedded down south of the river
would come into town and get drunk and gamble,
and this went on for weeks sometimes until a foreman and his men got paid off, after the herd was
brought up and the old man got the cash.

So all summer long the plains south of the little
board town between the Platte and the U.P. would
be dotted with cattle, herd after herd as far as you
could see.

There were flowers in the grass early in the season, and along the river the cowboys would go swimming and wash out their clothes, and when they
weren't riding night guard or getting drunk in Ogalalla, or when they were trying to save their money
for back home, they would sit around the fires and
tell lies and maybe do a little singing, or listening
to somebody else sing. And in the daytime they

would play mumblety-peg, with its eternal complications and contortions.

The biggest thing about it all was not the sky, or the plains, or the vast herds of cattle, or even the big slow river—it was the wind. The wind came out of the west, a thousand miles high and five thousand miles wide, and it never quit for more than a few hours at a time.

It blew away the blowflies and the deer flies and the horseflies, and sometimes it nearly blew away the horses too. It swept under the barroom door and sent the dust in little whirls, and it sucked the cigar smoke out of a rich man's mouth before he could inhale it, and blew the Bull Durham out of the poor man's cigarette paper before he could roll it. A pretty girl would come out from St. Paul to dance in the dance hall and in a week her lips were all cracked and peeling, dried out like buffalo bones. ·

Down by the railroad, where the buffalo bones were stacked higher than a man's head, waiting for shipment, the wind sighed in the gray piles, moaning in the honeycombed stacks.

The wind blew Nebraska all over the nation, hell, west, and crossways. A man could spit in the street in Ogalalla on Tuesday, and by Friday it would be in New York.

In the late afternoon, around four, they would hear the U.P. train—the regular passenger, coming down the long grade from Cheyenne, 160 miles away—long before the train would come in sight, the sound carried ahead for miles on the wind.

Gunfire was louder to windward, and a man shouting upwind was hard put. All night long, when the wind was bad, the flapping and banging of loose signs and shutters would keep the drummers awake, and every stranger. Then the men would go in the saloons, and the women in their back parlors, and everything human, hidden away from the wind, would get warmer and more close, and all would stand around drinking and smiling, and voices would boom out louder, as though in triumph at the victory of the human race over the universe. And all the time that they sang and blustered in the saloons, outside the big wind, that started in the entrails of the stars, would reach and boom and play with the roofs and rip off the shingles and rattle and ting and bang the shutters, while out on the plains, in the sod huts, some of the women, to whom the stars had come too close, knelt in the moonlight and bayed like hounds.

Late in the afternoon of July 9, Buford stepped carefully down from the U.P. passenger car, carrying only his small, locked suitcase, and faced the monumental piles of the bones of the dead giants of the plains.

The wind blew his silky beard eastward, and the brim of his hat flopped up. Down the slope from the tracks to the South Platte, the town lay gaunt and rattling, bone-gray clapboard mixed in with new yellow pine.

He felt the old gun stuck in his pants, its long muzzle uncomfortable in his groin, and started across the wide street toward the livery stable.

There were three horses tied outside the big door, and they all had Long's brand. Buford smiled.

"If it ain't my luck," he said, walking in. They had a fourth horse with a neck sling on, being shod.

Four wide, slow smiles. "Hello, Pappy," one tall one said. "Figured you'd be along. The old man's hotter'n hell."

"Screw the old man," Buford said. "Mr. Smith, I want a horse."

"He's waiting for you," a third one said. "He says if you got the goddam guts to come here, he'll kill you."

Buford laughed. "Go down to whatever saloon he's boarding at and tell him I've come down here to beat

him like a six-year-old boy. Tell him that. Tell him
I'm going to make him cry like a baby. Where is
he?"

"The Paradise," the short one said.

The horse in the sling was shaking all over with
fear, eyes rolled back. The smith touched a hot shoe
to the hoof. Blue smoke boiled up, stinking.

"That's a hell of a way to fit a shoe," Buford said.

"Yeah?" the smith said. "Who are you to come
into this town and start telling me what to do?"

"Any damn fool knows better than to burn a shoe
on. Any damn fool can take the time to hammer it
to a fit. Any damn fool, I guess, but Long's smith."

The smith stood up slowly and looked at Buford.

"Screw you all," Buford said. "You think that old
bastard boss of yours can say things about an Allen,
and you can sit there grinning like a bunch of crap-
eating cats. I'll whip the whole damn cheap outfit of
you right into the gutter. Now get going and tell
your old woman of a boss to hire himself a bed, because he's going to need one."

The four stood looking at him quietly, and the
smith too.

Without a word, the short one went to the door and
swung up on one of the three horses, and left.

"I want a horse," Buford said to the smith. "A
good heavy horse sixteen hands high. Seventeen.
Good and heavy."

"I ain't got such a horse," the smith said. "I ain't
got no horse at all."

"You mean to tell me," Buford said, "you can
stand there and lie to me, and turn away my trade,
just because I bawled you out properly for burning a
horse that way? You ought to be ashamed of yourself. You should have been bawled out long ago. Any
man with any self-respect would have told you off.
That's a cruel, lazy way to fit a shoe, and nobody but

a sloppy bum would do it. Now, by God, start running your business like a man and hire me a horse."

The smith stood with his face red. The others stood silent, stiff, their eyes lowered.

"You know I'm right, don't you?" Buford said, looking straight at the smith.

The smith blinked. "Yes," he said, "I know you're right." He turned and looked at the three hands leaning against the wall. They stopped smiling. "If one of you says one goddam word, I'll bust his head with these here tongs." He turned and walked back into the shadows of the big barn.

Buford smiled at the three. "Bums," he said quietly. "Sheep-lovers."

"You better watch yourself, Allen," the tall one said. "We ain't going to take much more."

"Trash," Buford said. "Country trash. Knifers. Back-country knifers. A bunch of skinny, underbred, cold-blooded plain trash. Start something, you trash."

The forge glowed quietly. The wind howled in the rafters. Buford laughed. "That's it," he said. "That's it. My back ain't turned—better wait."

The smith brought back a horse. It was a big, raw mountain of a horse, seventeen hands high, with a head on it like a stump. It came along jazzing around, snorting, head in the air like a wild goose, little red eyes peering down like mice out of a belfry.

"Crazy," the smith said. "But it's what you asked for, and I don't mind if he kills you."

"I notice you got a saddle on him without any help," Buford said. "I guess I can sit on it."

"He don't buck," the smith said. "He's just a damn fool. Last week he went straight through a solid board fence and never even felt it. Shied at a bit of paper. He ain't mean. He's just plain dumb and careless. Crazy."

"That's the kind of horse I like," Buford said.

"Now I want to buy a couple of light buggy springs. You got any such?"

"I have. Four bits apiece."

"Bring me two. About a yard long and an inch wide. Light ones."

The smith went back in the barn and came out with a couple of springs. Buford stuck them under his arm and pulled out a twenty-dollar bill. "What's the name of this horse? He looks a lot like Long."

"We call him Old Iron Ass," the smith said. "Have a good time."

Buford neck-reined the jag-boned mountain of a horse away from the barn. He touched him once with his heels and the horse rolled forward into a long, easy lope, ponderous and smooth as water. Buford reined him up and down beside the railroad twice, and then trotted down the slope toward the main street, where the dust was blowing harder than ever.

In Rooney's saloon there was plenty of noise, the stamp of boots and laughter, and a steady roar of conversation. Buford went up the wobbling stairs, tripped on an empty bottle, and went down the long second-story hall to the front of the building. He knocked on No. 47.

"Who is it?" a man's voice complained.

"Buford. Open up, Streeter."

There was a long silence.

Then: "Go away, Buford. You got my wire."

"Open up, Streeter," Buford said.

Bedsprings creaked. Then the door opened, and a short man with a large paunch stood back, holding it.

"Streeter, you are a heartless wretch."

The other blinked, twice, as though thinking this over. He had long gray hair brushed down smoothly, and the impress of his hat made a perfect shelf in it, all the way around. His eyes were dark, and drooped sadly at the outside corners. Still, the general effect was one of resigned dignity.

"I don't accept your goddam resignation," Buford said quietly in a small, nasty voice. "You hurt me, Streeter. You hurt me deeply. It's all right for these cheap bastards like Long to call me a thief, these picayune cattle buyers and scrambling cheats. But for you—for you—"

Streeter looked at him, dark eyes protesting sadly. "I did not call you anything, Buford. Why deny the facts? Why—why try to? Everybody knows it, everybody but me. Here I am, your agent, doing business in your name, assuming—assuming everything. And all of a sudden it appears you are not only broke but you have a million-dollar lawsuit on top of, of—on top, I say. And they—and they—are calling me a dirty crook—a crook, Buford, a crook." There was genuine grief in the dark eyes. "How could you, how could you? Your own friend. How could you? Lie to the others, Buford—but not, but not to me—not to me."

Buford raised the springs and slammed them against the board wall. Streeter's eyes opened wide.

"For the last damn time, Streeter, I am not lying to anybody! How could you believe it?"

He pulled his two hands down over his face and his beard, dragging them. His face was old and lined, sad and mournful, his big, handsome eyes drooped almost exactly like Streeter's.

"It's my enemies. Long, Dickson. They tried to ruin my credit. I was going to pay every cent. Can I count on you?" Buford asked humbly. "Your word, against my enemies. Say that you'll vouch for me against my enemies. Against this son of a bitch that's been spreading lies."

"Long?"

"Him and the other one too, the fellow that's got the attachments."

"The attachments. Oh, dear. You mean—what?"

"Vouch for me. With the sheriff. Bailey is such a damn gullible fool, he'll believe anything Dickson's man says."

"What? Oh, you mean this attachment fellow will come, and will come to see Bailey?"

"Well, what the hell else? He's got to have the law to enforce it all, doesn't he? If he ain't got the local law, why, screw his attachments."

Streeter's sad eyes twinkled at something in the distance. "Why, how perfectly true."

"And he got them by a fraud. A lie. I know those damn process servers down in Texas. You can buy them for two dollars a day, they'll swear anything. For two bucks they'll swear they served a summons on George the Third."

Streeter hummed.

Buford said, "Besides, if Dickson gets all those cattle, he's stealing your commission. What's three per cent of a million dollars, Streeter, old friend?"

A look of anger lighted Streeter's sad, resigned face. "The dirty thieves," he said with a jaded rancor. "My poor friend—of course, of course, I will vouch for you with Bailey."

Buford smiled, his white beard spreading. His big, handsome eyes were full of light and kindness. "Streeter, I knew you wouldn't let me down, old friend. And I won't let you down either. I have many devices—many plans, Streeter. Always another plan, my friend."

CHAPTER TWELVE

Ogalalla
Rooney's Hotel—Same Day
6:00 P.M.

Buford left No. 47 and went down the long, dark hall to the steps.

The wind was still blowing, creaking the rafters overhead, but downstairs it was quiet. Buford paused at the head of the stairs and listened.

There was still talking, below, but it was much softer. He sniffed the fragrance coming up the stair well on the draft—a delicate conflux of Old Bull, sweat, whisky, and horse manure.

He went down, with a caution that looked much like dignity.

Somebody below called. "He's acoming!" and all the talking died. Buford stood still, halfway down.

Then a long fellow with a fresh, red, scrawny face and tobacco-yellow cavalry mustaches appeared, smiling, at the foot of the steps.

"Bless us all to hell," the tall individual said. "It's Buford. Buford, I heard you was looking for a tussle, so I come here instead of waiting. Let's have a drink for old times' sake, before I mop up the floor with your hide."

Buford went on down, slowly, smiling gently.

The doors to the dining room and the saloon were crowded with men, waiting quietly. Nobody wore guns, except hide-outs like Buford's, and nobody knew who had those except the men that wore them. There was no gun on Long that Buford could see, but that didn't mean anything. There might have been a dozen guns in that crowd.

"What do you know about mopping, trash?" Buford asked. "You was brought up on mud floors, weren't you?"

Long's smile looked pained.

"I never robbed nobody, though," Long said.

"And I never sold out a friend the way you sold my note to Dickson—my worst enemy."

Long flushed and lost his smile.

"I heard from my agent," Buford went on, "that you've been calling me a thief. Ruining my character."

There had been a kind of suppressed enjoyment in the crowd, an anticipation of something more or less amusing, if bloody. The merriment had gone now.

"Your character," Long said, his red face hostile. His little black eyes snapped. "You owed me two thousand dollars, Allen. You ain't got a dime now, and you ran out on everybody at home. Hear that, you all?" he shouted at the crowd. "Everybody knows it."

"You damn chicken-hearted pimp, you sold my note for nothing. I was going to pay you and I am still going to pay you. Like this." Buford spat straight into Long's face.

Long gasped. His face turned bright red and his right hand dived into his pants pocket. It got stuck, hauling the derringer out, and Buford, smiling with joy, swung one of the springs and caught Long across the side of the neck with it. Long went down with his hand still in his pocket.

Somebody burst out laughing, and then everybody began to laugh. The front door opened and on a burst of wind and dirt, a small, compact man with a black beard and bright, hard eyes came in. He had a wide black belt with a big gun hanging from it. He pulled that out and stood there with his black bowler hat on straight, and looked at Long, and then at Buford.

"I'm Sheriff Bailey," he said. "What's wrong?"

Long was sitting up, swearing horribly in a low voice. The little gun was still stuck in the pocket of his tight pants, and he didn't have sense enough to let go so he could get his hand out.

Bailey went over and stuck his gun under Long's sharp, red nose. "Give me that, sonny," Bailey said matter-of-factly, "or I'll break your head."

Long looked at Bailey's gun. He sat there glaring at Buford, and then slowly got up. He got the two-shot gun out and gave it up.

"Now, listen," Bailey said. "This is a peaceful town. If you want to kill each other, get the hell across the river."

"He's a back-shooting son of a bitch," Buford said. "I'd never make it across the river. Here, Long," he said, and threw one of the springs at him. "You was in the cavalry too, as I recall. Go outside and get on your horse and I'll saber-whip you. A little contest," he said to Bailey, "a sporting event solely. No malice aforethought. Surely you can't boggle at a little workout with the sword?"

They began laughing again, and Buford laughed too.

"You got any guns?" Bailey asked, his hard, bright eyes unchanging.

"Who, me?" Buford asked. "If I was armed, don't you think I would have shot this skunk just now, in self-defense? Here I was, with nothing but these pieces of iron, helpless, with him pulling at that boudoir cannon."

"The hell with all that," Bailey said, without change. He looked like a bull terrier on the end of a chain, eyes fixed and intent. "Answer my question, yes or no. Have you got any guns?"

"Why, yes, Mr. Bailey, of course I have," Buford said politely, smiling and pulling his old Colt out of his pants. "Did you think I'd be crazy enough to come into this town without a gun?"

"No," Bailey said. "That's why I asked you." He took the gun and stuck it down his own pants.

Long was looking at the spring on the floor. He picked it up and worked it with his wrist, and a slow smile started. He looked up at Buford. "A damn good idea, you old sack of bull. I ain't had my hands on a saber for fifteen years. Come on."

He headed for the door, and the crowd followed.

Outside, Buford mounted Old Iron Ass and rode him down the street. He stopped and turned, holding his spring on his shoulder, and saw Long riding his nag down the other way. Long turned and faced him, and Buford could tell by the way Long's horse turned that he was a cutting horse, and fast.

The sun was going down, and the red light shone straight and flat down the wide, dusty street. A piece of paper whipped by on the wind, and Old Iron Ass let out a snort and jumped a yard. Buford said, "Sit still, you son of a bitch," and held the black mountain of meat down tight.

"Lord God Almighty," Buford said in the wind, "I ain't done this for a coon's age. God Almighty, let me whip that bastard good and hold my arm up, my God, because I'm old. Look at 'em! They're like a pack of dogs, waiting for him to slap me out of this saddle, God, and I'm alone—there ain't a man here that's my friend. Lord Jesus Christ, help me to best my enemies, and flog the bastard in the dust."

He saw Long lean forward, and he too leaned forward, giving his horse the rein. He kept the big bulk down to a neat, collected canter, though the brute was fighting the bit all the way, and he kept the spring trailing behind him, half raised, balanced.

He saw Long coming at him, Long with the spring in the air, ready for a chop, Long all set to do or die, and immediately Buford had a vision of Long's iron sliding down his, and that hard blade crashing into his knuckles. The son-of-a-bitch springs had no guards, of course.

All this time he was rolling forward on the old locomotive of a horse, and as Long raised the saber, coming full up on him, his eyes wide and glaring. Buford leaned far to the off side and swung Old Iron Ass to Long's left, passing on the wrong side.

Long let out a yell and went on, shouting curses and calling Buford a damned, dirty cheat and a coward. That was all right with Buford—Long had lost his initiative, and now he'd be on the watch for tricks—defensive.

Old Iron Ass was no cutting horse; he lumbered on down the street twenty-five yards before Buford, throwing all his weight to the off side again and ramming the old boat in the flank with his heel, forced him around in a circle so tight the horse almost went down on his knees. Long was sitting up there, faced around, shouting curses and waving his spring. Buford gave Old Iron Ass hell on the rump with his own saber. The crowd, lined along the walks, was watching intently.

Buford bore down on Long, and Long saw him coming. He put the spurs to his nag. He came at Buford not with that dangerous rush, but with a kind of wide-open caution, not knowing, now, what to expect, and he wasn't coming fast enough. Buford came in on him hacking, and beat Long's iron down, getting in a few heavy blows on the shoulder and back

as Long wheeled, but he couldn't work fast enough to
do it again, and Long was no fool. They sat there,
the horses scared out of their wits, rearing and shoving, with the iron ringing, smashing at each other.

Buford's arm was aching and the sweat was pouring into his eyes. He could see Long's iron, a black
yard swinging down out of the sky, and wished to
God for a straight sword. He knocked the blow down,
and he saw that Long knew he was tiring, because
Long was smiling and he had a nasty light in his
eyes.

Old Iron Ass was going crazy, and getting too hard
to manage. In his heart Buford cursed his tiring body
and his aching arm. His shoulder was going dead
from fatigue, burning like fire, and there wasn't a
damn thing he could do about it. That was what he
got for sitting in hotels while Long worked his butt
to the bone in the saddle. He couldn't keep it up, and
Long could.

Buford got his last chance when the knot-headed
horses wheeled away at the same time. He had Long
broadside for a moment, a moment that hung forever
in front of him, and Buford hauled off and whapped
Old Iron Ass on the butt with the spring as hard as
he could.

Old Iron Ass let out a shriek and charged, head
on, straight into Long and Long's horse, and went
right on over them without batting an eye. Long
went down in a sprawl of thrashing legs and stirrups, and Buford, hauling Old Iron Ass around, was
on him before he could get up.

Long didn't have a chance. Buford danced his horse
for fair, knowing that it wouldn't step on Long, and
from above, grinning through his tangled white
beard, he beat down on Long, beating his iron out of
his hand, and then beating him over the shoulders
with the flat of his spring. Long put his arms over
his head and tried to dodge, but Buford kept right

on top of him, slamming away while Long howled like a dog.

"You son of a bitch," Buford shouted. "I'll teach you to black my name." He slammed him on the head. Long fell headlong in the dust and lay quiet.

The crowd was silent. Buford rode Old Iron Ass down the street, along one gutter, close to the crowd, carrying his spring, and shouted out, "Now get this, you people. My name is Allen and I stick by my word. This man called me a liar. Any man that blacks my name again is going to get beat like a dog, just like that."

The crowd along the boardwalk drew back as he rode by, trailing the iron spring. His hat was gone, and his white hair stood out in the wind, and his beard, dirty and full of sweat, straggled down from his chin. With the red sunlight through that white hair, riding that black mountain of a red-eyed horse, and trailing that curve of black steel so close, nobody felt like saying anything back.

Except one man, who had ridden down the street and stopped in the middle, beyond where Long lay. He sat his horse, ganted and matted with dried sweat, and smiled as Buford rode toward him. There were four riders in the row behind him.

"A nice job," Spence said as Buford rode up. "I just got here. I believe every word you say, Mr. Allen. I know you will pay back every cent. I don't know what with, but I honor your intentions." He pulled a sheaf of blue-backed papers out of his breast pocket.

"These are attachments on your herds. I just rode the hardest sixty miles I ever rode in my life, but I'm going to get the sheriff now and ride back. Would you care to come along?"

Buford, with the sweat drying on his face, and his shirt clammy on his back in the cold wind, sat quiet in the saddle. He tried to say something and couldn't.

The iron spring in his hand was too heavy, and he

dropped it. He sat quiet, just trying to hold his head up.

Bailey rode up and said, "You gentlemen will have to check your guns. Town law."

"Why, of course, sir," Spence said. "In your office? We're leaving town again, though, sheriff," he went on. "We have papers to attach some cattle coming up the trail and I want your help." He blinked. He was having a hard time keeping his eyes open. The four men behind him sat stiff, their faces thin, their eyes red, almost asleep in the saddle.

"Now, boys," Buford said, "and I say boys because I know we're all going to be friends, why don't we take all this to Rooney's, out of the wind? There's no rush now. Everything can be settled legally. I need a wash and a few drinks. I reckon you could use the same, couldn't you, Mr. Spence? And your men?"

Spence looked at him steadily. "Do you mean that you're going to accept our papers, Mr. Allen?"

"Why, sir," Buford said, "that all depends on the nature of the papers, doesn't it? Naturally I'll have to have a look at them. Come along, out of the wind."

He went on up the street, not looking back.

The others rode after him.

CHAPTER THIRTEEN

Ogalalla
Rooney's Hotel
Room 47—7:30 P.M.

The four of them sat in Streeter's room with the last light of the red sun slanting through the dirty front window.

"Thanks for feeding my men," Spence said, sawing his knife into a large, rare T-bone which was half buried in two pounds of baked beans, canned tomatoes, and piccalilli. There were two open bottles of Old Croak on the table, and four water glasses half full, and two spare bottles on the floor, one on each side of Buford's chair.

Streeter sat on the edge of the bed nibbling a large dill pickle, and the sheriff sat calmly working through another steak.

"Good men," Buford said, faking diligently at his dinner. He was too busy thinking to do anything but drink. "Tough men. Especially that bird with the crooked nose. A man like that would walk straight through a brick wall if you told him."

"Forrest," Spence said, munching. "Isaac Forrest. Eyes like a hawk."

"Good name, Isaac. Now Isaac was an obedient boy. And Abraham! Do you remember Abraham? How God told him to cut off Isaac's head, and Abraham took him and was all ready to do it? Of course God supplied him with a ram, to save him from it—but Abraham would have done it. A good man, Abraham."

"Abraham who? Who are you talking about; who is this Abraham?" Streeter asked through a mouthful of pickle.

Buford looked at him with a large, serene blue eye. "Haven't you ever read the Bible, my old friend? I'd read the Bible twice by the time I was fourteen. My daddy was a minister of the Gospel. Didn't you know that? Came from Tennessee."

"Oh," Streeter said. "The Bible. Excuse me."

"Reminds me of your man Tucker," Spence said. "Tucker and Forrest would make a good pair in a fight. I couldn't get anywhere with your man Tucker. He claimed he couldn't read." He took his blue-backed legal sheets out of his pocket and laid them on the table. "I don't mean to be rude, Buford—you don't mind if I call you Buford?—but time is flying, and—"

"Tempus fugit," Streeter said, taking a drink from a tumbler.

"Shut up, Ed," Buford said calmly.

"Is he getting drunk?" Bailey asked.

"Hell, no," Streeter said, putting down his glass. "I'm getting sober. What you think? I was drinking for nothing?"

"Charming fellow," Spence said, as though Streeter were about four miles away on the end of a pin. "Point is, Buford, your good man Tucker is now about fifty miles from here. I saw him noon yesterday, and he was making twenty miles a day. Soon as I finish this fine steak of yours, I want to go back and take over that herd, and shunt 'em up to Cheyenne. But I can't get them away from Tucker without your okay—or the sheriff. If I leave in an hour, you understand, I can get to them by morning, even if I go in a buggy, which I intend. I want your cooperation, and I want it quick."

"I ought to be down on the street," Bailey said. "New herds come in today. Always got some new young fellers on the crews that want to shoot Yankees."

"Have another drink, sheriff," Buford said. "Take your mind off those Yankees."

"I can't," Bailey said. "One's aplenty."

"Leave a deputy," Spence said. "I want you to ride back with me and enforce these attachments—that is, if Buford won't sign a quitclaim himself, right here." He smiled. "Now."

Buford poured himself a refill. "Relax," he said. "What's your first name, my good friend?"

"Will."

"Will Spence," Buford said, with extraordinary satisfaction. "A fine name, a fine name."

"Will Spence what?" Streeter said, eating another pickle. He looked mischievous, his drooping eyes twinkling with some secret anticipation. "Chop off Abraham's head?"

"Ed, can't you for the God's sake stay sober?" Buford asked. "I need your advice."

"You don't need anybody's advice, Buford," Spence said. "You know Noonan, I'm sure. Do you admit that this is his signature?" He waved a paper in front of Buford's face.

"I acknowledge nothing except the time of day," Buford said, and lifted a forkful of beans.

"Those papers look legal to me," Bailey said. "It says right here, the Twenty-Second District Court, and that's a county seal, ain't it?"

"District seal," Spence said. "They're legal, all right. Ogalalla is county seat of Keith County, so Tucker's in your jurisdiction by now."

"Bailey," Streeter said, "you can't do this to our friend Buford. Buford is our old pal. Old, real old."

"Mr. Streeter," Bailey said politely, his black, hard eyes as sharp and expressionless as ever, "why don't you lay off that stuff? You know it's bad for you."

"Hulp," Streeter said. He beamed around at everybody. "This *is* my room, isn't it? Number four-sheven? Never saw it going around like this before."

"Is he a competent witness?" Spence asked Bailey. "Can he witness Buford's signature?"

"Anybody that can sit up is a competent witness in Keith County," Bailey said.

"Have you boys met before?" Buford asked. "I thought you were strangers, but I seem to detect a strange intimacy, or a singular singleness of purpose and mind. Anyway, I'll sign nothing. Will, why do you work so hard for Dickson? Why not work for me? You won't have to ride another sixty miles in a goddam buggy, for one thing."

Spence smiled at him. "You tempt me," he said. "I'd give a thousand dollars for a week in bed. What's your proposition?"

"I'll give you ten thousand dollars to deliver those attachments to me now. Across the table."

Spence shook his head.

"Twenty-five thousand."

"You haven't got it."

"I will have damn soon."

Spence shook his head.

Buford said, his voice getting lower, "Fifty thousand."

"You owe Dickson, altogether, damn near a million. Why would I sell him out for fifty thousand? I could take that one herd myself and sell it for a hundred thousand and they'd call it cheap."

"Is Dickson paying you anything like fifty thousand? At any time?"

"No, he gives me a nice salary, Bufe, and a commission on certain deals. I'm happy. I ain't rich, but I'm happy."

"In God's name, why? I'll give you a hundred thousand."

"I think this is bribery," Bailey said.

"Cogito ergo non sum," Streeter said, taking a quick one out of a bottle.

"I want no bribery around here, gentlemen," Bailey said.

"This ain't bribery, sheriff," Buford said. "This is a game of Mongolian fan-tan."

"A hundred thousand ain't enough," Spence said, taking a deep gulp of Old Croak. "You'd have to kill Dickson."

"My God, another Isaac."

"Not exactly. But Dickson doesn't like welshers and double-crossers. You ought to know him well enough to know what would happen to me."

"You look well able to take care of yourself."

"Not with Dickson. Nobody can stay awake all the time, and nobody has eyes in the back of his head. That's one thing about Dickson. He'll even things with a welsher if it costs him every cent he's got. He forgets everything else."

"You wouldn't speak so open in San Antonio, would you, Will?" Buford asked.

"No, and I wouldn't say it here either, except I know Bailey'll never get to San Antonio because he won't live that long, and Streeter won't because he's too—My God, look at him."

Streeter was sitting on the edge of the bed, turning yellow.

"It's those goddam pickles," Buford said. "Ed, for the God's sake, go to the window."

Streeter moaned faintly. He kept blinking his eyes and peering around.

"I'm willing to make a little compensation, though," Spence said. "If you sign those quitclaim deeds without any more fuss, I'll give you ten thousand cash, now. That's all."

Buford looked at the deeds—there were five of them—and slowly picked them up. He seemed to sink into deep thought.

"Streeter—" Bailey began.

There was a succession of hollow knocks as Streeter rolled off the bed and hit the floor, one loose bone after the other.

"Out," Bailey said. "How many drinks did he have?"

"Let's go," Spence said. "Come on, Bailey. My principal will pay your fee and plenty more for traveling. What's your fee?"

"Fifty dollars to ride that far."

"We'll allow you a thousand bucks for traveling expenses."

"That's too much," Bailey said.

"How do you know? You may get yourself shot up on this junket. That is, if Buford's son is doing what I think he's doing. I suddenly just wised up to what this little party is all about." Spence stood up.

"Now, now," Buford said. "Where's a pen? Who's got a pen? And what's your hurry?"

"Sheriff," Spence said, "be a friend and run down for a pen and a bottle of ink. Maybe Buford's softening up."

Bailey had a parting shot and left, wobbling slightly.

"Now, have a drink, Will," Buford said, "now, sit down, and have a drink. Don't go rushing off mad at me. After all, ten thousand's better than nothing, ain't it? And what did you mean, what my son is doing?" He looked old and bewildered. He picked up one of the spare bottles on the floor and poured some into Spence's glass.

"All this goddam stalling," Spence said. "The light just dawned. Feeding my men. What? Arsenic?" He laughed gently and sat looking at Streeter. "How could he get that drunk on four drinks, Buford?" He looked at Buford with twinkling eyes. Streeter was snoring jerkily. His face was green.

"What do you mean about my son?" Buford said, old and bewildered. He looked down at Streeter. "Silly ass. Never could hold it."

"I'll bet you a thousand your son is on his way down with your customers now, isn't he? He left Cheyenne last night to sell the herd and you came here to stall me. And every goddam minute you hold me here shooting off my mouth, your son's got that much more time to beat me to that herd."

Buford laughed sadly. "If only I'd thought of that. You overestimate me, Will, my boy. What a play that would have been! Selling those cattle right out from under your nose."

Spence said nothing.

"Have a drink," Buford said amiably. "After all, we can still be friends, can't we?"

Bailey came back into the room with a pen and a bottle of ink. "Rooney says be careful with his ink. He ain't got no more." He set them down on the table.

Spence pushed them across to the old man. "Go ahead, Buford, sign. Hurry up."

Buford picked up the pen. He dipped it in the ink, his hand shaking. He spattered ink on the table, and redipped it. He sat looking at the deeds, and at the pen, and slowly tears began to roll down his cheeks into his beard. He covered his eyes with his hands, dropping the pen, and wept. "For God's sake, can't you have pity on an old man?" he cried.

Spence laughed. In the midst of his laughter, while

Buford was weeping desperately into his hands, he swapped glasses with him.

"Sign, Bufie," he said, laughing. "Cut out the horse crap."

"For ten thousand? Ten lousy, measly thousand?" Buford quavered. There was mud in his beard as he raised his face, from where the tears had soaked into the dust. He looked old and bedraggled, utterly washed up.

Spence pulled out a fat wallet and showed the bills in it.

"Then let's be friends," Buford said. "Let's drink on it." He raised his glass. "All of it, and smash the glasses."

"A pleasure," Spence said, and lifted his. They drank, and threw the tumblers against the neighboring wall.

Sniffing, Buford signed three of the deeds. He put his hand to his head, and then shook it. He signed the other two. He sat there, blotting the ink with the tail of his shirt.

"Well?" Spence asked. "Hand them over."

"Another little drink," Buford said. His old eyes were keen as a fox's behind the rheum of his tears. He watched Spence with an expression of amiable timidity, pleading. He poured Spence's glass full.

"Well, what the hell are you waiting for?" Bailey said. "Give him the papers."

Buford put his hand to his eyes, and then looked at his hand, and blinked slowly three times. "Son of a bitch," he said softly.

Spence burst into a roar of laughter. He cut it off short and stood there grinning at Buford.

Buford suddenly sat forward, erect on the edge of his chair, and grabbed the edge of the table. He swayed.

"You damned old fool," Spence said, "why didn't you set that bottle down on the other side of your chair, where that silly bastard Streeter couldn't reach it? You might have known he'd foul you up. How could any man pass out that quick on four drinks, if it wasn't doped all to hell? This ought to teach you one thing—you can't outsmart me and Dickson. You can't possibly win."

Buford glared up at him, holding on to the table.

He half rose. "You son of a bitch," he said.

Spence moved.

Buford grabbed just in time, a split second before Spence's hands got to the deeds. He tore them savagely between his hands, and grabbed wildly, reeling, for the attachments. Spence seized the papers, and Buford lunged at him, fighting for them like an old lion, his beard wild and his clouding eyes wild with fury. He staggered into the table and Spence shook him off. Panting, Spence backed to the door, stuffing the papers in his pockets. "Come on!" he shouted to Bailey. He opened the door.

"Come back!" Buford shouted.

"I ought to throw him in the can," Bailey said.

"Come on," Spence said, "he'll pass out in a minute."

He and Bailey ran. Buford grabbed two bottles and staggered after them into the hall.

"You sons of bitches!" he roared. "You rotten thieves!" He staggered over to the stair well. The others were hurrying down the stairs. Buford hurled a bottle down the stair well at them. It smashed, spattering whisky all over.

"Damn you to hell!" Buford screamed. "I'll win! You can't, you can't beat—me!" He ran to the head of the stairs and hurled the other bottle. The swing carried him forward. With a cry, he fell, and tumbled down the stairs.

He caught himself and crouched panting for breath.

A face came up the stairs, and he squinted at it.

"My old friend," Long said bitterly. There was blood from a cut on his cheek, and the whole side of his face was a swollen, black bruise. "My old friend Buford."

Buford went limp; helpless, he slipped down the stairs. Long laughed. "He's drunk, boys!" he shouted. He grabbed one of Buford's feet and dragged him the rest of the way down.

Buford lay quiet, paralyzed, staring blindly up at Long and Long's men, fading into a swirling mist.

He heard their voices, from far away.

"Drag him out in the gutter, boys," Long said joyously. "Let the horses water on him awhile. Let him lie in the dung. I'll show him who wins."

Fury rose in Buford as hands grabbed him and lifted him up. Dark closed in.

In his ancient rage he wept, and even as he wept he slept.

CHAPTER FOURTEEN

The Plains 30 Miles North
of Frenchman's Creek
July 10—9:00 P.M.

There were ten men in the group riding along the next morning: Mike; Morton, who had contracted for the first herd; McCullough, who was buying the second; and seven of Morton's hands.

They were moving along at a good fast trot paralleling the broad trail of dust where the herds had gone ahead, and McCullough was still trying to post.

"Stand up in your stirrups," Mike said.

"Don't try to tell me how to ride a horse," Mc-Cullough said, his desperate, hopeless exasperation rising feebly over his exhaustion. "It's these damn saddles. Where in hell are we?"

Up ahead there was dust in the air, lying like a golden cloud. For once, the wind was quiet.

"There's a herd about four miles ahead," Mike said. He was beginning to smell the dust in the air.

"Our herd?" Morton asked. He was a hard rider, careless, stiff, and rough, and his horse was sweating all over, yellow foam beginning to churn in the heat-ing sun. The rest of the horses were plenty tired out, kept up in that steady trot; they had been going that way all night with only two breaks.

"Our herd?" Morton asked again. Tall, thin, his black eyes gazing ahead with happy expectancy, like an eager cadaver. Stiff as an arrow, he'd pound that horse down to the knees and never even notice, until it rolled over dead.

"Reckon," Mike said.

"Reckon!" McCullough said. "I'm through. I quit."

"You can't quit," Mike said. "You said you'd do this for me."

"I was drunk," McCullough said.

"Well, have another drink," Morton said. "Good for you, Mac. Wear that pot of yours down a little."

Morton pulled a bottle out of a saddlebag. A twenty-dollar bill fell out and floated back in the dust. "I'll be damned," he said. "Package must have bust."

"Ain't you going to get it?" one of the hands asked, riding along behind.

"Ah, the hell with it," Morton said. "Here, Mac, have a drink. Do you good." He held the bottle out.

"Leave him alone," Mike said. "One more drink and he'll fall out of the saddle."

"That's what I mean. Good for him," Morton said. "Teach him how to ride."

"Can't we stop this for a goddam minute?" McCullough asked, panting. He had a bad stitch, and the pain was screwing up one side of his face. "What's all the goddam hurry?"

"No," Mike said. "Only three more miles, Mac. I'll knock fifteen cents off your price. That make you feel any better?"

McCullough twisted, and looked at the loaded saddlebags, bouncing along behind him.

"No, by God," Mac panted.

One of Morton's men came up at a lope and held

the twenty-dollar bill out to Morton between two fingers. Morton took it, grinning. "Lee, you fall out by the side here with Mr. McCullough and ride him after us at a walk. You coming back down here anyway, ain't you, Mike?"

"Yes. Mac's herd is about a day down the trail. We'll ride back down for it after you get yours."

"Like hell we will," Mac said. "I'm going straight into Ogalalla. You leave me here alone with all this money? Like hell."

"It's fifty miles to Ogalalla," Mike said. "You'll never make it on that horse. You stick with me and buy your herd tomorrow, Mac, like you promised."

"You and your damn liquor," Mac panted.

There were seven riders behind them, eating the dust of the owners. They weren't amused by McCullough. He was nothing but a damn responsibility. They rode easy in the saddle, faces stiff with dust and sweat, fatigue showing in their eyes, but complacent in the face of a mild hardship.

"I'll take my money on to Ogalalla. Screw you and your cows."

"Two more miles," Mike said.

"How do you know it's the right herd?"

"Got to be," Mike said. "Foreman back there said so, didn't he? Got to be my herd."

He rode with a set face, and every rise of the pony was like salt in a burn on his buttocks. The saddle was too short for him, hired out of a livery, and the cantle pinched his behind. He rode forward, squatting on his crotch and standing, as he had been doing all night, ever since they put the horses down from the cattle car at Lodgepole Creek and crossed the South Platte in the dark. He kept thinking of that twenty-dollar bill floating away in the dust. There was about $160,000 in those saddlebags of Morton's, and more in McCullough's, since McCullough's contract was for $59 a head instead of $55.

"You and your goddam option," McCullough shouted, pain turning into rage. "I don't believe you got an option on any goddam ranch. It's some kind of a trick, just to get me down here with my money." McCullough was about to cry, and Morton looked at him sideways, enjoying it all.

They all lifted their noses. There was cow dung in the air, like snuff, bright in the nostrils. Then they came into the low-hanging dust, and it got thicker. The low bawl of the herd rose in their ears like the sound of water, and then they saw it, a dense, complex mass of dark under the dust, like a viscous liquid, churning and bubbling, flowing north slowly under its own smoke.

They were all lined out, now, through with their morning graze, and moving forward at a steady, bobbing walk, heads going up and down like pump handles. Stink, bawl, and dust.

Mike came up on the drag riders, and waved. The two men, recognizing him, waved back and yelled. The lame, the halt, the feeble, and the blind strung out behind for half a mile, and the drag men were letting the worst just fall out altogether, to be picked up by the next herd.

"It's ours," Mike said. He forgot the chafe, and sat up straighter, his face and his mind brightening.

He put the horse into a lope, and Morton followed him. The rest came on at a jog.

He and Morton came up on Tucker, and Tucker grinned. He stuck out a hard paw and shook Mike's hand, and then Morton's.

"We're going to tally out here," Mike said. "Right now."

They got the herd in a slow mill, stationed two tally men, facing each other across the trail, and let the herd slip through in dribbles, singles, and clots of two, three, and four cows coming through at a time. They tallied with knots on thongs, ten cows to

a knot. The booze was making Morton sleepy and
happy. He and McCullough, who had come up and
been helped off by two of Morton's hands, were sitting on the ground with their moneybags, knocking
off the bottle in a leisurely way, watching the tally.

Tucker beckoned Mike away from them. He
pointed east. "See that rider?"

Mike looked. The rider was a speck of black on the
yellow grass.

"Spence's man," Tucker said. "You remember
Spence—Dickson's boy."

"I know all about it."

"Well, Spence left here yesterday noon. If he rode
like hell, he'll be back here with the sheriff of this
county in a couple of hours. If he run a remuda with
him and killed a few horses—he might be here now."

"Tucker," Mike said, "just mosey down to the herd
and tell the boys to start shoving them through a
little faster. Just a little. And another thing." He sat
quiet, as Tucker waited, his cigarette dead in his big
mouth. "If Spence comes—there'll be trouble. And
he's got the law on his side."

"Not God, though," Tucker said. "As long as he
ain't got God on his side, I don't give a damn how
much law he's got."

"I don't want our boys hurt," Mike said. "I want
them back home with their money."

Half an hour later Tucker looked eastward at the
horizon. "See there, Mike."

There was a low feather of dust lying away across
the edge of the sky.

"After you pay your crew off," Mike said, "I want
you to go south and tell the boys on the other herds
to turn the cattle over to Spence. No shooting. We
can't fight the law, and I've run out of tricks."

"Ain't you giving up awful easy?"

"I've run out of buyers. You see the fat slob in the
check suit, lying on the blanket down there? He's my

last buyer. I was going to take him south. But it's too late now."

The herd was through and the tally men were riding up the slope toward Morton and McCullough.

The smoke on the east plain was bigger now, and Mike could see where it was growing, nosing along the earth.

"Won't be any more time to talk, Tucker," Mike said. "Somewhere in the Indian country there's two more herds. Three thousand head each. The old man's taking them to Montana—his own private outfit. Spence doesn't know about them."

Down on the blanket, Morton was going over the tally strings, checking them on a piece of paper. Mike's tally men came up with his strings and sat waiting. Down below, Tucker's men were keeping the herd in a big, slow mill.

"The thing is," Mike said, "the old man's lost his butt."

Tucker said nothing.

"We're going to try to save him those two herds. He's got to eat. Colby is driving them. You take over. You take them west and get lost, and keep on going north. You keep going, Tucker, because it's getting later in the year, and they're still south of Dodge. We got to get them on winter range in Montana before the snow starts—they got to be fat. So push the hell out of them. On up the Oregon trail. Take them over the Bridger cutoff."

"You got that winter range lined out? Where is it?"

"A place called Warhorse. Hell, I'll see you again before you get that far. I'll give you an extra two thousand, and you buy new rifles and plenty of cartridges, and don't let anybody take those cows away from you. Stay off the trail."

"Better sell 'em," Tucker said. "You got too much stacked against you."

"I thought of that. But where?"

"Dodge, of course."

"Spence has put the word out all over. There isn't a buyer on the whole trail that would touch those cattle, knowing about those attachments. Get me a fresh horse, and drive your remuda out somewhere and lose it. We don't want to leave any fresh horses around for Spence."

Tucker winked, and wheeled his horse down the slope.

Mike glanced at the eastward dust. There was a tiny black knot at the head of the stream, men and horses, indistinguishable.

He got down on his knees on the blanket by Morton and Morton said, "I got 2,906. What do you get?" There was plenty of booze on the air around that blanket, but Morton's eyes were as hard and black as a squaw's.

"2,908," Mike said. He was afraid his voice would shake with impatience, and he deliberately threw this into the settlement to foul it up. It was normal to have some kind of difference.

"Split the difference?" Morton asked. "Or do you want a recount?"

"I want a recount," Mike said, trying to keep his voice calm. Anything to keep Morton from noticing Spence coming, and holding up the payment.

"Oh, hell," Morton said, "don't be a hardnose, Mike. You mean we got to go through all that again for two lousy cows? What's two lousy cows?"

"A hundred and ten dollars," Mike said firmly and quietly. "I demand a recount. Or take my figure."

"Son of a bitch," Morton said. A recount would run more than 1,600 pounds of beef off that herd, even if it was only water. "I'll take your lousy figure. Do you do this all the time?" He scratched on a paper with a pencil. "Now how much do I owe you? I figure $159,940."

"You take my figure, I'll take yours," Mike said. "Count out the money, friend."

So they counted out the money, which came to 79 packets of a hundred bills each, and 97 loose ones. "Now if you'll kindly sign this bill of sale," Morton said, and Mike did, and it was done.

Tucker came up with a big roan and Mike strapped Morton's saddlebags on behind the saddle. There was a rifle in the scabbard. He pulled it out and checked the loading. Westward, there was a fan of dust in the air, where Tucker's boys were scattering the horse herd.

"I'd be obliged for a remount," Morton said, eyeing the big horse.

"Why, you bet," Mike said. "Tucker, you send a man up the line and see if he can bring our remuda back. You reckon your boys can handle the herd till we get you some fresh horses, Morton?" Mike asked in a kindly way. "Tucker, you take Morton's men and relieve ours, and help them get the herd lined out again."

"Northwest," Morton said, grinning at his cows. "Cheyenne way. Who the hell is that?" He was blinking at the east. There were men and riders now, clear in the sun.

"Looks like a posse," Mike said. "Maybe hunting some crook or other. Cow thief, maybe."

"Well, damn them, they better not run into my herd," Morton said. "I can't take no stampede now, with all my horses shot. Let's ride out and warn 'em off, Mike."

"Let's not," Mike said. "They've seen us. They're heading here."

He bent down and counted out Tucker's pay-money, gave it to him, and then began stacking the bundles of bills in the crook of his arm, like kindling. He stuffed it into the saddlebags deliberately, showing no haste.

He mounted and sat waiting, his eyes on the advancing riders. He recognized Spence at a distance, and saw a star flash on Bailey's chest. Behind them were Spence's five riders.

"The law," Morton said. "You guessed right."

Behind them, Tucker laughed. He had ridden up with his men. "Damn good guessers, all the Allens. Well, Mike, think we might as well mosey along?"

"Nope," Mike said. "We'll have to talk this one out, Tucker." He gently took his Colt by the butt and pulled it loose in his holster.

Spence and the others were coming through the grass, and Spence was grinning, with his blue-backed papers in his hand. They stopped, and their horses drooped, blowing hard and wet with sweat.

"All right, Mr. Tucker," Spence said, his smile brilliant, happy as a lark, "this is the end of your goddam trail. Here's the sheriff and here's the papers, and the sooner you get your ass out of Keith County, the better it'll be for you."

"Just a minute, sir," Tucker said. "Just as soon as I get leave from the teacher, me and the girls'll leave." He laughed. Nobody else did.

Mike got an amiable smile on his face as Spence looked at him. "Who are these gentlemen?" he asked, waving a hand at Morton and McCullough.

"Don't know," Mike said. "Never saw them before in my life."

"What the hell?" Morton said. "What the hell is this about? Are you arresting somebody?" he asked Spence. He blinked his bloodshot eyes.

"I'm attaching this herd, that's all," Spence said. "It belongs to me."

"In a pig's hind end it belongs to you," Morton said, rearing up in his saddle. "Is this trouble?" He looked at Spence and at his men, and at the law in front of him, and waved a long arm in the air, circling it. Four of his riders came up from the herd.

"Who the hell are you?" Morton asked Bailey. Morton looked about six stories tall, and his red eyes glared.

"I'm the sheriff of Keith County."

"Well, puke on Keith County!" Morton bawled. "I own these here cows, and if you lay a rope on one I'll see you all in hell. I just paid Mike Allen here for 'em and they're mine. Here's the goddam bill of sale."

Spence quit smiling. He looked at Mike and then back at Morton. "You've been screwed, my friend. Mr. Allen here never had title to these cows. They belong to me by court order, and if you don't believe it, here's the order."

He shoved the tattered sheets at Morton, and Morton took them and gazed in bewilderment at the seal and all the close writing, both in Spanish and English. He handed them back and looked at Mike.

"Well, I'll be a son of a bitch," Morton said quietly. "So that's why all the rush. You and your option. Give me back my money." His eyes turned cold and his face menacing. He was leaning forward in the saddle.

Tucker said, "Mike, I think it's time for us to fall back on Atlanta."

"Which the hell way is Atlanta?"

"Just follow me," Tucker said and, jamming in his spurs, he drew his Colt and, screaming like a Comanche, charged his horse straight into Sheriff Bailey. Mike and the others piled right in on top of him, firing into the air.

Bailey, his horse, and Spence went down and with Tucker firing his cannon over their heads, Spence's men turned in a panic. Tucker's party went on through and scattered screaming away down the slope toward the herd.

Morton and Morton's men began firing at them, and then, as Mike swung down on the herd, Morton stopped shooting and shouted. "Stop, you bastards!" he bawled in agony. "Don't do it!"

"Caveat Emptor!" Mike shouted. "Charge!"

They ran through the herd, firing, and back, breaking it into five terrified separate stampedes.

They pulled up in the clear and watched Morton's 2,908 cattle split in all directions, bawling in a crazy panic. In a little while the thunder died, and in the cover of the storms of dust, Mike and the rest headed north. They heard shouting behind them.

Mike swung his horse east, up toward a long, slow rise, into the sun. A mile farther, he stopped and looked back. Dust lay like smoke over a battle. Out of it, three small figures appeared, and headed toward him. They saw him and stopped at eight hundred yards. He saw the tiny puffs of rifle smoke, and then the bullets snapped over his head, and one struck the dust twenty yards short.

On his fresh horse he turned and headed north, toward Ogalalla, at a steady trot, all that was left of Buford's million bouncing lightly behind him.

One of the three riders followed him at the same steady trot. Mike pulled his rifle and stopped. He took a long hold on the rider and dropped one on him, and he saw the dust spit up where the bullet skipped on the ground, six feet to the rider's lee. After that, the other kept his distance.

Mike tried to shake him, but the other's horse was fresh. Mike remembered the single guard that Spence had left on Tucker. He slowed, and they rode that way, at a steady trot, about four hundred yards apart, all the way to Ogalalla, saving their ammunition.

CHAPTER FIFTEEN

Ogalalla
Rooney's Hotel
Room 47—July 10—9:00 P.M.

The lid was on in Ogalalla, with Bailey's deputy sitting on it. He'd go up politely to the newcomers and ask for their guns, and if they didn't co-operate, he'd pull his own and club them over the head, which was both surprising and humane.

Mike gave his up without a word and then went on to Rooney's.

The old man was lying on a blanket on the floor in No. 47. He was sick, his face slack and his eyes full of red veins on yellow white. He coughed and spat a lot in a china cuspidor and his hands shook all the time. Mike, with the saddlebags hanging from his arm, stood and watched him set down a bowl of bean soup on the floor and try to get up, and his heart turned in him. Buford looked ten years older.

"What the hell happened to you?" he asked quietly. He went to the front window. Spence's man was across the street, plain in the lamplight. He had no gun that Mike could see.

He turned back and looked at his father. The old man's clothes were covered with mud and gutter filth, bits of manure and straw clinging to the cloth, his beard stained with horse urine and more mud. His hair was matted with it.

"It was Long," Streeter said. He was lying on the bed, and though he was a lot cleaner than Buford, he didn't look any healthier. "Your father fed me and himself a Mickey Finn, yes, my boy, a Mickey, a true, real, honest Mickey. Then Long dragged him out and kept him lying in the gutter all night, down under the hitchrail."

"I am happy to say," Buford said in a hoarse voice, his throat full of phlegm, "that most of the time I was unconscious. Have you got a gun, my boy? I owe Long a call before we go."

"No. We're getting out of town as fast as we can."

"Not before I kill Long." Buford dipped his spoon into the soup and lifted it toward his mouth, and immediately shook all the soup over himself, out of the spoon.

He swore, and tried it again, this time holding the spoon with both hands. He got the soup down and held it down. "Filthy stuff. Surely God did not invent the bean. I'm just trying to get the strength to kill him. That's all."

"You better get the strength to get on your feet first," Mike said. "We got to get out of here. One of Spence's men followed me in. He'll get help. Spence himself'll be back here as soon as he can catch a horse. There's a train down at the station, loading cows. I saw it as I came in. It'll pull out pretty damn quick, and we're going to be on it."

"Have you got a gun?" the old man repeated.

"For God's sake, forget Long." Mike dropped the saddlebags and unstrapped one of them. "Put your mind on this. If you want to keep it, we've got to leave—now."

Buford looked at the packs of bills. "How much?" he asked dully.

"About a hundred and fifty-five thousand. I paid the boys. Tucker's going down the trail warning the other herds to give up. I'm going back to Cheyenne to pay the hotel bill."

"You would. How about the other four herds?"

"Not a chance."

Buford's fists clenched. "How about McCullough's money. Didn't you sell him the second herd?"

"There wasn't time. I was just lucky to get Morton's money."

"Can't we beat Spence down the trail and sell off the others?" the old man cried.

"There's Spence and all his men between us and those herds, Dad. Write them off." He went to the window.

"Streeter, haven't you got any kind of small gun?" Buford asked.

"Get out," Streeter said. "I've had enough trouble. Get your damn problems out of my room. I don't want any shooting."

"Pay him something, Mike," Buford said. "He's got some commission coming."

"I don't want your dirty money," Streeter said. "All I want is peace and quiet, yes, peace. Take your stolen money and get out of here. Yes, out."

Mike looked down at the old man, still ladling soup into his mouth, shaking half of it on his beard, where it blended slowly with the mud and the manure. "Is it?" Mike asked.

"Is it the hell what?" the old man snarled, showing a little life for the first time.

"Is it stolen?" Mike shouted, suddenly exasperated beyond words, fatigue, dirt, sweat, and failure flooding over him like a wave of solid sewage.

"No!" the old man roared, and they subsided.

"That train," Streeter said. "Go on. I don't want

your bodies on my hands. I've had enough, yes, enough trouble. Take your dirty money and go."

"I'm trying to go, you whining little shyster," Buford snarled. "My dirty money, he says, when he sees the end of it. Yes, we'll go. Just as soon as I finish this delicious bean soup." He slurped another spoonful, a little more deftly. "Go down and buy a ham off Rooney, boy. A ham keeps well. I'll need it on the way to Omaha. A good ham will—" He suddenly leaned sideways and threw up into the cuspidor.

Streeter moaned.

"Son of a bitch," the old man said. "If I only had a drink, I could keep it down. Son, get me a drink." He staggered to his feet and stood swaying. "The hell with a drink. Son, give me that goddam bowl."

Mike handed it to him, and he drank the rest of it, one swallow after another, and threw the bowl against the wall.

"I'll make that damn stuff stay down if I have to whip myself with a belt," he said. "Give me a thousand dollars."

The old man threw the money on the bed. "Clean up the mess, you sniveling little bastard," he said to Streeter, "and there's something for your goddam trouble." He went to the corner of the room and got his little locked suitcase.

They went out into the hall, the old man holding on to Mike's arm, and Mike carrying the saddlebags. They stood in the gloomy hall, looking out the end window at the man waiting below.

A train whistle hooted mournfully from somewhere.

"Let's go," Mike said. "If he's got a friend covering the back, we'll have to go out the side window."

They moved slowly down the hall. "I'll go back down there to San Antonio and cut Dickson's throat," the old man mumbled savagely. "I'll get every damn cent back out of him. Listen, Mike. You pay the damn hotel bill in Cheyenne and come after me. I'll wait for you at the Planters' in St. Louis. Bring my bags down with you."

"I'd better ride a way with you," Mike said.

There was no watcher at the back; evidently Spence's man didn't expect them to move so fast, or else he was covering both doors by turns. He might show up at any moment. They went out of the back yard, through the dark bulks of crates and barrels, hurrying as fast as they could.

The moon was out. They kept to the shadows, the old man moving at a slow, weak walk. He leaned on Mike's arm at every step, and still he mumbled.

"Has Spence's man caught on?" Buford whispered.

"Not yet," Mike said, looking behind. "Can't you go any faster? If Streeter should happen to turn the lamp out in that room, he'll know we've gone."

The old man was panting heavily, sweat running down his face. "Maybe he won't wise up," he breathed.

Ahead of them the gray mountains of buffalo bones rose beside the tracks. Up the line, the engine and cars were backing out of a siding onto the main line.

Mike guided his father in among the bone piles, and they moved slowly through them, surrounded by the maze of dead and motionless skeletons.

The train came slowly down the main line and pulled up by the station. The cars were full of cattle. At the end of the train, ahead of the caboose, were empties for some consignment down the line. In the caboose, somebody was singing.

For a moment Mike had the feeling he was lost in a maze, among the piles of bones. There were countless thousands of them, patiently collected from the plains, waiting for shipment by the carload—all that was left of the great northern buffalo herd. Who would have thought, ten years ago, that they could come to this? These mountains of death? He looked at his father's bent shoulders ahead of him. It was all the same, the endless herds and the immense delusions. In the end, they were all dreams and vanished in the air.

Mike followed his father into one of the empties. Alone in the moonlight, slatted by the bars of the car, they rolled out of town, eastward; silent, without arms. The son sat propped against the end of the car, his father's head on his lap, and he looked down at the old, tired face while the old man slept.

And he wept, alone in the rattling, empty car, his tears slow, without any sound, running down his cheeks, and from his chin falling silently into the dung in his father's hair.

PART TWO

CHAPTER ONE

On the Train Between
Seguin and San Antonio
11:00 A.M.—July 31, 1882

The train pulled out of Seguin, rattling across the
Guadalupe River bridge, and headed across country
for San Antonio.

"Listen," Buford said, trying to keep his voice
down, "for the last time, Mike, give me those saddlebags. I know Montrose'll say yes. I know it. I know
it. Right now there's an answer waiting for me at
the Menger."

Mike looked bitterly through the window at the
countryside, passing at a sedate pace. The train
rolled and bucked like a drunken cow.

"You're living on dreams," Mike said. "Montrose
was through when I talked to him in Cheyenne. You
were through when you didn't make the option date.
I don't care how many wires you sent him from St.
Louis, he's through, and so are you. Take my advice—"

"Take your advice," Buford said bitterly. "The
chick tells the hen."

"Take my advice," Mike went on. "You pay Terman the hundred thousand you owe him for those two herds Tucker is trailing now, the ones you're stealing, and sell those herds, and you've got some working capital. I'll just take the other forty thousand, or whatever's left, and that will give *me* some working capital. I'm going to marry Nancy Berry with that money, and that's that."

The old man bit his lip, his eyes screwing up with his agony. Mike was almost sitting on the saddlebags, crammed against the side of the swaying car. The old man's hands twitched futilely.

He was wearing a Panama hat, now, and was back in condition, except that he was thinner and there were heavy shadows under his eyes. His beard was fine and silky again, and he was wearing a pair of onyx cuff links, set, with simple dignity, in platinum.

He was wearing these black cuff links, he would have said, in mourning for the emerald ones, and he had made up his mind that he would wear them until he got the emerald ones back, along with Long's head, or whoever it was that had stolen them in Ogalalla.

"For the last time, son," the old man said gently, "won't you listen to reason? We're going to get home in an hour. I offered Montrose the whole hundred and fifty thousand, and I got to have it. I got to wire it to him immediately. Then you and I will go north and drive those herds up there to Warhorse. Won't we?" He smiled painfully at his son. "Won't we?" he coaxed.

He saw his son's eyes open wide, startled, and followed their look. His heart gave two heavy thumps, missed two beats, and then started in again at a fast pace.

Spence was standing at the end of the car, looking down the swaying aisle. Spence was smiling his eter-

nal smile. Behind him were two other men, and these
men wore stars.

Buford and Mike sat paralyzed.

Spence came down the aisle, holding to the seat
backs to keep himself from being thrown. His smile
was almost melting.

"My," he said, "am I glad to see you, Mr. Allen.
And Mike!" He stood there in the aisle, holding tight
to the seat back. Behind him the two officers stood
with feet apart, braced. "We've been waiting, Bufie
old pal. You have no idea how we've been waiting. I
assure you, no mother ever waited for her son as
Dickson and I have been waiting for you. Not a train
has gone through Seguin without one of Dickson's
boys on it, and an officer or two. Where is it?"

Buford smiled. His tongue wouldn't work. The
wheels pounded furiously. Nobody in the car was
paying any attention. It was useless to start shouting. *Murder! Police!* with the two policemen standing
right there.

In the silence, Spence's smile flagged. Out of his
pocket came two papers. "One for you, Buford," he
said, handing them out, "and one for you, Mike.
Warrants for your arrest. Now, where's the money?
The hundred and fifty-five thousand?"

Buford threw his warrant on the floor. "Go to hell,"
he said.

"All right, I'll go to hell, and you go to jail," Spence
answered. "I don't care. Did you think you could get
away with it? Why, the first thing Bailey did when
we got back to Ogalalla was get two warrants out on
you for everything he could think of—cow stealing,
fraud, assault with a deadly weapon—a few others.
However, if you hand over the money, all will be
clear. Restitution is all that is wanted."

"Screw you," Buford said. "You talk about restitution."

Spence stopped smiling.

"Arrest them," he said to the two officers. "Handcuffs. They're dangerous."

One of the officers pulled a pair of cuffs from his hip pocket.

"You think I don't mean it?" Spence asked, his face blank. "Where's the money? Hand it over and I'll tear these warrants up."

"You put a hand on me," Buford said nastily, "and I'll have you hanged. We ain't in Bexar County yet, and those two courthouse monkeys haven't got any right to anything until we are. Screw your warrants."

Spence blinked. The officers looked at each other.

"In other words, all you're doing now is plain robbery," Buford said. "Train robbery. Until we hit the next creek, we're in Guadalupe County and you can go climb a tree. Isn't that right, sonny?" he asked one of the officers.

The officer looked foolish.

"How far is it to the creek?" Spence asked him quickly.

"About three miles, I reckon."

"Pardon me," Mike said, "I have to go to the toilet." He stood up, with the saddlebags on his left arm. "My toilet articles," he said to Spence. "Would you mind moving the hell out of my way?"

Spence's mouth tightened.

"Come on," Spence said to the officers, "keep close to him. I don't know what he's up to, but I want him nabbed when we get past the creek."

"I have to go to the toilet, too," Buford said.

He got up and trod heavily on the officers' feet, swaying and falling onto them as the train pitched. "Pardon me," he said. The three of them went down in a heap. The officers swore.

Mike walked quickly away down the aisle.

"Get off of me!" one of the officers shouted, struggling.

"Excuse me," Buford said, struggling feebly to get up. He accidentally stuck his finger into one of their eyes. "I'm so sorry," he said, kneeling on the other man's groin. "I'm such a clumsy old fellow," Buford said sadly.

The officer with the outraged groin let out a howl and lunged to his feet, spilling Buford. The other one stood swaying, with one hand over his eye, weeping copiously.

Spence was right on Mike's heels. Mike reached the door in the end of the car and opened it. Dust, dirt, cinders, and smoke blew in, and he staggered out on the puny platform.

"Where are you going?" Spence shouted. "The can's back there, inside."

"Afraid to try it, on this train," Mike shouted. "Might miss!" Taking a deep breath, he leaped straight out from the platform toward the flying countryside, saddlebags and all. He promptly disappeared.

Spence let out a roar of rage, pulled a gun, and stood there helpless. There was nothing to shoot at, except Texas.

With a burst of bedlam, the train rushed over the creek, and Spence rushed back into the car. Everybody was huddled around the wounded officers, trying to comfort them. Buford was sitting handcuffed to the seat, smiling quietly.

Spence stood in the aisle and cursed steadily at the officers of the law.

"Take these things off me," Buford said complacently.

"I'll throw you in prison!" Spence shouted. "You'll never get out!"

"Don't be silly," Buford said. "You know very well Dickson will want to talk to me as soon as we get into San Antonio, and he's the last man on earth to want anybody dragged into the Little House with handcuffs on. Kindly remove them, before you anger your employer. You should save your bluster and threats, my good fellow, for lesser men than I. Besides, I am a friend of Police Commissioner Berry."

"Take them off," Spence shouted at the officers.

The two officers bent with their keys and unlocked the cuffs, trying to inflict as many minor abrasions and lacerations on Buford's wrists, in the brief time allowed them by the performance of their duties, as they possibly could.

CHAPTER TWO

At Keppelbauer's House
3:00 P.M.

Young Keppelbauer stood by his window with a glass of whisky in his hand. He looked exactly the same as he had in Dickson's house the night he got his deadline, except that his eye was no longer placid, nor his chin whiskers neatly combed. His paunch was still firm, but his cheeks needed a shave, and the bags under his eyes were the color of old liver.

He had been jailed once on an assault complaint falsely sworn by three of Dickson's men. He was now out on Dickson's bail.

Keppelbauer had not been to his office for four days. Midnight tonight was his deadline.

He had been hiding at home, watching a man out the front window who was watching his house. There was another man down in front of his office on Houston Street. It seemed that there were men watching him everywhere he went.

He wrapped up a loaf of bread and some cheese in a spare suit, and tied this with a string. There was no reason for using the suit as a wrapping, but he was not thinking clearly any more. He forgot to take any water.

He harnessed the last horse (he had sold all the others) to his buggy and, with the man watching, started down Navarro Street toward Houston, as though he were going to his office.

On Houston he turned west, and kept on going. He kept on right out of town, at a trot, and when he hit the country, he whipped his horse into a gallop.

An hour later, his horse was fagging out. He heard hoofs behind him and lashed the horse harder. Isaac Forrest and another man rode up beside him. Isaac Forrest shouted for him to stop.

Keppelbauer did not stop. He kept whipping his horse. Forrest's partner grabbed the reins at the bit and pulled the horse down. It stood there, drooping and gasping for breath, legs shaking, almost dead. Keppelbauer, with a white face, sat and stared straight before him with his bread and his cheese beside him.

"Don't you know," Isaac Forrest said, "there is nothing you can do?"

Keppelbauer's mouth twitched.

"Today's the thirty-first. Why try to run away? Didn't we catch you before? On the train?"

"I can't get the money," Keppelbauer said.

"Turn your rig around," Isaac said. His eyes were not unkind—they were just indifferent. Wide and bright like an eagle's, with that hard jut of nose between.

Keppelbauer's hands tightened on the reins.

"No!" he shouted, and slashing at the horse, leaned forward as though to force the buggy on. The horse lunged ahead, and the other man jumped his horse and grabbed the bridle. The buggy stopped short.

Keppelbauer, his face set, white and full of terror,

kept beating with his whip, and the horse reared and shook violently.

Isaac Forrest picked up his quirt and with a heavy swing brought it down across Keppelbauer's thighs. Keppelbauer let out a piercing shriek, dropped his whip, and sat there dumbfounded.

"Now turn around," Isaac said again.

Keppelbauer let out another scream of fury and pain to which this time was added surprise and outrage.

Isaac Forrest swung again.

Keppelbauer didn't have the breath to scream. He sat panting, gasping, almost unable to breathe, rocking in his seat, his face the color of paper ash.

"Turn it around," Isaac said, like a teacher, gently and patiently.

Keppelbauer dashed from the seat, leaping to the ground. He stumbled, picked himself up, and ran into the brush beside the road.

Isaac Forrest was after him, on top of him, his horse cutting Keppelbauer back as though he were a cow. The whip went up and came down, and went up and came down, on Keppelbauer's back, and Keppelbauer fell in the dusty road, back by his buggy, and whimpered like a dog.

"Don't you know by now there's nothing you can do?" Forrest said. The whip rose and fell. Keppelbauer writhed in the dirt, his smartly cut sack coat no longer neatly creased and businesslike.

"Nothing," Forrest said. "Turn your rig around."

Keppelbauer got up and staggered to his buggy.

"Nothing," Forrest said. He struck again.

Keppelbauer staggered and caught the edge of the dashboard.

"Nothing."

The whip rose and fell once more, and Keppelbauer sagged, clinging feebly.

"You won't go to the police, because they'll just jail you again on the same warrant, won't they?"

"Yes," Keppelbauer whispered. He climbed weakly up into the seat. He sat there, his head bowed. His eyes were shut and he was crying, his hands over his face.

"And they'll just turn you loose on our bail, when we want you, won't they?" Isaac said, like a patient teacher.

"Yes," Keppelbauer whispered.

"And there's nothing you can do," Forrest said. "Is there?"

The whip whistled, and slashed through the material of the buggy top beside Keppelbauer's ear. Keppelbauer shrank in terror.

"No," he said, barely making the words. "Nothing."

"We'll see you at the Little House at twelve."

"Yes," Keppelbauer whispered.

"Because there's nothing you can do, is there?"

"No, nothing," Keppelbauer said, sitting there. "Nothing. Please, just don't hit me again. Please!"

Isaac Forrest hung his quirt back on his saddle horn and rode away.

Slowly Keppelbauer drove back to his house, and went inside, and sat again in the living room, watching the man who was again across the street, and who was, again, watching the house, as quietly as before.

CHAPTER THREE

The Little House
Dickson's Office—5:00 P.M.

There was a catbird singing outside Dickson's office window. The garden lay lush and green down toward the little green river—an English garden, with Canterbury bells, foxglove, geranium, daisies, St. Johnswort, and bluebells.

Near the House there was a garden of roses. Dickson had them trained under gauze so that they grew with longer stems and richer colors. Everywhere in the Little House there were dozens of roses—red, pink, or white—in silver or crystal vases. He would allow no gold—nothing but silver or crystal was to go with the gray-and-white interior.

Somebody knocked on the office door and opened it. Spence stuck his head in. "We got the old man. The young one jumped off the train."

"That's fine," Dickson said. "You idiot. Well, put some of the boys out around the Menger. Isaac will do nicely. Did you get the money all right?"

"No. Mike had it."

Dickson's face turned just faintly pink.

"We'll get it," Spence said quickly. "Don't worry."

"I never worry, my boy. Bring Buford in."

Buford came in and looked around. "Lovely," he said. "Smells like a woman." He looked at Dickson. "A visitor, I presume. Not you, that is."

Dickson's mouth tightened and pinched. "Let's be pleasant, Buford. After all, we were friends for many months—"

"I see no need to be pleasant," Buford said. "You lied about me behind my back. You cheated my friends. You robbed me of almost all my money. You have ruined me. I see no need to be pleasant."

"Very well," Dickson said, sitting down behind his desk. "Let's be unpleasant. I give you until twelve midnight, this very night, to hand over the rest of the money you owe me."

"The rest. What do I owe you? You took my herds. What else do you want?"

"You owe me exactly $114,000, as the balance of the $300,000 of our private debt, not covered by the profits from your cattle. My dear Buford, I know you haven't got a dime except the $160,000 you got for that one herd. You owe me that too."

"$159,940," Spence said. "According to the buyer."

"So, altogether, you owe me $274,000, in cash. I am going to be generous," Dickson said. "I'll settle everything for that $160,000, Buford—if you'll tell me where those last two herds are."

"What herds?" Buford said.

"Terman's cattle."

"Never heard of them. Never heard of Terman, for that matter."

"Dear me," Dickson said, pulling open a drawer of his desk. "Must I prove everything? Is there no one I can trust?" He laid a piece of paper on the desk. "Promissory note by you to Terman. I bought it from Terman just last week. Let's grow up, Buford. You're surrounded. I have attachments on those two herds, now, and I want to know where they are."

Buford looked at the note, lying on the desk. He stood silent, wilting, and slowly his face lowered, clouding, the wrinkles in his forehead getting deeper and the lines around his eyes getting darker. "So he sold me out too," Buford said quietly.

"They were all cowards," Dickson said. "I, on the other hand, had perfect confidence in you, Buford. I still have. I know you'll pay me."

"It's not even a fair offer," Buford said heavily. "Those herds of Terman's are worth almost $400,000 and you want to settle, as you say, for $160,000, and the herds too. Such generosity."

In the silence the catbird sang, his voice trilling and warbling as the first gray of dusk rose from the river.

"Suppose I said," Buford said quietly, looking out of the window, "that I would pay you the $160,000 and you let me keep the herds. I have an option on a ranch, you see, in Montana. I offered the owner a down payment of $150,000. I could sell one of those herds and make that, and have the other left for stock. You see," he said looking down in a way that was almost benign, "you aren't leaving me any future, Dickson. What will I do? Drive a hack? It would kill me. I'm old. You're leaving me without a cent. Suppose I offer you everything but the two herds. I will give you all the cash Mike has."

"Why should I?" Dickson asked.

"I'm an old man," Buford said humbly. "Just leave me enough for another start." He stood there, gentle, old, meek, his handsome eyes smiling appealingly.

"Quit acting," Dickson said. "How many more herds have you got up your sleeve, Buford? You, who claimed you'd never heard of Terman. You're so full of tricks you bulge. You have a couple of million stowed away somewhere in a sack. I know your kind."

Buford stood quiet, his expression unchanged. "I'm not acting," he said. "God help me, I have acted. I have lied and pretended. I am not acting now, Dickson. I am begging. Look at me. How can you refuse an old man this? How little it is, to leave to an old man—an old fool."

Dickson looked up quietly. "Magnificent," he said. "Buford, you're tearing my heart. I love you."

"Then you won't?"

"No."

Buford looked down at him quietly. Then a kind of veil came down in his eyes, concealing, and he looked away. He licked his lips once, and stood quiet.

"Midnight," Dickson said. "You're over a barrel, Buford. I need the money, and I need it quick."

Buford cleared his throat. "There is one more possibility. I will give you everything, all the money and both herds, if you will buy that ranch and give me the job as manager. Just a job, for my old age. That's all I ask. You can take all the profits."

"What kind of profits?"

"I will guarantee you twenty per cent a year on your investment. A hundred thousand a year, with one herd. That is conservative."

"It's just crazy."

"They're making that now in Wyoming and Montana. On cattle for which they paid sixty dollars a head. These cost you thirty-five. I'd call it twenty-eight per cent. The market's going up. It's been going up for six years."

"I need my money fast," Dickson said, looking out at the garden. "I want to go back to England soon. With your money and these two herds I can just about make my goal. You see, Buford, you've delayed me six months. I can't forgive you that."

Buford's hands clenched and he looked down.

"Midnight," Dickson said. "I want the cash here, and a map showing the general trail of the cattle, and your son will ride north with Spence to locate them."

Buford stood looking at the floor.

"Don't look so hurt, Buford. Don't look so broken. You'll look fine on a hack, driving it around town. Think of all your friends, who'll hire you! 'Poor old fellow,' they'll say. But you'll do all right. You're only fifty-eight. I know it's just the beard that makes you look so venerable."

Buford looked up at him slowly, his face haggard.

"How can you say such a thing? Are you mocking me? Isn't it enough to break me, without mocking me?"

Dickson sat back in his chair and laughed. "Buford," he said, "you are delightful. Why couldn't we have been friends? You're much too good to be true."

A shadow passed across Buford's face. He was sagging. "Why do you say such things?"

"Because I know them. You're fifty-eight, and healthy as an ox. Your beard turned white in the military prison in—New Jersey. Is it New Jersey? Is there such a place as New Jersey? In February, 1864. Brace up, old boy, you've got decades ahead of you. Driving a hack."

Buford said nothing. He moved toward the door with a kind of shuffle.

"Midnight, old boy," Dickson called after him.

Buford suddenly turned back. "Mr. Dickson," he said, with all the mildness and humility of helpless old age, "you referred to a goal. I admire a man who has a goal. What is your goal, if I may ask?"

Dickson smiled. "Four million dollars. A paltry thing, but enough for a modest living."

"Let me commend your modesty," Buford said, and shuffled out.

CHAPTER FOUR

The Menger Hotel—5:45 P.M.

They welcomed Buford home to the Menger with the same genuine hospitality they had always shown—not excessively, but sincerely—which was the reason he had sold his house long ago, and taken to living in the hotel with Mrs. Allen. Why not? He could go sit in the patio with its old alamo tree and drink beer in the evening, hearing the remote thumping of the waltz bands over along the river, from the Casino and the Palm Garden.

"Do you have a wire for me?" Buford asked the clerk on duty. His fingernails rattled on the desk top in an insistent, repeated rhythm.

"No, sir."

The fingernails stopped. "Are you sure? Couldn't it have been mislaid?"

"Let me send over to the telegraph office, Mr. Allen," the clerk said, smiling. He snapped his fingers and one of the boys came scampering up.

"Is Mrs. Allen in or out?" Buford asked, moving

his cigar into the corner of his mouth. He never smoked more than an inch of any cigar, to keep the smoke from yellowing his mustache.

The clerk turned around and said, "Why, sir, I assumed you knew. Mrs. Allen left the hotel a month ago. About a week after you went north, Mr. Allen."

"She what?" Buford looked at the clerk in silence. "What do you mean, left? Checked out?"

"She rented a little house on Laredo Street, sir," the clerk said, "just between Paseo and Presidio."

Laredo Street, Buford thought. He threw his cigar into a palm pot. *Is she trying to shame me? Is that her way of criticizing extravagance, as she calls it? Living in some little Spanish flea trap? With some of those Mexicans of hers? Trying to make a fool of me?*

"The other side of the Creek?" Buford asked, shocked, "My God," he said to the clerk. "No wife. No telegram. Let me know when Mike comes. Right away."

"Yes, sir. What's the matter, Mr. Allen? You look ill."

"Nothing."

"Where will you be?"

He didn't know where he was going. "I?" He paused. He had a vague notion of going to see Berry. "Laredo Street. My God. Colonel Berry, too. Yes."

He walked out and stood on the curb outside, looking at the gutter. His left knee was shaking, and he felt weak and sick.

"Good afternoon, Mr. Allen," a man said behind him.

Buford looked around.

"Isaac Forrest," the man said, smiling. "Ogalalla. You fed me in Rooney's."

Buford's eyes narrowed. "Yes. I remember."

"We have a mutual friend. Thomas Dickson. He sent me to—to see that you were comfortable." Buford looked at him without speaking. For some reason, Isaac Forrest looked much bigger and taller on foot, in a derby hat, than he had on a horse.

"My orders," Isaac Forrest said, blinking his round bright eyes rapidly, "are to stay here and wait for your son. Do you see that man, over by the Market House?" He pointed a heavy, knobby finger across the Plaza. "He has been sent to follow you and see that you come to no harm. And Mr. Dickson told me especially to remind you about midnight. That was his word. Midnight."

Buford looked up at the high, hooked nose and the round eyes. In one instant he saw in them an absolute, implacable decision, and before it he quailed. The striking thing about Forrest's eyes, and what they showed, was a total lack of thought, of prudence, of hesitation. He was a man of total obedience, a soldier.

Buford's clothes suddenly became cold and damp, clinging to him. Some kind of bug seemed to be crawling between his shoulder blades.

"Indeed, indeed," he said in a confused way, looking around. Forrest backed a step, turned, and strolled off down the sidewalk. Buford was acutely conscious of the man across the Plaza.

He was suddenly sick with despair. He was caught, there was no way out. He looked away from the fellow, up, toward the sky. Birds were flying about in the trees. He stood and listened, escaping for a moment, just as he had stood in this same spot when he was four and five years old, and many times since, watching the ancestors of these same birds. For a moment he felt secure.

How beautiful his city appeared to him! With its little birds, the children of the towers and the gutters, flitting and darting in the evening sky.

Midnight.

The single word stabbed through him like fire. Where had it come from? The word faded away.

What could happen to him in San Antonio? Nothing. Nothing could harm him in the least. How could it? And then the truth broke through his careful web of delusions, and he saw with perfect clarity the dreadful certainty: there would be no telegram from Montrose, and he could not escape from Dickson unless—it was barely possible—he could bribe Dickson's men.

But where was Mike? Where was the money? If there were only someone left he could borrow from—borrow one more last time, scrape San Antonio to the very bone, so to speak, take all he could get, and run—

It wasn't lost yet. If only he could get to Warhorse and wave that cash under Montrose's nose, Montrose would change his mind. That was it. All was not lost, not yet.

He looked behind him. The little man was waiting.

And then it came to him, like the first gleam of rationality after a long delirium, quiet and clear. Colonel Berry might lend him the cash. Why hadn't he thought of Berry before? If Mike was going to marry Nancy Berry that made them practically related. He racked his brains. Why wouldn't Berry lend him the money? He could offer Terman's herds as security, as he had the bills of sale in his pocket this minute. And then—and then—

A gleam of positive hope brightened Buford's mind. It was all going to be wonderful again. And suddenly, like a final proof, it dawned on him why he had never borrowed money from Berry before, and why his credit ought to be good at Berry's bank. It was simply because he never had borrowed cash anywhere. All his debts were in accounts for real goods, cattle, supplies, horses, wagons, etc. He had never borrowed cash because he had never needed actual cash, in his business.

Oh, my God, Buford thought, *if only Berry will lend me $300,000.*

The bells of the Cathedral, and of St. Joseph's down by Blum Street, began to ring. Six o'clock. *Six,* he thought.

The bells stopped ringing, and the heavy tone lay in the ear like an almost inaudible droning.

Midnight.

The word struck through his mind like a saber, and he sank floundering into a pool of black fear, in silent agony. He had to get out, he had to get out—the words hammered through his mind. And what if Berry refused him? Where was Mike and the money? He had to have that $159,000 for bribes. And where was Mike?

He looked behind him. The little man was still there, apparently without a care in the world.

CHAPTER FIVE

Colonel Berry's Bank
on Houston Street—6:00 P.M.

Colonel Berry, sitting in his office, listened to the telephone ring, with something like malevolent enjoyment at the thought that it was wearing itself out. He let it ring until it stopped. He hated the thing.

The head bookkeeper knocked neatly on Berry's frosted-glass partition door.

"Yes, yes," Berry said in a husky voice, between a drawl and a groan. He was sitting at his plain, clean desk with his head leaning on his hand.

Outside, they were finishing up the general ledger for the day, and in a little while they would be gone.

The bookkeeper put his head in. "Buford Allen is here to see you," he said.

The Colonel sat tapping with one of his dried, emaciated fingers. He had a momentary stab of fear, for some unknown reason, since he couldn't possibly feel guilty about anything, and then a feeling of alert interest. He smiled slightly, his lined, pale face showing this merely by a rearrangement of wrinkles, a shifting of its papery crevasses.

Buford—that healthy fool. What kind of peace was there in this world, anyway? As soon as a man got some money piled up, just as soon as his undoubted genius in the quartermaster corps had finally been turned loose in the free market, he began to feel his belly falling out from under him.

What kind of a world was it, where no sooner were you through with your service than your own body began to give way? Was there any reason, any reward, in this? Any justice? If the government was going to give him a pension, why didn't they give him a new stomach, too? That would have been justice.

His stool had been black for two days, and last night he had vomited a red so bright and brilliant that it could only be described as splendid. And it hurt. Yes, it hurt, all the time, and worse and worse, gnawing hideously, exactly as though some small, blind, stupid animal were inside him, gnawing continually. Why? Why? What had he ever done to deserve this?

"Have Mr. Allen wait," he said, hating Mr. Allen inexplicably.

The bookkeeper nodded and pulled his head back.

"How deep was the grave?" the Colonel asked a vague shadow sitting in the corner, which the bookkeeper hadn't even noticed. It was the old Mexican the Colonel had hired to follow Dickson. "How many feet deep?" He had been sitting there like a lizard, so still that he looked simply like a heap of clothing thrown on the chair. In the office it was fairly cool, and as long as he sat still, the old Mexican's smell was hardly noticeable, not much worse than that of an old boarding-house hall runner. When he was moving around outside in the sun, it was like fourteen buck goats fighting in a Mexican shoe factory.

"How many feet deep, Io?"

Io held up three fingers.

"Just below Berg's Mill? Where they went that night?"

"Sss," Io said, almost a whisper, just the sibilant of the word "Si" hissing in the dusk, out of the corner. He sat there, his old brown hands folded on his stomach, across a filthy white shirt that had blue stripes running up and down.

"But you didn't see them bury the boy there. You didn't see Dickson actually putting anybody in the grave, or the Negro digging it?"

Io's heavy, square head, set on his shoulders without benefit of neck, moved from side to side like an owl's.

"But that's where they pulled the boat up, isn't it?" the Colonel said. He had to do all the talking, he had found out. "You saw them pull the boat up there, and go ashore—Dickson and the Negro, carrying the body. Then, yesterday, you found this grave under the brush."

Io said nothing. He had reported all this a week ago. Let the old Americano rehearse it in his mind.

"Did you find any tracks around the grave?"

"Sss."

The Colonel looked at him. The fact was, Io would make a first-rate witness. "Dickson's tracks? The Negro's?"

"Sss."

"You are well known around San Antonio as a hunter and tracker? You make your living that way?"

"Sss."

"And you will swear that the boy—what's his name—Hugh Buss, the young boy got in the boat, and they carried him out into the brush, after you followed them in the other boat, down there below Berg's Mill. And now you have found the boy's body, and he was stabbed. Well, that's all I need. But you will swear?"

Io looked very faintly troubled. *"Otro,"* he whispered and grunted at the same time, his voice heavy in his chest.

"Another? You mean besides the boy?"

"Sss," Io sighed, much relieved at the Colonel's neat perception.

"Who?"

Io shrugged.

"What did he look like? American? Mexican? Fair? Dark? Thin face? Fat face?"

Io held up five brown fingers.

"You found five graves?"

"Sss." Io suddenly yawned, his mouth opening very wide and his white teeth gleaming.

"My God," Colonel Berry said to himself.

"Un cemeterio secreto," Io said, suddenly breaking all bounds.

The Colonel put his hands up to his head and held them there. It was as though he had had a glimpse into some subterranean world, as though he had suddenly, with a great gift, seen a soul all the way to its bottom, and he shut his eyes to it. It had occurred to him, just once, that knowledge of one murder by Dickson would be a handy thing to have, in reserve. There was always the remote danger of blackmail by Dickson—the Colonel had always admitted the risks of his weaknesses. But the five brown fingers raised suddenly out of the shadows—

He turned away and swallowed. "The girl. Haven't you found her yet?"

"Sss."

The Colonel whirled around. "Well, why didn't you tell me?" he cried. "Where is she?"

Io drew a deep breath and sat forward. He was getting ready for a speech. He said, speaking clearly, in a rather cultivated voice, "Laredo Street. She is in the big white house with the green shutters."

The Colonel looked at him with a faint, kindly smile. "Thank God," he said. In the dark, two tears formed in his eyes. He brushed them away with the back of his hand. "Thank God. Io, isn't she pretty? Is she well?"

Io said nothing.

"What a charming girl. How did she get into a life like that? So sweet. She was always so nice, so kind. She wasn't like the others."

"Sss."

"Is she well? Does she seem—" He started to say "happy," and stopped. "Is she in good health?"

Io sighed deeply and shook his head.

"What do you mean?"

"Dead."

"What?" the Colonel asked faintly.

Io looked down and said nothing. There was no use repeating what he knew the Colonel had heard.

The Colonel stood up and shouted. "What? What? You damned liar, what? You lie! Stand up! Stand up! Damn you, why should you lie?"

Outside in the office, everything stopped. Everybody stood still, frozen.

Io stood up slowly. "I am not a liar." The Colonel stood there shaking, his mouth pinched as though he wanted to speak, or was trying to keep himself from doing so. His head shook on his neck, and his lips trembled. "Sit down," he whispered. "I beg your pardon. Sit down."

Io sat down with dignity.

"Dead," the Colonel whispered. "My God, dead." For a moment he covered his face with his two hands. "But why she?" he asked plaintively. "Why she? Why did it have to be she?" He sat looking at the picture on the wall, of the old-time officers in their fading group.

Io put one finger to his throat, or at least under his chin, where he would have had a throat if he had had any neck; he opened his mouth and made a loud sound like somebody throwing up.

The Colonel looked at him miserably.

"She was choke," Io said.

"What?"

Io put his finger to his throat again, stuck out his tongue, and waggled his head, again making that noise.

"For God's sake, stop that," the Colonel said, his voice shaking with anger. "How the hell do you know? If she was—was killed in town, I'd have heard. What about the police? The police?" He started to call Io a liar again, but thought better of it, and so repeated, "The police? The police?" as though his insistence meant something. "Do they know?"

Io put his forefinger to his head, looked as wise as he could, and tapped.

"They suspect?"

"Sss."

"Where is she? Where is she?" He kept repeating everything because, like a man in pain, who has to moan, he had to make some sound, any sound, just to ease the pain.

"The White House on Laredo Street. With the green shutters."

"Who did it?" the Colonel asked.

"In the street, I listened. I am following Dickson as you say. One night—two nights ago. She is upstairs. I hear Dickson. Talk, talk, talk. She screams, words, words. He says, 'Shut up, shut up, shut up.' She screams, mad, mad, mad." Io raised his eyes, whistled sadly, and sighed profoundly. "A little while. Then—out she comes—the window. But no screaming." He put his finger to his throat, stuck out his tongue, and again made that noise.

The Colonel shut his eyes. He squeezed them. He

opened them wide. "Get me the police," he said to nobody.

He stood up. "Get me the police!" he shouted.

He turned around and hit the bell on his desk as hard as he could.

The head bookkeeper came running in.

"Get me the police!" the Colonel shouted.

Already the shouts were having their effect on him, and he felt better, and also weaker.

The head bookkeeper ran.

The Colonel stood shaking. "Follow Dickson," he said to Io. "Wherever he goes. Don't lose sight of him. I'm going to dig up those graves. I'm going to arrest him, tonight. And I'll hang him. Hang him. Hang him."

"Sss," Io said, and rose, moving smoothly and easily. He moved like water, without effort, much more Aztec than Spanish. He made a small, courteous bow, in the country way, and then took a silent, Indian departure.

The assistant head bookkeeper came to the door and said, "Mr. Buford Allen is here to see you, sir," and immediately Buford Allen, smiling broadly, pushed past him and went up to the desk with his hand out.

There were tears in the Colonel's eyes, tears of sorrow and frustration and of solid physical pain, but Buford could not see that. "What do you want?" the Colonel cried out.

Buford stood, his smile gone, his mouth open. His hand dropped to his side. "Why, why," he said, and looked around vacantly, not knowing what he had wanted.

"Get out," the Colonel cried, trying to control his voice. It was too much, all of a sudden. "Get out of here, Buford! You have cost me thousands of dollars." This was not true, but the Colonel was saying it anyway, because here was a man who had cost many others thousands of dollars, a wretch who should be hanged. "I have lost thousands of dollars. Thousands, thousands. I don't want to see you again, there is nothing, absolutely nothing, I can do for you." And even when he said this, he was sorry for it, seeing Buford's face, the blankness, the lostness. But it was too late to change. "So go! Go on, get out!"

Buford's face was dead white. He stood speechless, looking at Berry. Then he turned and walked out, moving unsteadily, bumping the door frame as he passed.

Colonel Berry sat down with his head in his hands, and waited for the police. Vaguely he knew that the police could do no good. They would just hang somebody. The police never brought anybody back to life.

He listened to the sounds of revelry rise in the town around him, from the two Plazas up Houston Street. The fox gnawed steadily in his stomach. There was no way to stop it. What would happen? What was next? How little there was left, in any case, even if, by some miracle, they could stop the fox. If it wasn't the fox, it would be something else just as certain, a little later.

Nobody ever lived forever, everybody died of something. This notion, which he had known so long, but until now had never realized at all, stood clearly before him. Why? Why? What was it all for? If this was the way it ended, what was the use of beginning at all? What had been accomplished, in between? It was all some kind of stupid, insane joke. You had a cold and deceitful little daughter, and you found, incredibly, a little girl in some chance house, who was really a kind of daughter, who for some incredible reason was a little fond of you—or was it all an illusion?—actually did have some sweetness, some affection. And then she died. Why? Why? Why that particular one?

A key rattled in the front door. He looked up. It

was the head bookkeeper and the tall lean man with him was Cash, a lieutenant of the city police.

The Colonel said to Lieutenant Cash, "I want Thomas Dickson arrested tonight. On five counts of murder. You had a suspicious death in a house on Laredo, didn't you?"

"Yes, sir," Cash said to the commissioner. "One of the girls. It's Dickson's house."

"I think Dickson did that one too. Put a watch on that house, Cash."

"They're having a party there tonight, sir," Cash said. "Colonel Berry, this party is an open flaunting of the law. I know damn well the girl was murdered—"

"I can prove it," the Colonel said.

"Then let me use that for an excuse to bust a few heads, for once."

The Colonel said nothing for a long moment. "I'll meet you there at—when's the party?"

"Make it nine, sir." Cash left.

What could you do, the Colonel thought, in the end, but fight? Reason had no answer, at least for him. He would fight the fox as long as he could, he would fight it to the end, and even when he knew it would win, he would buckle down and hold on and continue to fight it, holding his breath against the moans, until the very end. What else could you do? It would get him—the darkness would come, and fighting did no good. And yet there was nothing to do but fight. Just hold on, and never give an inch.

He sat there waiting, his wrinkled mouth quiet and his jaw still.

CHAPTER SIX

Mary Allen's House—6:30 P.M.

Buford wandered down Houston Street from Berry's bank, heading west in a mental fog. There was only one place where he could go, one place where he was not an outcast, and he headed there without conscious intention, simply by instinct, like a drunk. He angled across the crowded Plaza to Dolorosa and then came back up Laredo to his wife's number. He knocked on the street gate. There was no answer.

Down Laredo Street, the big white house with green shutters had come to life. For some reason, all the shutters were open—an incredible thing, really—and light was streaming out from them in wide golden bands, breaking through the deepening evening. Lights and music. The music was a waltz, and he saw that a party was going on. Laughter came out, the laughter of women, high and sparkling; and deeper, that of men. In front of the house five carriages were drawn up, and saddled horses were hitched to the posts along the curb. The rest of the block was, as usual, in its Spanish way, dead quiet and totally deserted.

There was still no answer—but this was the right house. Buford pushed open the gate and went into the little garden, and closed the gate behind him. The moon was just coming up, and its light shot across the roofs across the street, lighting the front door of the little house before him. He looked around. It was a garden no longer—the place was piled with old furniture, chairs, stoves, tables, bureaus, commodes, all of it broken, with legs missing, rungs unglued, doors hanging by twisted hinges. On one side of the yard there was an open shed, with a carpenter's bench in it and some partly mended chairs.

He went up to the door and knocked. After a moment it opened.

He could see his wife in the doorway.

"Si?" Mary said.

The moonlight shone full on her handsome face. Then she saw his beard.

"Why, Buford!" she said, her voice—still so young—full of pleasure, surprise, and oddly, a little shyness. "Why, Buford, dear—come in, come in."

She stood back, and he went in. She closed the door behind him. He stood there, looking at her in the light from the kerosene table lamp, and they looked at each other in silence for a moment. He felt her warmth, which was her love, and there rose in him the discomfort of the memory of all his injustice to her, so that he was happy to see her, and didn't want to see her, at the same time.

He didn't kiss her, and she didn't expect it.

"Still the same Mary," was all he said.

"I?" she asked. "Why should I change? It has only been three months since you left."

"Yes. But everything else—it seems like such a long time." He looked around with a somewhat dazed expression. "What a place, Mary. I don't understand."

It was a large, square room with adobe walls, hand-plastered. There was a crucifix over the door, and another on the wall before him. There was a small statue of the Virgin by a little bed in the corner, and a single candle to one side, and a rosary.

"You really live here?" he asked. He had meant to upbraid her, to scold her, but as always happened, when he was actually in her presence, he could not.

The floor was dirt, packed hard and almost shiny with sweeping. On tables along the wall there were great heaps of clothing. Then he noticed, against the back wall, two small cribs. He had thought at first they were merely two crates—but now he noticed a movement in one of them, and recognized them for what they were.

He went over and looked down inside one of them. There was a tiny baby in it, well bundled up, sleeping on its back. It was sweating. He very gently took off one of the blankets. The crucifix was directly over the babies.

Mary was standing looking at them. "I have three more," she said, and nodded at the rear door.

"Where did you get them?"

She sat down at the sewing table. "People leave them."

"Here?"

"Everywhere. In the gutters. On the sidewalk."

"But what are you doing? Trying to start a new family or something?"

"No, oh, no," she said, rather sadly. "I keep them. We try to find families for them, or the sisters take them. But, you see, now that I live here, I find more than the sisters do."

She nodded toward the piles of sewing. "I have five Mexican girls now, sewing for me. You see if they know how to do anything at all, they can make a little living, and the sisters help them. They bring in the work from all over town. Mostly old clothes, mending—but sometimes seamstress work. Two of my girls are quite clever."

All Buford could see was cockroaches, scuttling along the base of the wall.

"It's a fad. It can't last. I know the women who go for this sort of thing—they all pitch in—but wait till your girls make a few mistakes, they'll get sick of it. The pious ones'll quit you."

"Of course, you're right," she said. "I know exactly how fickle human beings are." She smiled at him.

He felt the blood falling away out of his head and heart.

"But you see, if our 'ladies' fail us, the Archbishop will give us help—and, of course, we expect things to be a little difficult."

"Why did you leave the Menger?" he asked.

"Because I was embarrassed."

"Why should you be embarrassed?" he asked, his fist tightening. "We lived there for years, didn't we? And all of a sudden you left. Why? It almost looks like a separation."

Her eyes, blue and gentle in her handsome face, had a very open, luminous look. They were the eyes of a child, but very thoughtful, and at times very shrewd. "I was thinking of the bill. There I was, living on Mr. Menger, with the bill going on, knowing you had not paid it—"

"But I would have!"

"Would you? Why, Buford, I wired you myself that news about the suit. You surely don't pretend you have any money!"

"I have a hundred and fifty thousand dollars," he said.

"Is there nobody that has a claim to it?"

"Not a just claim," he said, with a confusion that angered him more than ever.

"So it's not really yours, is it?" she asked. "That is what I meant, Buford. That is the way I began to feel in Menger's—there I was going, every morning, down to Mass at St. Joseph's, and then I would go back to Menger's for breakfast, and contribute to a debt which I doubt very much could be paid. Buford, Buford. Don't look offended! All our lives, you have been living on debts. Debts and schemes, Buford. The only change is that the debts have got bigger and bigger, and the schemes to go with them. Why don't you face it, Buford? You're at the very end. You know, when a man's friends insist that he sign notes against his word, he is at the very end. Buford, why don't you let it all go? I watched you take the blanket off the baby then because it was too hot. Why don't you help me here? You could mend the furniture we get. Why not do something for somebody else, for a change, instead of always for yourself?"

They sat in silence, he looking at the cockroaches.

Then she went on: "So every morning I would go to Mass and Holy Communion, and in my heart it grew greater and greater, a kind of reproach, as though He were saying, 'Why do you continue taking what is not yours?' As though He said, 'You love Me, but don't you see that justice must come before love, before charity?' I thought, you can't keep taking Menger's food and lodging, knowing he won't be paid. No matter how fond he is of you, he will suffer all the same, losing that money; no matter how generous he is, he is in a business."

She looked down at her sewing. "So I left Menger's."

He was sitting up straight, his own face red. "That's preposterous. Absolutely preposterous. This is what this continual religion does for you. How can you get so crazy? Was it those priests? Your spiritual directors?" he asked, biting the words "spiritual directors" with a kind of sarcasm.

She glanced up quickly. "How pleasant it is," she said, her great, bright eyes looking right into him, "to see you so sensitive. Thank God you still have a conscience. It makes me happy, Buford. It only proves I was not a fool to fall in love with you—that my judgment was right, after all. Poor Buford." She smiled at him, and his anger, or what he tried to make into anger, turned into confusion again.

"Why don't you just give up? Why pretend? For some reason, you have always thought it necessary to live up to a certain preconceived notion, level, or whatever you call it. You never once have actually been what you actually were, or allowed me to be what I actually was. Always the grand lady! That was my role. But I was never grand; and that's why you hated me, I suppose. And even now I suppose it shocks you to have it known by me, that you hated me, at times—it goes against the pretense. You always insisted that I know nothing about Clara, and nothing about you—as though I could help it—as though I were some kind of a fool. Well, perhaps I was a fool to marry you, Buford. But I was not deceived. You still love her. I don't blame you! But I will never go to Montana with you."

"What? How can you say that?" he cried out. "After all I've gone through—My God, if you knew, right now, what I'm going through!"

"I can imagine your difficulties," she said, "and I already know all your arguments. The ranch in Montana is to be our last home—away from our creditors, with me there to take care of you, as I have always done, and Clara's grave there, also, for you to potter about and put flowers on. What a perfect picture of you! Forgive me, it is so comic: your tummy well filled, somebody else's money in the bank, and a woman to worship who can no longer be anything but virtuous. Forgive me! I suppose I do resent it, Buford. But how I tried not to! All those years."

"Clara has nothing to do with it," he said. "Are you telling me you are leaving me?" He was quite sober, quite matter-of-fact.

"No. You will be leaving me. I have a life here. I was born here. But I am telling you more than that, Buford. What is up there for you? Nothing. A strange country, without friends. You think it will solve all your problems. It won't. Oh, Buford, if only you would be humble! You could get a job at Menger's. What a wonderful desk clerk you would make! So affable, so charming, so tactful."

"Why are you mocking me? Why are you trying to hurt me?"

"I'm not, Buford. You're too old to start over in a strange country with nothing but the memories of a dead woman. It all comes from the devil—illusions and dreams. You will die alone, Buford, alone in the dark, without a friend. And without God."

"I don't know why you're saying this," Buford said quietly. "I have to go north. I have to push this thing through."

"Where are your emerald cuff links?" she asked suddenly.

"Stolen," he said. "In Ogalalla."

"You see, Buford," she said, "everything is going, little by little. I want you to live decently. There's nothing wrong in being poor, Buford. You and I could be happily poor, here."

"Poor!" he said, standing up. "I was poor once. My father starved to death. It took him four years to do it, but he starved to death, trying to feed us. A minister of the Gospel, living on handouts, riding a circuit for a forest-full of scrimping bastards. A meek and humble man, a man God must have loved indeed." A sudden fury shot up into his eyes. "Poor! I've been poorer than the dogs in the gutter. I know what that is, I loved my father, and I watched him die."

"That wasn't His fault."

"His? You mean God's? Who's blaming God? I'm only thinking of the people, the damned, mean, grasping, mealymouthed hypocrites always talking about charity, and handing him a skinny old hen and half a dozen pullet eggs on Sunday, for him to feed us with, and thinking they were serving God. Their God was the devil. Damn them all!" He started to shout and suddenly saw the babies, and checked himself.

He looked at his wife. "That's why I hate their souls. Poor! I'll make them poor, I'll grind their faces in the dust."

"And where are they now," she asked quietly, "the ones who starved your father, that you will grind in the dust?"

"You know where they are," he said. "They're dead." The anger died.

He looked at his wife, and the cockroaches. "But I won't be poor. Never. Never. Never."

He turned and went out of her house, and out of her garden, full of its broken and mended furniture.

He stood in the street, alone, facing the risen moon. The noise of the dancers, singing and hilariously shouting, came up the street from the big house. He stood there in a daze. Where was Mike? All he could do now was bribe Dickson's men.

His follower came slowly up the sidewalk. He was a short man, and had to look up to Buford, who was not tall himself. He said, "Listen, Pop, I don't mind following you around, but when are you going to eat? I'm getting awful hungry.

"I know everybody in that house," his follower went on. "Let's go on down the street and go in. They got a hell of a spread. Turkeys, hams, beef—you should see it; all kinds of booze. What say?"

Buford said nothing. The music grew louder. Why not? He had to eat. He couldn't lose this fellow. He couldn't go back to the Menger to wait for Mike. But Mike would come to see his mother, and this party was close by.

"Why not?" Buford said wearily, and walked down the sidewalk with the other. When Mike came, the two of them would bribe this little fellow—maybe tie him up and throw him over a wall somewhere.

A man stepped out of a carriage in front of them. He had a gun in his hand. "Step in, Buford," Spence said, motioning with the gun. "We'll wait here for Mike."

Buford said, his voice low with shock and fear, "He doesn't know where I am."

"No," Spence said, "but he'll come by and see his mother, won't he? Isn't he a good boy? Get in."

Buford climbed in.

Dickson, sitting inside, smiled gently. "Quite a little party, Buford," he said. "Do you know Mr. Keppelbauer? Keppelbauer, if you will stop moaning and sniveling for a moment, I would like to introduce you to somebody. A fool like yourself, let us say. Exactly." He climbed over Buford and got out of the carriage. "I'll just stroll to the Menger and see if Mike's shown up, eh? Ta-ta, boys."

CHAPTER SEVEN

Degen's Brewery—7:00 P.M.

Mike came into town on a farmer's horse, for which he had paid double. It was dark, and the moon was just coming up as he rode slowly up Blum Street from the east, toward the Menger. He got off the horse at the door of Degen's Brewery, which was just behind the Menger, down Blum Street, and knocked on the door.

Old Adolf Dallmeyer let him in. Adolf had a policeman's nightstick. He was eating his supper, liverwurst-and-rye sandwiches with pickles, and a big stein of Degen's best.

"Vell, vell, Mike," Adolf said, backing away from the door and letting Mike in. "What is this? A horse you on der highvay drags?"

"I fell off a train," Mike said. "Mind if I leave something here for a while?"

"Mind? Who, me? Vy should I mind? Leave anything. What? Your horse, is it?" He laughed a big, deep haw, haw, haw, and rubbed his stomach.

Mike had the saddlebags in his hand. All the way down from Cheyenne, through Pueblo and Dodge, over to Kansas City, he had never opened those bags, never changed the money into a suitcase, never thought of it, until he had paid his father's bill in St. Louis. He looked around for a place to hide it.

The brewery, with a single lamp high on one damp wall, looked like a cavern with its big barrels and mash vats. The place was warm and cozy, full of slopped water from the barrel-washing department, and the rich smell of the mash and the hops was everywhere.

"You take them," Mike said, handing Adolf the saddlebags. "Keep 'em for me awhile."

"Sure, sure," Adolf said, and slung them neatly behind his big chair under the lamp. "A beer, Mike?"

"No time," Mike said. He smiled. "Going to see my girl."

"Haw, haw, haw," Adolf laughed, patting his stomach.

Mike got back on his horse and rode up around to the front door of Menger's.

Isaac Forrest was leaning against the wall beside the front steps.

"Hello, sonny," Isaac said. "Been waiting."

"I hope I haven't been too long," Mike said.

"Where is it?"

"Where is what?" Mike asked, and walked past him, up the steps.

"The money," Isaac said, following him into the lobby.

"Is my father in?" Mike asked at the desk.

"He left a message he'd be at your mother's," the clerk said politely. He looked at the clipboard. "Mrs. Allen is staying in a house on Laredo." He wrote the address for Mike.

"Are the bags upstairs?"

"Yes, sir."

Mike started for the stairway.

"Just a minute," Isaac said, putting his hand on Mike's arm. Mike stopped.

"There's a warrant out for your arrest," Isaac said in a low, serious voice. "Don't give me the runaround, boy, or I'll have you chucked in the can. Where's the money? The boss has given your old man till midnight to kick through. It's up to you, sonny. So give."

Mike looked down at the hand on his arm, and carefully spat on it.

Isaac snatched his hand away and stood there, his eyes snapping. He wiped his hand on the side of his pants. "After I get the money," Isaac said. "Business before pleasure."

"I haven't got the money," Mike said. "A man in Baton Rouge has it. I bought two cassowaries with it. They died. I ate them."

He turned and walked up the stairs.

Isaac stood in the middle of the lobby with his big fists clenched. The clerk looked at him warily. Tommy Dickson, who had been sitting peacefully under a palm tree, got up and walked over to Isaac.

"Well done, Isaac," Tommy said, patting him gently on the shoulder. "You naughty kitten, go find your mitten, or else you'll have no pie. Evidently he's going to see his mother, as I thought. Just follow him around town. Sooner or later he'll lead you right to the money, wherever he left it."

Dickson sauntered out, swinging his cane jauntily.

CHAPTER EIGHT

Colonel Berry's House—7:15 P.M.

Nancy Berry put her hand over the mouthpiece of her father's home phone, that splendid toy of which she was so proud.

"Oh, dear," she said. "Daddy, it's Mike Allen. He's back in town. I thought he might be killed."

"How interesting," the Colonel said. He was sitting in the parlor, drinking a double bourbon and water, waiting for the fox to go to sleep.

"But what will I do?" Nancy cried.

"Do what you usually do when you get tired of them," the Colonel said. "Put your foot in the middle of his face and push. Hard."

"How can you say such a thing?" Nancy quavered, her hand still over the phone. "Oh, Daddy." She tried to sound sorrowful and aggrieved. But somehow the thought of putting her foot in the middle of Mike's face was so funny that she laughed. While she was still laughing, she took her hand off the phone so Mike could hear it. He would wonder why she was laughing. A girl had to keep them wondering.

"Oh, Mike darling. Oh, how nice that you're back!"

Mike said something.

"Tonight? Now?" she asked, with pretty dismay. "But Daddy's going out. There won't be anybody here—except just me."

Mike said something.

Suddenly all the charm and mirth vanished from Nancy Berry's face. She looked a little angry, and then, as Mike talked on, a little bored, and finally she smiled a smile of contempt. "Very well, darling," she finally cooed, "since I promised all that, come on over—in an hour." She put the telephone carefully together again and left it hanging on the wall.

"I thought you said Lieutenant Milford was coming over this evening," the Colonel said.

"Jimmie Milford?" she asked. "Oh, Daddy, don't be so quaint. Captain Barnes is coming over, not that little old Jimmie. That little old Jimmie Milford? Why, he's so silly. He threatened to shoot himself. Anyway, I want Mike to meet Captain Barnes. It should be amusing."

"One of them actually did shoot himself, didn't he?" the Colonel asked.

"You mean that little old Tommy Bragg? Oh, gracious, Daddy, you can't think he did that over me, do you?"

"I don't think anything," the Colonel said. "There is a point in life beyond which it does not pay to think."

She looked at him, wondering what he meant, or if he was just drunk. He sat there, bitterly enduring her. There was nothing he could do about it. It took all his self-control to keep from remembering her as a baby, as a little girl, in those times when she was so tiny, sweet, and happy. Maybe later, when she was gone, when she had carried her little whirl of private vice into somebody else's jurisdiction, was married, and had moved from the sphere of fornication into that of adultery, he would feel safe to remember those happy days. But he could not afford to now.

Her sweet, low, husky voice went on, talking about Mike, sticking him full of pins. A smelly cowhand, was the gist of it. The Colonel sat and drank. When he had finished, he got up and stood straight and still, looking at his daughter.

How pretty she was! Standing there in that evening dress. Her pale-gold hair, her blue eyes, her delicately pointed chin, her vivacious smile. It had taken a long time for his hatred of her conduct to kill his love for her.

Somebody knocked on the front door.

"Another sheep to the slaughter," the Colonel said. "What a carnage."

"What's that, Daddy?" she asked.

"Nothing," he said. "I'll run along. I suppose you'll be sending the servants home early. As usual."

"Why not?" she asked gaily. "Poor things, they need a rest."

"I should think they would," the Colonel said, and went out.

"Where are you going, Daddy?" she cried, running after him, affection on her face like icing on a cake. "If I need you?" She always said that. The six-year-old innocent.

"To a party," he said. "They're having a dance in a whorehouse down on Laredo Street." He said this with profound pleasure. It was the first time in his life he had ever used that word in the presence of a woman. With interest, he watched the lies coming and going on her face, nymphic glee chasing girlish wonder. "I'm going down there with Lieutenant Cash and get drunk."

At the door moments later the young captain,

turning upon the spit of her charm, himself, in turn, turned upon her the full force and beam of his own winning smile, telling her with his eyes that he adored her, while the old houseman, wheezing and snuffling, took his cap.

"You may go, Joseph," Nancy said. This rather regal form of address she used on the servants in front of Northern men, who wouldn't understand if she spoke to old Uncle Joe as one of the family.

Joe sighed, "Yazzum," and chuffing and wheezing painfully, padded slowly away down the hall in his old split shoes, which had large holes cut out of the sides of the uppers, to make room for his bunions.

"Darling," the captain said, opening his arms. "Darling." What he lacked in vocabulary he made up in expressiveness.

"Not yet!" she whispered, her finger on her lips, looking at him from the side of her eye. "Let's go out in the garden. It's so lovely in the moonlight!" What she meant was that they could both lie to each other better if they couldn't see each other quite so well.

CHAPTER NINE

Colonel Berry's House—8:30 P.M.

All the way across town in the carriage, Mike had been thinking about Nancy Berry. The two dozen red roses which he had bought, and which he held carefully suspended by the stems, filled the musty old box with their sweet scent.

He was not rich, he thought, but at least he had about forty thousand dollars, which was enough to start his own business. His father could pay for the two herds which were now going north secretly, and use them to start himself again, while Mike took what was left of the $160,000 and made his own way.

With Nancy. At least, that had been the plan—the "understanding."

Was there ever a girl like Nancy? A gay little girl, a flirt, in a way, but so tender, so delicate, so charming, with her little pointed chin and her golden hair.

The picture, for some reason, lacked life. His habitual response to it, of tender affection, was sluggish. He prodded it, and remembered Clara

Montrose. What was the matter with him? He had been in love with Nancy Berry for eight long years. He must be tired, that was all. Clara was just a friend. He loved Nancy. Yes, he loved Nancy. Maybe he didn't like her much, but he loved her. He sat suddenly astounded at this thought. How, indeed, could he have thought it? But he had. Was he crazy?

The carriage pulled up in front of the Colonel's house, and he got out and told the driver to wait. He was going to take Nancy for a ride, if the old Colonel would permit it. The thought of Nancy's forwardness—that innocent excess of desire, which seemed to him to be such an evidence of her love for him—crossed his mind, and he shut it away immediately. That was a problem that would soon be solved decently, and happily.

Nobody answered Mike's knock.

He knocked again, just a little longer.

He waited. He remembered Sister Margaret Mary, long ago cautioning the boys at St. Mary's College to say two Our Fathers before knocking the second time. He said two Our Fathers.

Then he knocked again, just a little louder.

There was a light on in the parlor, but there was not a sound in the whole house.

He stood there, surprise turning into a kind of unbelieving dismay. She had said she would be in, and for him to come over in an hour. Well, he was here, wasn't he? And where was she?

He began to be a little alarmed. The house was so still.

He went to the parlor window and looked in. There was nobody in the room.

He stood in the night, listening to the insects and the treefrogs, trying to think of what could have happened.

The silence of the house began to oppress him, and suddenly his whole attitude changed from the rather dizzy one of expectant excitement to a clear alertness, without any emotion at all, exactly as though he were again facing Spence on the trail north.

It was just barely possible that something was wrong. Still carrying the roses, he went quietly along the side of the house, looking at the windows, and at the second story.

In the rear there was the usual lawn, running down to the river, cut off from the neighboring houses and yards by hedges of oleander and mock orange. The moon was bright, his button shoes sank in the smooth grass, and the crickets hardly paused as he passed, so full were they of moonlight and the heat of summer.

He came around the back of the house, and there, in a kind of bower, across the lawn, where a lace vine grew, he saw his beloved Nancy in the arms of an army officer, who was kissing her. Then he noticed that one of Nancy's shoulders was bared, something he had never seen before.

Almost at the same time, Nancy saw him—almost, in fact, as though she had been waiting for him—and cried, "Oh! Oh! A man!"

The captain sprang to his feet, his hair and his wits in great dishevelment. He saw Mike. "You, there! Stand where you are."

Mike said nothing, and stood where he was.

"Who are you?" the captain demanded, jerking down his tunic and straightening himself out while trying to speak in a tone of military authority.

Mike moved slowly toward them, carrying the roses. "My name is Allen," he said. "I hope you will—I, that is—I had an engagement this evening with—" His head was swimming. He could hardly see.

"Why, Mike," she said, from the bower, "what an awful thing—Why, you know I told you I didn't want to see you again. How could you have come here, uninvited, when I told you—"

"You don't want him here, Miss Nancy?" the captain asked, whirling around.

"Now, Mike," Nancy said, "please don't make any trouble."

"I'm not making any trouble," Mike said. "I'm just standing here."

"Get out," the captain said. "I order you to get off this place at once. If you don't, I shall have the pleasure—"

"What?" Mike turned slowly and looked at him. "What did you say?" he asked dully.

The captain took two steps toward Mike, pulled back his fist, and hit Mike on the right cheekbone. Mike fell down. He sat there shaking his head.

"Stand up, sir," the captain said, "and fight like a man."

"Listen," Mike said, his head clearing, "I don't feel like fighting." He got up slowly and stood shaking his head again.

The captain swung once more, and Mike moved to the side with an expression of fatigue. "Please," Mike said, "I told you once I don't feel like fighting. Not at all. Can't you wait till some other time? Really, this all—"

The captain swung again. His tunic was binding him so that he puffed.

"Oh, for God's sake," Mike said. "You damn fool."

He sank one in the captain's stomach. The captain bent over, and Mike hit him in the side of the jaw. The captain had a head like iron. Mike had to hit him four times before he collapsed. When the captain finally lay out on the turf, he relaxed and started breathing again. Mike nursed his knuckles. He felt dizzy.

He turned and looked at Nancy. She was sitting in the bower, her face pale and pinched, without expression.

"Get out," she said sharply. "You are not a gentleman. Get out, you smelly cattle driver."

Mike stood looking at her. He couldn't believe it. He couldn't believe any of it. He stood there like a cow in a slaughterhouse, that has been hit once on the head, but not quite hard enough.

"Who is this man?" he finally asked. "I don't understand. I thought—Then you don't—Who is this man? Are you engaged?"

She laughed in a low, throaty voice. "Get out!" she said. "You idiot. Engaged! Get away, with your dirty cows! Go away! Go away! Do you think I ever cared anything about you?"

"With your dress half off," he said. "What's this?" It sank in, little by little. The harsh voice, the white, pinched face, the hate behind the words, and the words themselves. No matter how dumb he was, it had to sink in sometime.

"I knew there was some competition," he said, his voice trembling. "But—Do you know what you looked like? You and that man? You looked like a piece of raw meat with a big fat blowfly on top of it."

He whipped her across the face with the roses, paper and all. Petals flew.

"You dirty little tramp." She sat there, stunned.

He whipped her again, and the petals showered on the lawn. "You damn, dirty little bitch."

His eyes suddenly filled with tears, not for her, not for love, not for dreams, but simply from humiliation, from the feeling of filth, at being in contact with what he could now perceive. He saw himself with a dull certainty, for what he had been—a fathead. For the first time in his life he saw with absolute clarity that there was a distinct difference between what might actually be and what he wished to be, and that nothing in heaven and earth could make what he wished to be out of what was, if it wasn't that by nature.

He looked at the roses, still in his hand. He started to throw them down, and couldn't. They had done nothing. Why should he associate them with this little tart? They represented love—well, there was nothing wrong with love, and nothing wrong with roses. So why throw them down? The only thing wrong was his own fat head.

Without looking again at Nancy, who was now sitting there rigid with fright, he took the roses down to the river and, taking off the paper, threw them far out into the water. He watched them float away in the moonlight until they were gone, and then came back.

He stood in front of the paralyzed girl, who now was sure he was crazy, and was waiting for the worst, and said, "Please accept my apologies for my conduct."

His voice was quiet, cold, and heavy, as it had never been before. His face was heavier too, and it had a wholly new expression of profound reserve. He spoke with complete gravity and calm.

"Good-by," he said. "I am sorry, from the bottom of my heart, for having hurt you, in any way."

He looked at the captain, still lying peacefully on the turf. He stooped over and straightened the captain out a little, so that he looked a little more dignified. He sighed deeply.

He turned and walked away, back to the carriage.

CHAPTER TEN

Mary Allen's House—9:00 P.M.

"Have you seen Nancy Berry?" his mother asked.

"Yes, I saw her," Mike said.

He sat looking at his mother, and she sat looking at him, smiling quietly.

The heavy lines of his face softened and he smiled at her. He was sitting on the same chair his father had used. The sound of the dance band came up the street. There was something cold about his smile, something too reserved.

"What's the matter, Mike?"

"Nothing," he said.

"I hope—you mustn't mind if I say this—I hope you won't allow one experience to make you bitter. In fact," she said, looking at his face, "I know you won't."

"That's right," he said. The dance band in the big house down the street swung along, and a shriek of laughter rose and subsided.

"Marriage depends on making a sensible choice," she said. "Love is no substitute for character."

"Yes," he said, seeing through her, and seeing what she had not meant him to see, her life with Buford. After a moment he said, "Father still wants that ranch. He can't possibly get it. But he's still scheming."

"Yes. He told me."

"What is the matter with him? Why that one ranch in Montana, of all places? There's something between him and Montrose. But what?"

"I suppose I'd better tell you. Only I don't want you to be angry with him, Mike." She sighed. "You mustn't expect people to be noble—or even good. Buford—hasn't much character. Don't be angry with weak people, Mike."

"What's he done now? Anything new?"

"No, no. Do you know anything about a Clara Montrose?" she asked.

For some reason, he blushed. "Yes. I met her in Cheyenne. How did he know her?"

"That's the daughter. I mean her mother. Her mother was named Clara too. She and your father were engaged, here in San Antonio. That was in 1855—six years before the war." Her thread snarled. She straightened it.

"She lived here with her father." She sat quiet, not sewing. Then she said, with difficulty, "He was in love with her then. He's always been in love with her. I'm quite sure he's in love with her now. That's why he wants Montrose's ranch."

"That's crazy," Mike said. "What's the ranch got to do with a woman?"

"Because she died there. He isn't crazy, Mike. He just—he simply has never been able to get over loving that one woman. And I know he has tried. You see, he was always so impulsive, and he didn't have much head, for all his scheming. Your father isn't really a schemer, although he appears to be. I admired him so much—I haven't the slightest idea why, now. I suppose I thought he was so brave and dashing.

"He was engaged to her that spring, in 1855. He used to get drunk and ride his horses through town, scaring everybody. Buford was so wild that summer. He would get into fights and many people were afraid of him. My father said he hoped somebody would shoot him.

"And do you know, that was when I began to love Buford, I suppose, because I saw that everybody was against him—and I thought I understood him. San Antonio was such a little town then, Mike—everybody knew everybody.

"And I suppose he used to go up there to her house drunk—or half drunk. I don't know what happened. I really don't. But I suppose if I had been Clara, I would have done the same thing. After all, an engagement is supposed to be a happy time, and certainly she couldn't have been very happy. So that fall she broke their engagement, and Buford stopped drinking—not right away, but pretty soon. And he started courting her all over again, but of course it was too late.

"And besides, Montrose had come to town by then, and he was courting Clara too, and he was so distinguished—and so different from Buford." She stopped and thought, her eyes far away.

"Your father had a good deal of money then; he was trading in cotton with the English. He was more handsome than ever—such fine clothes! He bought those emerald cuff links then. And he started coming to our house more often, and he had stopped drinking, and I thought it was I who had made him stop. You see, I was nineteen, and so wise. Clara was engaged to Lieutenant Montrose. Your father and I were engaged that same year, and he used to take me to so many parties, and we had such a good time, and I really got to know Clara quite well.

"Everywhere we went, there was Clara, with Montrose, and I didn't notice it then, but I see why now.

"Actually, I saw the next year. Because when Clara married Montrose that next June, in 1857, and they went away on their trip, Buford and I—"

She stopped for a long time. Her face lost the remembering look, and became present. She said, rather stiffly, "Buford and I were married that summer. And when Montrose was transferred north somewhere, then Buford and I stopped going to all the parties and the picnics, and I began to understand."

She said, after a moment, "I want you to go north with him again, and take care of him. I know you don't want to go. But I am sure no good will come of this venture. Will you?"

He looked at her. "Why not? I'll leave my money with you—what I figure is my share. He can lose the rest."

"That's a good idea. He never let me save anything. Mike, don't be like Buford. Be humble, see the truth, and don't expect anything except what you deserve. Work hard, save your money, and try to be kind to the weak. Try to be like St. Joseph. Be a good man."

"All right," he said. "I'll try." He added, "The only trouble is, taking care of Dad, it's kind of hard to be good, sometimes."

"Well, you won't have too much longer. He's coming to the end of his rope. If he doesn't change, he'll crash. He's headed for a fall, Mike. Please try to help him."

"I'd better find him," Mike said, standing up. "Where did you say he was going when he left here?"

"He didn't say. But try the Menger. He always used to end up there."

* * *

Out in the street, Lt. Cash was staring at the lights of the big white house with a look of bleak hatred. Colonel Berry stood beside him, humped over, smoking a cigar. Four cops leaned against the wall, smoking cigars and talking. Somebody had brought out sandwiches and beer, and Lt. Cash had increased his popularity by knocking the tray into the gutter.

"Look at 'em, Colonel," he said. "God, how I hate their guts. I know what it all is, it's just Dickson's way of mocking the public. A murder in one of his whorehouses, so he produces a dance. Let me at 'em."

"How are you coming with the five graves I told you about?"

"They're digging at them now, Colonel. We'll know in a little while. Come on, let me at this. Just let me and my boys at this."

The Colonel said, "It's just barely possible those graves are innocent—Mexicans or somebody. We'll have to wait. I can't close down this place just because it's a whorehouse. You know that."

"I'd burn it to the ground," Cash said. He was a strict Presbyterian, and the open flaunting of the law infuriated him.

The Colonel thought a long while. "I guess you'd better have them take the girl's body back to the morgue. I guess we'd better have the autopsy. The doctor says that's the only way we can prove she was strangled before she fell out the window."

The thought of this was the one thing that was like a hot iron in the Colonel's mind.

Cash stood there fuming, chewing his mustache, his tall, lean figure tense and stooped. A buggy drove up.

"What did you find, doctor?" the Colonel asked as a little man jumped out of the buggy. The doctor shook his head.

"Colonel," he said, "three of them were stabbed

through, one of them was shot in the head. The other was so far gone I couldn't—"

"That's enough," the Colonel said. "Lieutenant Cash, I want you to get a warrant immediately for the arrest of Thomas Dickson for these six murders. I have a witness."

Suddenly he closed his eyes and stopped talking, because of the tears that came out of nowhere. The dance music from the house across the street had been working on him all evening. He had looked back on his delusions, remembering the little girl, of whom he had been so fond, who had seemed to him, in his age, so gentle, so meek, and even affectionate, in her way; and he had known them indeed to have been delusions, nothing but the wishes of his heart, his loneliness; and this had made the bitterness of her death even more bitter.

Underneath the heavy tears a flame of rage lit up, of hatred and revenge. "Go get 'em, Cash," he said. "Clean 'em out. Every damn one. And use your nightsticks."

A laugh came out of Cash's lean, hard mouth, harsh and joyful. "Come on, boys! Let's clean it out! Let's go!"

In a tight, sober group, grinning, the policemen ran across the street, toward the front door.

Somebody shouted the magic cry of "Cops!" and immediately panic spread and flying bodies jammed the door. Windows crashed, and men and women fled screaming out of the house and down the street, some still singing and laughing, scattering in all directions.

Cash came out and stood sweating by the Colonel.

"Cinch bugs," Cash said, laughing heartily. "Look at 'em," he cried with delight at the fleeing men and women. "Just like kicking a bed in a country hotel. Watch 'em run!"

Inside, the cops were cleaning up. The wagon had

come clanging, then a second, and they were bundling the wounded and the drunk and the unconscious in, packing them in like tamales in a pot.

"Never mind them," the Colonel said. "Get going. I want Dickson in the jail tonight."

Cash ran to his horse.

Down the street, Dickson was sitting quietly in his carriage.

Buford sat glumly in the corner, beside Spence. Dickson saw Mike coming down the street, and he pointed and nudged Spence.

Spence got out and pulled a gun. One of the police wagons clanged past, and then the other, and the hubbub quieted.

Mike slowed up, seeing the gun.

"Get in there," Spence said.

"I've got to find my father," Mike said.

"He's in there already. Get in. We're going to have a talk."

"The time has come," Dickson said politely, "to settle our accounts. Your father refuses to give up the money. There's only one alternative."

Mike got in. His father looked at him without expression. "Don't give them a cent, Mike. They're bluffing."

In the other corner Keppelbauer sat with his face in his hands. His sack suit was still covered with the dust of his falls under Forrest's whip. Sweat ran into his chin whiskers.

"Drive on," Dickson said, slamming the door.

The driver slapped the reins, and they moved from the light to the darkness.

The Colonel stood alone with the last of the carriages rolling away down the street. The lights of the house still burned brilliantly, but now there was total silence.

The Colonel's Mexican came by, trotting quietly on an unshod mule.

"Io!" the Colonel cried. "Where is Dickson?"

Io pointed down the street at the last of the carriages, which was turning the corner into Dolorosa. "There he goes. Didn't you know he was there all the time?"

The Colonel looked around for help. The street was empty and silent. He ran and got his horse. He trotted on down the street after Io, who was riding a safe distance behind the carriage.

The Colonel felt suddenly for a gun. He had none. He kept on, keeping well behind Io, so that the shod hoofs of his own horse would not be heard by the driver of the carriage, far up ahead.

CHAPTER ELEVEN

The Country West of Town
Same Night—11:00 P.M.

"You can run if you like," Dickson said. "However, you won't get far."

"This is a very poor joke," Buford said. His voice shook.

"I assure you, it is no joke," Dickson said. His voice was tight and strained.

They were standing in a triangle, back to back—Keppelbauer, Buford, and Mike. They were handcuffed together.

Buford's Panama hat shone white in the moonlight. The countryside was quite clear—mesquite and brush silver-tipped, shadows black and unmoving. There was no wind.

They were nowhere. It was just a small clearing in the brush west of town, four miles out and well off the road.

The carriage was silver-topped in the moonlight, and the horses moved gently, clinking their harness and bits. There were five riders sitting their horses

quietly in a rough circle around the three men, at a
distance of about ten yards. Dickson and Spence were
on foot, facing the three men in the middle of the
clearing.

How had they ever got this far? Mike thought, with
a kind of stupefied wonder. He was deathly afraid—
fear like pitch darkness inside him. First he had got
into the carriage. What else could he have done?
Spence had had the gun, and he had submitted, because Buford was inside. He couldn't run, with Buford in there, and Spence armed like that.

They had driven out of town, fast, with these five
horsemen around the coach. Nobody had said anything. But what could he have done then? Shout?
Who would have heard him?

Should he have jumped out into the road? But how
could he, leaving his father in there? So he had submitted to one thing after another, believing somehow that nothing much could happen in the end.
Even the handcuffs he had taken, because his father
could not have fought and run.

And so here they were now, handcuffed together
in the moonlight, and he could not believe what
Dickson was saying. How could it have gone this far?
Half an hour ago he had been walking down the
street—and here he was, helpless.

It wasn't a joke, but it was a threat. That was all
it was—a threat; they were simply trying to scare
the Allens into giving up the money. But in that
case, why was Keppelbauer there?

"Welshers," Dickson said, as though answering
him. "Welshers. Wretched, rotten suckers. You play,
you think you can bluff out of anything. Why should
I let you go? To spread the news that Dickson is a
soft touch? You're through. Through. And the world
is better off without you. Cover their eyes, Spence."

And Spence was walking around them. Keppelbauer was whimpering like a dog. He sounded like a lonesome little puppy, out in the cold, lost.

"This is absurd," Buford said. "It is preposterous and insulting. Do you think you are dealing with children, Dickson? Do you think for an instant you can frighten us into doing anything?"

"It's long past that," Dickson said quietly. Spence appeared in front of Mike holding a white bandage in his hands. Mike saw the bandage coming up, and right then he knew that this was more than a threat. He swung his foot and kicked at Spence's groin. Spence turned, and Mike's foot caught him in the thigh. Mike tried to get him again. The handcuffs yanked and tore and the three men staggered together. Keppelbauer fell down, crying.

Then Spence's fists were pounding Mike in the face, and he could see Spence's teeth glinting in a fixed smile, as the fists showered into him. He staggered, dizzy, and fell.

After a moment, he found himself on his knees, the bandage over his eyes. Keppelbauer was crying loudly, and Buford was cursing Spence and Dickson.

"How unresigned," Dickson said from far away. "One should try to die with dignity, at least."

In Mike there was nothing but sick horror at the suddenness of it. Dickson really meant it, and he was helpless, and so that was that. But it was the suddenness, the unpreparedness, that was horrible, the horrible knowledge of time lost, of things he would never now do. He became aware of a tooth rolling around in his mouth, and tasted sweet blood. He spat out the tooth and got slowly to his feet.

His father was still cursing, in a voice incredibly slow and cold and full of hatred—cursing not as swearing, but as calling down the solemn curses of God on their heads, damning them into the pits of hell. His voice went on, solemnly, low and rough, deliberately and with terrible, anguished sincerity.

"You see," Dickson said, "you people always think you can get away with it. Well, you can't."

It was incredible, and yet it was true.

"Wait," Mike said.

"I did wait," Dickson said. "Gentlemen, ride away. Ride away. You know I require privacy."

Horses' hoofs shoved sand. Mike could hear the grating and the crunching of gravel, and the squeaking of leather, fading away. How many were left?

"Mr. Keppelbauer is leaving San Antonio," Dickson said. "He is a bankrupt and he is running out on his creditors. Let's say so, anyway. To Venezuela. At least that will be the rumor. And the Allens—let's see—another trip—what does it matter? Bankrupts, too. They ran away to California—or is it Montana?—completely disappeared. Who cares? People are always doing it."

Suddenly Mike felt like laughing, and then this feeling turned into nausea. It was all quite unreal. And yet the fear was bigger than ever, a black cloud growing inside of him that would reach his mind, in a moment, and swamp it. What was coming? What was this silence? What was coming out of the silence?

"Dickson, Dickson, where are you?" he asked.

His father was whispering to himself.

"Here I am," Dickson said. He was off to the right somewhere, quite close.

Keppelbauer suddenly gave a sharp cry of pain and surprise, and stopped as suddenly, and fell. Mike felt his dead weight, dragging down on his left arm.

"Poor fellow," Dickson said, quite close. "And now you, my dear old friend. Why didn't you give me the money on time, Buford? It was a small thing, after all."

"I'll tell you where the money is," Mike said quickly. "You'll never find it if you kill us. I'll tell you, only just don't hurt my father."

"No." Dickson's voice was tight.

"Let us loose," Mike said, speaking as quickly as he could. "Take us back. I'll take you directly to the money."

"No!" Dickson said. "Damn you, do you think this is easy? Do you think I like to come out here? No! I gave you the chance—"

"You'll never find the money," Mike said. "You'll never find the herds. Think of the herds—$400,000. Half a million altogether."

"Don't do it," Spence said from somewhere. "Don't. Get the money. The money. Money, money, money. Dickson, get the money. Half a million. He's right."

Mike heard whispering somewhere, sharp hissing through the dark.

And then Spence said, "No, no, they're not. They didn't see you. They can't swear to anything. You can let them loose."

Feet crunched in the sand. There was a clicking sound and tugging at Mike's left arm, and he knew it was the padlock key. Suddenly the weight of Keppelbauer's body was gone, and then there was panting and grunting.

There was silence for a long moment. He heard the trunk of the carriage slam.

A hand seized Mike's arm, and the key slid and caught. The handcuff came off. The bandage fell down.

Spence was kicking dirt and sand over something on the ground. Keppelbauer was gone.

Dickson was stretching himself in the moonlight, like a cat, yawning as though he had just got out of bed after a long sleep. "Ah, what a beautiful evening," he said. "What a lovely drive we have had in the country! Come along, gentlemen, let's go back to the city, shall we? We'll pick up the money, and then we'll have a little talk." There was silence.

Dickson looked at Mike and his father with a

smile. "Let's have no further foolishness, my friends. As for Keppelbauer—do you see him? There are seven of us who will swear we never came here at all."

Buford was shaking. Mike could hear his teeth rattling. Buford suddenly sat down on the ground, and Mike knelt and held his old body up.

"Give him a drink," Dickson said. Spence brought a bottle from the carriage.

They got Buford on his feet and he stood there, licking his lips, looking around with a terrible fatigue.

"The carriage," Dickson said pleasantly, gesturing with his cane.

Mike followed his father into the carriage. The carriage swung forward, and the horsemen closed around it, traveling as before, a guard.

"And where are we going, Mike?" Dickson asked brightly.

"Degen's Brewery," Mike said.

CHAPTER TWELVE

Degen's Brewery—Midnight

They came back into town on Houston, down around the Cathedral, and up West Crockett toward the Little House. As they crossed Navarro, Dickson, looking ahead across the bridge, saw three men standing across the street from the Little House, plain in the bright light coming from the doors.

"Police," he said to Spence, and Spence sat forward a little. "Didn't you pay off on time?"

Spence didn't answer. He stuck his head out of a window and said to the driver, "Keep going, don't stop. Drive right past." He turned to Forrest, who was riding alongside with the five other men and said, "Ride right on past, Ike. Looks like trouble." Forrest smiled and glanced quickly around at the other riders. He gathered himself in the saddle, sucking his guts up and grinning.

Spence sat back. He and Dickson looked at the police through the window as they passed. The police were just standing there, one leaning against a wall, the other two against the lamp post.

"Most peculiar," Dickson said. "If I thought it would do any good, I would feel outraged. God knows we pay enough not to be bothered."

"It isn't that," Spence said, gnawing at a few bristles from his mustache. "Something's got fouled up with that girl—Joanne."

Dickson sat tense, perfectly quiet. "Absurd."

"It isn't absurd. It couldn't be anything else."

"It is something else," Dickson said. "I ought to go in the back door and find out."

"Get the money first," Spence said. "Forrest can go back and ask some of the boys."

"Is there, by any chance, anybody following us?" Dickson asked.

Spence turned quickly and looked out the back. There wasn't much traffic left that late at night, but there was enough to keep him from noticing Io, sloping along on his mule. The Colonel was too far back.

They went on past toward Alamo Plaza. "Send one of the men back," Spence said to Forrest out of the window. "Find out why the police are hanging around."

He sat back, and the carriage went on across the Plaza, on down Crockett Street, around the block along Nacogdoches, and then up Blum Street toward the Plaza again, slowing in front of the brewery door.

Dickson looked around the dark street. There were lights from the Plaza, but the carriage sat in a bank of darkness. Music came from the bands along the river, faintly through the summer night.

"Let's get out of sight," Dickson said. Spence poked a gun in Mike's ribs. "Get us in there," Spence said in a hard, low voice. "Don't try a break, mister. If there's going to be trouble, you'll catch it first."

Mike knocked at the door.

"Who is it?" the big watchman asked from inside.

"It's me, Mike. Let me in, Adolf."

"Oh, you, mine friend."

The big door slid back, and Adolf looked at the men behind Mike—Spence, Dickson, Forrest, and the other four.

"Vat is dis, Mike?" he asked. "I can't sell no beer now."

"We won't be a minute," Mike said. "Where's the saddlebags?"

A horse was coming up Blum Street, going hard. The rider pulled up in front of the brewery, and they all turned. It was the man Forrest had sent back to the Little House. He swung down and ran up to Dickson. "It's you they're looking for," he said. "Cash has a warrant out for you—for murder."

Dickson's mouth set in a pinched line.

"And I passed Colonel Berry," the man said. "He's coming along Nacogdoches Street. It sure as hell looks like he was following us."

Dickson glanced quickly down Blum Street. It was empty. "Get inside the brewery, everybody," he said. "You drive that carriage out of here," he ordered the driver. "And you keep your damn mouth shut, boy, or I'll cut your damn head off. Now drive like the devil—hurry! Forrest, you and your men get up the street and cover this door."

He turned and went quickly through the big doorway. Spence followed with his gun, herding Mike and Buford in after Dickson. He shoved the heavy door shut behind them. They heard Forrest and his men clatter away outside.

"Murder," Adolf breathed heavily, his eyes wide on Dickson. He half-raised his nightstick. "You?" It was too much for him. He was paid to manhandle breakers-in, not figure things out. While he was standing there trying desperately to think, Spence slipped around behind him and before Mike could lift a hand, yell, or move a foot, he had slugged Adolf across the back of the head with the pistol barrel. Adolf went down like a wet hide and lay in ponderous sleep on the black flags.

"I hope to God I didn't kill him," Spence said, looking down at him.

"What's the difference?" Dickson said. "One more won't matter." He turned and looked at Mike and Buford. His thin face with its high, fine nose was dead pale in the light of the single lantern. "After all I've paid, they wouldn't get out a warrant without evidence." He barely managed a smile. "Be careful, please. No noise. We're all on thin ice."

"Where's the money?" Spence asked in that hard, tight voice. "Get it quick, so we can get out of here."

Mike pointed to the saddlebags lying under Adolf's chair. Spence smiled quickly and, stooping, scooped them up.

"Count it," Dickson said quietly.

"Let's get out of here," Spence said, his beautiful white teeth released in a smile at last, shining in the lantern light. With the money in his hand, he seemed to swell again with self-confidence.

"Do as I say," Dickson said. Dickson's voice was sleepy and dull, and he looked tired rather than afraid.

"There's a way out the front, through the hotel kitchen."

A spot of red showed on Dickson's cheek, and his chin lifted a little. "You take my orders."

Spence held his eye for a moment; then lifting his eyebrows he looked away, patiently smiling.

"There's always time to run," Dickson said. "Only fools run because they're afraid. Count the money."

"It'll take too long," Spence said quietly.

"We've got all night," Dickson said with his icy stubbornness. "We're dealing with fools, Spence," he said, waving generally toward the Allens. "They may still be holding out. I'll hold the gun."

The sound of many horses came up the street. Spence stopped with the first strap unbuckled in his hands. Dickson stood with the gun on Mike and his father. They all listened. Voices came through the big, solid door, at first faintly, and then clearly. The horsemen stopped up the block.

"You, driver," Colonel Berry said outside, his voice faint. "Are you Thomas Dickson's man?"

"Get on with it," Dickson whispered, his eyes bright and his face alive once more. Spence undid the other strap.

Dickson turned and went, smiling, over to Mike and his father. Mike looked at the gun, pointed steadily at his stomach. He could try it, he could gamble. It wasn't more than five feet away. But he would have to take one step; he would have to bend his knees to jump, and that would be enough of a signal. Dickson had made sure to leave room for just that much warning.

Dickson smiled at him, reading his mind. "Don't try it. After all, while there's life there's hope, eh? Anything's better than being dead—and you know it, don't you." It wasn't a question; and Mike did know it, now.

Buford said nothing. He sat down suddenly in Adolf's chair and put his face in his hands.

"Before they break in here," Dickson whispered, "Forrest will battle them. I think we're quite safe."

The noise up the block, of talking, the blowing of horses, Berry swearing at the coachman, grew slowly. Inside, behind the massive door, there was no sound except the quick whisper of the banknotes as Spence counted, licking his thumb and not being very careful.

Colonel Berry had picked up the three men as he passed the Little House. They were all mounted in a minute, and he sent one for Lt. Cash and reinforcements. Hardly losing a stride, the Colonel and the two remaining men followed Io, hurrying a little to keep him in sight as he went down Crockett Street across the Alamo Plaza.

Up ahead, Berry saw Io stop, lighted by the moon at his back, at the corner of Blum Street. They caught up with him, and the Colonel, dismounting, looked around the corner.

"The same carriage?" the Colonel asked. The carriage, having left the brewery door, was pulling up toward the corner by the Menger Hotel.

Io hissed at him softly, and pointed a finger at something in the roadway. It was a dark black spot in the moonlit dust, about the size of a dime, but shaped like a tear. "Sangre."

"Keppelbauer," the Colonel said. "They put the body in the back. I could see that much. It's leaking. That's all we need. Come on. Hey, there!" he shouted up the block after the carriage. "Pull over there! Police!" The carriage stopped.

They remounted and went up Blum Street toward the carriage, which had pulled up just short of the corner of the Plaza, thirty yards away from the brewery door.

The colored driver was sitting in a huddle on top, his hands over his eyes. The carriage was empty.

Berry looked up the street toward the Plaza. There were half a dozen horses in front of the Gallagher building, but that wasn't unusual—late gamblers in the San Antonio Club, upstairs.

The Colonel saw Lt. Cash and four men gallop into the Plaza from South Alamo Street. He shouted. They didn't hear him, and rode on north beyond the Menger.

"You, driver," Colonel Berry said, "are you Thomas Dickson's man?"

The Negro, face buried in his hands, sighed deeply.

"Answer me," the Colonel said sharply.

"Oh, my Gawd," the driver said, his voice shuddering.

"He is, he is, you can see that," one of the police said.

"Open the trunk," Berry ordered. The clatter of Cash's horsemen dimmed, and then rose again, searching up and down the streets. Berry swore. He should have left a guide. At the rear of the carriage two cops worked at the straps and then opened the back.

"Lord Jesus," one of them said, holding a match. Keppelbauer lay there, his round face in a faint gauze of spiderwebs. Spiderwebs and dust covered his neat sack suit. The suit was black with blood.

"Run through, just like the others," Berry said.

Cash's people rounded the corner into Blum Street and Berry shouted again. Cash galloped up and slid off. He ran over to the trunk.

"Well," he cried, looking around, "where are the son of a bitches? This is enough, ain't it, Colonel? By God, they must be in the hotel. Old Allen lives there. Allen's as thick as thieves with Dickson, always has been."

"They killed Keppelbauer," Berry said.

"The two of them? Who?"

"They all drove out west of town. I don't know just what they did. I had to stay out of sight. But the two Allens and Dickson and the rest of Dickson's people were out there, and by God, Keppelbauer's dead, isn't he?"

"That makes them all accessories."

"Not old Allen," one of the cops said. "Old Buford wouldn't harm a flea."

"Oh, is that so?" Cash snapped. "Well, get the hell in the hotel and find him, if he's so damned innocent."

"He owed Dickson a lot of money," Berry said. "Get that driver down here."

"Oh, my Gawd," the driver said.

"Get down here, you," Cash shouted.

"Oh, my Jesus," the driver moaned, rocking. "Ah don't know nothing, boss."

"You know enough to keep your mouth shut, and that's plenty," Cash shouted. "Get down here. You want to hang? Get him off of there, boys."

Two cops grabbed and dragged him down.

"Oh, dear Lawd," the driver moaned, crouching in the street. He squatted down and put his hands over his ears, and rocked back and forth, crying, "Oh, Lawd."

"The son of a bitch knows," Cash said, wrath twisting his whole face. "Where did they go?" he shouted, stooping down beside the driver's head.

"Oh, Lawd," the driver cried more loudly, holding his hands over his ears. Cash stood upright. "Take that man's hands," he said to the two cops, "and hold them away from his ears."

The driver let out a quavering howl as the cops grabbed him.

"Now, now, now, boss, now, now, boss, now, boss," he cried twisting his head, the whites of his eyes flashing in the moonlight. "Now, boss, I ain't nothing but a pore old colored man, ah ain' done nothin'."

"You lying son of a bitch," Cash said. "You were driving this hack when they killed a man." He moved closer. "You helped in a murder. Where's your boss? You tell me and I'll let you go, boy."

"Oh, Jesus," the driver moaned. "He'd kill me, he'll cut off mah head."

"By God," Cash cried, "I'll hang you till your eyes pop out. You want the birds picking your eyeballs out, boy? I'm going to hang your boss Dickson, boy. You tell me where he is, and I'll let you go. You'll be safe."

The driver burst into tears, wriggling around, held

by the two cops. "He said he'd cut off mah head," he cried. "He'll do it too, boss."

"Get me a rope, somebody," Cash said in a brisk, sharp voice. "I'll hang the son of a bitch right now."

The driver fell to his knees. "Awright, awright, boss."

There were five shots, crackling on top of each other like a string of firecrackers. The red sparks of gun muzzles jumped in the dark, from the corner by Alamo Street, two more down at the other end of the block from the corner at Nacogdoches.

One of the cops said, "Oh," and fell against the carriage. His knees gave and he fell in the street, blood coming out of his neck.

"Son of a bitch," Cash said, drawing, and began firing at the corner of Alamo Street.

"Get in the carriage!" Berry shouted. The fire was pouring at them from both ends of the block, the bullets smacking through the wooden walls of the carriage body. One of the horses screamed and jumped, shot in the rump, and Berry scrambled up onto the seat, grabbing the reins.

The cops huddled behind the carriage, firing under the belly of it. Berry crouched in the driver's seat, shouting.

"Hold your fire, you damn fools," he shouted. "We haven't got any more loads. Get in the carriage and we'll make a run for it. Cash, get up here with me. I'm going to drive at the ones by the Plaza. Boys, get set. Wipe 'em out, by God. Kill 'em all. The hell with arrests."

He grabbed the whip out of the socket and swung at the horses, holding his gun between his knees. The horses lunged ahead and the carriage rolled heavily forward into the fire from up the block.

Cash shot into the fire, damping it, and they saw the men, now in the shadow, three of them in the street.

The Colonel fired at them, aiming as well as he could from the rolling carriage as he bore down on them. The bright-orange flames winked and the street roared with the gunfire, pounding back and forth between the buildings. The police inside the carriage were firing out the windows.

"If they kill the horses, get out and charge 'em," Berry shouted at Cash as they bore down on the five men. He saw one of Forrest's people fall, and then another. The others were running for their horses. He fired again.

The Colonel felt young. It was like the first skirmish he had ever been in, with a small band of Comanches on the Nueces River, as a lieutenant, in the days when he had thought of musketry only as a military formality. He was cool, the winking of the muzzle blasts meant nothing, he wasn't thinking of death, of the odds and the chances, any more than he had thought of them that day forty-five years before, and he crouched not in fear, but simply because it was the sensible thing to do.

His ulcer did not enter his mind, nor his daughter, nor anything, except the cool, fast action-thinking of a fighter, completely taken up with the thing happening at the instant, the job right now. It was a good enough feeling for an old soldier, to be fighting—he knew his tools.

So he died, with his enemies scattering before him like sparrows. One of Forrest's parting shots went through his left eye. The carriage stopped, the horses floundering in their tangled harness, and Cash held the old man up.

Cash felt a fume of terrible anger rise in him like the smoke out of hell; he wanted to stand up and swear, to curse his men, to reach out after the murderers and seize them. But he sat there, and the anger died away. Was that all it came to? A man you respected, a man you loved, a boss you worked for and sweated for and obeyed exactly, suddenly gone, leaving this limp, warm carcass.

A bit of knowledge flowed into Cash's head, as cool as moonlight. In the end, there was nothing but the job; it was the job that lasted. In the end, everyone died, all friends, all lovers, every man everywhere, and all affection passed away. Nothing remained but simple duty and the God who alone made it a duty and not just a dirty farce.

Cash said to his men, "The Colonel is dead. Go back to the station, Tom, and get out the whole force to cover the roads. Get on the telegraph and wire Houston and Austin and El Paso." His voice was cool, for once.

"They're gone," said the man who was named Tom. "You know how it is. If a man's got a horse, he can lose himself forever, fifteen miles out of town."

Cash sat quiet. "Do it anyway."

"We've lost 'em, Ben. Might as well face it. Better print up a reader," Tom said. "They won't hit a town till they get out of Texas. Dodge? Who cares, in Dodge? They got more'n they can handle right there in Ford County. But I'll wire 'em, Ben. Just you say which towns. Which way will they go? K.C.? San Francisco?"

Cash sat quiet. Dickson and his men had got clean away, except for the two dead. There was no use wiring. And as for the readers, who cared? West of the Mississippi, murder was much too common to attract much attention.

"Send out the readers, Tom," Cash said quietly. "We'll hear from Dickson some day. We can wait." Waiting, he thought, was the main power of the law, and if he never got Dickson and his people, he knew God would, who would outwait them all; and that was some consolation to set against the hard, hot pain of the Colonel's death.

CHAPTER THIRTEEN

Degen's Brewery—2:30 A.M.

Inside the brewery they heard the shooting and the shouting, the slamming of the fast battle, the clatter of hoofs and the slow silence, coming back again. Shooting wasn't unusual in San Antonio.

"What'll we do?" Spence whispered.

"Wait," Dickson said, taking the rebuckled saddlebags and putting them under his chair, from which he had turned out Buford. "Forrest will be back when the police have gone. We'll get horses and leave town. You'd better hit the watchman, Spence. He's coming around again."

Spence looked at Mike and Buford, standing together across the wide flags.

"What about them?" he said.

"Kill them," Dickson said.

Spence looked at them, studying.

Mike said, "My father's got two herds left, on the trail."

"That's right," Spence said.

"I remember," Dickson said. "I'm holding the notes on them. They're mine."

"They're worth about $400,000, delivered in Ogalalla," Mike said.

"I'm glad to hear it," Dickson said. "Where are they?"

Buford smiled a little. His face was coming back to life. "You'll never find them—without me."

"Maybe you've got enough money, Tommy," Spence said. "If we have to take these two out of here and go north after those herds—well, it might be easier not to. We could drop them in one of the mash vats—they wouldn't be found for a month."

"Delightful thought," Dickson said. "Think of all San Antonio quaffing the remains of the Allen family. Where can Forrest be? We have to leave before daylight. Where are those herds, Buford?"

The old man looked at Dickson heavily. "Do you think I'm crazy? If I tell you, you'd just kill us."

"And if you don't, I will," Dickson said. "So far I've never done away with anybody except for business reasons. But I am beginning to think that at times killing could be simply a dangerous pleasure. Didn't you ever feel like killing anyone? Haven't you ever been totally aggravated? You, Buford, have tried me dreadfully. The only trouble with killing people is that sheer quantity inevitably brings its own exposure, and there are always the police. Society is always so careful to preserve itself. One may well ask why. Surely being shot in the head is preferable to dying of cholera, or lying for years in bed soiling the sheets and making oneself a general nuisance to one's loved ones. I cannot imagine why people are in such a general rush to escape from death, when most of them make their lives so unbearable, all through their own stupidity. Take yourself, Buford. You'd be far better off dead. Where is that wretched Forrest? Spence, why don't you draw us all a beer, while we're waiting?"

"Do you want the herds?" Mike asked.

"Yes," Dickson said.

"Then you'll have to let us live long enough to find them for you."

"That's quite all right with me," Dickson said. "Please understand, my dear boy. I don't want you dead. There's nothing personal about it, really. Spence, I was not joking about that beer. I'm thirsty. Here, I'll hold the gun on them."

"All right," Buford said, rubbing his beard. "We'll find the herds for you."

Spence found a row of sampling steins on a shelf and they listened to the beer spurting from the taps. He came back with four of them, full.

"Buford's got a bunch of men with those herds," Spence said.

"Naturally," Dickson said. "We have a bunch of men too."

"How are you going to keep Buford from tying up with his men, and standing us off?"

"Don't be silly, Spence," Dickson said.

"I'm not being silly. We'll find the herds. Then the Allens will have at least a dozen men to help them, and they're all loyal. They always are to their bosses."

"Oh, God, virtue again," Dickson said. "Is there anything wrong with a pitched battle?"

"You can't fight around cattle," Spence said. He looked at Mike and smiled. "Mike taught me that. If you start shooting, the cattle stampede. So what will happen is that Buford will force us to trade with him. We can have him or the cattle, but not both."

"There's many a way to kill a cat," Dickson said, sipping his beer, and eyeing Buford. "How long will it take to find them?"

"Maybe a month."

"Then you're assured of a month of life. That should make you happy." He drank. "Let me see, you had an option on a ranch. You told me about it. Suppose you give me that option, Buford?"

"Oh, God," Buford said, and shut his eyes.

"It isn't any good," Mike said. "The date's gone."

"As I recall, you said you could buy it for $300,000. What's it worth?"

"I could have sold it in Cheyenne to some son of a bitching Englishman for half a million," Buford said.

"Then so could I," Dickson said.

Buford sat down on the steps leading to the upper level. Only one thought came to his mind through the fog of fatigue and spent fear and failure. Dickson couldn't be trusted. Nothing he said could be believed. The only thing he would respond to was money. He looked up at Dickson. Dickson's eyes were steady and cold.

"I want that ranch, Buford. The option. I had a certain goal—of money, you understand. With your cattle and this ranch, I can clear enough to go home. I could even sell the ranch in England—everybody's dying to get rich in the cattle business these days. Give me that option, Buford, and I may let you go."

It was a lie, Buford thought. He would never let him go, not now. He would kill him just as soon as he had sucked him dry. And Mike, too. There was only one possible escape—to find the herds, to join forces with Tucker, and then to fight a battle with Dickson and his forces. The only thing that would keep Dickson from killing him before he got help was the hope of getting money.

"Give me the option, Buford," Dickson said. "I suppose you have it on you."

One idea rose in Buford's mind: Escape. Everything depended on getting to Tucker.

"Spence, search him," Dickson said. "I'll hold the gun on Mike."

Buford looked up with a start. Spence was coming toward him. He stood up, angry blood rising to his head, and then he saw the gun on Mike and his heart stopped for a moment.

"Wait," he said quickly. "I'll give it to you." He took the option, in its envelope, out of his inside pocket and handed it to Spence. He smiled bitterly. "I hope you have more luck than I did with it."

"We'll be partners," Dickson said, reading the option. "So I can act in your name."

Buford watched his son's face as Mike looked steadily at the barrel of the gun. "Yes," he said.

"Spence, suppose we got half a million for that ranch, if Buford says it's worth $300,000? How would you like to go to England with me? We'd pay off Forrest and the others handsomely, and you and I could go. You could manage my estate. This last coup would do it."

"The option's no good," Spence said, handing it to Dickson. "Date's past over."

"I know a man in Chicago who knows a lot about changing figures."

Somebody tapped on the door. The four men froze.

"It's me, Forrest," a low voice said outside. Spence opened the door and Forrest came in. "I killed a police commissioner," he said, grinning. "The whole town's gone crazy. They'd lynch us all, boss, if they could."

"Did you get horses?" Dickson asked quietly.

"Hell, yes, and for these two buggers too. Stole them right off the rail down in front of Wolfram's. They're waiting down in the alley."

"All right, we'll be down directly. Go back and wait for us."

Spence shut the door behind Forrest, and Dickson faced Buford.

"Now, Buford, old man," Dickson said, "one last little thing. If I were in your shoes, I would try to play along until you got up to your herds, and then try to join forces with your driver's men. Then, if I were you, I'd stage a battle, and try to get free. Am I right?"

Buford's chest sank. He looked at Dickson, trying to keep his face from showing anything.

"Sensible idea," Dickson said. "You're quite convinced I'll kill you as soon as I get your cattle and your option. So I can expect some desperate measures as soon as you can try them."

"I don't know what you think," Buford said, "and I don't give a damn. All I know is that you can't get those cattle until I find them for you and tell my man to give them up. And if necessary I'll drive those cattle to the north pole before I give them up. I ain't going to get killed."

Dickson looked at him quietly. "Time will tell us everything. I can't keep you from joining Tucker, naturally, since he has the cattle now. But I can keep you quiet, my poor old friend. Spence, you are to take Mr. Michael Allen tonight and ride north by yourselves. Take two guards to relieve you. Forrest and his gang will go ahead with Buford. You keep Mike and Buford apart, and if either of them makes trouble, kill the other. Now, find the herds and sell them. Then go on to this town named Warhorse and wait there for me. I'm going to make a little trip to Chicago first. Everything clear?

"Now, Buford, you will go along with Forrest and find the cattle. And you'll keep the peace, understand? Because if you start a battle, Spence is to kill your son. They'll be in touch—Forrest and Spence. Do you understand?"

Buford looked at Dickson, his eyes full of hopeless hate.

"Michael will be our little hostage," Dickson said. "To keep you on your good behavior, my dear Buford. Run along, Spence. Take Michael with you. I'll deliver Buford to Forrest before I go."

Buford looked at his son, and then back to Dickson. "I want a private word with him," Buford said.

"Quite all right," Dickson said. "Climb those steps over there. We'll stay down here. But stay in sight, old man. I've got the gun on you."

Buford led Mike heavily up the steps, and in the dark confusion of vats and tanks, turned to face him.

"What are we going to do?" Mike whispered, looking at his father.

"Nothing," Buford said. His mouth shook weakly. "He's got us where the hair is short, boy. All we can do is play along."

"How long?" Mike asked.

"As long as we can, boy. Listen, they won't hurt you if I don't start anything. And I won't start anything. Listen, Mike, get this through your head. You'll get nervous, all by yourself, wondering about me. But keep this in your mind, always. Dickson can always be bought. He'll do anything for money. As long as we have the herd, he won't hurt me. He won't hurt me as long as Tucker and I are with the cattle, because we'll stampede 'em and he wants the money."

"He'll try to sell the cows in Ogalalla," Mike said.

"I know it," the old man whispered, his breath uneven and short. "That's where I've got to win. I've got to make them drive those cattle all the way to Warhorse. Listen, son. We neither of us can make a break until we're together again, understand? He won't kill me until I've given up the cows, and I've got to work it so I don't have to give 'em up till I'm with you again, understand? And I'll do it. Only, for God's sake, Mike, sit tight. Don't blow up. Wait. Trust me. Will you, for God's sake, just trust me? Tucker and I won't let them sell in Ogalalla. We'll make them drive on north. For the last time in our whole lives I ask you, Mike, please trust me. Will you?"

Mike looked at his father's haggard old face and smiled gently. "Sure, I'll trust you."

Buford took his son's head between his two hands and kissed him on the cheek. "Good-by, Mike, my dear old boy. I swear to God I'll get you out of this. We'll make it."

He turned and stumbled back over the pipes and buckets, and down the stone steps. Dickson took him by the arm and led him outside, and Spence and Mike were left alone.

"Come on," Spence said, smiling. Mike went down the steps.

"It's a long way from Frenchman's Creek," Spence said, his handsome teeth showing in his handsome smile. "But I've got you over a barrel this time, sonny. There won't be any tricks this time. Stand over there." He gestured with the gun to the wall. Mike moved back against it.

Spence knelt by Adolf and went through his pockets.

"Five bucks," Spence said finally, standing up and pocketing the money. "Not much, but then, every little bit helps, doesn't it? Get going, sonny," he said, waving the gun toward the door. "There's a long road ahead for us, and you'd better be goddam careful if you want to see your old man again. Move." He waved the gun again, smiling, and Mike moved.

CHAPTER FOURTEEN

On the Trail,
Headed Northwest
September 18–25

It was late in the season when Forrest's gang, with
Buford under guard, neared Ogalalla six weeks later,
still with no news of the two lost herds.

They would get a hard frost on the plains at night
and wake up, teeth chattering, and huddle around
the fire, murdering each other in their hearts, waiting for the coffee to boil up. Buford and Forrest and
two others—a blond fellow named Sheffield and a
black-haired one named Irving—kept one fire, and
the rest of Forrest's men another.

The smoke from the cow chips stung their bleary
eyes and made their dirty faces draw and crawl, and
they would hunker there, some miserable, some getting meaner all the time, some wishing to God for a
drink.

They hadn't found the herds, and it was beginning
to look as though they wouldn't, and Forrest's face,
as he looked at Buford nowadays, was losing its
placid soldier's look and getting colder and harder.

Buford looked right back at him across the dirty little fire. He was getting mean himself and he sometimes enjoyed the feeling.

They had hit the south Platte west of Ogalalla on the seventeenth, and all the men—there were ten in Forrest's party and two in Spence's, riding herd on Mike a day behind—had expected to go into town and kick hell out of somebody just to relieve their feelings. But Spence had ridden up from behind and put the lid on them. They were all too hot to show and nobody was to go into town. One man, a new hand under Forrest, agreed secretly with the others to go into town for whisky, and he did; and when he got back Forrest beat him till he blubbered like a baby, lying on the ground with his nose pulped and his left ear half torn off. That's what soldier Forrest handed out for disobedience, under Spence's orders, and Spence watched it with a smile.

They dropped this poor wreck at some nester's, and went on across the river, following Buford's directions to go up the Oregon trail, and it was Spence's smile and his politicking art that made every man in the crew agree that the beaten man had got what he deserved.

They had Buford to hate, too. They all knew he was trying to find six thousand head of cattle, and the idea got around that he was trying to diddle somebody when he didn't. At first it was a joke, how the old man was diddling Forrest and even Dickson. In the Indian country they had begun to make bets each day, and by the time they hit the Kansas line, they had started a big pool on guessing how many days it would be when they hit the herds, and then at the Nebraska line they started another on how many weeks, which was not quite the same thing.

At Frenchman's Creek, where Tucker had diddled Spence last July, things started to go sour, and Spence's mood of suspicion traveled down through the men, and they began to watch Buford as though they were beginning to think about eating him.

They were all lousy by that time, partly because they camped dry a good deal and couldn't wash, and partly because most of them didn't like to wash, and when a non-washer was guarding Buford, he wouldn't go with Buford down to the creeks or holes, so Buford couldn't wash either. They changed the guard on him every four hours, just as though he were a prisoner of war. If he got a washing guard, it was at a dry camp.

They kept him riding all the time—no rest for the wicked, Forrest said. Every day he would ride out with his guard west, crossing trails, and circle back, and another team would ride northeast and circle back. Forrest sent out parties, gone for three days, cutting way west, a hundred miles, one time, and still they found nothing of a B A hair brand, which they were looking for. They didn't ride far to the east, because Buford had given orders to Tucker to take the herds west off the trail.

There was a rule, put down by Spence, that neither of the Allens was to be given any news of the other. Mike would ask about his father, a day ahead, and Buford would ask about his son, a day behind. But as far as they were told, the other might as well have been dead.

By the time they started up the Platte on the Oregon trail, the bacon was maggoty and the weevils had all hatched out in the cornmeal, and Buford got the worst. He didn't mind much. He was so hungry from riding out constantly that he would have eaten grasshoppers. They would kill a straggler cow almost every evening, carrying nothing, leaving what was left from dinner for the coyotes, just like a pack of wolves.

They ran into other herds going north to the sweet-grass country, five hundred cows, a thousand cows, three hundred cows. Batches bought in Cheyenne or Ogalalla and being taken north over the Bozeman trail and the Oregon trail for fattening and breeding purposes. Nobody had seen any B A hair brand, and on the twenty-fourth of September, when they were nearing the west border of Nebraska and about to cross over into Wyoming, Buford was beginning to get a little desperate.

There were times when he thought he was crazy and the whole hunt a delusion. He would lie stiff in his sweat, full of saddle aches and pain, and begin to believe that he had relayed some other kind of order to Tucker. He knew perfectly well he had sent a map to Tucker, showing a change of route to the west, even setting up a rough schedule. And yet, had he? Maybe he just thought he had. Maybe he had dreamed up that map, to convince himself there was a herd somewhere. Maybe it was just his imagination, a delusion born of fear, something to keep himself from getting killed.

Day after day they nosed northward, riding hard, but not making much progress, because they were cutting trails back and forth all the time. Sooner or later, he would run out of days, there would be an end somewhere up by the Yellowstone. And what then? He could see Forrest looking at him one day, the last day, and what would Buford say?

Let's go back, he would say, and look again. We must have missed them by a hair, Forrest. Spence would be there too, for the showdown.

Let's go back, Spence. You know how easy it is to miss a herd of cattle.

No, Spence would say. No. There wasn't any herd, Buford. You were lying.

And Spence would smile.

And there, at the end of nowhere, they would close in.

Your man Tucker sold you out, Buford, Spence would say. Your faithful Isaac.

He had heard Spence and Forrest planning things.

Spence said, "Old man Allen's got to be allowed to go up to this Tucker and tell him to turn over the herd. So we can't kill him. If we kill him now, Tucker will never hand over the herd. I know. I tried him once."

Forrest said, "Don't be a damn fool. Allen will never tell this Tucker that. Not if he gets that close."

Spence said, "I've got his son."

Forrest said, "The old man's a tough son of a bitch. Look at it square, Spence. He knows you want the herd. Killing the kid isn't going to get you the herd, is it? Hell, no. The old man will just make this Tucker fight, then."

Spence said, "I don't think so. The old man will cave in if I threaten about his son. He'll order Tucker off the herd."

Forrest said, "Bull turds. You got him figured for a coward. He ain't. He's a mean old son of a bitch and he's getting meaner and tougher all the time. I give him maggoty bacon to eat and he just looks back and chaws it up like he was saying, 'The same to you.' I say kill him now and battle it out with Tucker."

Spence answered, "We'll lose the cattle."

Forrest: "Not for long, if we win. Battle over, we can round 'em up again."

Spence: "If we win. We can't take a chance on losing, Forrest. Dickson doesn't like losers."

So for weeks Buford never knew when they were going to kill him, or if they would. Any day, the man riding herd behind him, on his big circles, might have orders to shoot him in the back and he'd never know when it was coming.

But Buford knew one thing. Much depended on just how they found the herds, if they ever did. They

might locate the herd and ambush Tucker—kill him
at three hundred yards. If the country was such that
they could hold the cattle easily, they might risk a
battle. If they came on them at night, with most of
Tucker's riders sleeping, they might massacre the
lot on the ground, and then be free to catch the stampeded cattle again.

On the twenty-fifth they were getting near Fort
Fetterman, where the Bozeman trail left the Oregon
and went northward. Buford and Irving were cutting
to the west and they saw the long dust of a big herd
and rode toward it, coming up toward the drag as
usual so as not to scare the leaders. They cut into
the trail it was leaving, and then, looking back, saw
another dust about four miles south and three miles
behind, about the same size, and a pain of hope shot
through Buford's heart that almost made him sick.
Irving saw it, too—two big herds about the same size,
traveling fairly close together, but off the beaten
track, and probably far enough off so that their dust
couldn't be seen.

Irving closed up on him, drawing his gun as he
always did until they saw the brand.

"Take it easy," Irving said. "If it's them, set your
goddam horse, old man, or I'll plug you. If we spot
the herd, we ride back pronto and report. That's orders and don't forget it."

They weren't going to let him get close enough to
wise Tucker up, with only one of Forrest's men
around. When he talked to Tucker, if ever, Forrest's
whole gang would be there—they'd made sure of that.
"Identify the herd," Forrest had said, "and then report back to me."

Buford rode up the trail with Irving's gun on him,
eating the heavy dust. They began to pass stragglers, and his heart dropped. There were a few odd
brands, pickups, stragglers from other herds gone by,
but the mass of the lame were all branded a fancy

cross on a box and a diamond around another box. It looked like some Englishman's brand, dreamed up in a hotel. They'd ask, now, if the foreman had seen a B A herd somewhere, sometime.

Irving put his gun away; they rode on at their constant jog-trot, cutting aside out of the herd, up past the bobbing, stinking cows through the fog of dust. The off swing rider showed ahead, vague through the glittering dust. This man turned around, hearing the quick chop of the ponies' hoofs, so different from the rumble of the cattle. Buford saw the face, and knew the man.

It was Tucker's cousin, a kid named Green. The kid kept riding in his station, but half-turned in the saddle, watching the old man come; and then the kid held up an arm and waved, and his white teeth showed through the haze of dust.

Irving was riding on Buford's near side, so his gun would be handy in case the old man tried something.

"Know him?"

"Sure I know him," Buford said, his heart pounding. Maybe it wasn't the Green kid, after all. He didn't dare look up. Maybe it was just another Texas hand that knew the old man by his beard. They all knew old Buford Allen with his free and easy drinks.

Buford glanced again at the fancy English brand bobbing along on the fifty cowhides he could see, and then looked at the kid again, and knew it was Green, and saw through it all at once. He felt like crying and swearing at the same time, and then he knew there wasn't time for either, that he had to do something fast. Tucker had just doubled the B back in a box, and doubled the A downward in another box. He'd done it to hide the herd, on his own initiative.

All Buford could do was wink at the kid with his right eye, the one Irving couldn't see.

"Hi, Mr. Allen," the Green kid called as they rode up.

Buford winked again. "Hi, kid," he said. "Who's your boss?"

The kid looked silly for a minute, and Buford winked again, and the kid saw it.

"Get him for me, will you? Just ride up ahead and tell him I want to talk to him."

Irving caught something in the air. The kid's grin was fixed now, unnatural-looking. He turned and loped his pony ahead and Irving looked at the old man.

"What the hell's up?" Irving asked, his hand on his gun. "Why did you send that kid off? This your goddam herd?"

"Of course it isn't," Buford shouted in a rage. All over, inside, he was jumping and seething with feelings and contrary emotions. "I just know that kid," he said, "and I know the foreman, and I know he'd rather ride back than have me barging up in front. He's that kind."

Irving looked at him with wide, comprehending eyes. His gun came out. "You're the boss, ain't you? I seen it in that kid's eyes and no foreman would ride back for no stranger, no bum like you look. Let's get out of here. Move. Move, by God, or I'll kill you."

Two men were coming back down through the dust, the kid and another, and two more behind, at an easy lope.

Irving moved in fast, pushing his horse close to Buford's.

"Go on and kill me," Buford said. "You'll live just about one minute, sonny."

"Drop them reins," Irving said, jamming the gun into Buford's kidneys.

Buford opened his left hand and the reins fell on the ground. The pony stopped stock-still, scared of stepping on them.

"They doctored the brand is all," Irving said quietly. "You probably knew it all the time. What the hell. I got this gun in your back, old man, and if you or them makes one bum move, you're through."

Buford saw Tucker's dirty black hat come out of the fog, and then Tucker's big grin with a dead cigarette hanging on it, and Tucker pulled up six feet away.

"Stay back," Irving called over the rumble of the cattle, and showed the gun.

Tucker's hand just started for his own and stopped. He raised his hands a little, just for peace, and then his eyes began to glance around, feeling for his own riders' positions, beyond the dust and the herd. The two other riders crowded up behind him and sat there too, looking at the gun, held steady on the old man's back.

They sat there and the drag went by, and presently there was one little calf limping along with its mother close by, and then they were gone, and there was nothing left but the amber sparkling dust and the stink, and the bawling rumble of the herd fading as silence grew.

Irving laughed a silly kind of courageous haw, and said, "Jesus, what a fast one. Get this, girls, I'll shoot the old goat at the first move."

Tucker sat placidly, his face a little peaked, watching his boss and Irving. The Green kid's face was working with a mixture of outrage and complete uncertainty.

Tucker said, "Do you mind if I take this butt out of my mouth?"

"Spit it out," Irving said.

"They got us over a barrel," Buford said to Tucker.

"Who?" Tucker asked.

"Dickson and Spence."

"I remember Spence."

"They got more than a dozen men. We've been looking for you for a month of Sundays."

"I suppose they got their goddam judgments again," Tucker said.

"No. But they're going to try to get the herd. And they got Mike over a barrel. Thank God you changed that brand, Tuck. It would have been a different story."

"What's different about it now?" Irving said. "We're going out of here. These gents are leaving us right now. I'm getting your reins and then we fade away."

"No," Buford said. "I'm not leaving."

"You'll leave or you'll die, by God," Irving said, jamming the gun.

"Go ahead and shoot," Buford said, sitting tight.

Irving looked at Tucker and Tucker's men, and they looked back.

"Send a man up toward the river, Tucker," Buford said. "He'll find Spence's outfit—all riders, no wagons. Tell them we found the herd and to come on over. We're staying here, Irving."

Irving looked back at Tucker.

"Go on," Tucker said quietly to Irving. "Shoot the old man. We got four guns here, and we're just waiting for you to get off that first shot. You'll get off just one, sonny. That's all."

Irving sat there looking like a calf trying to eat two pails of mash at once.

"We better just sit here," Tucker said soothingly, "until your friends get here. We won't shoot you as long as you got the boss covered, but you ain't going to shoot either, are you?"

"All right," Irving said, and sweat came out on his forehead. His face slacked off in a sick way and he blinked. "I'll wait."

Tucker sent off a man, and they listened to his horse's hoofs, hard across the ground, fading.

They sat in the bright sun, with the dead grass waving. The cow pies dropped by the herd sat and baked and stank and wild flies droned. The horses stamped and switched their tails.

"What we going to do, Buford?" Tucker said.

"Shut up," Irving said, jabbing Buford with the gun muzzle.

"You can't make me shut up," Buford said. "You can shoot me, but you can't shut me up."

"That's right, sonny," Tucker said placidly. "Shoot him if you want to. We're right here, waiting."

Irving said something that sounded like "Jesus" and sat there sweating. He was having a hard time and his arm was getting tired.

"Can I roll a cigarette, please," Tucker asked politely. "I'm dying for a smoke and I swear that I won't start nothing."

"No," Irving said. "Don't move. I'm getting nervous, so you be goddam careful."

Tucker said, "Boys, everybody just keep your hands high, will you? We don't want Nervous here to lose control of the situation. Buford, what's the story?"

Buford gave it to him.

Tucker said, "So what do we do?"

"Wait. But remember one thing, Tucker. The herd is what they want. As long as we got the herd, they won't do anything. We got to stay close to the herd, or they'll just blast us loose from the ground. They don't want to lose that herd, Tuck. Remember that always."

"Then let's go," Tucker said.

"No," Irving said. "We stay here."

"I'm going," Buford said. "I'm leaning over and getting those reins, and then I'm leaving, Irving. You ain't going to be very safe if you let me and that gun of yours get separated."

"You stay where you are," Irving said.

"Don't bluff, sonny," Tucker said. "You ain't deal-

ing with kids. That one shot in there is all you got
between you and hell, and you know it."

"Oh, Jesus," Irving said in an agony. "All right,
you old son of a bitch, get going. Let one jump out of
that horse, though, and by God, I'll plug you! I ain't
fooling!" he shouted.

"I know you ain't," Buford said evenly. "I'll be
good, don't worry. You goddam monkey, just wait till
I get you off my back."

"Ride up ahead and get all the men you can,"
Tucker said to the Green kid. "Get all the riders off
both herds except just enough to hold the points, and
hurry back." The Green kid left at a dead run.

Buford rode after the herd at a fast walk, and the
others rode well ahead of him, leaving Irving in control.

They made it to the herd just twenty minutes before Forrest and Spence caught up.

All Forrest's men were there, the full camp, and
they pulled up to a walk forty yards behind Irving.
They could see Tucker and his men, riding twisted
in their saddles, ready for anything.

Forrest started to pull his gun, and Spence shouted
sharply, "Don't!"

"Why the hell not?" Forrest said.

"We'll lose the cattle."

"We got the odds."

"What the hell of it? We can't kill 'em all," Spence
said. "If there was four left, they'd keep the herds
busted from now till doomsday. If any of you men,"
he shouted to the bunch behind him, "goes for a gun,
I'll shoot the bastard myself."

"Well, what the hell are we going to do?" Forrest
cried out over the din of the herd.

"Talk," Spence said. "Goddam it, I see it now.
Goddam it, that fox Tucker changed the brands to
hide the herds. And that fool Irving didn't wise up

fast enough and the old man Allen did. Goddam the luck. Goddam it all to hell."

He started ahead at a walk, keeping forty yards behind Irving.

"What're we going to do?" Forrest asked again, bewilderment in his face.

"Talk," Spence said again. "We'll just have to wait till they're bedded down, that's all."

They rode that way for five more hours, down the long, hot afternoon, each side watching the other, Tucker's men riding backward with eyes like hawks. Nobody made a move, nobody smoked.

In the middle, Irving rode doggedly on Buford's near side, quartered behind him, his horse's withers almost touching the other's flanks.

I must be crazy, Buford thought, and then he didn't care. A gun in his back, he had the situation half under control. He wasn't underneath, for the first time since he had left Ogalalla so long ago.

They rode that way till sundown, till the big herd slowed onto the bed grounds that had been picked out, just south of Fort Fetterman, near the river.

Spence and Forrest made a camp by the river, a hundred yards from Tucker's chuck wagon, and while they were starting the fires, Spence rode quietly out into the open toward Buford and Irving, still sitting alone in the middle of nowhere. Tucker saw him coming and rode out to meet him.

They sat their horses, each about fifteen yards from Buford, and talked.

Spence said, evenly, "I've got your son, Buford. You've pulled a fast one on me. I admit it. But I've got Mike."

"And I've got the herd," Buford said. "You'll never get it until I give Tucker the order to pull out his men."

"I can see that," Spence said, his voice calm and level. "And when do you plan to do that? Why don't we do it now? I'll bring Mike up here tomorrow, and we can make the exchange right here. I don't want Mike, Buford. That was Dickson's idea."

"Don't pull that," Buford said. "You're all bastards."

"We can swap right here," Spence said. "Irving, put down that gun and get over by the fire."

Irving looked up in surprise, and so did Buford.

"I've got thirteen men," Spence said, "and your son and you aren't going anywhere with those cattle without me and my thirteen men. It's purely a question of when we swap, isn't it, Buford?"

Irving dropped his arm with a groan and turned his horse away into the dark.

"Yes," Buford said.

"And you know you can't get Mike away from me," Spence said. "Any more than I can get the herd away from you." He smiled in the deep dusk. "So let's trade."

Buford was sitting there on his tired horse, looking northwest, up toward the Big Horns, and beyond them to where Warhorse would be.

"Come on," Spence said. "Let's trade, Buford, right here. You and Mike will be safe, and I'll have the herds, which you owe Dickson anyway. You can go home, and I'll sell the herds the way I'm supposed to."

Buford said nothing. He was thinking of Montrose's ranch and, deeper yet, of a certain place, perhaps under some tree, where there was a mystery he had not solved. Nobody else in all the world would understand it, how an old man would wander all that way to a woman's grave, as though it were a fire, a little warmth, in his old age.

He thought of giving up now, of getting Mike back. But he knew Mike would be safe as long as he controlled the herd. Mike could wait.

"It might be wise," Tucker said in the dark. "Nobody's been killed yet, Buford. It might be a wise thing to quit now, before somebody gets killed."

It was like climbing up one of those long talus slopes in the mountains, Buford thought, trying to reach the top. One struggled and slipped, but kept on struggling. A man had to, because at the bottom there was nothing but darkness—one of those god-awful canyons, cold as death, a trap.

"We're going ahead," he said quietly. "I'll trade you in Warhorse, Spence, maybe; we'll see what happens."

It had fallen into his hands, now, hadn't it? Buford thought. Who could say what might not happen, in the time ahead? A man was a fool to give up.

Spence said, his voice tightening, "Oblige me by trading now. What have you to gain?"

"We're going on north," Buford said quietly. "We'll take the Bridger cutoff and go on to Warhorse, and see how your boss Dickson is making out with getting that ranch."

Spence sat there in the dark. "There's your son, Allen," he said coldly.

"He's a good boy," Buford said. "He'll sit tight."

"Accidents can happen," Spence said in the dark.

"They'd better not," Buford said. "Not if you want these cattle. If Mike gets hurt in any way, we'll fight you, Spence, and to hell with the cattle. And even if you win, you'll never be able to collect 'em. Tucker and I'll shoot you down one by one, pick you off if we have to follow you for the next twenty years. Don't forget it."

Spence sat quiet, the heavy, quiet words still sounding like echoes in his mind.

"All right," Spence said patiently. He had felt like screaming for a moment, but even now he managed to smile, even though nobody could see it. "Warhorse it is, then," he said. "God help you when Dickson gets hold of you again. I'll have to let him know about this."

"Just tell him," Buford said, "I'll trade in Warhorse."

Spence turned his horse away in the dark, and Tucker said, loudly and clearly, while Spence could still hear, "Greenie boy, we'll set a double guard around the chuck wagon. If anybody comes near in the night—shoot him and the hell with the cattle. We don't want to get murdered in our beds."

Buford sat in the dark, his eyes on Spence's distant campfires.

"They'll have riders all round us," Tucker said in the solid black. "They'll be watching us like a hawk, Buford, and the first slip, they'll be on us. If we let them get the drop, we're through. We'll have to stay out of canyons and such, and just travel as though they was Indians, because they'll murder us if they get a chance. I wish we had more men."

"We got enough," Buford said. "If we're careful."

He sat quiet in the dark, thinking one thought, over and over, like a kind of prayer he was sending down the trail, to Mike. How many miles away was he? Sitting with some stinking guard watching him, hunched over some lousy little fire?

Sit tight, Mike, he thought. *Sit tight, boy. With a few more breaks like this, we may make it out yet.*

That night Spence left Forrest to cover Buford, Tucker, and the herds, and rode on north, taking Mike with him, to Warhorse, where Dickson was waiting.

PART THREE

CHAPTER ONE

In the upper room of the old stage station in the town of Warhorse, Montana, two weeks after Buford had found his two herds, Dickson stood looking at a large, clumsily drawn wall map of Montana Territory. He had taken the original from Buford. It showed the probable course of the two herds, and their location to date.

Harris came up the stairs and entered the room carrying a tea tray.

"Good morning, Harris. All rested after your trip?" Dickson said cheerily. "Toast right? Perfect!" He merrily spread some strawberry jam on a piece of toast and began munching. "What did you think of the United States of America, coming up on the train?" he asked.

"A remarkable country, sir," Harris said in his British voice, and poured Dickson a cup of tea.

"And how did you leave my mother?"

"Very well, sir. Since you asked her not to write

you, she sent a verbal message. She has only fifteen hundred dollars left to live on."

"Oh, bother," Dickson said. "Well, she can apply for charity. Can't send her a dime with the police watching her. Did you take a boat down the river as I suggested?"

"Yes, sir, just as you suggested. At night."

More feet pounded up the stairs. Somebody knocked at the door.

"Come in, come in," Dickson called out in bright good humor.

Spence entered with Irving behind him. Irving was unshaven, dirty of face, and smelled powerfully of horse sweat and fresh manure.

"Why on earth don't you bathe before you come up here?" Dickson asked crossly.

"I just got in an hour ago," Irving said heavily.

"I thought you would want to hear his report right away," Spence put in.

"Go on," Dickson said, looking at the map. "Where's the herd? What's up?"

"They were just turning off the Oregon trail when I left," Irving said. "Three days ago. Forrest said to tell you he was right on schedule."

"Thirteen more days."

"Yes, if they don't run into trouble west of the Big Horns. There's a lot of small rivers to cross there."

"I'm figuring on the twentieth. He's got to hold to that date. Who're you going to send back, Spence?"

"Weaver's had a week's rest," Spence said, "he's due for a trip."

"I'll send a written message," Dickson said. "What about Tucker and old man Allen, Irving?" he asked.

Irving smiled slightly. "The old man's getting cocky. He's sassing Forrest night and day, hogs all the firewood and the best water places."

"He's a fool," Dickson said. "I suppose he thinks just because he outsmarted you when you found those herds together, he's got the upper hand. Well, let him dream. Does Forrest want anything? Guns, ammunition, more men? He can have anything but whisky."

"Nothing," Irving said. "They're saving their cartridges, except for a little hunting. Don't you worry about Forrest."

"Fine, fine," Dickson said. "All right, Irving, run along and, for heaven's sake, do take a bath. And don't get drunk. And stay out of the town saloons. You can go, Harris. Leave the tea things."

Irving grinned and left, Harris following him.

"Things are coming to a head, Spence," Dickson said. He pulled Buford's option out of his pocket and looked at the date. It was a new one: October 9. It was a delicate piece of forgery, indeed a matter of pride to its author in Chicago, whom Dickson had visited on his way north.

"The judge will rule on this tomorrow," Dickson said. "I've got the town sewed up. But we can't have any slips. I've got two suckers down in Denver—an Englishman for $500,000 and a Scotsman for $450,000. We can't afford to miss."

He looked at Spence. "I gather Montrose wouldn't even talk to the Allen boy when I sent him up to dicker. What do people say? Does anybody believe old Montrose? Anybody at all?"

Spence looked at the hooked rug on the floor for a long moment. "I'm afraid," he said, "when it comes to actually throwing Montrose off his place, he'll find too many friends. Even if they believe that date, and think Montrose is just trying to welsh out of his option—later they may remember it and have doubts."

Dickson smiled. "About what I thought. So we've got to have a clincher. Montrose has to become a scoundrel. We've got to make him thoroughly untrustworthy in the eyes of the town. It has occurred to me that he might murder somebody—or better yet, fall under suspicion of it. Remember that plan we made for killing Vickers? Nasty little fellow anyway—much better off dead if he only knew it. It's a bit daring, Spence old man—I know what you're thinking—but we need something dramatic. Shall we use Sheffield—to do the job?"

Spence shrugged. "He's due for a turn."

"He's been getting a little cocky, hasn't he? Maybe it's time to remind him of a few things. Tell you what, you get Sheffield and meet me down by the pigpen in half an hour. I'm going to talk to our little ward Michael. I have a little plan for him, too. Come along."

They went downstairs together.

"Good morning, good morning, Humboldt!" Dickson cried, stepping lightly through the big downstairs barroom. "Go along, Spence," he said.

Humboldt was sitting in front of the fire, drinking a weak grog.

"Good morning, Mr. Dickson," he answered. "I've put the boys hard to work digging that barbecue pit, and the fire will be going soon." This was a pure lie. He had just waked up, with a terrible hang-over.

"Leave all that to Harris, my dear fellow," Dickson said, marching briskly by, and went out the back door. Humboldt was a political investment.

With the Northern Pacific railroad having gone through town, and building west—the work trains went up and down every day—the stage station was deserted of trade, except as a local saloon, and the owner, Humboldt, had been delighted to sell out cheap, especially as Dickson kept him on as barman and general caretaker.

Dickson had made the station house a charming place, with American furnishings, a bit of bright paint and varnish, and a good deal of copper, brass, and Revere silver, as well as hooked rugs and other products of primitive native crafts.

The stage station was located on the main street (the only one, in fact) of Warhorse, in what was left of a grove of cottonwoods. The whole town lay along a large creek which joined the Yellowstone River four miles south of town, and the stage station, around which the town had grown, was a natural center.

There were a number of saloons besides the bar in the station, one general hardware and dry-goods house, one feed and grain house, one livery-and-wheelwright combination, a small bank, and a building which contained the offices of two lawyers, one of whom was the county judge.

The county court and the town marshal's office were in the same building, and both used the same log jail in the rear. There was one small church, a schoolhouse, and a new building which was to house the new library.

Dickson's rear yard was quite large, the bare earth running sixty yards down to the creek, spotted with cottonwood trunks gnawed by horses customarily tied to them. Along the creek lay a big corral, and the old barn which had been used for the relay stock for the stages, and next to this was the pigpen and a small henhouse.

The pale autumn sun, sharp in the frosty Montana air, was warm and gold on the yellowing cottonwood leaves. Wood smoke made a pleasant, spicy odor, and the men digging the barbecue pit were joking together, their voices clear in the bright air.

The tables for today's barbecue, an affair to which Dickson had invited practically everybody in town, had been set up the day before, bright new pine planks, their oozing sap covered with newspapers. Everywhere there were evidences of a lively social life, which Dickson loved, although the place now was so nearly deserted.

The stage station had, in fact, become a kind of

men's "clubroom" with card tables and billiard table (although Dickson was not now running any professional games). The walls had been decorated with old arms, Indian weapons and trophies, and some good heads of game.

What Dickson had done was to introduce the pleasures of an easygoing country house or hunting lodge into a town which had known nothing but hardship and barrenness. People came and went freely through it, always welcome, and Dickson was always the open, genial, pleasant, and cheerful fellow who had plenty of money and knew what to do with it.

He had bought a large organ for the church, and he went there regularly and sang loudly, at least for the five Sundays he had been steadily in town.

Everybody knew his business. He was an Englishman who, like many other Englishmen, was investing his money in cattle. He had an option on General Montrose's ranch, and he had six thousand head of cattle coming up the Bozeman trail, due to arrive about October 20. They also knew that Montrose did not intend to sell, despite the option, and little by little Dickson had brought them to believe that Montrose was trying to lie out of his contractual obligations.

In five weeks Dickson had made himself better liked than Montrose had in thirteen years, for Montrose was a cold, reserved old fellow, inclined to be harsh and critical in public, and never sociable.

The general opinion was that Montrose was a typical old army crab who seemed to think he was better than everybody else combined.

Dickson, on the other hand, simply assumed that everybody was just as good as he. He just ignored all differences. He never, for instance, kept wine off his table just because the people in Warhorse held wine drinking in contempt.

The fact was, he educated the people, and they naturally enjoyed the process, since they weren't aware of it. The men of Warhorse now almost enjoyed drinking brandy in the evening at the Station House.

Dickson had accomplished all this in six short weeks by being breezy and friendly and persistently aggressive in being generous. In Dickson's company they all felt gay and above themselves.

And, of course, behind all this charm there was money. How could anyone possibly criticize a man who believed in the public good and gave a library to the town, and a beautiful organ to the church, and yet did it so casually?

Everything that Dickson did had been deliberate, or at least conscious, except one thing. There was one factor which was working on him of which he was quite unaware.

This was the fact that it was fall. It was the first autumn Dickson had seen since he had left England, and he loved it; and this love, which was a reflection of his love for England and Lamont, colored his whole feeling, his whole attitude, in an entirely unconscious way.

As the leaves began to turn, and the nights to grow more chill, and as the boughs of the aspens became bare, Dickson had even begun to dream of keeping Montrose's place as an investment, in exactly the way many Englishmen were dreaming. Instead of selling it he could very well live in England and keep this for a summer hunting place.

It was the color of the leaves that moved him most—a thing which he never realized, and which was therefore all the more potent. Warhorse, because it was autumn now, reminded him of England and Lamont; the chill of autumn, the hard frost of morning, the clarity of the air, this was England again, as he had not seen it for years—or almost England.

For all his years away from England had been
spent in the tropics or in the semitropics, in Jamaica
or in San Antonio, or New Orleans or Cuba. So he
looked now at the yellowing leaves and sniffed the
wood smoke and, rubbing his reddening hands
briskly, he felt an old love stirring.

CHAPTER TWO

Behind the Station House
Same Morning

Mike Allen was walking up and down between two of the cottonwood trees, his hands in his pockets, moving with a rough restlessness. He had been under guard, living in the barn, for a week. Beyond him, sitting at one of the new picnic tables, was one of Dickson's men, holding a steaming cup of coffee between his hands. Farther down the gentle incline toward the creek, the man named Vickers was leaning against the pigpen looking at the swine.

"Ah," Dickson said, strolling up to Mike, "our Damon and Pythias, as usual!"

Mike stopped pacing.

"What is it today?" Mike asked. "Horseshoes again? Or mumblety peg? Aren't people beginning to wonder just what I am supposed to be doing? Don't they ever ask who I am, and what my name is, and why I am followed around by Stringer or somebody? Isn't there any gossip?"

"Not so loudly, my boy. As far as I know, nobody

in Warhorse finds you at all interesting. But be careful, or I may have to lock you up in the house—voices carry remarkably in this delightful mountain air."

Vickers was coming up from the pigpen, hobbling hurriedly on bowed, spindly legs, his small, angular body moving with nervous energy, almost twitching. He looked from side to side, his blue eyes darting everywhere as though on the watch.

"Hey, hey," he said, coming up. "What goes on? Good morning, Mr. Dickson, good morning. Mrs. Vickers sent her very best. Say, did you know the old sow was blind? I was poking her with your stick, and I saw her eyes—plumb poked out, Mr. Dickson."

"An accident," Dickson said. "An unfortunate error on my part. I was simply scratching at her snout, and—well, she made a false move. False moves are always expensive. Eh, Mike?"

Vickers' manner changed to acute wariness as he eyed Mike, and then in an instant his expression became sad. "Today's the day, Mr. Dickson. My note. It's due. My God, what will I do? Eh? You know if Montrose didn't keep robbing me, I'd have plenty of money."

"My dear fellow, you know I have always had complete faith in you. No one understands better than I the difficulties of having bad neighbors. Now, Joe, you run along up to the bank and entertain Mr. Curtis a few minutes, will you? It's nearly ten, and he'll be there. I'll be along and perhaps we'll work something out."

"You know he'd take my ranch, don't you?" Vickers said. "I couldn't help thinking—Eh?" He blinked quickly, pale blue eyes beseeching, promising, and doubting all at once.

Dickson laughed gently. "Why worry, Joe?"

A pale smile broke out on Vickers' face. The wiry stubble on his chin spread and seemed less dark. He licked his lips and nodded. He spat, with sudden force, and started off again, grinning now to himself.

"Charming fellow," Dickson said. "Now, to you, dear boy," he began afresh, turning to Mike. "Come along, let's walk down to the pigpen while we talk over a little job for you."

Mike sat still, looking up at Dickson with remote coldness.

"What is it now?"

"Another visit to the Montroses."

"They wouldn't even see me."

"Oh, yes, they will. It's quite obvious the girl is fond of you."

Mike looked wretched. "There's no use talking about it," he said. "They told me not to come back again."

"You think she is disgusted with you, through with you," Dickson said. "But let me tell you, it is quite different. Love in a woman is like a flower—"

"Shut up. Keep your filthy mouth shut. What do you know about love, you lousy bastard?"

Dickson turned white, and then two round red spots appeared on his cheekbones, like pats of rouge. They stood facing each other for a moment, and then Dickson took a breath. He had a little difficulty controlling his voice, which he could not wholly keep from shaking.

"Listen to me, you wretched yearling bull, you hulking backwoods oaf. There comes a time when nothing, not even common sense, will restrain me. I have put up with you and that stupid old fool of a father of yours for the sake of the money he owes me. But there will come a time when I can endure no more, and I shall turn loose on you and on your miserable, wretched little group. I shall turn loose, I shall strike you all, I shall thrash you bloody in the dust—" His upper lip was lifted and his white teeth showed; his eyes sparkled with sheer vicious fury. Then he stopped himself.

They stood in silence, and then looked away from each other. Dickson took three paces away and then three paces back.

He lifted his eyebrows. He looked about at the yellow leaves. "A lovely day," he said. His voice still shook. He looked around again. "A sparkle in the air, a chill."

He said, "Have a care, my boy. Remember, I too have my animal to control. Now, let us discuss these matters civilly. Shall we?"

Mike looked at him. It was the first time he had ever seen Dickson angry, and it was as though, between two delicate, parted curtains, he had seen a lean, pale wolf ravening, a naked, hairless blue-skinned wolf with pink eyes, held by a slender golden chain.

"As I was saying," Dickson went on, trying stubbornly to keep a light tone in his voice, "love in a woman blossoms like a flower, and don't think I am being personal about a lady who so obviously has your approval. I am merely making an objective remark.

"And just as nothing can keep a flower from blooming—not wind, nor storm, nor worm—so nothing can prevent a woman's love, once she has conceived it. She can hate you, think you a wretched coward, a villain, she can despise you—and yet, how unhappily! For she still loves you.

"Well, so, if I may be permitted this quite impersonal observation. Miss Montrose despises you, and yet I think you can still go out and talk to her and her father without being shot through the head. Something I cannot say for myself. Come along. Don't balk! If you won't come quietly, I'll have you dragged bodily, my boy."

He strolled on down toward the pigpen, Mike following. "At any rate, you are going out there, this very morning, and offer the good General a cool $75,000 for his ranch. It is his last chance. I shall take it by legal force tomorrow."

"Suppose I tell everybody that option date is forged, instead."

"My dear boy, that's just what Montrose is saying. Poor fellow! If only he could prove it! But of course he can't and neither can you, because, of course, he really did give Buford an extension."

"That's a lie," Mike said.

"Philanthropists never lie," Dickson said. "Ask anybody. The town doesn't want to believe I'm a liar. And why on earth should they believe you, if they won't believe the General himself? Anyway, if Montrose sells the ranch to me today, we shall save a lot of trouble. Surely he will appreciate my courtesy."

"I can't think why not," Mike said.

"Oh, come, let's not be sarcastic," Dickson said. "Good morning, Joanne," Dickson said, leaning on the pigpen fence and addressing the old blind sow. She stiffened with alarm at the sound of his voice.

"What's wrong, Joanne, darling?" he asked. "Why don't you speak to me?"

The sow in the mire grunted and turned swiftly toward the teasing voice, her teeth showing in a snarl. Her eyes were empty, the little lids fallen in, the short blond eyelashes sticking out all awry.

Leaning on the fence was a six-foot pole with a sharp prod in the end of it.

"Why, Joanne, darling," Dickson said sweetly, "don't you love me any more? I think we will eat you today at the barbecue."

Dickson picked up the prod and reached in. The pigs stampeded in panic. Dickson jabbed one of them in the rear and it jumped three feet, sprawling on another. Dickson laughed heartily, and wiped his eyes with a big, snowy handkerchief. "See how they run," he said. "Silly beasts. Don't they know they can't get away?" He jabbed another.

"Well, trot along out there, my boy, and make your offer. If Montrose has any sense, he'll take it."

"I thought you offered him $100,000 and he refused on principle."

"Oh, dear, why be so dense, Mike? This $75,000 is your offer, Mike. If he accepts your offer, I shall not press my option, and you shall transfer the deed to me. The whole point is simply, through you, to give Montrose a chance to get out in such a way that he won't lose face openly by having to submit to me."

Dickson poked another of the pigs. They stood trembling against the other side of the pen, which was too small for them. They were all quite thin, worn down by constant teasing. Suddenly one of them charged, with the speed of lightning, against the fence in front of Dickson, and fell, champing its jaws furiously, into the mud. Dickson stepped back, his eyes alight. "Savage little beasts, aren't they? Don't they know they can do nothing? That one over there—the fattest one. I will name him Keppelbauer. Here, Keppelbauer, boy—come here!"

Mike looked sick. "All right," he said, and walked slowly away.

Dickson reached over the fence and deftly jabbed out one of Keppelbauer's eyes.

As he leaned the stick back against the fence, Spence and Sheffield came around the other end of the barn from the bunkhouse, walking slowly together, talking.

"I told him the plan about Vickers," Spence said.

Sheffield looked at his boss without particular interest. "Suppose I do it? It's a hell of a risk."

"Aren't you paid well?" Dickson asked easily and pleasantly. "I haven't bought the police here, no. But the country's wide open. You're safe."

"It ain't only being safe," Sheffield said. "It's just that it's a big job, that's all."

"No bigger than Roarty or Madison, or that fellow in New Orleans," Dickson said, with the same smile.

Sheffield's eyes dodged, and he colored slightly.

"What was his name?" Dickson asked lightly. "I've forgotten. But, of course, the New Orleans police haven't. They could find it somewhere."

Sheffield's color grew bright. "What are you trying?" he cried suddenly.

"What are you?" Dickson asked calmly.

They looked at each other for a moment, and Sheffield's eyes dodged again.

"I have fifteen men now," Dickson said. "I've picked you, personally, to give an opportunity to. What are you trying to do? Hit me for a raise, just because this is particularly important, urgent—and there isn't much time? Is that it, Sheffield?"

Sheffield glanced at Spence, and his eyes ducked even more quickly. "No."

"Are you becoming unreliable?" Dickson asked, moving a step closer. "Having ideas of your own?"

Sheffield shifted away slightly. "No. No, not that, Mr. Dickson."

"When I bailed you out of that jail in Baton Rouge you liked my proposition, didn't you? Enough to jump the bail? You owe me two thousand dollars on that count, my dear Sheffield, and if I may say so, you owe the Baton Rouge authorities around fifteen years on a manslaughter charge, if you haven't forgotten. I assure you I haven't."

"Listen, I didn't mean anything," Sheffield said. "I was just kind of nervous, that's all."

"Nervous?" Dickson asked, moving another step forward. "Don't you trust me? Don't you have confidence in my ability to take care of you? What do you mean, nervous?"

Sheffield shook his head sharply. "I don't mean nervous. I didn't mean that."

"Afraid?" Spense said. "Are you afraid, Sheffield?"

"Hell, no."

"You like your pay? The regular five-hundred-dollar bonus?"

"Hell, yes."

"You want to talk to Forrest about it? The soldier? A private talk?"

"No. I like Forrest. I don't want to talk to him."

Dickson stepped close. "Listen, don't think, Sheffield. You're well off. Lots of money. Easy work. A man like myself to take care of you. Don't make the mistake of thinking, eh? Let me do all the thinking, eh?"

"Yes. All right, Mr. Dickson. All right. Jesus, what did I open my mouth for?"

"Then go saddle some horses for yourself and Spence. Spence will explain everything as you go along.

"Here's what's going to happen, Spence," Dickson said as Sheffield hurried away. "You know how Vickers has always accused Montrose of stealing his cattle. This afternoon Sheffield will shoot Vickers, and it will look as though Montrose did it or one of Montrose's men—as though Vickers had caught them red-handed. Do it just as we planned it before. And just because Vickers is a damned old fool and has been accusing Montrose of stealing his cattle, half the people in town will believe the setup. Then tomorrow Judge Frank can rule my option is good in court and that Montrose forfeits, and turn the ranch over to me. And then who's going to believe it if Montrose keeps on saying I forged the date? He'll have enough trouble talking himself out of a suspicion of murder. Do you think that will do it?"

"The only thing is," Spence said slowly, "you

might push Montrose too far. Killing somebody is always a big thing. It scares people. Do you think we really have to do it? Is it really necessary?"

Dickson smiled pleasantly, his handsome, aristocratic face full of charm and affection.

"My dear Spence," he said in a gentle voice. "To make sure of getting this ranch, I'd do a lot more. What's one little man? Are you a Christian or something? Vickers is just sixty-eight cents' worth of blood and bone as far as I'm concerned.

"I want Montrose to do all his shouting about whether or not he's a murderer—not about fraudulent option dates. And why shouldn't we arrange this insurance? For the sake of sixty-eight cents' worth of blood and bone that moves and squeaks and sounds like a man? When I was a boy, we used to catch mice in flour barrels and chop them up with butcher knives, on the run. It was jolly sport. A pity killing Vickers has to be so secretive, so mechanical."

He looked at Spence with twinkling eyes. Spence's face was troubled. "Calm yourself, dear boy. There's nothing cheaper than human life. The supply is so much greater than the demand. Now, run along, Spence. I'm going to the bunkhouse to prepare the boys for coming events. And remember, the main thing—I want Mrs. Vickers to see the brand on Sheffield's horse—don't forget."

"Ta-ta, Joanne." Dickson waved to the pig, and strolled away.

CHAPTER THREE

The Railroad Station
Same Morning

In all his years of being on the dodge, since he had fled from Jamaica, one of Dickson's greatest problems had been the safekeeping of his growing fortune.

Above all else, his fortune had to be in some form which would allow him immediate flight, for he knew that for him, calamity was instant. He had always foreseen, and discounted, the collapse of his small criminal empires through some human error of his own; he was far too clever to believe that he could frustrate the law forever at any one place, and was content to enrich himself at a succession of places for limited times, being quite happy with losing all the battles with society, as long as he ultimately won the war.

But this implied a succession of escapes; and hence his fortune had to be highly portable. He could not bank it; the police could easily stop his credit. He could not hide it, as he might easily find himself barred from a particular part of the country. He could not carry it as currency, which was too bulky, and also liable to depreciation; nor as gold, which was too heavy. His solution was not very satisfactory, but he could devise nothing better.

Dickson had a large suitcase in his room, upstairs, locked in the closet. The closet had two locks. In this suitcase there was a great deal of money, but only a minor part of it was in cash.

A good part of the three and a half million dollars was in English notes, some of it in French bills, and some in Russian rubles; most of the cash was in U.S. Federal gold notes. This was for current and emergency use.

But the bulk of Dickson's fortune was in diamonds. Thus, while most of the suitcase was filled with ribbon-tied packages of paper notes, the greater part of his money was contained in seven canvas sacks, lined with velvet, in which were smaller packets of diamonds, each packet in tissue. He could have carried most of his wealth in his pockets if he had been forced to do so. None of his diamonds was very remarkable, none of them large. But they were all first-class stones, all perfectly cut; each of them would bring a full price and could be sold without any question anywhere in the world.

Out of the suitcase Dickson now took three hundred separate bills and put them in a large envelope.

He ran down the stairs and out onto the main street. Harris had his horse ready for him, and he swung up easily. He went down the street toward the railroad station at a nice trot, posting elegantly on his English saddle.

People stopped and stared.

Dickson swung down at the yellow railroad station, almost the newest building in Warhorse. The agent doubled on the telegraph key, and he was working at it now, his face blank and absent as he wrote down a message.

There was nobody else in the office. Dickson waited. The big railroad clock ticked on the wall—brand-new, shiny brass pendulum swinging jauntily. A brand-new pot-bellied stove sat confidently in the middle of the waiting-room.

The key stopped rattling.

"Good morning, good morning, Lee, old boy," Dickson said gaily, leaning on the counter. "How's our little woodpecker?"

Lee turned around on his swivel stool. He slowly pushed back his green eyeshade and looked at Dickson. He had a quiet, pasty face which looked stone-cold, and a wide mouth with thin lips. He looked at Dickson now, his face a perfect, observant blank. This masklike quality meant little. Actually, he was a family-loving, warm-hearted man, and Dickson knew he was. He had a young wife and two small daughters, and they had just moved into Warhorse with very little money. The railroad was paying them mostly in prospects, with which it was paying nearly everybody at that time. The blank face concealed worry about the future. Lee had the habit of worry, a small vice which seemed to him to be founded on prudence and foresight, but which actually had its source in timidity. His mouth barely twitched, a movement which Dickson took as a warm smile.

"I heard our books had arrived, John," Dickson said. "Thought I'd look in." Lee was the kind of man who was reassured by being called by his first name. Also, he liked the "our" books, as though Warhorse were just one big family.

"They did," Lee said. "Over there." He nodded his head an inch toward a pile of boxes in the corner.

"Mrs. Frisby said she's going to send a man down late this morning. Coming to the barbecue, I suppose? Don't forget to bring the girls—everybody's going to be there." Dickson laid a small envelope and a piece of paper on the counter.

Lee saw them and blinked. He looked afraid.

He came over to the counter, picked up the envelope delicately, and looked inside.

"What now?" he asked in a low, husky voice, looking quietly at Dickson.

"Nothing much. Just sign the receipt, John."

Lee signed the other piece of paper. "What am I going to tell the old lady? I haven't told her anything yet. I've been thinking and thinking. How am I ever going to spend the money without her knowing it? How am I going to explain it all?"

He glanced out the window to see if anybody was near.

"When the time comes to build your house, just pull a surprise on her," Dickson said. "Say you had it saved up from years ago. She'll think you're a smart man. They always respect you more if they think you've put one over on them. Just take your envelope, Lee, old boy."

Lee slipped the envelope into his pocket.

Dickson gave him a folded paper. "Here's a phony message from the police in San Antonio. An answer to the one Montrose tried to send. He'll be in today, I think. Give it to him."

"He's been in every day," Lee said, and took the sheet of paper. He read it.

General Lucius Montrose Warhorse Montana Regarding your inquiry September fifteen this office re Thomas Dickson subject is prominent citizen this city very highly regarded in all quarters known for civic activity no charges

*of any kind have ever been made against him
and he has highest local reputation personally vouch for him as gentleman of highest
character*
*Benjamin Cash Asst Chief Police San Anto-
nio Texas*

The impassive, pale face did not move. Lee nodded.
He glanced out of the window again.

"I want that copy back," Dickson said. "No sense
in leaving my autograph around."

He leaned forward across the counter, a little
closer to Lee. "You see, my dear fellow, we have to
understand each other. Always remember, no matter
what you might be tempted to do, I have your re-
ceipts. So, far, for three thousand dollars."

Dickson smiled. "Did you by any chance, actually
send the General's wire asking information about
me? I mean, the motive of curiosity must have made
it very tempting."

"No," Lee said. "I didn't send it. I gave it to you,
didn't I?"

"Yes, you did," Dickson said, and knew that Lee
was lying. He smiled. "The reason why I told you
not to send his wire was because if the police down
there got any inquiries about me from here, naturally they'd assume I was here, wouldn't they? And
they would most naturally wire the local sheriff,
wouldn't they? You see, if I am exposed here, you
will be too. That's why I told you not to send it, even
to satisfy your private curiosity. Much too dangerous."

He watched the skin of Lee's face turn a shade
paler.

"The important thing is to let me know of any
messages, John," Dickson said patiently. "I can handle anything—answer anything. But if they don't get

any answer in San Antonio, they may start using the mails, and then we're through. We can't control the mail, can we?" He smiled.

Dickson took his receipt and put it carefully into his wallet. "See you at the barbecue," he said. He reached a hand toward Lee and, with one forefinger, very gently tapped the back of Lee's hand, which was lying beside the phony message from San Antonio. "Don't make the mistake of taking me for a fool," he said, in a quite ungenial voice.

Lee looked up slowly into Dickson's eyes and dropped his own quickly again. "No," he said. "I won't, Mr. Dickson."

Dickson strode jauntily back to his horse.

Lee went to his sending desk and from the bottom drawer took out a cigar box. He opened it and took out a message, which was still in rough copy, as he had taken it down from the key.

It read:

General Lucius Montrose Warhorse Montana In answer your wire September fifteen you are advised that Thomas Dickson is notorious character wanted urgently by this office on six charges of murder in first degree he is professional gambler also wanted for extortion and on numerous other counts if you have knowledge of his whereabouts we request you advise your local authorities to arrest on our charges and we will mail warrants and requests for extradition immediately upon your advice by wire here he is probably accompanied by William Spence and Isaac Forrest both wanted as accomplices and on other charges and perhaps by others known to us urge you to use caution in dealing with these men as all are dangerous will greatly appreciate any help

you can extend us in apprehending these in-
dividuals
Benjamin Cash Asst Chief of Police San An-
tonio Texas

Lee heard the hoofs of Dickson's horse trotting
away up the main street. He sat at his desk and
wiped his cold face with both hands. There was a
light dew of sweat on it, in spite of the chill air.

He went to his key and sent this message:

Benjamin Cash Asst Chief of Police San An-
tonio Texas
Sorry cannot assist you as Dickson and others
left here two weeks ago were last seen in Da-
kota Territory near Deadwood and thought to
be heading east will advise you if I receive
any further information
                                    Lucius Montrose

Then Lee took out a pen and wrote on a telegraph
form: *Dear Sheriff Bolt: In case I am killed, this will*
explain why. I am sorry I ever got mixed up in this. His
pen scratched and spat. His hand was shaking. *I was*
a damn fool but I needed the money. Lee stopped and
thought. It wasn't true that he had needed the money.
He had only thought he had needed the money. But it
was too late to change the wording, just as it was too
late to change the deed. *I am in too deep in this to come*
out clean, but this is so you will know the truth. The
money is in the bottom right-hand drawer of my desk
in a cigar box. I haven't even been able to spend it. The
pen dug in with a bitter incisiveness on the last words.
The peculiar thing about the note was that it explained nothing, even when he took the rough message
describing Dickson and put it in an envelope with his
note.

He addressed the note: *To Sheriff Bolt. In case of*

my death. John Lee. He put the sealed envelope into his inside pocket and sat quiet. It felt like a bomb, and at the same time, it was warm and comforting. But the thought of giving it to Bolt made the blood drain out of Lee's head and hands and feet, leaving him feeling hollow. He sat helpless, trying to get up the courage to do what he had to do.

CHAPTER FOUR

Curtis's Bank
Same Morning—9:45 A.M.

Joe Curtis, the banker of Warhorse, had one assistant, who did all the work. It was a good thing this young man, named Lewin, liked banking and figures, because business in Warhorse had picked up a great deal with the coming of the railroad, and he had plenty of both.

The savings deposits had taken great jumps, but nothing in comparison to the commercial loans. The fact was, as Lewin had pointed out twice to big, fat Joe Curtis, if a depositor like Red Timmons, who ran 10,000 head of cattle, pulled out his money, it would be very dangerous indeed. If not disastrous.

"If we need cash, call somebody," Joe Curtis said.

"We can't. You know as well as I everybody's up to the hilt. Who the hell can you call, when the money's all in nails and boards? There won't be any income from all this expansion for another year, Joe."

Joe lolled back in his chair, which tilted and swung

in all directions. He had a heavy black mustache and
heavy black hair, and his eyebrows shelved out in
great tufts. He was heavy with fat of a rather loose
kind, and his voice had a harsh, rattling quality as-
sociated with the constant quaffing of bourbon.

"For God's sake, Lew," he said, clearing his throat
and shooting a load at the spittoon, "do you want to
be a goddam clerk all your life, or a banker? The
railroad won't let us down."

"Listen," Lew said. "If we don't collect a couple of
those short-term notes like Vickers' before Saturday,
we can't meet the railroad payroll, and if that happens, everybody in town will come yelling for his
money, and we're sunk."

Beads of sweat crept out on Joe's forehead and
rolled down into his bushy eyebrows. "Hush, Lew,"
he said. "Hush. Those are forbidden thoughts. You've
got to keep your mind healthy, son. Healthy."

"Healthy like being drunk all day. No thanks.
Take a tip, Joe—try a few forbidden thoughts once
in a while, it keeps a body sane. We got too much
out on loans. For one thing, we'd better foreclose on
Vickers. We can sell that ranch fast, it's all flat land,
first class, and plenty of water."

"Dickson is backing Vickers. For some damn reason they're friends. I can't foreclose the little bastard."

"Foreclose and sell it to Dickson. That'll give us
some cash. Besides, it's right next to Montrose, and
Dickson wants that. It's perfect."

"Do you think it's possibly true that Montrose is
stealing from Vickers? Or having his men do it?
Maybe the old boy is really doing it."

"Who cares?" Lew asked. "All I care about is the
deposits. I have to look the damn balance sheet in
the face every day, and it makes me sick."

Curtis heard boot heels coming quickly along the

board sidewalk. He wheeled around in his chair. "Here comes Vickers now."

"Shall I let him in?" Lew asked.

"Hell, no, let him wait. It ain't ten yet and I don't know what to do with him, anyway."

"Renew his note?"

"Well, we need the money, don't we?"

Vickers knocked on the door, timidly and urgently.

Joe Curtis sat still. Lew waited.

Vickers hobbled rapidly back to the saloon, cussing to himself. Then Lewin saw Dickson trotting up the street.

"Bet you five he's coming here," Lewin said. "He knows Vickers' note is up. You really want to put his money in the kitty—I mean, the deposits?"

"He won't leave town. The General'll sell."

"How do you know?"

"I just know."

"You mean you got the Judge to go for that option, is that it?"

"There ain't nothing wrong with that option," Curtis said.

"Montrose says the date was changed. He says the date was July fifteenth, and it's been changed by somebody."

Joe Curtis spat in the cuspidor. "Montrose is a contrary, nasty, mean, stuck-up old bastard that keeps his money in his sock. He's just lying to throw us off, 'cause he doesn't want to sell. Changed his mind."

"You mean you'd rather have Dickson around town than Montrose," Lewin said, his face committing nothing.

"Well, wouldn't you?" Joe asked, his big voice rattling. "Dickson is a friendly man, for one thing. He's forward. Look at this library. And I believe his option is good, and I'm going to back him up, and so is the Judge."

"How do you know?"

Joe spat. "Well, I was playing cards with Dickson and the Judge last night. Just a little private game, down at the Station House. The Judge told me when we was riding home. He told me he thought Montrose was just trying to lie out of his contract, that's all."

Lewin looked at his boss. "The Judge's account is down to seventy-five dollars. He's taken out three thousand in the last four weeks. His savings, I mean."

"So what?" Curtis asked coldly.

"Don't get sore. Just look facts in the face," Lewin said.

"Everybody knows Dickson lost two thousand to the Judge. Are you implying the Judge is in the hole? Why, everybody knows the Judge won two thousand bucks off Dickson."

"Sure. And how much has he lost since? If he hasn't been losing, what's he been doing with his account? He hasn't bought anything around town. He hasn't sent it anywhere. So who's got the Judge's money?"

"What's that got to do with the price of beans?" Joe asked.

"You know damn well what it's got to do with the price of beans," Lewin said.

Joe leaned forward. "Go on, I want you to say it out loud. What's that got to do with the Judge's decision on the option?"

Lewin said nothing.

"Go on, tell me," Joe said. "Put up or shut up. Are you slandering two good men—the Judge and Dickson both?"

Lewin looked at his boss with a faint spark of fright. "Now, don't get sore, now, Joe," he said. "I'm just trying to work for you. You're putting a lot of chips on Dickson, and you don't really know anything about him. What about that wire the General sent to San Antonio last month—the one he says he will show everybody?"

"Well, what about it?"

Lewin said nothing.

"More dust kicked up by the General in a tantrum," Joe said. "He's just sore 'cause he's got to sell his ranch, is all. Just sore and slandering. Don't be a slanderer, Lew."

Lew's mouth closed tightly.

"Lew, you know as well as I do," Joe Curtis said, noting the closing in of Lewin's mind, and turning gentle, "that Warhorse is going to grow big by big thinking and by big people. We want people like Dickson here. If it comes to a choice between Montrose and Dickson, we'll take Dickson. Montrose was the first man in this country, and if it was left to him, there'd be nothing today but him and the Indians, this very day. Dickson is a happy, cheerful man with plenty of money and business sense. We can gamble on Dickson. I'm sure of it." There was a prophetic light in his eyes.

"All right," Lewin said. "You're the boss. Thank God I don't own any stock in this bank." He stood up.

Outside, Dickson swung down from his horse, and Vickers came hobbling back along the walk from the saloon.

Joe Curtis stood up as Dickson came in, followed by Vickers.

"Good morning, there, Joe old boy!" Dickson cried out cheerily, and extended a hand.

"Good morning, there, Tommy old son," Curtis boomed in his rattling voice, pumping Dickson's hand up and down with heavy warmth. "Sit down, son, sit down. Vickers, find a seat, will you?" he said, as though suggesting that Vickers could find one out in the shed behind the bank. "What's on your mind, Tommy? Anything I can do for you?"

"Well, Joe," Dickson said, letting his lean, neat length down into a chair against the partition, "our friend Vickers here tells me he's in a tight, as we say out here in God's country. That right? Note's up. Six thousand, he says. So I thought I'd come in here and"—he pulled out his wallet—"just take up Vickers' note for him, and make it a personal matter between him and myself. All right, Vickers?" he asked, beaming. "All right, Joe?" he asked again, turning and beaming at Curtis. He pulled out six neat, clean thousand-dollar bills, and laid them on the desk.

Curtis beamed broadly.

"Now just charge my account for the interest, will you, Joe? And sometime you just stick that old note in the mail to me. All right?"

"Well, I should say so," Joe said in a low, warm voice, exactly like an old Southern mammy crooning over a hurt pickaninny. He picked up the six bills with dear love and tender affection.

"Kind of figured," Dickson said, using the subjectless verb in true Western fashion, "Vickers and I would work together when I take over the General's place tomorrow."

"Yes, by golly, it is tomorrow," Joe said. He pulled out a drawer and took out Buford's old option. "That's right, so it says, right here. October ninth. No getting around that." He lifted his heavy, smiling face and winked lightly at Dickson. "Is there?"

Dickson pulled out his big envelope and laid it in front of Curtis. "Three hundred thousand dollars. Set it up in escrow, Joe. That takes up the option without any question."

Joe Curtis looked in the envelope and shut his mouth. He saw the denomination and riffled a finger over the packets. He half-shut his eyes, to keep them from bugging.

"Surely does, Tommy," he said in a slightly weak voice. He wondered for a moment if he should not call Tommy "Mr. Dickson" from now on, and immediately revolted at the servile idea. "I don't mind saying, Tommy, Warhorse is mighty proud to have a man like you in its midst. Mighty proud."

Vickers blinked and smiled, looking with childish happiness first at Curtis and then at Dickson.

"Come along," Dickson said, taking his arm. "We'll just ride out and look your place over. Especially your fence line. We'll probably take that down altogether, eh? We'll pool our cattle and we can operate more cheaply that way. So long, Joe! See you down at the barbecue this afternoon! Bring the missus and the kids!"

They went out, the long and the short, the short hopping and dancing, as happy and excited as a child.

Joe Curtis sank down into his swivel chair with a deep sigh and dragged a bottle out of his desk.

"Lew," he called, and Lewin came in.

"Did you hear all that, Lew?" Curtis asked benignly, taking the money out of the big envelope and showing it. "Never mind putting this in escrow, boy. Put her right on deposit. I'm going out and make some more seven-per-cent loans."

CHAPTER FIVE

Montrose's ranch lay back between two great spurs of the Warhorse Mountains, fenced only at the lower end where the hay land lay flattening out down toward the Yellowstone.

Warhorse Creek, which started high in the mountains above Montrose's place, ran down through it for twelve miles to the fence along Vickers' place, and then another nine miles to the town.

As Mike, followed by Irving, rode up the ruts toward the mountains, he could see small scattered bunches of Montrose's cattle, dotted over the steepening country. They left the hay land, and the grass thinned, and as he climbed along the road beside the rushing creek, he could see easily enough why Montrose ran only a thousand head while everybody was saying he should run four.

Four miles farther, Mike caught a glimpse of the summer headquarters, far up the canyon. They had passed the winter house, down on the flats, to which

Montrose had not yet returned, and the road began to get into rough upland, by-passing boulders and running over exposed gravel. They were entering the big head canyon, which narrowed as it rose toward the far blue peaks, covered with black forest.

The summer house was in clear view, far up. It was built of logs with a tin roof laid over planking.

Mike stopped at a new gate across the road. It hadn't been there the last time he had been up. He got down and opened it, and they went through. On the upper side of the road, there was a kind of barricade or small fort built of rocks. There was nobody in it.

They rode up before the big log house and swung down. There was no one around.

"You wait here," Mike said. "I won't be long."

"Take your time," Irving said, rolling a cigarette and sitting down against the house. "There ain't but one way out of this canyon."

Mike went up the wide plank steps and crossed the creaking porch. He knocked at the big plank door.

The big door opened and Herbia looked out at him. She gave a kind of hiss, her heavy lips drawing back a little, and seemed to shrink.

"You ain't wanted here," she said. "Get out."

"Herbia, tell the General I want to see him."

"You get out,' Herbia said, her voice rising. "You ain't going to trouble the General no more. Miss Clara said if you came you wasn't—"

"Herbia," the General said from behind the door.

Herbia dropped her eyes and moved back. The door opened wider and the General stood there, dressed in the same tight black coat and smart trousers which he had worn in Cheyenne. At this range, though, Mike could see the shine on the seams and the threadbare edge of the coat cuffs. The General was wearing a gun and he had his coat tail tucked up inside the gun butt, leaving it handy.

"Get out," the General said in a voice like an icicle. "I drove you off once. This time I'll shoot you off."

"General," Mike said, "I am not armed, I'm bringing a message. I ask you to believe I have no part in this business. I've come up here to try to help as much as I can. I ask you to believe me."

"I have been subjected to too much trickery," the General said. "You are a tool of Dickson's. You came here the first time pretending to be our friend, and we found your offer was just a lie. Why come here again? Do you think we are fools?"

"I'm a prisoner," Mike said to the General. "I have been for two months. A hostage. I told you that before. Why don't you believe it? I want to help, but I can only do so much."

"It's a trick. I do not dare believe it is anything else," the General said. A look of indecision and confusion, momentary weakness, crossed his face. "Deception, everything has been deception, from the beginning."

"Wait a minute, Father," Clara said from inside the room. "It's a little too much to believe that this is a trick. Surely not everyone is a master of lies. If Mr. Allen did not want to help us, as he says, why would he come up here again? Surely he knows that if we threw him out once, we can do it again." Her voice was hardly bitter, very much controlled.

"What is it you have to say, then?" the General asked. "Say it, and go. We're leaving for the party— Mr. Dickson's great social event—to try to improve our social standing. I'm afraid it's a little too late."

"Do you mind if I come in?" Mike said, gesturing in Irving's direction.

"Such secrecy," the General said. "Come in, then. I suppose I shall have to endure it. My daughter insists on politics. Let this be part of politics." The General looked almost sick with disgust, and then suddenly a look of surprise crossed his face as he stepped back. He said, in an almost civil voice, "You know, I cannot understand your patience under insults. God knows I have insulted you enough to keep you away from here. Why do you keep coming back?"

He stepped back out of the doorway. Mike went in, taking off his hat. Herbia shut the door, and the gloom of the big room closed in on them.

"The truth is, I am simply ashamed," Mike said. "I can't afford to feel insulted, General. Nearly everything you say is true."

"And I might say, I am ashamed *for* you," the General said. "You are a most peculiar mixture of humility and asininity, if I may say so. You come up here apparently abject, offering to help. How on earth can you help, with that armed dog at your heels, if I may ask? I cannot follow your line of reasoning. You remind me, in fact, of a puppy on a string. Now what is it, please? What is the message?"

Mike looked at Clara. She looked back, directly, for a moment, and then dropped her eyes. Mike had the feeling, for a moment, that the General, Dickson, the whole mess was a game—that the only real thing in the whole business was the instantaneous feeling that came over him, when they looked at each other, of—of what? He knew that she was happy when he came, and he knew that she knew exactly what he was feeling. It was as though each of them were suddenly looking through a hole in the dense wall of their accustomed human reservations and amenities, straight into the eyes of a perfectly charming friend who understood everything, and with whom there was little use for words. It made him happy just to be here, and it made her happy, and the peculiar thing was that it was making the General happy, in spite of everything. That was why the horrible mess in which they were all involved seemed for a moment quiet unreal. That was why the General had suddenly begun to abuse him—because he liked him, in spite of himself.

"Dickson told me to offer you $75,000 for your ranch. In my name."

"Bosh. That is merely insulting."

"I know it. But I want to offer the balance in my own notes. I want you to give me title to the ranch, and I will fight Dickson."

"What kind of chicanery is this? What on earth good are your notes?"

"The point is," Mike said, laboring on, "that if my father and I—" Why was it always so difficult to talk to the General? The same thing had happened in Cheyenne, the feeling of dreadful mental labor, to outline his plans clearly. Then it occurred to Mike that he only had this difficulty when he was being specious, or trying to be clever. It was difficult to be a fool with General Montrose, and easy to be sensible. It was as simple as that.

"Your father and you," the General said. "You mean, you two would take over my problem with Dickson, and fight shoulder to shoulder, sparing my daughter and myself, while accomplishing what Buford still wants to do—rob me. You would defeat Dickson, operate the ranch successfully, and pay off your notes to me, while I lived in Mt. Holly. How extremely noble in conception, if I may say so. Didn't I tell you once we all had our illusions? Yours seems to be that it is possible to be virtuous simply by having good intentions. Why, it seems to me that you and your father are responsible for this whole incredible mess. You've come up here into a peaceful country like a swarm of locusts, you and your father and that wretched creature Dickson. You and your father have loosed a horde of villains on us all, simply from your father's incredible greed and your incredible weakness.

"That fellow Dickson is now in the process of actually trying to force me out of my simple rights. What in God's name are we coming to? Why, he has bewitched the entire community. He has turned all their heads. And you are with him. That is the fact you cannot deny. You are actually enjoying his hospitality.

"If you were to come here and endure our privations with us, the calumnies of people we once called friends, I would be more inclined to believe your protestations of friendship. And yet, I do believe your protestations, but what else are they? As I said, you are exactly like a puppy on a string. You can take your incredible offer and go to hell with it."

"Father," Clara said, "I am getting tired of all this ranting. I am simply tired." She sighed heavily. "I can't help feeling there is something good behind Mr. Allen's feeble moves."

"Ranting?" the General asked. "Have I been ranting? Herbia, do get me some coffee, will you? Bring Mr. Allen a cup of coffee."

His face suddenly became tired. "This wretched business," he said, looking almost vaguely around. "It's the ruin of everything. I feel myself slipping, and I cannot understand why. All of a sudden, this filthy fellow Dickson is upon us, and how did it all happen? He is ruining me among my friends, and they believe him. Those incredible accusations of that poor fellow Vickers. It's simply fantastic. The whole world is slowly turning upside down."

"Dickson's bought them," Mike said.

"He's bought you too," Clara said.

"No," Mike said. "All I can do is wait. Don't you understand? I can't do anything until my father gets here. The only thing I can do is persuade him to give it all up and clear out, and I can't do that until he comes."

Herbia came in with the coffee cups on a tray.

" 'Scuse me, General," Herbia said. "You'll be mad if I don't tell you. There ain't no more of that."

"Of what?"

"Coffee, suh. No more hardly nothin'. Flouah. Beans. Hawss radish. How'se ah goan laht the fah 'thout no matches?"

"Never mind, Herbia," Clara said. "We're going to get everything this afternoon."

The General turned to Mike. "Even if you could make the ranch pay well enough to pay off your notes, you would still have to beat off that devil Dickson, and how could you do that even as well as I? So what do I have to gain by your offer? Surely the ranch is in better hands than in those of men who have already proven themselves unable to cope with this Dickson. Your father—poor, greedy, muddling fellow—and you, a young man of decent inclinations and not half brains enough to implement them—what on earth could you do that I cannot do? My God, Mr. Allen, how can you sit there and endure what I say?"

Clara's cheeks were faintly pink. There was a light in her eyes, a subdued glow. She could not escape Mike's look. It did not embarrass her, but it made her feel far too beautiful.

"Because I want to help you."

The General smiled thinly. "Would you fight for me? Against your father? If it came to that?"

Mike looked at him astounded. "Why? Believe me, all my father wants is to get free from Dickson."

"Are you sure? He could get free easily enough, by giving up those herds you told me about. Are you sure he isn't planning still to get my ranch?"

"How? How would he do that?"

"How do I know?" the General asked. "You said he had a dozen men, with this man Tucker. He could do a lot with a dozen men—fight Dickson himself, for instance. Or me. To get the ranch."

The blood drained slowly out of Mike's head. "He couldn't be such a fool. He learned his lesson in San Antonio."

The General shook his head. "In all his life, Buford has never learned a lesson. I told you he was pursuing an illusion, didn't I? He lives on hope—on dreams. And he always bounces back. Wait and see, my boy. As for you, you're going to have to learn to go your own way—alone. Honor and justice at times require one to step squarely on the faces of his friends, and even of his own father. I say again, you are a puppy on a string, sir, and I give you one simple, all-inclusive counsel: Grow up."

The General stood back from the table, and Mike knew he was through. He rose slowly and wearily. "Thank you for the coffee," he said.

"You may also tell Dickson that he will never get my property by any means. I do not say, even over my dead body, as he shall be the one who dies, not I. I suppose you noticed the new gate, and my rather neat little sentry box."

Mike said, "Do you mean to tell me you are getting ready for an invasion?"

"What else? I am not a general for nothing. I can read that fop's mind like a map. Tomorrow he will try to get a judgment against me and he will succeed simply because Judge Frank owes him money. Frank owes everybody money. He is an habitual moocher. Dickson will try to evict me, and I shall resist, and I assure you it will take at least a troop of cavalry to get me out of here." He held the door open.

Mike did not get another look at Clara. He crossed the porch and went down to his horse.

Irving got up. For a moment, Mike had an almost irresistible desire to smash him in the face, gun and all. With a bitterness that burned like alkali in the mouth, he kept the impulse down and mounted his horse. They rode out without speaking.

Mike knew he would never have a better chance to get away than now. Irving was quartered to his rear; but Irving wasn't wary. Mike's long weeks of patience and good behavior had put all his guards to sleep. If he could get away from Irving—

The future opened up in Mike's mind, and he saw how little chance he had, even if he did get away. He had no way of killing Irving. Even if he was able to get away, Irving would reach Warhorse as soon as he hit the Yellowstone, and Dickson would put ten men on his trail.

And where would he go? They'd know he would have gone to his father. What else could he do, except try to warn Tucker and the rest, and start the battle now? And if they lost the battle, he and his father would both be dead, and Montrose left at Dickson's mercy.

It was a hopeless situation. But Mike knew that nothing ever worked out as any man foresaw it, ever. Things happened—accidents, lucky breaks. A man had to try, to give the breaks a chance to happen. A man had to do something. He had found out that night in San Antonio that nothing was worse than simply accepting what the enemy made you do.

Mike's horse didn't have much nerve, it was a decent, good-natured animal out of the livery. What he needed was a wild one, an easy shier, a cat. But he did the best he could. He hauled back on the reins and rammed in his spurs at the same time, rearing his horse and wheeling it toward Irving, trying to throw it on Irving's mount. Mike's horse was slow, but Irving's wasn't. It dodged backward away from the forefeet pawing over it, almost throwing Irving over its neck, and Mike brought his horse down and wheeled away down the road, beating with his heels, leaning low over the horn, as Irving fought to get his own horse under control again.

Mike was fifty yards down the road when the first shot whipped over him. He glanced back. Irving was off his horse, standing, holding his hand-gun at aim, steadying it by holding his right wrist in his left hand.

The second shot hit Mike's horse in the rump, and the third hit it in the spine. The horse dropped, throwing Mike over its head, and they plowed down the road together through the dust.

Irving stood there, seventy-five yards away, smiling quietly. Mike sat there in the dirt, listening to the horse scream.

Irving remounted, and trotted up. He shot Mike's horse through the head and it stopped screaming.

Irving put his gun away and picked his quirt off the horn. "Get up, you simple bastard," he said to Mike. Mike slowly stood up. His shirt sleeves were torn out where he had landed in the gravel, and the torn skin of his arms burned like acid.

Irving pushed his horse forward and brought the quirt down through the air, lashing across Mike's shoulder. Mike's vision turned black with the pain and he staggered backward.

"March," Irving said, pushing forward with the horse. The quirt came down again, and Mike staggered forward down the road.

"You'd better learn, you son of a bitch," Irving said with quiet fury. The quirt lashes whistled and Mike's back ached, his hands rising in the air. He seemed to dance a few steps, and broke into a trot.

"You damned, dumb son of a bitch," Irving said quietly through his teeth. "You'll learn. By God, you'll learn. Pulling a thing like that on me. I might have lost my job."

It was some time before Irving's temper sank again, and by that time Mike could hardly see at all. He staggered forward down the long, dusty road in the burning sun, his hat gone, blood collecting slowly in the burning welts on his back.

It hadn't been any use. He hadn't thought it was going to work. But a man had to try. Sometimes things broke right.

And sometimes they didn't.

CHAPTER SIX

Vickers' Ranch—2:00 P.M.

Nine miles down the creek from Montrose's ranch, Mrs. Vickers sat in her house, wiping the tears from her eyes.

For the first time in five years, she was perfectly happy. Her husband and Dickson had arrived with the joyful news about the note being taken up, and for an hour after they left together in the direction of the fence line, she wandered about the house in a dream.

At first she dreamed of curtains, new curtains on the windows, and then she began to dream of new windows, and then she began to dream of a small, but very neat clapboard house, painted white, with green shutters, just like the one she had left in Indiana. It was then that she felt as though an immense weight had been lifted from her back—she literally stood up and breathed more freely for the first time in years.

When Dickson and Vickers came back, she was

brewing a pot of fresh coffee. She felt the tension in the two men; then she noticed the big round ball of fresh hide which her husband was carrying.

"Got him, Martha," was all Vickers said. "Got him. Look." He unrolled the hide on the ground in front of the house. "Look there," he said, pointing to the raw burn of new branding-iron marks. "Took a shot at us, he did."

"Who?" she asked.

"Montrose."

"Probably not Montrose himself," Dickson said from his horse. "Probably one of his men. Looked about the size of Fred Hand."

"Don't matter," Vickers said shortly. "Look," he said to his wife, pointing a dirty finger at the big, sprawled brand. His meaning was plain enough. The old scar of V, with a bar under it, had been altered to that of an M by the addition of two legs to the V. "Doctored my brand and took a shot at us, too. There was two of 'em. Gitcher dress on," he said. "I'll take this to the party. I'll show them all. We'll see who was the liar."

Dickson smiled at Mrs. Vickers and took off his hat. "I'll ride along," he said. "See you later."

Vickers rolled up the hide and put it in the wagon. He hitched up the wagon while his old lady ran inside and "got her dress on," a phrase which included everything from washing her feet to dabbing a touch of flour on her tanned cheeks.

After he had hitched the horses, Vickers went inside and sat down with a cup of coffee.

Suddenly a thought jumped up before him, and he sat quiet, his confidence draining, fear beginning to shrink him again. He remembered that all his accusations against Montrose were actually lies. He had been lying so long and so consistently that he had built up an actual belief in his stories. But now, as he sat alone, the belief broke.

He barely moved. He was afraid. This sudden proof, this hide which he had skinned off his own cow, now had the effect of unnerving him. Could it be really true that Montrose was robbing him? He sat in numb confusion, knowing in his heart that the idea of Montrose thieving was absurd. Something was false. But surely not the evidence of the hide? Then what was it? He faced a gray cloud of mental paralysis. He either could not think at all, at this moment, or the thought he faced was too terrible to entertain, and hid itself behind a curtain of wool. In all the five years he had run stock on this place, he had never had a single good reason to suspect Montrose; yet this in itself had in some way seemed to him all the more reason to suspect Montrose of villainy, for surely his calves did disappear.

He was, in fact, too lazy to ride his own range, and therefore many of the calves were weaned without a brand. These were mavericked by anybody who had the nerve to do it. The fact was that the whole idea of Montrose robbing him had been conceived in Vickers' head for the purpose of detracting from the General's superiority as well as excusing his own laziness.

The very lack of proof was an asset, in a peculiar way, because people had never seriously believed Vickers' hints, insinuations, and secret accusations, and this meant that Vickers could repeat them endlessly, which was what he wanted to do. His purpose was not to see justice done but to escape it himself.

In his heart he knew that this hide was an incredible thing, not real at all. He knew vaguely that it did not mean what it purported to mean—he knew that this event had a hidden significance. But he did not know what this hidden meaning was. He suddenly gave up, under the pressure of fear and indecision. He would take the hide to the party. Let the others decide what was the matter, if anything really was.

His wife came out of the bedroom in her one good dress. She had a smile which was quite beautiful, of which she was unaware. She looked like a young girl, as she had looked when she was fifteen, in her first real dress—excited, timid, eager, but brave, for the first time adventuring into a social world where anything romantic and exciting might happen.

"Pretty," Vickers said, and she turned pink with pleasure.

They went out and got into their wagon, Vickers chewing his front teeth incisively, looking boldly and clearly ahead, and also from side to side.

They drove down the road.

Half a mile farther, Mrs. Vickers was startled out of her dreams into a stunned blankness by a shot, close to the road.

She turned her head toward the noise, and saw her husband falling forward onto the dashboard. The horses, panicked, plunged into their collars. She saw the man with a smoking rifle and a red neckerchief over his face.

She also saw the Montrose horse brand on the horse's shoulder, as the rider turned and quirted the horse away.

Then the wagon horses were flying down the road, and her husband was lying in a heap at her feet, rolling and jolting with the roll and rattle of the wagon as it hit the potholes.

She stopped the horses. She sat there looking at her husband. There were two holes—all she could see was a trickle of black blood—one on each side of his head, small and somehow obscene, hideous and final.

A few birds came back to rest.

The horse flicked a fly off its ear.

She began to scream.

CHAPTER SEVEN

The Barbecue
The Station House—3:00 P.M.

It was understood in Warhorse that the Montroses had not been invited to the party that afternoon.

General Montrose had indeed been invited, but quite privately.

Therefore, when the General drove up beside the Station House in his buggy, with Clara sitting beside him, and followed by the small retinue of his four hands, there was a general hush that went like a wave of wind over the throng, and the temperature dropped a few degrees as eyebrows rose and looks were exchanged.

The four Montrose hands who had accompanied the buggy rode off down the street, obviously toward one of the saloons. It was well known that the General encouraged drunkenness and gambling on his ranch.

At this first big party of Dickson's everyone had begun by feeling wonderful and had progressed upward. The roast pig was delicious, and so was the beef, and the steak sauce, made by Harris, was something fascinatingly exotic.

There was beer, there was bourbon, and there was wine, and the ladies delighted themselves in exchanging guesses as to what local maiden would end by snaring this remarkable man, while the husbands exercised their newly acquired wine lingo, sagely judging this wine and that as they passed from bottle to bottle.

They were on their best behavior, they had come dressed in their finest, but the jealousy and hatred which the ladies had concealed beneath their complimentary remarks on each other's new silks and feathers soon dissolved in a general animosity toward the cause of dear Mr. Dickson's difficulties, which bolstered up the general feeling of self-satisfaction.

The arrival of the General put a stop to all this geniality. Mr. Dickson showed some confusion and surprise, but he recovered himself and hurried forward like a true gentleman, hand extended and with a most hospitable smile on his face.

General Montrose had been primed by his daughter. He had been forced into this, and he was doing his best not to show it. But as he helped his daughter down from the buggy, and saw Dickson hurrying forward with hand extended, all his resolutions and discipline of mind dissolved in a mixture of fear and bewilderment. It was incredible that this proven enemy was actually going to shake his hand. But what was he to do?

Clara, even while she was stepping down, read all this in his face, and as Dickson came up, she managed to turn her ankle and give enough of a cry to concentrate all the General's concern on her welfare rather than his own.

With a flutter of concern, Dickson caught Clara's other elbow, and with pretty gratitude she batted her eyes at him, at the same time inwardly shuddering.

"I am so happy that you could come, General," Dickson said.

The General managed to smile. "We feel especially honored," Clara said, her voice incredibly sweet in her father's unbelieving ears. How could she do it? he wondered. But somehow she infected him also with a feeling that it was possible to utter complete nonsense with the greatest ease.

"Let us hope," Dickson said, contributing abundantly to the nonsense, "that all our differences will be ironed out. I know, I am sure, that they are merely the results of misunderstandings."

"Indeed, indeed," the General said in such a voice that the words could be taken as affirmation or complete disbelief with equal ease. "Why, Dickson, I see that you know everybody. Look, Clara, all our friends." He gazed over the crowd.

It reminded Montrose of truce meetings between the commanders of hostile forces, during which everyone treated everyone with the most perfect courtesy, rendering compliments and tributes to valor, serving drinks and food if available. The day before, each had been desperately plotting the other's destruction, and both would have been profoundly moved with gratitude if the other had been smashed to bits by a stray cannonball—but here they were, soft-soaping each other like two rival mothers at a spelling bee.

The General accepted a bourbon and water, and he actually tried a sip. He had sworn he would simply carry a drink around until they left, but would eat or drink nothing of Dickson's. He and his daughter slowly walked through the crowd of chattering ladies and sedately conversing gentlemen, who were wandering around the tables and sitting in groups.

Nobody noticed as Mrs. Vickers drove up beside

the General's buggy and sat there. Dickson saw her first, because he was expecting her. He saw the two legs, in gray trousers and black boots, hanging down from the side, the toes dirty and dusty where they had brushed the bumps.

Mrs. Curtis, spreading caviar determinedly on a cracker, saw Dickson's look and followed it with a jerk of her ostrich-plumed hat.

She said, "Why, why, what's that?" And other ladies looked, and then others. All of them, unbelieving, saw the feet and the legs, hanging down.

One by one, voices shut off in the middle of words as eyes saw looks, and followed. The thought of *drunk* flashed by and went, impossible because of the way Mrs. Vickers was sitting there. Without thinking, they knew she would never have come there with a drunken husband. And there was the wrong kind of pain in her face—not worry, not shame, but a gaunt, stretched look that was far different.

With what breath she had in her lungs, Mrs. Vickers screamed; and then she bent over, huddling in the seat, her hands over her face, rocking, moaning uncontrollably.

Dickson was the first one to move. He ran up the yard to her, mounted the wagon to help her down. Other men ran, and then a few women. They got her down from the wagon and carried her to one of the benches. They poured whiskey into her throat, which almost strangled her. She stood staring about at the crowd of worried faces and clung to Dickson.

"Mr. Dickson!" was the first thing she said, and they saw how she clung to him, her poor yellow hands dragging and clutching. She leaned her head against his chest and closed her eyes.

There was a crowd of men around the wagon, looking at Vickers' body.

"They killed him," she said.

"Who?" one of the men asked. Dickson said nothing.

"Montrose. I saw the horse." She told all this as though it were a secret, a little story, which she was telling to her father. And even though the others asked the questions, she addressed only Dickson, her voice low and intimate, as though the others were not there.

They heard her answer, and they sat and stood absolutely still, shocked out of thought.

Montrose heard it. He stood quiet with his daughter.

Down at the wagon, men were spreading out the hide. They came back up, dragging it through the dust.

"What's this?" one of them asked. "Mrs. Vickers, there was a hide in the wagon. A blotched brand." The speaker looked at Montrose once. "What does it mean? Somebody ran a Montrose M over the Vickers V, you can see it easy."

"The hide," she said. "Yes, that was it. They came back with the hide. Mr. Dickson, you remember."

Dickson said nothing.

A cold wind came over the yard, and they noticed that the sun had gone down behind the Station House roof.

"Won't you tell us?" one of the women asked. Many of the women, their faces drugged with shock, were fumbling to put on their veils and shawls. It was over, the party was all over. Where had it gone? Many of them were half drunk, and the shock of Mrs. Vickers' screams and the sight of the body had left them stupefied.

The Sheriff came up, walking quickly on his short legs, abrupt in movement. He had taken one look into the wagon with his sharp black eyes, his square, grizzled head turning quickly like a bird's, and seen enough.

He sat down next to Mrs. Vickers, his blunt, square hands on the knees of his shiny black trousers, and said, alert and at the same time trying to be gentle, "The hide, Mrs. Vickers. What is the hide?"

"They found it out on the fence line," Mrs. Vickers said, almost sleepily. It was easy to rest there on Mr. Dickson's shoulder.

"Montrose forged the brand," she said. "My husband said so."

The Sheriff looked up at the General, who was standing with Clara, apart from the crowd. "You'd better come over here, General Montrose." The General advanced slowly, and Clara followed. The women and men drew back to let them pass, farther than they need have drawn.

"My husband said it was him branding the cow," Mrs. Vickers said from far away.

"The General himself?" the Sheriff asked.

The General's mouth was tight. He was trying to contain himself.

"I don't know."

"This is—This is—" The General started to say "absurd," but murder was not absurd. He thought of "outrageous" and the Sheriff said, "General, please wait."

"A man shot him," Mrs. Vickers said. "I didn't see his face. He had a red handkerchief. But I saw the brand on the horse. Yes, I saw that." She burst into tears. "I know that one—just like the hide. Montrose's horse, it was Montrose's horse. Oh, my God, my God," she wept, and kept on crying, "My God, my God," over and over.

By now half the men and nearly all the women had left. Only the most sober remained. They looked at Montrose all at once, their eyes steady, wide, and waiting.

The General said, "Why, why, surely—surely you don't believe—Sheriff Bolt, surely this is some trickery—" He shot a look at Dickson. "It is not true. I deny every implication. Why, I was up in my head-quarters all day. I have witnesses. It is simply—simply—fantastic."

The Sheriff looked at him alertly, a small, square, troubled bird. "I rule out now a personal accusation. Nobody accuses you personally, General. But—a man, one of your men—" Immediately there obtruded on his mind the possibility of collusion between the General and one of his men, and he shut it out.

"Mr. Dickson," the Sheriff said, "why does she keep on addressing you?"

"Because I befriended her husband, I suppose."

"Is that all? There's nothing more?"

"I must say I was a witness to the branding," Dickson said, with a troubled look. "Vickers and I rode down his line this morning. You know, I took up his note at the bank and we were discussing some plans. We saw two men at work over a cow—in fact, one of them shot at us. But I have no idea who it was. No idea at all. They turned and ran. We went up to the cow. It was tied. Vickers took off the hide for evidence."

"Where is the Judge?" the Sheriff asked.

"He's home," somebody said. "Sick."

"Somebody get him," Bolt said.

"I'll go," Curtis offered, and waddled toward his horse.

The Sheriff sat still. He detested the presence of these people. It was no longer their business. And yet if he moved the proceedings away from here, he would have to ask the General to come to his office and that would imply an accusation, the shadow of an arrest, and he did not want to imply this.

So he said, "Didn't you see the face of the man at all, Mrs. Vickers?"

"My God, my God," she said rolling her head wearily. "No, no."

"But you saw the brand on the horse."

"Yes," she whispered.

"Someone should take care of her," Dickson said. "Would one of you ladies be good enough to take her to your home?"

Two of the women helped Mrs. Vickers away.

The General was left with a large group of men. They stood silent, and a change came over them, now that all the women except Clara were gone—a quickening of eye and a sobering and hardening of mood.

"I would like to say now—" the General began. "I want to—I deny every charge. The whole thing—this whole thing—"

"What charge?" a man asked quickly. "There's been no charge." This with a gleam of eye, as though he had said something very astute.

"Why, by God," the General said, his own eye glinting, "you know what I mean, and there had better be no charge out of this. It's all a pack of lies!"

"Lies?" the same man said. "By Mrs. Vickers? Is she in any condition to lie?"

"What about that hide?" another asked. "Is that hide a lie? Vickers has been saying for years you were stealing his cattle. Look there, at your brand on it."

"Are you accusing me?" the General asked, his face turning pink, as he took a step forward.

"Father," Clara said from behind him.

He turned quickly. "Get in the buggy."

"Father, please," she said.

"Get in the buggy."

She turned and went.

"Let's have it out here and now," the General said, "and enough of stabbing in the back and tattling behind doors."

"Have what out?" another voice asked. The eyes

were watching him, all except Dickson's and the Sheriff's. Dickson sat there, his face remote, saying nothing. The Sheriff listened.

"Tomorrow it is to be decided by our local judge," the General said, "whether I shall keep my ranch or whether I shall be forced to give it up on the basis of an option agreement which I claim is not valid. Why is it so apropos that I am today accused of murder?"

"Nobody has accused you of that," Sheriff Bolt said without looking up. "Don't exaggerate."

"Don't mince words," the General said.

The Sheriff winced. Why did the General have to make himself unpopular? After all, the Sheriff was in the position of authority here, and should be respected; and Bolt did not want respect for himself, either, but simply for his office. "I am not mincing words," he said stubbornly. "I have not made a charge. All we have is a fact. We have a murder. Somebody murdered Vickers. The murderer was riding a Montrose horse."

"And I say that somebody might be anybody who stole a horse to make it look like me or one of my men."

"And what enemy do you have who might do this?" Bolt asked quietly.

"Any man who might forge an option in order to force me out of my rights, and who might want to turn public opinion against me."

"And who do you mean?" Bolt asked gently.

The General looked down at Dickson.

Joe Curtis rode up, bulging over his fat mare, with another man. The other was a lean, shrewd-mouthed old gentleman with wet eyes and a red mouth.

"I mean Dickson," the General said. "I know, I swear by God, that either he forged that option or else he knows it was forged by someone else. It is not the true date."

"And so you accuse me," Dickson said, smiling faintly, "of killing Vickers. What, if I may ask, is the connection?"

The General stared blankly at him. What, exactly, was the connection? He was excited, he was upset, he could not find it. His mind was suddenly a total blank. Someone laughed, and then another, and his confusion became worse. And yet he had thought of the reason, just a moment ago.

"It seems to me," Dickson said very gently, patiently, without the slightest animosity, "that you are overeager to accuse someone else of a crime. Do you accuse me of it?" He remained sitting. He did not intend to make any attack on Montrose, even to the extent of physically standing up to him.

"Perhaps you have in mind," Dickson said in the same quiet, gentle voice, "that I helped out Vickers with his mortgage, and then murdered him so that I could obtain his ranch."

There were smiles and a few chuckles.

The General stood helpless. He could not think. Somewhere, behind this, there was a reason. Why couldn't he see it? He had seen it so clearly just a moment ago—the reason why Dickson had done this.

"Perhaps you feel that I am so evilly inclined," Dickson said smoothly, smiling just a little, "that the deed fits me too well to go wasting. After all, if I did forge that option, I might be capable of murdering a poor little man I had befriended. But why?"

The General could say nothing. He looked with miserable fatigue at his daughter, sitting in the buggy. Why had they come to this wretched party? Why were politics necessary?

"This accusation," he said, faltering for words because of a weakness that for some reason was undermining him, "this accusation of thieving from Vickers. It was always unfounded. You all know that. The very idea that I—" He stopped. "Do you make a charge, Sheriff? I thought I had reasonable friends here, with a sense of justice to which I could appeal. I shall have to turn to the law."

"General," Bolt said, "you know I can make no charge. There is no accused and not even a suspect. Somebody forged a brand and Vickers was bringing in the hide as proof. Somebody murdered Vickers. He rode a horse with your brand. I could hang the horse—if I could find it—for being an accomplice, and that's the end of it."

"Well, by God," the General said with a great flood of relief, "you are a fair man, Bolt."

"I, for one," the lean, wet-eyed man said from his horse, "would like to state another opinion." He glanced at Dickson and back. Everybody turned, and waited submissively.

"It is my opinion that the option is not forged," this man said.

"That's right, Judge," somebody said. "That's right. We all knew that."

"It is my opinion that it is a valid contract," the Judge said, licking his lips as though he had eaten a piece of candy.

"It occurs to me," the General said in a loud voice, "that you are prejudging a case which has not yet come to trial."

"I am not prejudging it," the Judge said in a mechanical voice. He looked quite ill, as though he were forcing himself to speak while nauseated, as though he had liver trouble, or a very bad hang-over. "I am merely stating an opinion. That does not become a judgment until tomorrow."

The General smiled bitterly.

"Will you appear?" the Judge asked.

"At what?" the General asked, contempt plain on his face.

"The suit. Mr. Dickson has brought suit. Tomorrow morning at nine o'clock."

"How can he have brought a suit, when the option date has not arrived, and I have not yet officially refused to comply?" the General asked.

"Nevertheless, he has brought it," the Judge said, like a gray mechanism.

"And what you have written, you have written. What kind of law is it that borrows so against the future, and assumes what does not even exist?" the General cried out. "By God, this stinks of your own affairs. Your damnable Honor! You always were a borrowing scoundrel, as I recall. Whose debts are you paying off now, may I ask? Whose debts?" He was shouting.

"Here, here," Bolt cried, standing up. "We can't have this."

"Contempt of court!" somebody cried out.

"Is this a court?" the General shouted. "Contempt of nothing! I say it man to man, I smell a stink of borrowing here, I know him to the bone, a conniving rat, a wretch—"

In his fury he was almost beside himself, his ancient cheeks pink, his eyes glittering.

"A pack of scurvy jades, trash, full of your wretched pomp, your civil judgments—I say to you, be damned."

"Be damned, is it!" one voice cried, while the others turned between fright and anger. "We'll see who's damned, by God! Get out, you damned old crow, you're not one of us, you never were."

"Will you respond?" the Judge asked quietly in his dead voice, his watery eyes looking at nothing, or perhaps a leaf upon the dust, his mouth firm and unflinching.

"To what?" the General asked, his voice shaking as his rage receded, letting in a trickle of fear. "Your wretched improper summons? Summons me at the proper time, you judge of nothing." He walked away, past the Judge, past Curtis, toward his buggy.

"Nevertheless," the Judge said, "I would suggest you stay in town overnight, as the trial will open at nine in the morning."

The General stopped, and turned back toward the crowd. "And where," he asked, his voice clear and unmoved, "would I stay, after thirteen years? Which one of you will have me overnight?"

Not one of them answered.

"Which one of you?" the General asked again. "Which man is still left uncorrupt enough to lend me his roof for one single night?"

They said nothing. In that crowd there were, in fact, six or seven who wished with all their souls that they might say something, might sing out, "I will!" But they did not; they were afraid of others around them.

"My friends," the General said. He no longer felt that trickle of fear, as he looked at them. "True friends! A wretched huddle of sheep. So much for politics." He turned on his heel and strode back to his buggy.

He picked up the reins and drove with Clara to the railroad station. He went in and asked abruptly, interrupting Lee at the sender, "Have you got an answer to my wire yet? About Dickson?"

Lee got up without answering, and handed him an envelope. General Montrose opened it with trembling fingers and read, and as he read, his anger and his excitement died. He finished, and his shoulders sagged. He looked once at Lee, hardly seeing him, and his face had become old, with the first signs of feebleness. He let the telegram fall to the floor, and turned and went out.

Lee looked after him. He wanted to cry out. He lifted one hand from the counter, and the cry was at his lips. But he could not. The buggy drove away, and Lee's hand fell. He looked at the paper on the floor, and then covered his face with his hands.

As the General drove up the main street again, his face bitter, he saw one of his men run out of one of the saloons, followed by the others, and then a pack of other men. They were fighting in the middle of the street, and horses tied near them danced and pawed. The Sheriff was running toward them, and other men.

"Already," the General said, whipping up the horse. "They've started already. Those are Dickson's men fighting ours. You see what's going to happen, Clara."

And then, suddenly, it came back to him—the connection between Dickson and the murder, the reason why Dickson would murder a man he had befriended. All Dickson was doing was making it possible to drive the General, without mercy, out of his holdings. He had cast suspicion, and he would feed suspicion, and the General saw the wisdom of this, for suspicion was more dangerous even than a charge, since it could not be answered in court. The suspicion that he, General Montrose, was a murderer, or the boss of murderers, would make almost any act of Dickson's justifiable. For now Dickson could do anything to Montrose and his men and get away with it.

The men had stopped fighting, driven apart by the Sheriff and other townsmen. The General's men had mounted their horses. The General got out of his buggy and, taking his foreman, marched into the one hardware store.

"Give me all the 30-30 cartridges and forty-five Colts that you've got," he said to the clerk.

"I haven't got a one," the other said.

The General flushed. "Then this is the first time in thirteen years you've run out."

"That's true, General," the other said simply. "I was bought clean out this morning. Mr. Dickson bought every cartridge in the store, and it'll be a month before I get another shipment. Why don't you ask Mr. Dickson? I asked him what I'd do with my customers, if they came in; he said, just send them to him."

The General very slowly smiled. His wrinkles were deeper, as though his flesh were shrinking. His eyes had lost their boldness and their light. He was getting back the look he had had in the war, a look of quiet shrewdness and patience. The bombast, the wrath, the ire, all that pap for the peacetime garrisons, was gone.

"Thank you very much," the General said gently and humbly. "When the opportunity arrives, I will call on Mr. Dickson and get what I need."

CHAPTER EIGHT

The Station House
October 9—8:00 A.M.

At eight o'clock the next morning, an hour before the hearing was to begin, Dickson was lying in bed in the Station House. He had sent the word about, the previous evening, that he was ill—nervously ill, he let it be known—and the dear ladies, with a most pitiful rush of compassion, attributed this, as he had intended them to do, to the coarse attacks of General Montrose at the barbecue.

There was not a wife in town who had not become enraged at the dinner table, when told of the insufferable calumnies broadsided by the General at the community as a whole. "Huddle of sheep" was the thing that stung worst.

The next morning some of the more gentle ladies brought Dickson some delicious broth and home-made crackers for breakfast, inquired about his health, and noted, with much cooing, the volume of Keats which Dickson had laid, face down, on the bed cover. They asked him to read them a poem, and in his most elegiac voice, somewhat faint, to be sure, he read them "La Belle Dame Sans Merci."

" 'And there we slumbered on the moss' "—*How daring*, the ladies thought, *to read this in mixed company!*—" 'and there I dreamed, ah woe betide, the latest dream I ever dreamed on the cold hill side.' " Ah, how they longed to comfort this noble young man, as each of them was sure that she alone could do it.

" 'I saw pale kings, and princes too, pale warriors, deathpale were they all; who cried—"La Belle Dame Sans Merci hath thee in thrall!" ' "

He ended his reading here, as the rest of the poem was just so much morbid rubbish, as far as politics was concerned.

The dear ladies left in a body, cackling like excited hens.

He was so handsome in bed!

The Keats had kept everything on a high level, and it was all so deliciously depressing—the poor, dear young man might die because of that vicious beast, the General. There was a furious hiss of horrified whispering all over town. Could it possibly be true that Montrose had been behind that brutal murder?

Mrs. Judge Frank took the trouble to drop in at court, where the Judge was busy brushing his black robes (it was, in fact, the very robe in which he had been graduated from a small college in Kentucky) and admire his astuteness in favoring Dickson.

As for the $2,500 which the Judge owed Dickson for private gambling losses, that had never been mentioned by Dickson. The Judge knew it never would be. How wonderful it was to deal with well-bred people!

Seven of the dear ladies trooped into the courtroom and settled themselves, bringing out their crocheting and knitting. They had been visiting the sick.

Oh, how sweet it was to be charitable to the sick! Especially when they read poetry, and, above all, did not moan, stink, and complain.

By this time Dickson had recovered enough to ride over to the preacher's house, where Mrs. Vickers had stayed the night.

"But you see, Mrs. Vickers," Dickson said gently, settling down with a cup of hot tea which the minister's wife had given him, "we want to do you justice, my dear. Are you sure you can't remember which one it was?"

"But I didn't see. He had a handkerchief over his face."

They were alone in the front parlor.

"Yes, of course, but surely you must have had a glimpse of his eyes. Were they brown, like Fred Hand's? You know Fred Hand, the biggest of Montrose's men. Surely you've seen him dozens of times in town here. You remember his brown eyes? He has a kind of square forehead, with wrinkles going across. Remember?" He sipped his tea, smiling and waiting.

Mrs. Vickers sat thinking, her eyes vacant.

"You remember the man's eyes," Dickson went on gently. "They are round, and smiling—like Fred Hand's. You remember, but of course they would not have smiled while he was shooting. It was a big man, wasn't it?"

"Yes," Mrs. Vickers said, "he was a big man. And he did, yes, he did have brown eyes. Yes, I remember." She remembered nothing of the kind, because she had seen nothing of the kind. In the fury of that moment after the shot, all she had seen was smoke, a blotch of red where the handkerchief had been, across the rider's face, and the brand on the shoulder of the horse. That was all.

But she remembered from other times, Fred's eyes, and the wrinkles, and as she thought, the two images became merged in one image, so that the clarity of the true image of the murderer was lost, forever confused with that of Fred Hand. It had happened, as Dickson knew it would happen—as he was making it happen, like a painter, painting one image over another.

"His hands, as he held the rifle," Dickson went on gently. "You remember Fred's, how big and rough they are. Just the hands for a mean man, a rough man. You remember his ring? That big silver ring with the turquoise in it? The blue-green stone. Perhaps he was wearing that—perhaps you remember it now."

Mrs. Vickers sat trying to remember.

"On his left hand," Dickson said. "The hand that was out in front, holding the barrel of the rifle. Not the hand that pulled the trigger—the other hand, the one nearest you. Do you see the ring?"

"Yes," she said. "Was it? It might have been. I don't remember."

"A blue stone, in silver—blue-green. In the sun, it might have showed. Or perhaps you only saw the silver, not the stone."

"Yes, he might have been wearing a silver ring. Yes, he might have. Oh, dear. Did he? No—no, I don't—But did he?" She put her hand to her forehead. She had imagined a ring on that hand, and now she could not get the ring off the hand, she could not remember it as it had been actually—quite bare. But because the image was now there, she began to see it as the remembered image, and she said, "Yes, he might have been wearing a ring. In fact, I think now I did see something. Yes. But not the stone."

"And he was a big man," Dickson said, passing over this point easily, to something obvious.

"Oh, yes, very big, like Hand."

"You see, it could only have been one of those five men, riding a Montrose horse."

"Yes," she nodded. That was quite clear.

"And he was a big man, so he was either Fred or the General. All Montrose's other men are small. Remember?"

Her eyes lighted, and she raised her eyebrows in surprise. Why, yes, she suddenly realized with pleasure at the thought, that was true. It had to be true. "Yes," she said, "the other three are shorter men. But it wasn't the General."

"No, it wouldn't have been the General," Dickson said, "because the General's daughter says he was up at the house. So who must it have been?"

"Why," she said, again with that pleasure she found in making a logical deduction, "it must have been Fred Hand. It couldn't have been anybody else, could it?"

He left her with this thought. He knew she was imagining Hand's face, and trying it on the face of that mysterious rider, perfecting his forgery for him.

"It was him, I am sure of it," Mrs. Vickers said. "Oh, why didn't I realize it before? It must have been him!" Her voice rose, and grief re-entered. "Oh, how could he have done it! Why? Why?"

Dickson led Mrs. Vickers out the front door, toward the Sheriff's office.

CHAPTER NINE

On his return from Montrose's headquarters, Mike
had been moved from the barn quarters to an empty
room on the second floor of the Station House, and
he had been kept there, with the door locked and
with a guard to watch him.

The room had one window facing the main street,
and another facing the rear yard, and he had been
able to see the party, and hear some of what the
General had said when he was shouting, but he did
not know what was happening, and nobody had told
him. He did not know that Vickers had been murdered. He had seen Clara walking about during the
party, but he had been afraid to wave to her.

It seemed to Mike that Dickson was quietly getting ready for a final battle. At first, Dickson had
had only two men in Warhorse, Spence and Irving.
Irving had ridden back to the herd, and had been
replaced not by one man, but by two. One of these
had in turn acted as a courier, and the other had

simply stayed in Warhorse. As the herd drew nearer,
Dickson had little by little weakened the party of
men riding under Forrest, and added these men to
his force in Warhorse. The closer Buford got to Warhorse, the less need there was for a strong party to
keep him from making off with the cattle. Dickson
could reduce that guard to all but two men, or even
one, and that would be enough, when Buford was
only two days' drive away, for Buford could not possibly escape with the herd when he was that close.

This meant that Dickson would have almost the
whole of his pack in Warhorse on the day that Buford arrived—a strong, rested force of well-armed
men, ready to take on Buford and Tucker, with their
trail-weary crew, who had been riding fagged-out
horses. Meanwhile, Dickson was keeping his growing force of men out of sight down in the barn quarters, and would not allow more than three at a time
to go out on the main street, or into the saloons.

Sitting on his rope bed by the window, Mike saw
the General come into town, this time with a wagon,
and without Clara, and ride with his four men up
the street. He saw the Sheriff come out of his office
and talk to the General, and watched them talk in a
gathering crowd for five minutes. Mrs. Vickers and
Dickson were mixed in it for some reason.

The General turned to Fred Hand, the big man in
the rear, and spoke to him. Mike saw Fred Hand get
off his horse and follow the Sheriff into his office next
to the county court, and he attached no significance
to this. All he could surmise from the crowd was that
they were holding the option hearing. The guard
would tell him nothing.

He sat with his guard, drinking coffee and playing
cards. There was nothing to do but wait. He had seen
them lug the cases of ammunition up to his prison
room the day before, and assumed Dickson had
brought it into town. He had no way of knowing that

it was the town's whole supply. Spence had objected to storing the ammunition with the prisoner as being too risky. But Dickson pointed out that the ammunition was useless to Mike, who had no weapons, and it saved a guard. Dickson had no doubt that Montrose would steal the cartridges if he could. There was a case of 30-30 and one of .45 besides twenty-five pounds of Ffg black powder in one keg and ten pounds in cannisters.

Mrs. Vickers accused Fred Hand in the street, in a cool, steady voice, and the Sheriff adjourned to his office to get away from the crowd. Mrs. Vickers looked at the turquoise ring on Fred's finger, and her eyes lighted exactly as though she had seen it before, on that dreadful occasion.

"The ring," she said. "I saw it."

"Are you sure?" Sheriff Bolt asked, sitting back easily in his chair. He always made a point of looking sleepy at such a moment, it kept people relaxed. He wasn't afraid of Fred Hand, who was a big, easygoing and good-natured fellow, powerful and amiable.

"Yes," Mrs. Vickers said. "I'm sure."

Her manner impressed Bolt. If she had said, "Of course I'm sure," or "Why, certainly, what do you think?" he would have retained a doubt of her sincerity. But her simplicity, her calm, her actual subjective certitude, had a deep effect.

He looked at Hand, and at the General. "How about it?"

"Couldn't be," one of the General's other men said. "Fred was with me all afternoon yesterday, brushing the horses and such, until we went down with the General."

Dickson looked at the other men. "Is that true?"

"Well, whatya think?" one of them asked angrily, as though Dickson's question had been an insult. "Of course it's true."

"You saw them? You saw them together all that time?" Dickson asked.

"Why, yes, of course," the man said, reddening. "How about it, Joe?" He turned to the other hands.

They agreed unanimously. It was this which increased the shadow of doubt in Bolt's mind. None of the General's men had meant to lie, but they had lied. The first one was telling the truth, but the others were lying. Bolt didn't know why.

Dickson did. Dickson had known that the second man had been offended when he had asked him to confirm the first man's alibi—as Dickson had intended that he be offended. To his simple country mind, the question had seemed like an accusation of lying, and he had followed up the second question with another angry affirmation, just because he wasn't going to "let some son-of-a-bitch Englishman make a liar out of him." But this, in fact, was what Dickson had actually done. On a ranch the size of Montrose's, all of his four hands couldn't possibly have been within sight of each other in the middle of a working day, and everybody knew it.

Montrose's men stood there, looking at Bolt, realizing that their unanimity had had the wrong effect. But to retract would have weakened their position still further. So they stood there, angry and stubborn, looking at Bolt. This was what Dickson had wanted—an appearance of collusion.

"But that can't be," Mrs. Vickers said, in the same calm voice. "Because I saw him."

"What about it, General?"

"Well, what about it?" the General asked back. He had been watching Dickson, and he knew he had a war on his hands. If fear of the Lord was the beginning of wisdom, fear of the enemy was the beginning of strategy, and the first rule of strategy was not to commit yourself unless you had the advantage. His damn-fool employees had committed themselves in a bucket. Let the Sheriff answer his own questions from now on.

Bolt sighed. Everybody was lying. It didn't matter; there were whole counties in Montana where nobody had ever been hanged for murder, because of alibiing relatives. Nobody would ever hang Fred Hand.

"Well," Bolt said, "he has been accused, General, and that makes it a legal matter. I can't let him go."

"You can't convict him, either."

"I ain't even going to try to," Bolt said. "But there's got to be a trial."

"All right," the General said. "Throw him in jail. How about it, Fred? Could you stand a few days in the clink?"

"How's the food?" Fred asked.

"Not bad," Bolt said. "I eat it sometimes."

Dickson was happy. He knew he could never convince Bolt by himself that the General was a thief or that Hand was a murderer. He didn't even want to. What he wanted to do was to stir up emotions and suspicions, particularly in the women, and the women could ride rough on their husbands until it was a domestic necessity to concur. Again, it would not be crime or vice that would get rid of the General, but the sanctity of the marriage bond.

The General took off his hat and bowed respectfully to Mrs. Vickers. He left the office without looking at Dickson and, followed by his men, went into the court next door.

CHAPTER TEN

Courtroom Same Day—9:00 A.M.

Judge Frank came into the courtroom and sat down amid the usual gabble, and everybody stirred and resettled themselves. The doors were opened and people kept coming in, scuttling as though they were late for church.

"We have here an option agreement between one Buford Allen and you, General Montrose, by which he contracts to buy, and you contract to sell, your ranch property upon the payment of $300,000 on or before October 9, 1882. It is today October 9, 1882. I have here a record of deposit by Thomas Dickson, acting as agent for and partner of Buford Allen, of $300,000. The court would like to know, Mr. Dickson, is it your intention to buy this property in accordance with the agreement?"

"It is," Dickson said, standing up and smiling pleasantly.

"General Montrose," Judge Frank said, "is it your—"

"No," the General said. "Decidedly not."

"Do not interrupt the court," Judge Frank said. He was doing beautifully. Mrs. Frank beamed at him with approval and love.

"General Montrose," Judge Frank began again, with that smooth, mechanical order of thought which sounded so dead to the ear, "is it your intention to sell your ranch in accordance with the agreement?"

"No."

The Judge shuffled some papers. The mechanism had hit something. Then he recalled what he had planned.

"Mr. Dickson, do you claim that this is a breach of contract?"

"I do," Mr. Dickson said. "I ask that the court enforce the contract with a judgment giving me this property."

"The court," Judge Frank said, "sees no reason why this contract should not be enforced. General Montrose, do you have any answer?"

"The date on that contract is a forgery," the General said. "I do not accuse anyone of anything. I state the simple fact that it is a forgery. I state that the original date was July fifteenth. I state moreover that that date was passed by and the option right forfeited by Buford Allen. I have here three telegrams from Buford Allen asking for an extension of that date, and I offer them in substantiation of my claim. You will note that Buford Allen asks for an extension to September fifteenth. If the true date of the contract was October ninth, why would he ask for an extension to September fifteenth? You will see that the telegram was sent from St. Louis." He marched up to the bench and laid the papers before the Judge and retired to his former position.

The Judge looked at the telegrams. He was obviously nonplused.

The General asked, "How do you explain that,

Your Honor?" He could not help a smile, and this was his undoing.

Judge Frank felt himself stimulated by this prick of scorn, and he said, "I accept these telegrams in evidence but I must point out that they do not refer to any particular agreement. They request a general extension until September fifteenth. An extension of what, may I ask?" He looked up.

The General's face turned pink. "Of the option in question."

"That is not stated here," the Judge said. "Nothing is specified in these telegrams. There is no evidence that these telegrams refer specifically to this particular option. They might refer to some other contract entirely outside our knowledge." He smiled and pushed the telegrams to one side.

"Holy God," the General said, "how many contracts would I have, I would like to know?"

The ladies looked at each other with profound shock. What had burst from the General as a genuine prayer, they took as sheer blasphemy.

"That, I would not know," the Judge said, smiling mechanically with his firm mouth. He blinked his wet eyes twice.

"What kind of flummery is this?" the General cried.

"I warn the General against this sort of language," the Judge said. "Another outburst, and I shall hand down a substantial fine for contempt."

The General turned from pink to red, but he kept his mouth shut.

"I take it," the Judge went on smoothly, "that the General means these telegrams to substantiate his assertion that the contract has been forged. Is that so, General?"

"You bet your damn—" The General stopped himself. "Yes."

"Then we have a question actually of whether the

contract date is forged. These telegrams, because of their lack of specification, do not constitute proof, or indicate anything at all. They may suggest something, but we cannot render a judgment on the basis of suggestion." He smirked. "Mr. Curtis, you have carefully examined this contract?'

Joe Curtis stood up. He cleared his throat and coughed, looked around for a spittoon, and found nothing. He swallowed. "I have," he said solemnly.

"Have you found any evidence of tampering?"

"No, I have not."

"Mr. Lewin, have you examined this contract?"

Lewin stood up. "Yes, I have."

"Have you found any evidence of tampering?"

"No, I have not." He sat down.

"Are these men experts?" the General asked. "I say, let the whole thing go to Helena for judgment."

"The time will come when you may appeal," the Judge said. "But not until I have rendered my verdict. These men are experts in that as bankers they are accustomed to inspect signatures and other writing for validity. I should say they are experts."

"Well, by God," the General said, "since I do not owe them any money, I feel perfectly free to say that I shouldn't say they are anything of the kind!"

"You are entitled to your opinion, but that is hardly evidence. I judge that this contract is valid. Furthermore, there is no reason in evidence why it should not be carried out. I therefore order you, General Montrose, to surrender your title to your property in exchange for the money on deposit in Mr. Curtis's bank."

"By God, you are too hasty," the General said. "Get Buford Allen here. Let him testify as to that date! Mr. Dickson, where is Buford Allen? I have heard he is driving your cattle here. How far away is he? How soon can he be reached?"

Dickson had not thought of this. He hastily sorted

out the lies possible in the situation and said, with an appearance of ease, "The fact is, I am not sure how far away he is."

"That has nothing to do with the case in any event," Judge Frank said.

"And why not?" the General barked. "It seems to me most essential."

"Why, Mr. Allen's testimony could not gainsay the testimony of experts, could it? If he were to say that these telegrams referred to this contract, and that it had been forged, he would be asserting the incompetence of our present witnesses."

For a moment the General stood dumbfounded. "Did I hear you rightly?" he asked finally. "Are you asserting that an actual party to the contract is not a reliable witness to it?"

Judge Frank blushed to the ears.

"The fact of the matter is, if Your Honor will allow me to speak," Dickson said hurriedly, "the fact is that Buford Allen told me that this contract, which you now have, is actually a new contract granted by General Montrose in answer to Mr. Allen's request for an extension." This story had occurred to Dickson as a flash of inspiration. He knew it was good instinctively. It was beautiful.

"That's a damned lie!" Montrose shouted, his face a deep red. "I never granted a second contract."

Dickson looked at the floor and said nothing.

"It is you who are lying," the General cried. "You or Allen, I don't know which."

A murmur of protest rose in the courtroom. The General was being uncivilized. Dickson stood silent, looking at the floor.

The Judge banged on the bench. "I warned you once, General."

"Where is Michael Allen?" the General asked. "He has been living with Dickson. Surely he can give an account of this matter."

"I don't know where he is," Dickson said. "He left town last night. I presume to see his father."

"I demand that his father be subpoenaed," the General said.

"I ask," Dickson said in a humble, quiet voice, "that Your Honor render a judgment on the basis of this evidence, rather than prolong the affair. Mr. Allen is my partner in this matter. I think I can be taken reliably as his spokesman, without subjection to insult."

Judge Frank sat behind his bench and thought. At least, he appeared to be thinking. He looked at the faces of the men he knew, at Dickson, Lewin, Curtis, and all the others. He looked at the faces of their wives, and of his wife. He knew what they were thinking, he could feel it. He could feel easily enough when he was approved by his peers, and when he wasn't.

He knew, furthermore, that nothing in the world would make him more popular, nor more quickly bring the forgiveness of his social lapses and sins, than to follow the judgment of the audience.

"In rendering this judgment," he said, "I have to take into consideration a number of factors. First, we have the testimony of experts that this is a valid contract, and, on this basis, I must rule that it must be fulfilled. Second, we have certain other evidence that this may not be a valid contract, but this evidence needs substantiation which cannot at once be made available."

He paused. During this pause, he was thinking: *Why should Buford Allen testify differently from Dickson? They are partners. Therefore, I can assume that Allen will back up Dickson, and even if this comes to appeal on the basis of new evidence, I shall be in the end confirmed in my judgment. All I have to do is find some justification for excluding that ev-*

idence now, which is plausible enough to please the court of appeals in Helena.

He said aloud, "In the meantime, we have an urgent reason why this judgment should be made now, rather than have the case continued until we can reach Mr. Allen, and that is the expected arrival of the cattle belonging to the plaintiff, an investment which will suffer damage if it is not taken care of properly, care which requires possession of the ranch in dispute. Now, it might be contended that any damage to the cattle could be taken care of in a separate suit. But in considering the general welfare of those involved, and the values at stake, it seems to the court that judgment should be rendered for the plaintiff. For the plaintiff should not be required to undergo certain damage as the result of continuing the case, while the evidence at hand is for him, simply because the defendant makes a claim to have at his disposal certain evidence which in any case would not be in itself wholly conclusive, and which could not be expected to bear the defendant out.

"Therefore the court orders that the defendant comply with the conditions of the contract, and transfer title to the plaintiff this day, and that he make available to the plaintiff all the property, and all access to it, and use thereof." Judge Frank knew the end of his hour had come, and he hated to see it. "Mr. Dickson, have you ready a deed describing this property?"

"I have," Dickson said, pulling a fat packet of papers out of his inside pocket. "It is a transcript of the county record as far as the description goes."

"Have you examined this deed, Mr. Curtis?"

"I have," Joe Curtis rumbled.

"It is an adequate deed?" the Judge asked, pursuing the silly rubrics to the very end.

"It is," Joe Curtis said.

At this point, Sheriff Bolt, watching the General's

face, saw what was coming, and he prudently left the court.

The General said, "I refuse to comply with your judgment, and I shall take this whole matter immediately to Helena. Furthermore, I shall bring a charge of malfeasance and incompetence against you, Mr. Frank. I desire to put Mr. Allen on the stand and force the truth from him. You should continue this case, and you are—"

Frank smashed his gavel on the bench. A tear rolled down his cheek and he dashed it away. He felt no grief—it was simply that the ducts of his tear glands, which drained into his nasal passages, were chronically swollen by horse dander, and would not drain. Nevertheless, he gave the impression of being stricken with grief, and the courtroom rumbled with sympathy.

"Sheriff Bolt!" the Judge cried. "Where is Sheriff Bolt? I fine you herewith one thousand dollars for contempt of court, General Montrose. You shall not leave this court without paying it or going to jail. Where is Sheriff Bolt?"

"If I submitted to this court," the General shouted over the uproar of voices, "I should soon find myself without a head. I shall leave it when I damn well please." His three men got up from their places and stood there. None of them was armed, but nobody moved to stop them.

"Sheriff Bolt!" Judge Frank cried out. "Find him!"

The General turned and walked toward the door. His men followed him.

"Stop him!" the Judge cried.

The General and his men disappeared.

Mr. Dickson said, "I should like to ask the Judge to appoint a deputy in the absence of the Sheriff— Mr. William Spence, a reliable, honest, and efficient man whom I can personally recommend for what duty you require."

"Thank God, yes," Judge Frank said. "By all means, Mr. Spence, you are hereby appointed."

"I also ask Your Honor for an order of eviction, which will empower the Sheriff to oust General Montrose from his holdings. His attitude of hostility makes such action necessary."

The Judge faltered.

Three men came back, leading Sheriff Bolt. Joe Curtis, Lewin, and others crowded around the bench where Dickson was standing. There was an atmosphere of relief and excitement, and their expressions were happy and victorious, and at the same time surprised. The thing had been done, the issue raised, and whether all had been good or not, the General had been told off.

"Sheriff," the Judge said, keeping safely on his bench (not for physical safety, but simply to preserve his official status), "Mr. Dickson wants an order to evict the General. In view of my judgment, it seems to me entirely appropriate."

Sheriff Bolt looked at Spence and Dickson. Spence was smiling pleasantly, and Dickson looked sober and rather regretful at all this.

"The General won't evict," the Sheriff said. "I heard him, out there in the street. He said he'd fight till either him or us was laid out dead."

"He can't talk like that," Curtis said. He looked at Bolt as though he were lying. Immediately the thought flashed from eye to eye that the Sheriff was trying to get out of an unpleasant duty.

"The law must be carried out," Judge Frank said.

Bolt looked up quietly. "That's perfectly true, but there's ways and ways of doing it. The law ain't designed to get people killed. The law is to protect the peace. If I go up there and the old man shoots anybody, it makes him a murderer. I don't want that. There's got to be some better way, some way that don't force anybody into doing anything worse than what's been done. Things are dirty enough now." For some reason he looked at Dickson.

"Very well," Dickson said, giving in easily where he could, as he always did. "I am not a hard man, God knows. You all know that. I don't mean the General any harm."

"Of course," Curtis murmured, patting Dickson on the shoulder. "We know that, Tommy. We're for you."

"So let him stay until he gets ready to move out," Dickson said. "But give me the legal ability to use the place. I mean, let me use the conveyances and the stock, which I will need. Give me a judgment against the personal property on the place, and the ability to attach it and enter. Surely that will cause no trouble. Spence will see to it that no trouble is caused."

"Spence is your new deputy," the Judge informed Bolt. Bolt looked at Spence without expression.

"I will give you a general attachment on all his personal property," the Judge said. "God knows I do not want to precipitate some kind of battle with the General. Maybe in time he will see reason."

"How much time are you giving him?" Bolt asked.

"My herd will be here the twentieth," Dickson said. "I would like to have Montrose gone by then."

"We'll give him until the nineteenth," Judge Frank said. "That gives him ten days."

Bolt said nothing.

Spence said, "Your Honor, I would like to have two more men as deputies. Montrose may try to sell some of the stock. We will have to have men to watch the fence line. There's no telling what he might do to damage the property—or make off with it."

"By God, that's right," Curtis said. "I wouldn't put nothing past the old bastard, after what he said today. Give Spence enough men to do the job, Judge."

Judge Frank asked, "Who do you want? Give me

their names, and I'll include them in the same order."

"Isaac Forrest," Spence said. "Joe Irving. Robert Sheffield."

"Do I know these men?" Bolt asked. "I don't know them by name, at any rate."

"They are all my men," Dickson said.

"It seems to me the town should be represented," Bolt said. "This seems to me to make it a party affair."

"They have worked under me," Spence said. "Since they are only temporary deputies, why not let them be my men? They will do the job more efficiently."

"That's right, they're temporary," Bolt said, grabbing at this straw. He knew he couldn't oppose Dickson and Spence. He knew he was adrift as soon as he saw that the Judge had appointed a deputy without consulting him. "How long is temporary?"

"Oh, two weeks," Dickson said, again giving easily where it didn't matter.

"All right," Bolt said. "Come on. I'll give you your stars, and you will be entitled to wear arms. But I warn you—I shall hold you accountable."

Spence said nothing, and followed him like a lamb.

Spence got Irving and Sheffield and gave them their stars and told them what to do. The General was up the street with his men, and they were loading their wagon full of groceries, staples of all kinds, an immense supply. They had armed themselves out of the wagon.

The General rode off, alone, down to the railroad station. He went inside and sent a wire to Helena, asking for military help and a proclamation of martial law. While he was inside, Spence took his horse and rode back up the street with it. He put it in the Station House barn.

When the General came out, he saw his horse gone

and, in a confusion of bewilderment and rage, hurried on foot back up the street.

He found his men in one of the saloons, having a drink on completion of their job of loading the wagon, and he ordered them outside.

The wagon was gone, with its load of supplies.

The General and his men stood looking up and down the street. Their personal horses were gone, all three of them, as well as the one Fred Hand had used, which they had been leading.

The General saw the Sheriff coming down the street with Spence.

"Sheriff, where is my wagon?" the General said. "Somebody has stolen our wagon and all our horses. Is this some kind of silly practical joke?"

"No," Bolt said heavily. "It ain't a joke, General, it's damn serious. The court ordered us to attach all your personal property. And I might as well warn you, you're to be evicted in ten days." He stopped and looked at the guns on the hips of Montrose and his men. "General, I see you have armed yourself. I trust you will not start any trouble in this town." He knew perfectly well he couldn't get the guns away from those four men, and so he didn't ask for them. "I would be obliged if you would leave this town at once, and don't come back until you're peaceful."

The General looked down at him, and at Spence and the other two deputies behind him. "I don't choose to start a fight," the General said. "But I want at least decent treatment. I want our personal horses back, and my wagon."

"General," Bolt said doggedly, "they were taken on a court order. They are the property of Mr. Dickson now. Take my advice, and don't leave nothing around loose. The only things we can't take are the things you actually got in your hands. Do you understand?"

"But I need the supplies," the General said, his

voice rising. "Keep the wagon, but give me the supplies."

"No," Dickson said, coming up, "not the supplies, General. And I might as well warn you, your account at the bank has just been blocked pending a settlement of this affair, and the stores have been warned about it, so you have no credit in town."

"Are you trying to starve me out?" the General cried.

"General," Dickson said, smiling gently, "I am only trying to get my property. My money is waiting in the bank for you, any time you wish to pick it up and leave. All you have to do is ask for it. Three hundred thousand dollars."

The General flushed. "That I shall never do," he said. "This is far beyond a matter of price or value. I shall never give up what is rightfully mine, or give in to thieves and—for all I know—worse." He turned and started to walk down the street.

"Wait," Bolt said. "I'll lend you a horse." He looked angrily at Dickson, and Dickson realized he had tripped up on something. He didn't know what it was, exactly (actually it was the feeling among these men that to take another's horse was the worst thing you could do to him, legally or not) but he knew he had to put it right. "I'll give you the wagon," he said. "Spence, hurry and get the General's wagon."

Spence ran.

"I'm not a hard man," Dickson said. "I have no intention of being mean about things."

Spence came back with the wagon, at a trot.

"Where are the supplies?" the General asked.

"I said I would give you the wagon," Dickson said. "But not the supplies."

The General smiled bitterly. He climbed onto the wagon seat, and his men got into the back. He drove off without another word.

Bolt was left alone in the street. He wandered

slowly back to his office. Words kept repeating in his head. Thieves and worse; thieves and worse.

He was fundamentally a simple man, and he could no longer follow this affair through all its legal windings. All he knew was that the General, a man after his own heart, was being jimmied out of his property by a set of people whom Bolt did not actually know at all. Who were they? They had been in Warhorse only five weeks or so.

Bolt was different from most of the people in Warhorse. He was somewhat seclusive, like the General, by nature, but he also had a political reason for being so. As Sheriff, he had to maintain respect, and he could not cultivate anyone too intimately, or permit obligations to grow up. He had to keep himself somewhat aloof. For this reason, he knew nothing of the associations of Dickson with everybody else, and he did not share their enthusiasm for Dickson, simply because he had not been subjected to Dickson's influence.

Somebody came in his office door. Bolt looked up from where he was sitting. It was John Lee.

Lee took an envelope out of his pocket and handed it to the Sheriff.

Bolt thought it was a telegram, and started to open it. Lee saw this, and said, "Don't. Don't open it," and left the office as suddenly as he had come.

Bolt looked at the writing on the face of the envelope: *To be opened only in case of my death. John Lee.*

He tried to read through the envelope. He couldn't. He slipped it into the top drawer of his roll-top desk. What crime had Lee done? For of course, people never left this kind of envelope with policemen unless they had committed some crime, or were involved in one. If the fool would only tell him, it could be solved. But that was it—they were all fools, the kind who were ashamed, but not ashamed enough.

At that moment, Dickson was down in the telegraph office, waiting for Lee. When Lee came in, Dickson asked what the General had been doing in there, and Lee told him. He handed Dickson the General's message to Helena, and Dickson took one look at it and tore it to shreds.

Lee said, "I told you a lie, Mr. Dickson."

Dickson said, "I know you did."

"I know all about you," Lee said. "I got the answer from San Antonio."

Dickson waited. It didn't look like blackmail. Lee didn't have the right expression for blackmail. Lee was afraid, his white face weak and stiff.

"I just wanted to tell you, Mr. Dickson," Lee said in a low, weak voice, forcing himself to speak, "that I gave that information to Sheriff Bolt."

"Yes," Dickson said. "Sealed in an envelope. To be opened only in case of your death."

Lee's heavy-lidded eyes opened a little wider.

"Poor boy," Dickson said, smiling. "Did you think I meant you harm? Haven't I paid you well? You're worth a lot of money to me, John. Why should I hurt you?"

Lee's lower lip trembled, and then he wiped at it with his hand. "Why?" he asked. "Ain't I the only one that knows?"

Dickson said nothing. "Perhaps you were wise, John. Anyway, let's be friends." He smiled engagingly. "You don't tell on me, and I won't tell on you."

"Yes," Lee said, leaning against the counter, and looking sick to his stomach. "I guess that's right."

He watched Dickson go without hatred. He was too sick with fear to hate anything, even himself.

That night Dickson sent a rider for Buford Allen, who was at that time presumably crossing the Bad River and going down it to the upper waters of the Big Horn—about 220 miles away. It would take three days to reach him, riding hard, and when the rider got there, Buford would probably be at the crossing of the Big Horn, south of Norwood Creek—that is, if the cattle could be pushed that fast through that country. They could make it back to Warhorse in something over two days. If all went well, Dickson figured, Buford should be in Warhorse by the 15th or 16th, which would give him four days before the herd arrived.

While Dickson had counted on the General's sense of principle to save him his $300,000, he was not quite prepared to push things to an outright war, and he would gladly settle with Montrose for $75,000. He thought that Buford might be able to persuade the General where Mike had failed. In any case, the effort would look well.

He had another reason also, which was that he wanted Buford publicly to state that the option was not forged. It was the only weakness in his case, and he wanted it removed.

And lastly, he wanted to divide Buford from Tucker. Tucker was a strong hand, but like all the Isaacs of history, he was not much use without his boss.

Everything was going simply beautifully.

CHAPTER ELEVEN

The Last Days of Warhorse
October 10–17

During the next six days, while he was waiting for Buford, Dickson did a number of things to improve his position. Indignation was not enough. What he needed in the hearts of Warhorse was fear.

So the night of October 11, the day after Vickers' funeral, he ordered Forrest, Spence, and Irving to take their horses and ropes and break Fred Hand out of jail.

Spence and Forrest, in the dark, called each other by the names of the General's men, and since they did this in whispers, poor Hand could not know that the names were false.

They yanked the barred window out of the frame, and left a horse—one of the horses taken from the General—and of course Fred Hand climbed out, since there is no consideration to a man in jail which is greater than immediate freedom.

If he had refused to run, he would have served the General well, and done Dickson immense damage, but he did not refuse. He climbed eagerly out, jumped on the horse, and dashed away.

Spence, Forrest, and Irving, seeing him pounding out of town, immediately set to work shooting it up. In fifteen minutes—just the time needed for Bolt to wake up, get out of bed and get his clothes on, and wake the neighbors—they had smashed every store window along one whole side of the street and thrown the window displays into the gutter, broken into the hardware store and stolen four rifles, and smashed all the showcases and dumped the shelves in five other stores. They worked fast and efficiently.

Bolt appeared on the scene and fired at them in the dark—there was only starlight and the first sliver of a new moon—and they fired back, and would gladly have killed him if they could.

Two other men arrived with rifles and added to the shooting, and then three more, and by that time the three vandals decided it was time to escape, so they galloped out of town on the Montrose road and, four hours later, came back into town from the other direction, crossing the creek just before dawn and sneaking their fagged-out horses into Dickson's barn unseen.

The next morning, October 12, a town meeting was held in the courtroom, and it was decided to send Bolt up to the General's headquarters to ask for the surrender of the three men (three had been seen in the dark) as well as that of Hand. In the court there was no oratory. The owners of the wrecked stores had come down at dawn and counted up their damage in silence, and they remained in silence. Dickson welcomed this with a sigh of relief, for he knew that this silence in the men and women meant that they were seriously thinking.

They were adjusting to a new conception, which was that the General, instead of being merely a bore, a crank, and finally a senile recalcitrant, had become a positive danger to them all. A couple of them suggested that the General had gone mad. Others thought merely that he could not control the scoundrels he employed. Others ridiculed this, and said it had been an act of vengeance for the seizing of his horses.

But whatever they said, their tone had changed. There was no emotion except bitterness, and under that there was a deep undercurrent of uneasiness. Bolt returned and said he had been met by a shot from the stone fort at the new gate.

The General had denied his accusations. He said that he had fired Fred Hand on his return, as he would not harbor him, since harboring a man who broke jail while awaiting trial would injure his own position. He denied that his men had broken Hand out of jail in the first place, and that they had left the ranch that night at all.

This was greeted with the most bitter derision as a barefaced lie. The General at least could have admitted what he had done. In every heart in Warhorse, that next day, there was an ache for revenge that spread to their backs. That night, all the store owners slept in their stores with loaded shotguns, and Curtis sat in his bank with two cowhands he had borrowed from one of the ranchers. Nothing happened, and this increased their anger, for by now they positively wanted revenge, and had almost hoped Montrose would try another raid.

The worst thing had been the shooting at night. Nobody had been hurt. But it was plain, now, that the General was out for blood, and was taking the offensive. It began to be rumored that he had never been a general at all; that he had been a Confederate general in disguise; that he had been running a rustling business on a grand scale; that his daughter was entertaining all the men in the mountains, etc., etc. Nobody again asserted he was mad, as this would have made him inculpable, and so robbed them of retaliation.

Dickson knew that sooner or later they would begin blaming him, if they didn't get their hands on Montrose—for, after all, it was Dickson who had, by his purchase of the ranch, brought all this on the town. So on the morning of October 14 Dickson sent Spence and Forrest and four other men (by this time his gang had grown to seven) up to the General's ranch and they tore down ten miles of fence in one afternoon simply by roping the fence posts and pulling them down, ten rods at a time. The General evidently saw the dust, or had a patrol out, for at three o'clock in the afternoon he and his three remaining men opened fire on Spence's party, wounding one of them. Spence answered this with rifle fire, and then with a charge, but Montrose was well placed and drove them off with hot fire, wounding another.

The two wounded men were taken back to Warhorse and the ladies fought to nurse them.

Bolt went again to the General the morning of the fifteenth, and was stopped at the old fence line. The guard was a stranger to him, and the General, to whom he had been taken by another stranger, informed him that he had hired two gun fighters to protect his interests.

The General pointed out that the Judge should have continued the case, knowing there was additional evidence, that his ruling was illegal, and therefore any action upon it was illegal.

Bolt answered by saying simply that there existed a state of war which had to be suppressed somehow, and if the General did not surrender and get out, he would be driven out, even if killing was necessary.

The General simply refused to go.

Bolt asked him if he intended to take on the whole town and county of Warhorse?

The General calmly replied: Yes.

There was nobody in Warhorse equal to this decision. They could not match it. But their silence burst out in a bitter rage when Bolt told them, and then Dickson knew he was free to do what he chose.

The first thing he did—the next day, the morning of the sixteenth—was to run off a hundred and fifty of Montrose's cows and donate them (everybody agreed they were his property) to the town of Warhorse to be sold for cash to cover the damages, and to insure any more that might occur. He got away with these cattle with nothing worse than a few shots from Montrose's patrol—a lone man who was riding the line and could not possibly stand off Spence's party nor get to the General in time.

This act greatly heartened the people of Warhorse, and they turned to Dickson as a leader. Bolt, clearly, was incompetent—all he could do was talk.

Judge Frank issued the order to evict the General, dating it the 16th instead of the 19th, and Dickson nobly said that he would hold off, and protect the people of Warhorse, while giving the General the last possible chance to get out. He made it clear that on the nineteenth he would take his men and advance into the General's territory and lay siege to the headquarters. He was trying to avoid a battle with the General, partly for political effect and partly because he might suffer so much damage in forces that he could not easily cope with Tucker, which would soon be necessary.

That night he had Spence kill one of the townsmen, the hardware-store owner, by the simple method of shooting him through a window. Spence then set fire to the house, and to the one next door, by throwing burning tar on the roofs, and in the ensuing shooting—wild as usual—he and his men escaped, after killing a Montrose horse which they had stolen and leaving it for evidence. Thereafter, the people went to bed at dark, or nailed blankets over the windows.

Some of them came to Dickson and begged him to go and kill Montrose. The fear which Dickson needed was blossoming nicely.

By this time, October 17, everybody, including Bolt, had forgotten the original issue.

The last thing in the world they wanted was interference by the military and a declaration of martial law. When Bolt suggested this, they denounced him openly as a coward, incompetent, and even feeble-minded. They wanted revenge—not safety.

On the night of the 17th, Buford arrived, his horse a wreck, and he not much better. The herd was then crossing the Clark Fork of the Yellowstone sixty miles away, and it was due to arrive the evening of the 20th, right on schedule.

CHAPTER TWELVE

The Station House
October 18—8:00 P.M.

The silver of the moon had widened during the week,
and Buford got a general idea of Warhorse as he rode
up the main street behind Dickson's rider, followed
by the packhorse.

He had come because Dickson still held Mike hostage, but he was full of confidence. Tucker held the
herd, and had his orders.

Buford could see nothing of the damage done to
the stores; the broken and gutted windows were hidden deep in black shadows. There was hard frost in
this valley, and his feet and hands ached and tingled
with the cold.

They got down in front of the Station House, and
Buford limped after the rider on his numb feet. Dickson's man went in ahead of him, and the heat of the
big room poured into Buford like whisky. Then he
saw Dickson, standing on the other side of the big
flaming hearth.

"Welcome," Dickson said. "You look magnificent, Buford. A wayward Santa Claus."

"Keep your stupid wit to yourself," Buford said. "I'm hungry. I've ridden my butt off because you wanted to see me. Now what the hell is it?"

"Troubles," Dickson said. "Harris," he called toward the kitchen. "Troubles, Buford. Final complications. The General is pigheaded. He won't leave."

"That's your business," Buford said. The heat was making him more tired than ever. He stood there, feeling unwilling to sit down in Dickson's house. And yet, where else was there to go?

"True," Dickson said. "But I need help. You once mentioned a job on this ranch—as manager. If you help me, Buford, I'll offer you the job and twenty-five per cent of the business. I'll be quite frank. You have control over those cattle. I can't get them against your will. If I try to take them by force, you'll stampede them, and I'll never get them rounded up again. A pity cattle are so nervous! They never get used to gunfire, it seems. Well, Buford, I'm willing to compromise with you all down the line—for your help. How about it?"

Buford said nothing. He just stood there, his beard gray with trail dust, his face brown with wind and sun, his cheeks flat, almost gaunt. "Where's Mike?"

"Harris, get Mr. Allen some supper. Everything of the best. And hurry it up, too. Come in, Buford, you can't stand there all night. Come and sit down by the fire. Have some supper, and then I'll show you your room."

"Where's Mike?"

"I think he's upstairs, in bed."

"Didn't he know I was coming?"

"No, he didn't. I have nine men here now, Buford," Dickson said. "By tomorrow I shall have eleven. I trust the herd is on time? It'll be here the twentieth? The day after tomorrow?"

"Yes," Buford said. "Let's get it straight, Dickson. My man Tucker has orders to start the shooting the same day he fails to get a written message from me. You don't think I came here unprotected, do you? He will break up the herd and start a war on you. Understand?"

"I understand perfectly. It could be quite a battle. But who ever wins a battle? We can both win if we cooperate, Buford. Come and sit down. I really do need your help."

Harris came in with a tray. He had half a rib roast, bread and butter, and part of a cold chicken, with a bottle of wine.

Dickson sliced beef and began making Buford a sandwich.

"I need a man of military experience," he said, busily cutting. "Do try that wine, Buford. It was horribly shaken up coming across the country on those dreadful roadbeds, but it's recovered remarkably well. General Montrose insists on being defeated bodily. Like all men of excessive principle, he is hidebound in strategy, and will not retreat. I can't say I am sorry for his nobility of soul; it saves me a tremendous lot of chasing him about over those ghastly mountains. He has entrenched himself with a force of four men and his daughter. They are nearly out of ammunition. But still, he can hurt us. I need your military gifts. Your rank was major, was it not? At the time of Appomattox? Remarkable word, Appomattox. Sounds quite Aztec."

"At the time of Appomattox, my rank was mud, like everybody else's."

"You have an excellent opportunity to beat General Montrose, Buford. I want you to do it. Our position is perfectly legal." He finished the sandwich and offered it to Buford. Buford took it.

"You want me to drive him out of his place?" Buford asked, and stuffed part of the sandwich into his mouth.

"Not exactly. As I said, I have nine men. I want you to go with Mike tomorrow and try to reason with Montrose, and get him to give up. After all, nobody likes bloodshed, do they? But if he won't surrender, you're to give him an ultimatum. If he doesn't surrender, we will attack at noon the day after tomorrow." He carefully explained the situation to Buford, while Buford ate.

As he listened, Buford began to smile. Dickson watched him relax.

"I thought you'd feel better about things," Dickson said, "when you found out why I sent for you."

Buford looked at Dickson. Evidently Dickson was finding himself a little out of his element—at least he was losing control of the situation enough to ask for help. The tables were slowly turning. If they turned far enough—if he got enough breaks—Buford might even be able to take Montrose's ranch and then turn on Dickson and vanquish him. This seemed vaguely feasible because Dickson seemed so meek and friendly, smiling and making that sandwich.

"I'll think it over," Buford said. "Where's Mike?"

"Right at the top of those stairs," Dickson said. "See you in the morning."

Dickson waited until the door to Mike's room had closed behind Buford, and then turned to Irving, who had been waiting. "Keep a watch down here," he said. "I'm going to let them wear arms tomorrow—but don't let them get away from you. If they try, just kill them."

"What about Tucker and his gang?" Irving asked. "We can't—"

"Suppose you were Tucker?" Dickson said. "Suppose you received a message from Buford that all was well? Suppose you thought the writing might be forged? Copied? What would you do? You can't be

certain, you understand. Would you start the battle
and lose all your boss's cattle? Or would you wait
until you made sure?"

"I guess I'd send a rider up here to make sure,"
Irving said.

"Certainly you would," Dickson said. "And that
would be too late. That's why Buford's arrangement
with Tucker is foolish. He thinks Tucker is protect-
ing him, but it won't work out that way. I'm going
to keep Buford under guard from now on. Tomorrow
you'll send one of the men to Tucker with a message
from Buford—a fake one—that everything's all right.
Even if Tucker's suspicious about the writing—who
cares if he is? He won't just leave those cattle alone
with Forrest; he'll send a man here to see for himself. And that's all the time we need. So you just do
as I say, Irving, and don't worry about Tucker."

When Judge Frank and Mr. Curtis arrived at nine
o'clock to play Boston, Dickson told them of the arrival of his partner, and how his partner would not
stand for any more delay. Dickson had pleaded with
him, so Dickson said, for patience, but Allen would
not hear of it. Allen demanded immediate surrender
by the General, and had sworn that he would go up
and wipe the General out. He was going up tomorrow to deliver an ultimatum. There was nothing
Dickson could do to stop him. Allen was a rather
rude fellow, and had not cared to meet Mr. Curtis
and the Judge. He had gone upstairs to bed, half
drunk.

A feeling of comfortable friendliness enveloped
their lively game. Dickson had not needed to explain
anything. As the day for Montrose's eviction had
neared, Curtis and Frank, in spite of their hatred for
Montrose and the murders committed by his men,
had begun to feel at heart a sense of bewilderment.

The situation was really bigger than their powers, although they would not admit that.

"And the option?" Frank asked. "Will your partner swear to the validity of the option?"

"Oh of course," Dickson said. "That goes without saying."

The Judge and Curtis settled back in their chairs with a deep sense of relief. They were safe. Whatever the Governor might do, upon investigation, if worse came to worst and Montrose and his people were slaughtered, the people of Warhorse would be exonerated completely.

"It's murder," Mike said, after his father had finished telling him about Dickson's plan. A wind had risen in the night, and ice-cold air sifted in around the windows, through the walls.

Buford didn't even hear him. He sat by the little stove in the middle of the room, baking, a bottle of whisky, which Harris had brought with his things, on the floor beside him.

"It couldn't be more perfect," Buford said, smiling to himself. "It's come at last. Two whole years, Mike, I waited in that damned prison camp. He used to come down there through the camp on his big horse and inspect us. General Montrose and his aides and staff. Inspecting the Flower of the South for lice. There we stood shivering at attention, and he—a two-bit quartermaster general—inspected us for lice. They never got rid of the rats, and all winter long the floors were either mud soup or ice, but every month on the dot he would come down and try to find a louse. And of course he did. But he made it such a crime."

"So now you're going to murder him because you had lice and he had none," Mike said from the bed. "He beat the hell out of you in the war, so now you're going up there with a pack of cutthroats and kill him."

"What?" Buford asked. "What did you say?"

"I said, it is murder," Mike repeated quietly.

Buford's face turned red. "It's a legal eviction. Dickson got a judgment!"

"How?" Mike asked quietly.

"Who cares!" Buford cried. "The court's the law here, isn't it?"

"You know damn well your option expired. Montrose says Dickson forged a new date."

"What does Dickson say about it?" Buford challenged.

"He says Montrose sent you a new option."

"Well, maybe the hell he did! And Dickson waylaid it. Maybe it came to San Antonio after we left. It must be good or the court wouldn't approve it."

"Maybe Dickson bought the court," Mike said.

"Why do you argue?" Buford asked. "The whole town is behind Dickson. He's told me. Montrose's men murdered a man here in town. They wrecked the stores. They burned two houses. Maybe Dickson is a son of a bitch, but Montrose is worse. Let Dickson and me beat hell out of Montrose, and then I'll beat hell out of Dickson alone."

"But you're not going up there," Mike said, "and neither am I."

Buford turned and looked at him. "I don't think I can force you, Mike. But I want you. Dickson needs our help. This is our chance. With a decent break, we can get the ranch for ourselves; we can fight Dickson when Tucker comes. That's all I want—this last chance."

"I'm sick of what you want," Mike said. "All our lives we've been in trouble because of things you wanted. Mother wanted me to keep you out of trouble. What good have I been? None. What can I do? Nothing. But I won't work against the General."

"The General," Buford cried. "You sound as though you like the old bastard."

"I do," Mike said. "He's a true gentleman, and that's more than you ever were."

Buford's face twitched. He blinked at his son, and a sudden sense of grief welled up in Mike as he looked at his father's face. "I'm sorry," he said.

Buford took a breath that sounded like a gasp for air. "Yes, but you're right," he said, short of breath, forcing the words as though he had been hit in the stomach. "I never was a gentleman. You're perfectly right." He looked around vaguely, pain in his face. "Mike, what else am I to do?"

"Quit," Mike said. "Leave with me, tonight. We can break out of here, run away."

"Where?" Buford asked, looking around. It seemed to him that the windows were unnaturally dark.

"Back home," Mike said, but his voice was flat. Buford wasn't even listening. "No, we can't do that either. We've brought this on the General, we've got to help him. It's our fault, all our fault. We'll have to help him out. We can go over to him. We'll warn Tucker and go to the General's."

Buford was silent. He was thinking of a place of darkness, not listening to his son. He was thinking of his own father, long ago, preaching in the woods of East Texas, at the little meetings he had held on his circuit, sometimes in a tent, sometimes in a barn, sometimes under the trees. "And there shall be weeping and gnashing of teeth," he had said, and something about casting into the outer darkness.

To be cast into the outer darkness—that was the end of all ends, the vast, final, terrible perishing, the irrevocable oblivion—and yet not oblivion, for there was weeping and gnashing of teeth.

When Mike talked of leaving, this was what Buford saw—outer darkness staring him in the face. He had faced it handcuffed to Keppelbauer that night, and many nights after on the trail. Where was there to go? Suppose he did quit, as Mike said. He would have nothing, no money, no friends, no home. What was he to do? Desert this last promise, the prospect of a ranch, a final home? A place where the woman he loved was buried—a place to live, safe with many cattle, with plenty to eat and nothing to fear. How could he desert this?

And how could this be wrong, when it was so perfectly fitting and proper? For here now, too, he would bring an old enemy to his knees.

In all sincerity, Buford weighed it as well as he could. It seemed to him that his case was perfectly just, and yet, under the bottom of his heart, there was a pit of darkness, an abyss into which he could not look, a profound questioning of all his reasons, of his most basic justifications. How could he look into that? For that would be to question his own soul, his whole life. To question that would be to cast himself up like a leaf in the wind, at the mercy of an unknown judge. For Buford's most profound assumption, the thought which from childhood had been the premise of every judgment, was simply that money was the best thing in the world, the greatest possible good. Of all the people who had listened to his father, there was probably no one who had learned less than Buford. The only thing Buford had learned from his father was that if you were poor, you starved.

So Buford knew he had to go on. There was nothing else to do. How could he turn back? And yet there was something now which dragged at his bones, a dreadful fatigue, which was new to him.

That was it—he was tired, he was old, and he was thin. The fat of his years had gone, and the passions which had lived on the fat had shriveled as his belly had shriveled, and all the justifications of passion were dried and gray.

And yet he had to go on, tomorrow, up to Montrose's.

A flicker of his old resentment rose, and with it a slight sense of pleasure. There would be triumph in that, at least.

With that thought, Buford sighed and thought he was at peace.

And yet, underneath, something, somebody within him was crying out, out of darkness, protesting in anguish. It was himself, the secret part of his mind that knew there was a truth to be faced, but which it was perdition to face, which it were better to die than face.

And he thought this was bodily fatigue.

CHAPTER THIRTEEN

Montrose's Ranch—October 19

In the morning they went up toward the mountains, the old man at the lead, followed by his son, and then by the nine fighters, all silent. A match flamed here, a horse grunted there, someone coughed, but nobody talked in the cold.

They were heavy with arms, each bearing a pistol and a rifle and a belt full of ammunition.

The ground was hard with frost, just barely warming under the thin morning sun, and there was a fringe of ice along the shadowed bank of the creek as they splashed through, passing Vickers' place.

In the rear of the band rode Spence and Forrest, with orders to kill Buford and Mike if anything went wrong.

Buford had forgotten the thoughts of the night before. Now it was morning, and the air was bright and hard as steel. All Buford needed was a saber heavy at his side, and he would have felt happy.

He saw the new gate and the stone fort. A small

puff of white smoke appeared in front of the little fort, and a bullet cracked high over their heads, like a whip snapping.

Buford held up his hand, halting his band, and went forward with Mike, holding up a white handkerchief.

The two of them waited for an hour in the increasing sun, the horses stamping with flies, until the General came down with his other men in answer to a gun signal.

The General had taken his time as a matter of policy, but he was most civil as he let Buford and Mike through the gate, and closed it, and left his four men in the fort. They kept two of Forrest's men under their guns, as hostages.

The General took them into his house cordially enough. He invited them to sit down, and they did so. They sat in silence, looking at each other, the bright sun cutting into the gloomy darkness of the big room, while Herbia went, on orders, and got coffee.

"It's not much good," the General said, when Herbia came back with the steaming cups. He was slightly amused by the ambassadors, who didn't seem to know what to do. Didn't they realize that every worthy war conference should take on the aspect of a ladies' tea party? "We've been brewing the same pot of grounds for almost two weeks. But it is all I have to offer."

He smiled at Buford, inviting conversation, but Buford seemed to be confused and ill at ease in Montrose's actual presence.

"How strange to see you under arms again, Buford," the General said.

Buford sipped his coffee as politely as he could, still finding nothing to say.

"I confess I find a certain pleasure in a state of war," the General said easily. "A pity we never had the pleasure of meeting on the field, isn't it? I expect your memories of me are very bitter; it must be most humiliating to be a prisoner of war; although God knows I did my best to see that you people were kept well fed and decently clean. Cleaner than in the field, at least." He drank some of his own coffee. It tasted like a very weak dilution of church ashes, hemlock, wolfbane, and bat droppings, but it was attaining a certain respectability of its own, purely by virtue of its age.

"It was humiliating to us both, in different ways, I suppose," the General went on, filling the heavy silence. "I resented it so when they took me off the line and put me in charge of that prison camp, Buford."

Buford colored slightly. He felt increasingly uncomfortable.

"No doubt you gentlemen have some final offer for me," General Montrose went on, smiling steadily. There sat the Allens, their faces increasingly dull, apparently unable to swing into the subject matter. "Perhaps I should let you make it. Or perhaps I can save you the trouble. You wish my surrender. I reply I shall not. You then give me an ultimatum"—Buford blushed—"I must be gone by a certain time, or you will attack, well supplied with legal formalities and ammunition. What is your deadline, Buford? When waging war, it is best to get on with it."

"I am instructed to give you until noon tomorrow," Buford said woodenly.

"How well put. You are instructed. The typical military evasion of responsibility. Nobody knows anything but the chief of staff, and he won't be back till Wednesday. You are greedy, Buford. Very greedy." It was suddenly becoming impossible to remain civil in front of that stiff, pink face of Buford's. "I tremble at the magnitude of your gall."

"If you prefer," Buford said, "I will fight you personally with any weapon you may choose."

"And make an affair of honor out of an affair that has no honor, is that it? What a wealth of choice your virtues afford you, Buford. Leave the room," he said suddenly to Mike, his eyes flaming. "I wish to tell your father a few things in private."

"Let me tell you, Buford," Montrose said as the door closed, "that I shall never give up. You know that, and I suppose it affords you pleasure, to get what you regard as revenge. But what am I to say to you? You can win. Yes, certainly, you will win. The best I can promise you is a dreadful damage, and believe me, when you come up that canyon, I will do you as much damage as I can, before you slaughter us. But I shall not permit you to take a false satisfaction in your victory. You are going to know the truth. For you are a fool, Buford.

"You are a blind food, and you are quite capable of going ahead and committing the most atrocious crimes with a perfect blandness of conscience. There are some criminals who know and enjoy their malice, like Dickson, and there are others who commit everything with a most genuine sense of virtue. How well I know you, you wretched little soul. You are transparent because you are simple, and you are simple because you are ignorant. You are a creature of the woods, with simple thoughts."

Buford's face was red, but he made no move. He sat there with his mouth slightly open, looking steadily at the General. The General went on, talking in a fast, low voice, which seemed to be amused at times, and at others, shaking with rage, yet always subdued.

"How satisfying to an empty soul it must be, to revenge its rotten little pride in just this way. It was pride that got you into the war—but never mind all that. But I suppose it is Clara, most of all, isn't it?

That's where your pride hurts the worst. That is the reason, isn't it? Because she is buried out there on the hill. I suppose all these years you have hated me for taking her away from you, for I suppose you have lied about that as well as everything else. That was what you said the last time you came up there drunk, wasn't it? After we were married. That you would get her back, that I had deceived her and lied about you.

"What need was there to lie about you, when you were making a public fool and nuisance out of yourself? But you lied to yourself then, and of course you have lied about it ever since. As though she loved you! As though any woman could long love such a rude, uncontrollable savage.

"But if you think that you shall come here and lord it over my place after killing me, you who covet the bones of my wife like some dirty little maggot, remember when I tell you that she detested your memory, that she despised you for humiliating her by your conduct, and that you caused her nothing but sorrow and grief when you were engaged, and nothing but unease forever after, because she believed you might hurt me—even though I knew you were too much of a coward to do so.

"And if she never visited you in prison, know now it was not because I prevented her, as you accused me, but simply because she did not want to see you. Do you understand? You fool, she loved you once, better than she ever loved me, but you ruined that. It was I who made her happy, it was I she loved in the end."

The General's eyes were weary and wretched. Buford sat in a lump, his face empty.

"I spit upon your dirty little soul, Buford. You come up here like a swine out of nowhere, nothing but a rampant snout, to devour me and gobble up all that I have. What are you but a grunting pig? Full

of desire and appetite, always snouting around after
some new bit of garbage, scheming how to crowd out
your brothers at the trough? What have you ever
done but fill yourself with things? What did you ever
give to anybody else but trouble? Even to your own
poor son, who can't help loving you. Why are you
alive? Why did God create such a wretched mimic of
a man? A true swine, grunting with benign lusts and
witless sentiments, with not a ghost of honor. Now
get out of here, you wretched little comic, and go tell
that swineherd Dickson, your master, I shall slaughter as many of you as I can and as God wills. And if
you win, and live, I command you now to remember
everything I have said, and know that if in heaven
she looks down and sees you maundering about her
grave, she will spit upon you with the angels. For
you are purely of the devil, and there is nothing good
about you at all. Now get out."

The General stood up.

Buford rose and stood still, his face empty and flat.
How should he stand it? For what the General did
not know was that Buford knew that all he had said
was true, and had always known it. All his feeble
roofs came tumbling in, and there was nothing left
on him but dirty rags.

The General turned and left the room.

"So I am saying good-by," Clara said, standing on
the edge of the little canyon, looking up at Mike. "I
am not condemning anyone. What is the good of that?
All these things happen, and God knows who can
sort it all out, the good from the bad—only God himself, I suppose. But I am saying good-by, because—"
What was there left that she could say? She had come
out of the house to say good-by, and all the reasons
for all the good-bys there ever were could not prevent the parting.

He looked down at her. "I love you," he said. Down

across the rushing creek a horse in the corral stamped. "I always have loved you, since the first day I saw you when I was sitting on that porch in Cheyenne."

A cold wind came down from the mountaintops, which were covered now with gray mist.

"A funny kind of love, wasn't it?" she said. "It was there all the time, but it never got anywhere. I was waiting, all those months, hoping you would come. And then you did come. And now it's over. That's a funny kind of ending, isn't it?" She wanted to cry; she knew he was going, but she didn't want him to; so she kept on talking.

"I used to think if things worked out that far, they'd work out all the way, but that isn't so, is it? I suppose all over the world there are thousands of people like us. Things end, they fail, people starve, people are killed, and who ever thinks they will starve to death or be murdered? But they are. And love doesn't always have a happy ending, though I thought it must because it is so lovely. The funny thing is, we are starving now, almost, up here. All the game has gone down the mountain. It is going to snow. There isn't much left to hunt. And we're almost out of ammunition." She knew it sounded odd to keep on saying things were "funny" and yet that was the only way she could express them, and make them speakable at all.

"Well, listen," he said, "I just want to tell you this isn't the end." He looked down at her quietly. "I can't go on with this. I don't know what's going to happen, but I can't fight your father. Do you mind if I call you Clara?" He had never called her anything, as far as he could remember. He had carefully avoided being forward or verbally intimate, and yet it had always seemed silly to call her Miss Montrose, for some reason; so he had called her nothing.

"Yes," she said. "Call me by my name. Go on. I want you to finish what you were saying. All of it."

"I said I loved you." They stood looking at each other. The cold wind sighed in the firs, and the creek talked below.

"I love you, too, Mike."

He put out his arms, and she came into them, and he held her for a moment, not tightly, simply sheltering her, feeling the wind on his back, and her, warm inside his arms.

"I won't let you down," he said. "I've got a kind of plan. I need a derringer. Have you got one? And the buggy."

"My father has a derringer under his pillow," she said. "Don't you want something bigger?"

"No. I've got to have something I can hide."

"I'll get it. He won't miss it until tonight."

"I'm coming back tonight, Clara. I'll take the buggy down to bring the ammunition in, and I'll be back tonight."

She ran for the house.

He ran down the path that led to the corrals, across the creek.

Buford Allen came out of the big log house and stood on the porch. His eyes were dry and sunken. The cold wind flicked his beard. His cheeks were hollow and lined. He listened to the cold winter wind and listened to the words of the General, quite clear in his mind. High above him, as he lifted his beard and looked at the mountains, the dark peaks towered like judgments, hiding in the mist. A scatter of snow fell.

He had never seen anything so cold, nor so great, nor so powerful. The longer he lived, the smaller he got, it seemed to him. His enemy had already won the victory. Was there nothing in the end but to become small, to return, at first a child, then dumb, then deaf, then blind, to nothing?

Everywhere the snow grew, like the dancing of a million tiny spirits, and then it began to die, leaving a fine white powder in the crannies of the blown ground.

Within himself he felt the first faint stir of anger and resentment at the General's words, and he stood there in the freezing air, regarding these sparks with contempt and derision, because he could see that they were the beginnings of illusion, the beginnings of lies, erecting themselves again in his own defense, like snow building and obscuring the towering mountain. It was as though there were two people in him, one swiftly recovering his position with lies, the other regarding this artificer with derision.

He was a swine. All his life he had been a swine. He had the heart of a swine. He saw himself with a snout, in swill, or scheming how to get more swill. It was all he had ever done.

But if he was a swine, what were the others? Were not all men, then, swine? And if they were, what else was there to be?

He suddenly saw his father's face, the wide, white brow, the eyes, big like Buford's, but different—open, understanding, and smiling. What did he seem to be saying, patient and loving as he preached, he who had starved because he had no time to hunt? Nothing. The face, smiling, faded.

"Come on," Mike said from somewhere.

Buford looked down from the porch. Mike was sitting in the General's buggy. "We've got to go," he said. "Dickson's waiting for an answer."

Dickson. Suddenly Buford felt sick. All the strength drained out of his back and he felt like falling down the steps onto the ground. Dickson. All his bones ached.

He went slowly down the steps and climbed into the buggy. "Tie my horse behind," he said in a low voice to his son. "I'm getting too old to ride."

CHAPTER FOURTEEN

The Station House
October 19—At Night

All that day the sky darkened. There was no wind, and the cold grew, and everywhere in Warhorse there was the sound of axes and handsaws as the people hurried to finish up a last bit of woodcutting.

Mike and his father sat in the upstairs room. They had come up from the buggy to thaw out, and when Mike had started to go back to take care of the horse, he had found the door locked. That had been at two o'clock. Mike had spent the whole four hours since in needling the old man, who was sitting again by the stove.

The whisky bottle, so thoughtfully provided by Dickson the night before, was gone. There was nothing to do, nothing to eat, and nothing to drink.

"Warhorse," Mike said. "So this is what we've got, after all these months." He too was waiting for Dickson to come and hear their report, but with a different purpose. The derringer was warm in his pocket. "Last July you were eating oysters in Cheyenne, remember? You almost had your hands on a million dollars. And now you're in a little room, locked in like a tramp in a jail, without a dime. Waiting for a pimp to decide what to do with you. Do you still think you can outsmart the world? Do you?"

In desperation Buford put his hands over his ears and leaned his elbows on his knees. It had been going on for hours. The words came through his hands. Even when he put his fingers directly into his ears, they came through. There was nothing bitter in Mike's words, no resentment, nothing but simple fact.

"All your life you've been trying to get rich. Not just well off, not just comfortable, the way most men do, but rich—stinking rich. Why?"

The old man pressed harder.

"Do you want to lord it over everybody else? Is that it?"

Buford lowered his head still farther and groaned. "Leave me alone," he said. "For God's sake, leave me alone," he said. "Is this why I had a son? So he could shame me in my old age?"

"The same old steamboat," Mike said. "Only this time, you're going to sink with it. You know that, don't you? Dickson will kill us both, just to get us out of the way."

"You're a coward. You're a silly little coward, Mike. He won't kill us." Buford dropped his hands and sat up. "That's what's the matter with you."

"I know Dickson. I've watched him twelve hours a day. He'll kill us both without a thought. Do you remember Keppelbauer? He would have killed us that night, except for our money. He would have killed us the next day, if it hadn't been for the herd. But tomorrow he'll have the herd, and we have nothing left that he can get. He's a devil. And you're a fool. When a devil gets hold of a fool, who wins?"

"You lie!" the old man shouted. His eyes roamed

around the room, seeking for some escape from the constant sting of the quiet words. "I've got ten men and Tucker. I can beat Dickson any day."

"Locked up in this room?"

"I'll get out. I'll get a horse."

"Try the door. The horses are all in the barn, down by the bunkhouse. Try."

Buford rubbed his face miserably. "Tucker's got my orders. I haven't been able to send him a message today. He'll come tomorrow. He'll know something's wrong."

"Did you tell Dickson about this message-sending plan?"

"Of course I told him," Buford said. "To warn him."

"Well, if you told Dickson, he sure as hell has figured out some way to outsmart you by now. Tucker'll never show up. Or if he does, it will be too damned late. Don't you know Dickson is smarter than you by now? Smarter than all of us put together?"

Buford got up suddenly and ran to the corner where the firewood was stacked. He grabbed up a piece and turned on his son. "Shut up," he said in a lower voice. "I can't stand any more. If you don't shut up, I'll beat you, I swear it. I haven't beaten you for fifteen years, but I can do it again."

"Go ahead," Mike said. "Why don't you kill me? That would put you in good with Dickson, and maybe he'd give you Montrose's ranch after all."

Buford moaned and turned away. He dropped the piece of wood on the floor and sat down again, covering his ears.

"What about Montrose?" Mike asked. "Haven't you got any feeling at all for him? You've brought all this on him, absolute ruin. He can't possibly escape. Wouldn't you feel better fighting for him? After all, if we're going to get killed in this business, we might at least get killed trying to make things right.''

Buford sat still, trying to ignore the voice.

"Why not admit it's our fault," Mike said. "You started it, and I kept you going. So why not admit it? Why not do what Mom's always talking about? A little penance for our sins. A lot of penance for our sins. They used to teach us that at St. Mary's. We'd have to pay for everything wrong we did, even if we got forgiven. So let's pay. You know something? If we went up there and helped old Montrose fight off Dickson—even if we get killed, which we probably would, it might keep us out of hell."

The old man made no move.

Snow began to fall. Mike could see the hard little pellets, coming down dry and tiny, bouncing off the window sill into the growing dark. It must be about seven o'clock.

"There ain't no hell," Buford said, remembering his father in the tents and barns, and all the hell-fire sermons he had heard and hated.

"You can't prove it. Suppose there is? Suppose it's a hundred-to-one shot. A thousand-to-one shot. For God's sake, do something decent for somebody else for once in your life."

"Didn't I give you the Remington pistols?" Buford suddenly shouted, at his wit's end.

"No," Mike said.

"I did, I did, I swear I did."

"No, you didn't," Mike said quietly. "You said you were going to, and I guess you dreamed it up that you did. But you never actually did."

"Oh, Jesus," the old man said, and put his hands over his face.

Mike shut up. His throat ached with talking. He'd done all he could. There wasn't anything left he could say, he'd said everything twice.

He felt the derringer in his pocket.

Mike went to the window. The horse and buggy were still below, there in the street. There wasn't a single reason in the world why Dickson's people had left that horse out there in this cold, but they had. Maybe because it was in front of the house, and the hands kept to the back.

Feet came evenly up the stairs, a key turned in the lock. The door was kicked open. Harris came in with a big tray. The smell of hot food filled the room.

"Well, well, Harris," Buford said, with feeble warmth, the light of fakery arising in his old eyes.

Mike looked at his father distantly.

In the end, what could a man do? As he had thought in Cheyenne, Mike thought now, a man couldn't just kick his old father in the teeth. It was true, children had to overlook the faults of their parents when they grew old, and help them when they needed help.

But there was a limit, and he had passed it long ago. No child ever had the right to condone or excuse or help a parent in sins and follies. His father wouldn't come. He was still lost in some delusion, he couldn't see the truth of what he was doing, and he couldn't be stopped. So, standing there by the window, watching Harris serve the food from the serving dishes to the plates, watching his father's face, he said good-by in his heart. There was no good crying about it. The older you got the less crying you did.

Dickson came into the room—he had come up the stairs without a creak, like a cat—and watched Harris finish serving.

"Eat! Eat!" Dickson said. "Come on, Mike, a man needs food before the battle, and tomorrow we fight. Tomorrow you lead our forces."

Mike looked at him and said, "A good idea."

Harris went out, and Dickson closed the door. "I

just thought I'd come up and go over our plans, gentlemen. I suppose Montrose refused to budge."

Buford nodded. "Absolutely."

All Buford did was nod and listen, as though approving what Dickson proposed. The main body was to go up the main road and engage Montrose in a fight at the stone fort, and two men were to go up each side of the canyon and take them from the rear. However it developed, whether the fight was at the fort or at the house, there was to be no open assault by Buford, and no retreat by Montrose. The whole plan was based on Montrose's tendency to stick and fight a pitched battle. Wherever it happened he was simply to be surrounded and kept under slow fire until either killed or forced to surrender for lack of food and water. If he fought from the house, he was to be burned out. He was not to be permitted to surrender, but was to be shot on giving himself up. Dickson was quite carried away by the prospect.

Buford balked at the idea of murdering Montrose after his surrender, and Dickson allowed this change.

It didn't matter to Dickson. The only reason he was up here at all, talking to these fools and disclosing his intentions, was simply to make sure that Buford and his son got out in front, where they could be easily dispatched by Forrest at the beginning of the fight. Why not accede to Buford's scruples? By the time the General gave up, Buford would be dead, so the General could be murdered without hurting anybody's feelings. And, of course, Buford, dead, would take the blame for all the violence and, as a corpse, would hardly care.

"That's a fine plan," Mike said. "An excellent plan. But I'm going to change it." He put his hand into his pocket and casually took out the derringer.

Dickson saw it, and he turned pale, his face stiffening. "How careless of me," he said in a cold voice. "I might have known something like this would happen, with a woman mixed up in it. You were always unstable, Mike."

"Keep your mouth shut," Mike said. He spoke in a quiet, steady voice, not wasting an ounce of energy. "Please understand me, Dickson; if I did nothing but kill you now, I would do a tremendous good. If I killed you now, I would put an end to this whole thing, but your people would get me and my father for it, so I'd better wait for a better chance. But remember, I will do so with pleasure, if you make a single sound. Do you understand?"

Dickson looked at the two barrels of the derringer, and then at Mike's calm eyes.

"I understand perfectly," Dickson said.

Buford simply sat and stared, his mouth full and open.

"Now, listen," Mike said. "We are going down the stairs, with you just in front of me. You will be carrying the case of rifle cartridges, and I will be carrying the other. I warn you now that if you make a single sound or a single sign to the guard, I will kill you on the spot. Do you understand?"

"Yes. I understand perfectly."

"You will go out the front door in front of me. You will put your case in the buggy, and take the reins. I will put mine in, and get up beside you. You will then drive the buggy out of town on Montrose's road. And don't forget, at any time, I shall be most pleased to kill you. My only difficulty is that scruple about murder."

"The Christian ethic," Dickson said, "prevails again." He was getting used to the gun, and cheered up. "I advise you to kill me, my dear boy. If I ever get back, I shall make it hard indeed upon your old father. I take it you are joining Montrose with all our ammunition. For that alone, I would have all his teeth pulled out with a pair of pliers."

"You take it, and you have got it. You can do with

my father whatever you please. Whatever you do, he's got it coming."

"What's that?" Buford asked.

"I'm fooling, Buford," Dickson said. "Just fooling."

"Will you come along with me?" Mike asked Buford politely. "I don't intend to argue that matter any more. Make your choice."

"You're a fool," Buford said, his face turning red. One fact in this crisis stood out in his mind. He might lose the ranch. All scruples and pangs of sentimental conscience had vanished in this pinch. In his heart, he hoped Mike would kill Dickson out on the road. "I am not coming," Buford said.

"He's just a boy, Buford," Dickson said. "He'll get over all this. I'll forgive him. Best be patient. Best be calm."

"Get up, Dickson," Mike said. "Do what I told you to do."

Quietly and obediently, Dickson went and lifted one case of cartridges. Mike took the other and managed to get it up on his hip. Dickson opened the door and went down the stairs. Mike followed him, keeping as close as he could so as to keep the guard from seeing the derringer.

Sheffield was on duty. He watched them without a move, Dickson in front leading the way out the door, Mike following with the other case. There was no sound, no movement on Dickson's part, that Mike could see, but he knew Dickson had made some signal, probably with his eyes, because he could see Sheffield stiffen and sit forward slightly.

The snow was falling steadily, still the fine, blizzard pellets, almost ice, granular underfoot. In the dim light from the Station House windows, Mike saw Dickson climb into the buggy, and he followed.

"We have no lights," Dickson said with some satisfaction.

"You get the horse on the Montrose road," Mike said. "He knows his way home."

Dickson flapped the reins gracefully and they went off down the street.

Two hours later the snow eased and stopped. The night was perfectly still, but no longer perfectly black.

A fat slice of moon appeared, and suddenly the whole country was almost blazing with its cool, serene light, glittering on the icy snow. At the same time, the air became sharper, colder, and tiny sounds became audible—the very distant barking of a dog and coyotes, coming through the creaking of the buggy wheels.

Then he heard Sheffield, far behind.

"Pull off the road," Mike said. "He can see us now, and he's probably got a rifle. I'll have to ambush him." They were going along the creek. "Hide the buggy behind those willows," Mike said.

He got out of the hidden buggy. "Lie down on the floor there," he said, and Dickson obeyed.

Mike waited with the derringer. The faint sound of hoofs came nearer. He kept in the trees until the rider came into view, keeping the gun on Dickson's prone body until Sheffield was almost abreast. Then he swung the gun and, taking as careful aim as he could in the moonlight, he fired.

Sheffield stood up in the saddle. The horse bolted from under him, and he fell into the road. Mike leaped on him and held the gun against his forehead. Sheffield was dead. The bullet had hit him in the ear, eighteen inches above the point of aim. It was just so much luck he had been hit at all, as Mike knew it would be, with that little gun, but he was hit and that was that.

He took Sheffield's arms and his mackinaw and laid them by the wheel of the buggy.

"Get out," Mike said. "I am going to enjoy myself,

for a change. Perhaps it is my memories of Joanne and Keppelbauer, and the rest of those pigs. It is probably that I am part swine myself, Mr. Dickson. But I am going to mark you, permanently.

"Before I do, get something straight. The General and I are going to fight you, and keep on fighting you. You're depending on him to get cornered. But I'm going to change his mind. You won't catch us in any house, or any fort. There won't be any siege. We'll let you have the place, and pick you off one by one from the trees. Do you understand? In other words, you're getting a war, not a battle. And more than that, if you try to run Tucker's herd in there, we'll run it out again. We'll run you and your damned cows to rags. It's you who'll be burned out of your houses and shot as you come out of your doors—not us. Because as soon as I get to the General, I'm going to make him put you on the defensive. And as soon as I get the warrants from San Antonio, you'll be hanged. What ever made you think you could win, in the end?"

In the snow he beat Dickson, hammering him until he was helpless. Dickson was no fist-fighter. He made a few aimless swings, and collapsed.

Mike picked him up, and with one precise and well-balanced blow, smashed his nose flat on his face.

Dickson lay in the road, his blood black on the moonlit snow.

"It's only about ten miles back to town. If you get up on your feet before you freeze to death, you can make it by dawn."

He turned and went back to the buggy. As he drove it back onto the road, he stopped for a moment and looked down at Dickson, who was sitting up, his nose still bleeding. It would never be aquiline again.

"I'd hate to see you freeze before I got the chance to shoot you in a fight," Mike said. He threw down the mackinaw, and drove off toward the mountains.

Dickson sat there in the powdery snow, his nose hurting as nothing had ever hurt him before. The cold was freezing it. He got up and put on the mackinaw. He stripped the jacket and the shirt off Sheffield's body, and held the shirt over his face. Looking down at the body of the servant who had failed him, he was overcome with fury. He kicked the corpse as hard as he could, kicking the head this way and that, and if he had had any kind of a knife, he would have mutilated it.

Panting, he staggered off down the road toward town, moaning slightly with the pain of his nose and his beaten body. He hurried as fast as he could. Certain changes would have to be made, quickly.

CHAPTER FIFTEEN

Buford's Prison—Same Night

Buford had gone to the door, which Mike and Dickson had left open. He had stood there, his mind empty, and watched Sheffield come quickly up the stairs, gun drawn, and close the door in his face.

He sat down on the bed where Mike had been, and listened to the silence, and then to the wheels of the buggy creaking away. The stove glowed hotly in the middle of the room, its heat fiercely penetrating the air for about six feet on each side, where it died against the solid wall of freezing air.

For a long time Buford sat there, thinking of nothing, looking at nothing, and then, very slowly, like the trickle of icy rage melting, loneliness crept in and he sat silent, wondering at it.

Where was Mike? He looked around. It was a senseless question, he knew quite well where Mike was, just then. But he looked around and asked it, because suddenly Mike had gone in a new way, and for the first time in his life Buford realized that Mike

had never really left him before and that he had
never been lonely.

And now the presence was removed, the Mike who
had been holding his elbow for years, who had never
let him stumble—unimportant Mike, amusing Mike,
the slightly contemptible Mike; for, of course, he had
abused him in a casual way, and nobody can help
feeling contempt for people they can abuse, even
when they love them.

Mike was gone, not sent but departed of his own
will. Mike had left him.

He looked around the four walls, freezing in the
icy air. Where were they, that he had never seen
them before? As he was for the first time alone, for
the first time he began to feel something new, a
slight fear of the world itself. Suddenly the world
was smaller, sharper and clearer, and these walls,
which he had simply taken for granted, now took on
a strange aspect, as though slightly threatening. He
was lonely and he didn't know it, because he had
never been lonely before. He was surrounded by the
world, and there was no fellow at his back.

Mike, Mike, he kept saying over and over inside
himself, the unspoken, inaudible spiritual word repeating like a cry, as though in him there were a
soul, stranger to himself, groping in a dark place,
crying the name of a friend who had gone. *Mike,
Mike;* crying down the unseen corridors of an interior world where all the true things finally happened, not confusedly as with the broken and
accidental images of the outside world, but simply
and completely. *Mike, Mike;* crying backward
through all the lost years, and he could not remember a time where there had not been Mike, somewhere near by, following, listening, serving.

Now and then a heavy billow of wind, coming out
of nothing, smote the house, and it creaked. Trees

popped with the frost, and the fire in the stove shook
and fell, sighing and spitting. The red was darker,
and Buford got up and added more wood to it.

He stood in the middle of the room, listening. For
what? To the silence. It was a new silence, a death,
there was nothing but silence and the cracking of
the trees. Silence was nothing, and into it the heart
spent out, and died.

And Buford began to weep, partly with loneliness,
with age, with weakness and fatigue, and partly from
simple self-pity; but mostly because of shame and
remorse, as he looked back on all those dead years,
and remembered all the things he had not given his
son, and all the things he had not done for him, in
his pride and his vanity and his self-centeredness.
The son was always a shadow, following faithfully
and with devotion. Not a face full of love and gratitude, with eyes shining, clear and well-remembered,
but a shadow.

And there was nothing that could be done now. It
was all too late. All the times for giving had passed
and Mike was gone.

He was gone indeed, and if he had died, the going
could not have been more complete.

He remembered him suddenly, in short blue pants
and a white shirt, getting into a rowboat on the
river—he must have been about four years old, or
five—scrambling into the boat with four other boys,
shouting and laughing, and starting away down the
green water toward St. Mary's, where they tied up
the boats every day, and went to school.

He remembered the tiny body when Mike had been
born, and how Mary had held it, and loved her one
baby, smiling. And always, wherever he had gone,
there had been Mike, following along, slowly growing bigger and bigger, joked with, and yet hardly
noticed, talked to, and yet never heard, a kind of

smaller shadow. Little by little, a bigger and bigger shadow, which gradually had begun to hold him up.

Buford sagged, sitting alone like an old bag of potatoes on the edge of the rope bed. Mike was gone, Mike had gone.

He got up in a sudden fury and seized a piece of firewood and, in simple tantrum, flung the chunk against the wall. It shook the wall, bark flew from the chunk, and it fell with a heavy thumping; and afterward, there was the same silence and the same cold, and he stood again, listening to nothing.

All kinds of things suddenly beset the old man, shame, a vision of himself hopelessly entangled in the final ends of his own shameful weaving, a sudden vision of the future opening before him and closed out again by panic, a shaking of anger, a weakness of despair.

He slipped off the bed and sat on the floor, resting his head on the edge of the bedframe, his eyes shut. A vast whirl of things flew up, like leaves in the winter wind, visions of things past, of dreams and plans, of money lost, money sought.

The cold crept up through his buttocks, and his bones ached. He let them ache, and damned them. There was nothing to get now, with which to glut himself, no hope left; he had nothing left but the stinking corpse he had tried to fill up, a rotten, feeble existence which he had once vaunted and adored. What was this, sitting on the floor? Just garbage, fit for hogs, and he was nothing but a mockery for thieves and swindlers to laugh at.

He fell on the floor and put his forehead on the dirty boards, and said, *God help me. My God, I will not get up, I will die here on the floor, unless you help me.*

And then he remembered his little suitcase, very clearly.

He got up. *What? What?* He asked himself in surprise. He was going to do something, but he hardly knew what it was.

He went straight over to the little suitcase. He was still surprised. He did not know what he was going to do, and yet he also did know, before he did it, and he did it with quiet purpose. He moved with extraordinary ease, without fatigue, with a smoothness and certainty which he had not felt for years, and picked up the suitcase.

He set it down on the bed and opened the door of the stove. He opened the suitcase, and without any emotion whatever, with just a simple, clear purpose, he put the picture in the fire, and the letters, one bundle after another, until the suitcase was empty. Then he closed the suitcase and set it on the floor.

He watched the picture and the letters burn up and crumble, and closed the stove door.

And then he knew he had to follow Mike; all the clouds of illusion parted and he saw what was really at stake, with a sober, simple common sense—not a few thousand animals, a piece of the earth, or money, but something much simpler.

He looked down at an internal vision of a great black chasm at his feet, the edge of murder. If he went forward he would fall into nothing, darkness forever, crumbling, dissolving, hating himself forever, utterly ruined. What he had been about to do could not be repaired, and ruining Montrose would not have been a means, it would have been an end. And he himself would have been lost in the dark, where cattle and money whirled like dust, with all the other vanished illusions. The thing that was at stake was simply himself, his innermost being.

He walked to the door and tried to open it. It was

locked. He shook it. He threw himself at it frantically, trying to smash it with his shoulder.

Outside, a voice said, "If you don't stop doing that, I'll come in there and beat you over the head, old man." It was Irving.

Buford knelt by the door and held his head in his hands.

CHAPTER SIXTEEN

The Station House
October 20—6:30 A.M.

My dear General Montrose, Dickson wrote on his very best rag paper, as he sat exhausted in the big room of the Station House, barely able to move the pen with his still-numb hands. *I have come to realize the impossibility of pressing our present situation* (what he meant was "inadvisability" but he decided to throw the General a bone or two) *and I would like to meet with you in the presence of the citizens of Warhorse to try to make some kind of settlement of our difficulties.*

Surely we both must realize by now that to pursue our present course must end in disaster for all concerned, and that neither of us can expect to gain. May I suggest, nay, entreat, that you and Mr. Michael Allen come to town this afternoon for a public or private discussion of our difficulties. I will arrange a meeting with the town leaders for four o'clock.

As to what may be proposed, I am of completely open mind. I have not permitted myself to formulate

*any demands, but continue to hold in first esteem the
needs of the public welfare, with the single purpose of
preventing bloodshed. Most sincerely, Thomas Dickson.*

He stopped shaking with the cold, and sleep was
fogging his mind, together with the pain of his broken nose. He had staggered into town at six o'clock,
and the town doctor had come and stuck padded bits
of shingle up his nostrils in an attempt to straighten
and raise the wreckage of that once-classic feature,
and he had become slightly habituated to the intense
ache.

It was now half past six. Dickson sealed the letter
and handed it to Spence. "You waste any damn time,
Spence," he said, by way of godspeed, "and I'll cut
off your silly ears." Spence went.

Moving with legs of lead, Dickson followed him
and watched him gallop off down the street with the
letter. Dickson felt as though he were about to drop
through the floor, and doubted if he could make it to
his bed; but it would be noon before the General got
the letter, and he would be able to cope with the
situation again by that time. Dickson started to shut
the door, and then saw something which drove all
the fatigue straight out of him, and left him cold
with alarm.

Lee was sitting on the steps of the Sheriff's office,
his head in his hands. From the position, from the
very fact that he was sitting there, alone in the dark
of dawn, waiting under the morning star at the Sheriff's place of official business rather than going to his
house, Dickson knew everything. The fool had gone
noble and was going to confess. And like all the am-
ateurs there ever were, he was bungling it.

In a fury that almost blinded him—there was a
limit to what a man could stand in twenty-four
hours—Dickson frantically searched the room for a
pistol, found none, and ran to the kitchen for a knife.

He ran out of the house holding it under his coat. He slowed to a walk as his panic faded—there was nobody around to see anything.

As he approached Lee, sitting huddled on the snowy steps, apparently in a stupor of self-abnegation, Dickson managed to smile.

"Up early, John," he said, coming up. "How about a cup of coffee, old man?"

Lee looked up at him with eyes dull with shock.

"I—I—" He looked around. "Oh, my God."

"A damned shame I was awake so early," Dickson said. "For you, that is. Come along, dear boy." He was trying desperately to keep on smiling. "Come along and we'll think things over." He showed the knife and glanced hurriedly around. There was still nobody about, but there was no telling when the miserable rodents would come out of their holes.

Lee looked at the knife. "You wouldn't dare," he said, and the dullness of his eyes cleared a little with a kind of shivering confidence. "You wouldn't dare. You know he has that letter."

"My dear boy," Dickson said, hardly able to withstand the impulse to whip off one of the fool's ears, out of sheer spite. "I know very well Bolt has the letter. I searched his office last week and I couldn't find it. But I shall never harm you. I merely want you to come in out of the cold, John."

"No," Lee said, "you don't dare kill me, and I won't go with you."

"Listen to me, my dear boy," Dickson said, moving up close, his bloodshot eyes glaring on each side of his swollen nose, which was now a pitiful blue, "I am reaching the point where I would kill you for the sheer fun of it. If you force me, I will knife you to death here in the street and burn the Sheriff's office and get your silly letter that way. I shall then break a window in the bank, and swear I caught you trying to rob it. The silly asses will give me a medal for killing you. Now, come along."

Lee stood up, his face wretched, his confidence gone.

"Never fear," Dickson said. "I won't harm you— until I get that letter." He put the edge of the knife suddenly across Lee's bare throat, and pressed the edge against the skin. Lee made a peculiar choking sound, like the squawk of a chicken seized from a roost at night.

"Walk," Dickson commanded, and put the point of the knife in Lee's side.

Lee walked. Together they went back toward the Station House, Dickson's left arm around Lee's shoulder in the most companionable manner, his right hand holding the knife against Lee's ribs.

He drove Lee up the stairs to Buford's room and locked them in together. Then he sent Irving for Forrest.

When Forrest came, Dickson was standing in front of the fire, trying to keep his eyes open in order to keep from falling.

"Forrest, there is a change of plan. Mike Allen got away last night. He killed Sheffield. He might be coming into town this afternoon for a peace talk. You take two men out and wait on Montrose's road for them, and when they come, if they come, kill them. Take shovels with you. I want them buried right there. No bodies, no questions.

"Now, send two other men to wait on the road south out of town. They might come that way for some reason. Not likely, but possible. And three men to the north road. I want all Montrose's people ambushed and dead before anybody sees them. If they happen to come in any other way, I'll be waiting for them with two parties, one in the hardware, one in the library. Send two men to each of those places now, Forrest. And don't fail. If any of them get by, or get away—" He moved up close to Forrest, his eyes glaring, and Forrest instinctively backed away from the ferocity he saw in those two eyes.

He turned and, wobbling on his spent legs, headed for his bed.

CHAPTER SEVENTEEN

Buford's Prison
October 20—7:00 A.M.

Buford and John Lee were standing behind their door, listening. Dickson's words, though somewhat distant, were clear enough.

Lee and Buford looked at each other.

"One of us had better get out of here," Lee said. "One of us has got to warn the General."

Buford looked at his little suitcase and rubbed his cold hands together. There was not much wood left, and he was saving it. His hands trembled. In the growing morning light, hungry and still tired, he felt older than ever. "Maybe Montrose won't come down," Buford said. "Surely they're not fools enough to trust Dickson."

"Aren't you a fool?" Lee asked.

"What?"

"If you weren't a fool," Lee said, "you wouldn't be here, locked in. The whole town's fools. I'm a fool. Why shouldn't they be fools? We're all used to believing people. Dickson made us all believe him. Fools."

"And how did you get in here?" Buford asked, rubbing his trembling hands continually. "What was your particular folly?"

"I sold my soul," Lee said. "For three thousand dollars."

"Is that all?" Buford smiled, a wintry, old man's smile. "Have you got the money, my boy?"

"Yes, God help me, I've still got the money," Lee said, looking far off through the window with sad, half-closed eyes.

"Then I'm the biggest fool here," Buford said, "because I sold mine for a million, and I haven't got a damned dime. But I don't think Mike's a fool. He ran out, last night. A good boy."

He looked at the little suitcase, and suddenly gave it a kick, sending it bouncing across the dirty floor. "A good boy." He walked around the room restlessly, grinning in his old man's way.

"If I could get out," Lee said, "I could tell the Sheriff. I wish I had let him kill me in the street. It would have been better. The Sheriff would have found out." He told Buford about the letter he had given to Bolt.

"Maybe I could tie those blankets together and get down from the window."

"There's another window below," Buford said. "You'd go down your blanket and the guard would see you. You think they haven't thought of that? The only chance you have is to jump and run like hell. It's fifteen feet down there. You might break a leg. But you might not, either."

"You see," Lee said, "if it hadn't been for me, none of this would have happened. I thought I was poor. I thought I had to have more money."

"You did?" Buford said. "Isn't that funny. All my life, I've been thinking I was poor. It's the great

American crime, being poor. We both had the same thought, and now look at us. Pigs in a pen." He snickered. "Two skinny swine. Have you got a knife?"

"No. What are you going to do?"

"I was going to try to cut the lock out of that door. No good jumping out of the window and breaking a leg. If we had a knife, we could start to work and cut the lock out of that door and get out."

"How long do you think we've got to warn them?" Lee asked. He was standing at the window.

"Afternoon. Maybe three o'clock. They couldn't get a message and get down here any sooner. One of us has got to jump," Buford said. "Go on. From what you say about that letter, you're worth more dead than alive anyway. Nobody knows me. If Dickson shot me, who'd care?"

Lee sat there on the bed. "Yes," he said feebly.

"It's only fifteen feet," Buford said. "I fell out of a barn once. Only broke my arm. You're young."

Lee sat still, hunched on the bed. "He'll kill me."

"You deserve killing," Buford said. "Go on and jump."

"My two little daughters," Lee said. "Who's going to take care of them?"

"Go on and jump, son. It'll do you a world of good. Teach you how unimportant you are."

Lee looked at him miserably.

Heavy feet came up the stairs, the door was unlocked, and Irving came in with a shotgun in one hand.

"Party's going to begin soon," Irving said, slamming the door and setting a chair against it. He sat down with the shotgun across his knees and smiled broadly. "Boss said to me, if they make a sound, just shoot off their goddam heads. Never mind the goddam noise, he says. Just blast away, and I'll say it was the ammunition caught fire in the stove." Irving's grin widened mightily.

"Why all the blasphemy?" Buford asked. "Kindly keep your damn dirty mouth shut while in here with your betters."

The grin fell like a wet towel.

"The first rule of them all is not to use the name of God in vain, you dumb-looking son of a bitch," Buford said. "He didn't say anything about just plain vulgarity, so I can call you a dumb son of a bitch as long as I want."

"Why you damned old crow, I'll—"

"Shut up," Buford screeched in sudden fury. "You big damn slob of a backwoods farmer, put down that gun and fight me." He grabbed up a chunk of wood and shook it at Irving. "I'll beat in your head, you flea-ridden bastard." He was shaking with rage and frustration.

Suddenly Irving burst into a roar of laughter. He laughed out one long breath, and then Dickson's voice said from down the stairs, "Kindly shut up. All of you. Immediately."

Silence fell.

After a while, Lee got up slowly and wandered over to the window.

"Get away from there," Irving whispered harshly. "Boss says no shouting at the people. Get back on the bed or I'll blow your—" He glanced at Buford. "I'll blow your damn lousy guts out," he finished.

"You're learning, stupid," Buford said quietly, with a gentle, infuriating smile. "The fear of the Lord is the beginning of wisdom. For such a clod-faced bastard as you, you're pretty smart.

"When I was a boy," Buford said quietly to Lee, "the first time I dived, I just ran and held my nose and shut my eyes. It was noisy and sloppy, but it got me in the water."

Lee dropped his head. "Yes," he said. "I know. Just don't badger me. I know."

Irving spat on the floor.

It was then noon.

At three o'clock Buford heard Tucker's voice in the street and jumped to his feet. Irving raised the shotgun at him. He stood silent. Dickson was talking to Tucker in the street below.

Dickson said pleasantly, "Why, they went hunting, Tucker, old man. Jolly good to have you here; fine thing, right on schedule."

"Never mind all that," Tucker said. "You send a man and bring Buford back. In a hell of a hurry, too, buster."

"I will," Dickson said. "And Buford and I will ride down there. Just as soon as they come back. I know Buford'll want to look at the cattle."

"I got twelve men," Tucker said. "I'm ready for anything, Dickson. Buford had better show up quick and Mike with him. You understand?"

"Don't worry," Dickson said. "We'll be there. I'll send somebody out to find him right now. Where are you camped?"

"Half a mile south, down on that big meadow by the creek. Hell, you can't miss six thousand head of cattle. And you'd better not fail."

Tucker turned his horse and loped off down the street.

At four o'clock, Dickson came up the stairs and knocked on the door. Irving got up and opened it. Dickson, not entering, said, "I just got a message, Irving. Montrose'll be down at seven o'clock. Come on. I need you in the hardware store. I'll keep a watch on these two from downstairs."

They went out and locked the door.

"Seven," Buford said. "We got till five, Lee."

"You heard him," Lee said. "He said he was going

to keep a watch from downstairs. Whoever jumps is going to get killed right there in the street."

"Why don't you ever learn?" Buford asked. "If you're going to do it, do it now. Every time you wait, something happens, like Irving coming up here, and then it's too late. I'll give you till six to jump, and then I'll do it. I can't do much good, nobody knows me. But at least I'll try."

"All right," Lee said wretchedly. "All right. Just leave me alone, will you? I'll do it."

CHAPTER EIGHTEEN

Buford's Prison—Dusk

At about six o'clock, with the last streaks of the bleak winter sunlight coming through the window, Lee stood up straight from the bed and cried out, "Oh, Christ, oh, Christ!"

He let out another cry, without words, just a wail of hopeless beseeching, and ran to the window. He had intended to make it a heroic dive evidently, but as he neared it, he quailed. He jerked up the lower sash and put his leg over the sill, and then, holding to the sill with both hands, put the other over. He let himself down outside as far as he could, and then shouted, "Bolt! Bolt!"

It was the worst possible time of day for him to have done this, just as six-thirty in the morning had been the worst possible time for him to confess to Bolt in the first place. Almost everybody in Warhorse was home eating supper. There was one woman walking down the street. She stopped and looked at Lee hanging from the window. Her mouth opened and she screamed timidly, and ran for her life.

Lee dropped. He cried out sharply.

Buford ran to the window.

"Bolt! Bolt!" Lee shouted, trying to raise his wail of pain to some volume. He was hobbling away up the street, hunching along, dragging one foot, hopping on the good one, and then, with cries of pain, dragging the other. He fell and began scuttling on all fours. There was nobody in the street at all.

A door slammed below Buford. He saw Dickson come out with a rifle. Dickson raised the rifle. The shot cracked in the empty street and Lee fell on his face. He rolled over and lay there, twenty yards from Bolt's office, and rolled back and forth. Dickson aimed carefully again, and fired. Lee lay still. His upraised hands flopped down onto the roadway.

Bolt came running around a corner out of an alley. He had a sandwich in one hand, and a pistol in the other. He stood looking at Lee, and then at Dickson. Dickson ran up the street toward him, carrying the rifle.

"The damned thief!" Dickson shouted. "Sheriff, arrest him!"

The Sheriff did not move. Dickson reached the body. He looked up from it to Bolt, and as the two looked at each other, the Sheriff's eyes expressing nothing, Dickson's rifle came up and covered him. Bolt had been totally perplexed by the spectacle of the dead Lee and Dickson with the rifle. He didn't like Dickson, but that didn't mean anything. It was only when he looked at Dickson's eyes that he realized something completely foul was in the air, and then it was too late.

"Drop that pistol," Dickson said.

Bolt looked at the black end of the rifle bore. There was nothing he could do. He knew perfectly well, from Dickson's eyes, that he would shoot, and he wondered why he didn't. He dropped his gun.

Bolt remembered the letter. Suddenly a dogged anger came up in him. He looked once at Dickson, and then turned his back on Dickson and walked back to his office, his sandwich still in his hand. Dickson ran after him.

As Dickson ran into the office, Bolt was opening the letter.

"Drop that!" Dickson shouted desperately.

Bolt read on. When he was finished, he put the telegram in his pocket.

"Give me that," Dickson said.

"No," Bolt said. He didn't understand why Dickson didn't shoot him, and he was waiting for the bullet.

Dickson looked around desperately. In one blow, his edifice of lies had fallen. He was known. And yet it had been so sudden that he was still caught in the lying. He still had the habit of depending on lies. The problem was to get the Sheriff out of sight.

Bolt made a sudden dive for him. Dickson shot wildly and, dodging, evaded Bolt, and as Bolt fell and slid on the floor, Dickson clubbed him on the back of the head.

Bolt lay moving feebly and groaning. Dickson got the telegram out of his pocket.

"Get up or I'll kill you," Dickson said, prodding with the rifle. "Walk. To the Station House."

The Sheriff got up and staggered out of the office, Dickson behind him.

Bolt walked straight ahead.

"Hurry," Dickson said, his voice shaking. His one hope was to cover things up. Killing the Sheriff was one thing that he could not distort.

Dickson forced him into the Station House and up the stairs to Buford's room. He slammed the door on them and locked it.

He stood on the stairs where they could hear him mumbling. "My God, my God," he kept saying. Then he ran down the stairs shouting for Harris. It had occurred to Dickson in that moment that the worst might come to the worst. A wise man always kept a line of retreat open. A saddled horse was worth a million dollars at certain times.

Buford and Bolt looked at each other.

"You're the Sheriff?" Buford asked. "Montrose is coming into town. That bastard is ambushing him."

"Why didn't he kill me? I caught him red-handed in a murder. Jesus, now I see everything. Jesus, what fools we've been."

"You ain't any bigger fool than me," Buford said. "I've been trying to get out of this room all day, and I just saw the answer right in front of my face. Look there by the wall."

The last flare of sun died, and the shadows began to creep up the street. Men were calling to each other, asking questions about Lee's body lying in the street.

"There ain't a damn one of them knows the truth but me," Bolt said. "If Montrose comes into town, they'll gang up on him. Jesus, what a pack of fools."

"Get out of my way," Buford said, and set the chair against the door. "I guess the ball has opened."

He opened three one-pound cans of black powder and set them on the seat of the chair against the door and then poured loose powder out of a fourth around them. He brought four heavy pieces of wood from the woodpile and stacked them over the powder, to direct the force of the blast against the panel.

"For God's sake," Bolt said, "for God's sake."

"Upend that bed and lie down behind it," Buford said. "Open the windows to let out the blast."

"You'll blow the whole place up," Bolt cried.

"What of it?" Buford answered, busily smashing

out the windows. "If I had a little more powder, I'd blow up the whole goddam town."

He went to the fire, shoveled out a panful of coals, and carried them to the chair by the door. He dropped the coals into the wood, and ran.

Mike and Montrose, with their four men and a small wagon loaded with hay, came into Warhorse through back lots. They had left the road outside of town as a precaution against ambush. The wagon bumped and heaved over stumps and rocks, but it got through. They were carrying eight one-gallon cans of kerosene and had two torches, unlighted—sticks wrapped with old cloth, wired on, and soaked in the oil. They were all heavily armed, carrying two pistols apiece and one rifle each.

"Here's the orders," Montrose said as they dismounted in the dusk. "Mike, you go down to the south end of town and ride up the main street and draw their fire as we planned. I'll wager there's eight of them in town now, and that means you two boys will have to work fast. Remember, they'll be in a crowd somewhere, waiting for the showdown, because Dickson will have to figure we might have got through, or scared off, or might even bring the attack on him. So he'll have posted his men somewhere to meet us, on the chance. We've got to find out where, in order to work our plan, and all we can do is draw their fire. Mike, don't ride down that street too damn fast. You've got to give them a chance to shoot at you. Keep low, and don't give them time to aim, and you'll get through all right.

"You two boys," the General said to the gun fighters, "keep in the alleys till you see where the gunfire is coming from, after Mike rides through. Run around to the back and fire the back entrance of their place and when they get burned out the front, Joe and I and Mike will catch them coming out into the street. Joe will have the hay burning in the street to give us light to shoot by. We'll cut down the odds right away.

"We'll kill as many as we can, and meet in the church and then run for the woods. You got it? The object is not to fight a battle, but to hit and run. Reduce the odds. Tomorrow we can hit them again. But now's our big chance. So long, boys."

He turned his horse and headed up the street toward the north end of town.

The two gun fighters and Montrose's third hand went off into the dark, carrying their cans of kerosene and torches. Joe headed the wagon south, Mike riding alongside.

In the Station House, Buford and the Sheriff lay behind the bed, holding on to themselves.

Just as Buford was getting ready to get up and dump some more coals on the powder, the place blew up.

All they knew was a terrible blast, and then they found themselves coming out of a stupor into a blinding, whirling hell of sulfur smoke and heat. Buford saw a flame through the smoke. The twenty-five-pound keg had gone off, too, from the concussion. The door was blown out. The room was burning.

They staggered up and pawed through the smoke to the door.

The Sheriff kicked the burning wreckage of paneling out of the way and half-fell down the stairs. He ran out shouting. Buford tried to kick out the fire, and then ran down after him.

He saw the weapons on the wall and grabbed down an old saber. The remains of the burning paneling fell down the stairs behind him, coals and embers rolling across the room. He dashed for the door.

At the south end of the street, Mike pulled up and sat in the shadow of a house. Joe drove the hay wagon out into the roadway. He had the lantern in his hand.

"So long, boy," Mike said as Joe slapped the reins.

"So long, son," Joe said, and the wagon creaked off.

Up the street there was the roar of the explosion. The flash shot out from the second story of the Station House, and then the dark jumped back again. Joe's horse reared. Joe beat it down and raised his rifle, ready.

"Go on," Mike said. "Never mind all that. Follow the orders."

Joe slapped the horse up again, and Mike sat forward in the saddle. The one problem he had was whether to run straight up the street, or to identify himself in some way.

He began to say his prayers. They all came back out of nowhere at once, all the ones he had learned as a child, in school, from his mother.

The smell of black powder came down the street, and then he saw his father, walking unsteadily toward him in the gloom of the winter evening. The old man's clothes were smoking, and his face and arms were black with burned powder. The flames shot out of the Station House roof and the red light glowed around on the trees.

"Dad," Mike shouted, and spurred his horse out into the road.

"Jesus, son, get out of here," Buford said, stumbling up. "They're all laying for you and Montrose."

"Where?" Mike asked.

"I don't know."

"I've got to draw their fire so my boys can locate them," Mike said. "Then they'll take them from the rear."

"Mike, wait. Tucker's camped south of town. I'm going to get him. Don't ride down that street, boy. You'll be killed for sure. Oh, God, where's a horse?"

"I can't wait," Mike said, pointing at Joe's wagon, trundling up the street toward the church at the north end of town. "It's too late to change the plans now."

Hoofs were beating up the street from the direction of the railroad station.

"It's the other ambush," Buford said. "Give me one of those guns, boy; I got to get me a horse."

Three riders came up the road, and at the same time, light streamed down the street, and they saw the wagon load of hay go up in flame. The loose horse ran up the street, dragging tugs and lines, and they saw Joe scuttling for an alley. The bright flame spread everywhere, towering fifteen feet. Mike handed his father a pistol.

The three riders came on fast, the flame-light shining on bits and leather, and Buford fired. Mike put two shots into them. They slowed up, panic-stricken from the gunfire in their faces. Two of them turned and ran back down the road, and Buford had the bridle of the third, and was shooting straight into the rider's face. The rider toppled out of the saddle, and Buford climbed up. He sat there for a moment, waving his saber at his son, laughing, with the red flame firing his white beard and hair. He turned the horse and beat it into a run with the flat of the saber.

CHAPTER NINETEEN

In the Town—Evening

Mike bent over his horse's neck and put it into an easy lope, keeping it well gathered up and rolling. He headed for the burning wagon, keeping to the right, and forty yards from it he let out a yell that sounded all the way to the church. He put his spurs to the horse and let it out, and it lunged forward, passing the burning Station House at a dead run.

At the same time, gunfire burst from one of the dark buildings and bullets snapped above and behind him. He spurred the horse into a second line of fire, a second volley pouring at him, and as he passed, the horse died on its feet, shot in the neck.

Falling, it slid on its breast for fifteen yards, sending Mike flying through the air another ten beyond. Mike scrambled up and ran on with the bullets snapping at his heels.

He made the door of the church just as the ambush party from the north road galloped into town. They saw him dash into the building, and opened fire.

Montrose was lying on the floor in the doorway. He opened fire on the three men in the party, and they broke and ran for cover, smashing into the two closest stores. They began to fire back into the church doorway, and Mike dragged one of the heavy benches into the doorway for cover.

"Take a window and keep moving," the General said, rising and running to one of the small panes on each side of the door.

Some men were coming from the hardware store, and then flames began to jump up from the back of the library. There was shooting down the street, from behind the buildings.

"They'll be coming out," the General said. "Where in hell is Joe?" He was ignoring the firing from the two nearest stores.

A man ran out of the hardware, and then another, into the light of the burning wagon. Then two out of the library.

"Take the hardware," the General said, and fired. Mike shot at the first one on his side of the wagon. A man on each side dropped into the street. The others stood still, turning, looking for the firing. Mike and the General fired again. The General's man dropped and began crawling away, and Mike's ran down an alley.

A bullet from the near stores smacked through the wall and caught the General in the leg. He fell to the floor and cursed.

Somebody came in the back of the church. "It's me!" Joe hollered. "The bastards chased me all the way here; they're in the woods, two of them. Mike, you hold that door, I'll cover this one."

The firing fell off, except in the rear, where a rifle kept up steadily.

Mike moved over to the General's window. "Damn the luck," the General groaned, "we can't run now. They'll rush us."

"You bleeding much?"

"Hell, no. It's not much of a hole." The General dragged himself to the doorway.

Suddenly a long flame poured up the side of the church, showing in through the side window.

"They're all around us," the General said. "They'll burn us out."

The firing began again from the near stores, hard and steady, and Mike saw men running out of the doors under cover of it, heading for the sides of the church.

"They'll be shooting in through the windows," the General said. "You run, Mike. I'll kill a few."

Four stores, besides the library and the hardware, were burning now, as well as the church and the Station House. The street was brighter than day and hot as summer.

Down the street men and women were hurrying with buckets and washtubs, trying to save the rest of the stores. The sparks were flying high, coals falling on all the roofs.

The rush started, men pouring in on the front door from both sides. The General was firing fast into the huddle. The rush fell back, and then it came on again. Mike slammed the doors shut and shot the bolt.

Outside some of Dickson's men were shooting in through the walls. Mike and the General dropped to the floor. The gang in the street had got a beam from somewhere, and they began to ram into the doors. At the second blow, the end of the beam came through the panel, and Mike fired through the hole, driving them away from the ram.

From down the street a hammer of hoofs grew, and outside, the crowd of men began to shout, and the firing rose hotter, but it was away from the church. Mike ran to one of the windows. Dickson's men were flying from the porch and Tucker's gang was whirling and wheeling in the street, men jumping and running for cover, firing as they ran, Tucker in the middle, shouting. Tucker with a pistol charged his horse straight into one of the bunches of men beside the church, and back through it. Mike saw his father run his horse back past the church, his old saber raised, his teeth grinning in his beard.

The Sheriff and Lewin joined Tucker's men, who were dismounting and running for cover. Curtis was down the street running out of the bank with boxes of papers. Back under one of the store porches, well protected, Dickson was shouting at his men, firing a pistol. He shot Tucker out of his saddle, and Tucker rolled and ran out of the way of the loose horses. The horses ran down the street, neighing in panic, and the firefighting citizens scattered before them, and came back, shrieking and weeping and shouting and cursing each other while the flames roared steadily.

Out in back, Buford ran his horse through the brush and the trees, where the two rifles were spitting at the back door of the church. He ran down one of the men, breaking his arm with the saber, and the other rose out of the brush and ran for safety. Buford ran the horse straight over him, wheeled, and rode back to the church. He ran inside.

The old man was crazy with delight, his eyes danced. "Oh, Jesus!" he shouted. "Come on, Mike, get the General out of here before he gets fried."

He grabbed the General under the arms, and Mike took him by the feet, and they ran out of the door and down the steps, into the shadows behind one of the stores.

Buford looked up and saw Dickson down the street, in the act of shooting at one of Tucker's men. Buford fired and ran toward him, and Dickson turned.

Dickson fired back at Buford, and Buford ran on, shooting. Dickson's gun snapped empty. At twenty feet he hurled the empty pistol at Buford. It caught

the old man square in the forehead and he went
down, stunned. Dickson ran away toward the Station
House. He saw Spence run into the Station House
ahead of him.

In the Station House, the whole bar was burning,
and the smoke was too thick for Dickson to stand
upright. He ran in, panting, and got a fresh gun from
his office.

The fire was climbing up the banisters and eating
already at the treads. Smoke poured up the well and
through the open bedroom doorway.

He heard Spence cursing furiously above the roar
and snapping of the fire.

Dickson leaped up the burning stairs and into the
bedroom. Spence was just coming out of the closet,
his clothes scorched and his eyes streaming from the
smoke and heat. The locks had been shot out. He
held the suitcase in both arms. One end of it was
badly burned and partly burned bills were slipping
out. He held a gun awkwardly in his right hand.

"Where are you going with that?" Dickson asked
sharply.

Spence said nothing for a moment. The two men
stood staring at each other.

"I thought," Spence said, "things were going
wrong. I thought I'd better—"

"You thought you'd beat me to it," Dickson said.
"You lying son of a bitch, I should have known what
you were waiting for."

Spence dropped the suitcase and raised his gun at
the same time, but Dickson fired first. He fired again,
and Spence dropped where he stood, his hands over
his belly, groaning. His hair caught fire from the
smoking cracks in the floor and he screamed. Dickson stooped and tried to beat the flames of the suitcase out with his hands. He grabbed it up and ran.
The whole room was on fire.

A small shower of money fell out on the staircase,

and at that instant, Dickson's hair also caught fire. He, too, screamed.

He turned and ran down the stairway, holding the burning suitcase under one arm, beating at his burning head with the other. Halfway down, his leg went through a burned tread and he tumbled the rest of the way down, wrenching his knee badly, the suitcase rolling ahead of him out into the big room.

In the middle of the room, the suitcase fell open and the money poured out, bundles tumbling over each other, burned ribbons breaking, bills sliding in heaps. Dickson made it to the suitcase, his burned, bald, red head oozing water, and his face twisted in a grimace of agony.

He grabbed up the little sacks of diamonds, stuffing them frantically into his pockets. It was almost impossible to breathe with the heat and smoke scorching his lungs. He had to crawl close to the floor.

A ceiling joist fell behind him. He jumped up and ran for the back door, and just as he reached it, another beam fell flaming before him, and he fell over it.

He scrambled to the burning doorway, then got out into the air. He ran on down the slope toward the barn, where Harris had saddled three horses. Half blinded by the smoke and heat, he ran into one of the cottonwood trees, and stood there peering around, his clothes smoking and glowing like tinder. He stumbled on into the dark, away from the fire.

Buford burst into the burning barroom of the Station House just as Dickson went out the back. He charged in, his arms over his head, jumping over the fallen beam, and saw the suitcase standing in the middle of the floor with the burning money around it.

With a cry of horror he fell on his hands and knees, choking with smoke, his eyes streaming, and frantically clutched for the bills. He grabbed handfuls of

money and stuffed bills wildly into his pockets; more
handfuls he stuffed into the front of his shirt, burning himself in frantic haste. His fingers burned from
the flaming bills, and he uttered shriek after shriek
of pain, and yet still he fought to get more and more.

He stood up finally, clutching money to his breast
like leaves, burning francs, pounds, dollars, rubles,
every kind in fringes of flame, charred and un-
charred, the bills dribbling from his arms in show-
ers.

He staggered forward. Beams crashed about him.
In a burst of panic he ran for the back door. The
whole second floor came down behind him, and he
fell on his face outside in the open air, the money
flying in all directions. He got to his knees, trying to
beat out his flaming clothes and the flaming money
at the same time.

He heard a shot. Down the slope, Dickson stood in
the dark with the flaming house at his back, his
burned, bald head making him cry out. His knee
buckled under him as the panic of the fire left him,
the wrench too bad to stand. He sat down on the
ground twenty feet from the corral fence, the pistol
in one hand, his handkerchief in the other, barely
sixty yards from the waiting horses.

"Harris!" he shouted, looking wildly about. The
streams of tears from the smoke and burns were
slacking a little. He saw Harris's vague shape climbing the fence.

Harris ran up and stood over him, the red of the
fire flickering on his black face, pink on the whites
of his eyes.

"Where's the money?" Harris asked.

Dickson saw the knife in his hand and swung the
pistol toward him. At the same time, Harris swung
down the knife, driving at Dickson's chest. The knife
caught Dickson in the shoulder as he dodged, and
Dickson shot Harris square in the face. Harris fell

without a sound and Dickson struggled to his feet. He limped toward the fence.

Down the slope, Buford saw Dickson stagger toward the corral fence, and then he saw the horses beyond it.

With a hoarse shout, Buford got up, raising his gun. Dickson was awkwardly climbing the fence. He turned at Buford's shout, saw him outlined against the fire of the house, and, standing with his feet on one pole, his knees balancing him against the top rail, he fired back.

The bullet cracked past Buford's head, and Buford rubbed the smoke tears out of his eyes. He aimed with all the coolness he could manage, and squeezed off carefully.

Dickson cried out sharply. For a moment he stood there, and then he fell backward, arms whirling to save himself, on the other side of the fence.

Buford ran after him, gun ready, bills falling out of his clothing as he hurried.

From beyond the corral fence a scream rose, a single, throat-tearing shriek of agony and fear, rising straight into the night. Buford stopped, frozen with horror at the sound.

It rose again, dizzying Buford for a moment, and then he ran forward again.

Dickson lay on his back in the pigpen. In his panic, his eyes still smarting, and bewildered by the dark after the fire, Dickson had climbed the wrong part of the fence. He lay on his back thrashing and kicking wildly while the pigs attacked him, squealing and grunting with fury.

Buford in a panic of terrible haste fired through the fence. He killed one pig, and then another, and then the gun snapped empty. He threw the gun furiously at the nearest pig, and looked around desperately for something to drive them off with. He found

Dickson's spiked stick, and jabbed futilely at the nearest pig with it, but it paid it no attention.

The horrible screams of despair, agony, and fear rose more and more weakly and finally ceased, as Buford, numb with horror, helplessly watched. It was too much for him. He fell to his knees, exhaustion overtaking him as the screams died. There was no sound left now but the snuffling and grunting of the pigs as they rummaged and gorged. Buford covered his face with his hands, and still he could see it, the horrible, mangled wreckage of what had been Dickson.

He vomited, kneeling there with Dickson's money sticking out of his pockets and out of his shirt, money he had owed, stolen, and fought over. And there was the man he had shot, whom he had tried to kill, and now, suddenly, all the hatred, misery, fear, and desperation Dickson had caused him was gone, wiped out in an instant, gone in the horror of what had happened to his enemy.

He knelt there, padded with Dickson's money, stupefied under the shock of his death, and he remembered his father's face for the second time. Suddenly the money felt like a great load of the most disgusting filth, as though there were toads and leeches clinging to him, sucking his blood, and it seemed to him that all these bills were covered with other people's blood and crimes.

He began to pull it out of his pockets and let it fall to the ground, shaking it free of his fingers. He pulled the stinking bills out of his shirt until he was free of it all, and it lay in the dirt beside the mire of the pigpen.

He could see his father talking to the people now, his mouth forming inaudible words. He was talking about love, and Buford remembered it now. He had always been talking about love, that was all. Telling the people about love, about the love of God for them, and the love they should have had for each other.

That was all he had ever talked about, and he had died of it, starved because he was too busy preaching on the circuit to stop and hunt. That was all he had said, what Buford had never wanted to hear: that love was all any man could ever get, and ever give. That there was nothing else to be had, in the end; that love was everything, and that all the rest was shadows.

Buford stood up. He opened his eyes and looked at his enemy in the slime—hardly even a man any longer, a poor, pitiful shape of bloody bones, helpless in the mire, slowly sinking, as the beasts gnawed and crunched, slowly disappearing, with all Dickson's fortune, in eighteen inches of muck.

Buford went down to the creek and, sitting on the edge, washed his hands in the icy water. He took off his shoes, and washed his feet, and then washed his face and his beard, and then his bare chest, and when he was through with that, he wandered quietly back along the barn, no longer even hearing the pigs, not even noticing the money. He stopped by the barn and looked at the fire. The heat of it spread all the way to the creek, making the winter night comfortable, and he listened. He noticed that it was snowing again, the tiny flakes coming down soft this time, and slow.

Up in the town, the shooting had died. Dickson's men had scattered with a pounding of hoofs, flying like dark bats in all directions.

Women, weeping and some of them hysterical, men talking in a daze, wandered about as though lost. The whole town had burned, except the houses off the main street. There was nothing left of Warhorse except two long lines of hot coals and naked chimneys, stoves standing alone or overturned. As it snowed, the people instinctively held their hands out to the warm coals of their possessions even while they cursed and wailed.

Buford stood alone and watched them, from within the shadows of the cottonwood trees. He quietly regarded one simple fact: All this ruin, desolation, and death was one man's fault.

His.

CHAPTER TWENTY

Montrose's House
October 23—Noon

The one thing he had come to Warhorse to find, Buford thought, he had not even seen: Clara Montrose's grave. He sat at the long table in the main room of the General's house, drinking a cup of fresh coffee. He was going to leave now, and he could not go without seeing it, and yet he couldn't even ask where it was. Not any more.

"Three thousand head go to you, General," he said. "For God's sake, sell them and give the money to the people in Warhorse. Just to keep them off my trail. Tucker told me how bad the feeling is."

Buford looked at his son, sitting on the other side of the table, and at Clara beside him. He pulled two bills of sale out of his pocket. "The other three thousand go to Mike and Clara. I won't want any cows in San Antonio. Give me two dollars, Mike." He shoved the bills of sale across the table. "I'll take two bucks, and two horses as well, and I'll ask you to pay off Tucker when he gets well, and all our men. You and Clara keep the rest, with my blessing."

"You'd better wait until we can sell part of the herds," Mike said. "You can't go home broke."

"I don't want any of the dirty money," Buford said. He had seen it burning by the handful, like leaves. He sat remembering Dickson's death, and the smell of the mire of the pigpen, and the feel of the money in his hands.

Mike rolled two silver dollars across the table. Buford got up and stood looking at Mike and Clara. "Come and see your mother. After you get married."

Mike nodded.

"I wish—I wish—" Buford said, looking down at Mike. "I wish that all these years—when we were together—I could have been—"

He stopped. How could he say it? The past was all gone and it could never be changed now. It was lost for good.

He went over to Mike and kissed him on the cheek. He turned and went out on the porch, with his two dollars clinking in his pants.

Mike came out after him, because he did not want to sit there, the way he felt.

He watched the old man go down the steps, and then followed him. He held the old man's horse while he mounted. "Dad. Don't think I ever looked down on you. I never did, I never will. If you want me—I'll always be here."

The old man looked at him, and Mike saw his smile. "I know, Mike," he said. "I always loved you, too."

He turned his horse and went away down the road, with the packhorse following.

He rode on down the canyon, letting his horse amble, loose-jointed, the packhorse moseying along behind.

He sat slumped in the saddle, his knees open, and as he looked down at the greasy, cracked old reins in his left hand, and at the worn leather of the pommel, and felt the loneliness beside him where Mike had been for so long, he wanted to stop and die.

To move on, into that gaunt world before him, so wide, so empty, made him cringe inside himself, huddling back. It was a motion that made no sense, this aimless drifting forward into nothing.

Buford, helplessly gripped by the terrible fatigue in himself, the exhaustion in the face of his futile future, pulled up the gray horse and sat there, his eyes shut. He was out of sight of the house, and the brave front he had made, the erectness of spine he had maintained, all crumbled. Out of sight, need he be brave? Everything in him, his heart, his memories, his habits of cheerfulness and optimism, cried out to go back up the road, to stay with his people, to see his grandchildren. And yet it was impossible. He had destroyed their town.

Where was her grave? Surely there was one good thing left, surely he would feel again the happiness of her presence, in some way. He could hear her voice in his mind now, and feel the lift, the happy peacefulness it had always given him.

He picked up the reins and the gray horse wandered on down the ruts. Trees and granite passed, and as he emerged from the wall of the mountains, the growing distance behind him made a quieting of all his feelings. The sky, limited till now to a wide V between the mountain spurs beside him, opened out, and the whole expanse of the country lay before him.

A dry, cold wind, bitter off the snow, blew down the canyon, and whirling around the granite escarpments above him, beat at him in gusts. Far below him the icy water of the creek washed and rattled over the boulders, and there was nothing around him but cold, silence, and loneliness.

Home! Home! he thought. *If I could go home, if I had a home—if there were one place in the whole world where there was a fire waiting, and food, and a roof which was mine; where there was even a dog to wag his tail at me and pant a welcome; how much I would give for that much of peace, a simple place, somewhere in this hideous wilderness.*

Suddenly he saw, off to his left, on a brow of the mountain which bore three pine trees, a little fence enclosing a square of ground about twenty feet to the side. Immediately he knew what it was, and pulled up.

He sat looking at it, forgetting everything he had been thinking and feeling. A kind of hope, a distinct sensation of love, came up in him, like new life.

That was it, that was the thing he had come so far to get.

He almost laughed to himself—destitute, on a charity horse, beaten, broke, and futureless, he was seeing for the first time what had brought him to this end.

He left the road and guided the gray over to the little fence. The bare, dead grass waved in the chill wind, the ungrazed stalks rising high and shining in the sun out of the inch of snow that was already melting. There was a plain headboard on the one grave. That was all.

Clara Montrose.

He got down from the gray and went over to the headboard, feeling that remarkable alertness and expectation.

Under the pine trees, the deep bed of needles had caught the snow, and the grave was quite bare. Somebody had hoed it, during the summer, to keep the weeds off.

There it was. What else had he expected? A simple, bare, clean grave, quite smooth on top, about six feet long, as usual; no different from any other grave.

He knelt down beside it, not out of any reverence, but simply to be closer to it, to see it in more detail.

What was there? The icy wind cut down off the cliffs through the pines. A patch of bright sun struck down on the bare ground. No sound, but the soft breathing of the air in the pine needles above him.

All the bright expectancy, the actual, physical emotion of love burned in him, like a light held through a long night.

What had he expected?

He put his hands down on the earth of the grave and brushed the dirt. There was nothing—just damp earth, a few twigs and needles. A momentary seizure of anguish came over his mind and lifted like a hand again. A voice in him cried out, *Are you there? Are you there?* exactly as to a living person—as though she herself had been waiting, somehow alive, for all of death, in that place.

Why don't you answer?

How many years he had dreamed of this, the comfort, the happiness of being with her, in some mysterious sense, as though he and she could talk across death in some mysterious, but quite real fashion.

And he had never once questioned his dreams! Not once. Always there had been the illusion of the possibility of somehow feeling her presence again, in some way.

And there was nothing here but dirt. And down below, just bones. The bones of a body that she had left. Not a thousand miles below, or a thousand feet, not at some extravagant distance which would have left him the seed of another illusion—but merely six poor feet below, so close, indeed, that it was horrible.

And that was death—a simple departure. Oh, how the earth stared back at him, that blank, bare space of dirt, with what cold vacancy. He dug his fingers into the dirt, scratching it, as though indeed it did conceal something, somewhere; but there was nothing in his hands but dirt, the same simple black stuff that he could have found anywhere. He dug them in again, and held his dirty hands up in front of him, and there he knelt, with nothing in his hands but dirt, as he had knelt by the place where Dickson died, with nothing in his hands but burned paper, a uselessness of filth.

He stood up, his mind vacant and quiet. The wind blew about him, clean and fresh. He looked down at the grave again—it was still vacant. It meant nothing to him. And then he looked out across all that vast country, seeing it from high on the mountain; it, too, was empty. He imagined all the trails that he had followed, leading him to this place—the years of the war, the years after, years of struggle, by one means or another, to gain this one point, eventually, to be, as he thought, with her.

And all wasted. All of it gone, with nothing to show, and he was here at last, and it was nothing, nothing at all. And there had never been anything.

He had loved something, surely. The love was real enough. But if a man could love something that didn't even exist—And then he realized that what he had loved had really existed—the illusion had existed, that was all. The love was real enough. And yet, if it was real, why was it so lost? Why had he come all this way for nothing?

The hostility of the country bore down on him, like the chill of the wind. It would stand no loitering. There was no welcome on this earth for any man; wind and cold and hunger would drive him on from place to place as long as he could move, and in the end the silent, savage, relentless indifference of his enemy, the world, would drive the very soul out of his body.

And yet he loved.

He went, blown on by the wind. He picked up the reins of his horse, and led it and the pack animal back to the road. He stood there, unable to summon up the will even to climb back on the horse. He stood by the gray, the reins in his hands, head bowed, and slowly, because there was no other living thing at all, he leaned his forehead on the neck of the horse.

And then he realized with perfect simplicity that of course the peculiar quality of his own life was actually to be loving something; and then he saw, for the first time in his life, that everybody else was busy loving something, even Dickson—whether it was money, or card games, or women, or horseraces, or cats, or antique furniture, they were all blundering around after the objects of their various loves.

Then he thought, *It was not even Clara that I loved. There was nothing actually in her that I loved, but something about her that I thought was there—something I read into her, just as I imagined that there was something in Mary that I loved, only that was not quite so great an illusion. Clara simply suggested something to me that was lovable; it was not herself, for she was not particularly good, or intelligent, and so on. And no doubt that was why I got drunk— because I knew in my heart it was an illusion.*

Ah, yes, he thought, *I wanted the illusion.* And then he saw the truth of it—that he wanted to love, but he had never found anything good enough to love except an illusion. And if this was so, then why did anybody love anything? Why had God put it in his heart, why did it exist at all, for what purpose?

He began to think that he saw the answer. But the actual thought that came into his mind was quite different. It came suddenly, as a realization that he had no friends in San Antonio, and no future. He couldn't start in business again there, for everybody who had trusted him had lost money on him. True, he owed nobody, since they had all settled with Dickson for his notes, and Dickson had died. But still, they would not receive him again.

Suppose I go back? he thought.

Why shouldn't people despise me?

Isn't it just?

Don't I see the justice of it in myself? Is there anything else that I have a right to, except being despised? For if I did all these evil things, then surely there can be no relief for me, until I have paid. And how can I pay now, except just to bow my head and take it? Surely, if I give up, if I bow, God will have mercy.

Why had he thought of that? Buford looked around quickly. He was not in the habit of such thoughts; and yet it had seemed most reasonable to him, and the idea of God's mercy had even brought tears to his eyes. But why was he thinking such things now? Well, what else? In the end, when everything else was lost, there was nothing left but God. In the end, all the vanquished turned to God, when the rods of fortune had beat them flat.

If I go home, Buford thought, looking up, looking far away, *if I go home and endure their spite, and their contempt, and their scorn, and endure the worst of all, their damnable kindness, I will have done the just thing.*

But he did not think of justice as an idea, he did not really think consciously at all. It was an ache in his bones, as though the marrow of his bones themselves ached and cried out for justice.

He began to think of another dream, and he watched it carefully, to see if it was an illusion. It was simply to live at peace, not attempting great things, not living over chasms, not inducing others to risk themselves; but simply to live in peace. And this meant to live fairly. And if he, for instance, heard of anyone who needed help, to help him, and so keep the scales balanced.

His heart began to brighten. He climbed laboriously back on the gray, and clucked to it, and they ambled on down the road.

He did not look back toward that grave. He was

thinking new thoughts, jumping ahead again, dreaming dreams. Who could tell what might happen? (when he had labored through the penance he had just begun)—Mary had five Mexican seamstresses. Without a doubt the pious ladies of San Antonio could be eased out of—or rather, persuaded to donate—sewing machines, used, or perhaps even new.

Your Excellency, he began, addressing the Archbishop in his imagination, *don't you see what this means? Production of cheap dresses for the poor, by the poor—very modest profits, so much for the other diocesan charities, so much for myself as manager—Good God, Your Excellency, a man must live, and a little to put by—ten sewing machines, your Excellency! It's all for the poor—am I not poor? And if, as St. Paul said, a servant is worthy of his hire, am I not your servant? And if, like Zaccheus, I give half of what I get to the poor, if I get more, will not the poor profit as much as I? Your Excellency, think of it! Twenty sewing machines!*

So he rode down, his white beard shining in the sun, his old eyes bright and alert, sparkling with thoughts and imaginations, ruminating plans and dreaming of rewards—but of a strange kind, for these rewards would be just.

The icy wind blew after him, blowing up dust and dirt over his back, but he rode along unaware of it, his mind turned inward. The wind tugged at his coat, flapping the tears in his clothing, tugging his beard, but he paid no attention.

The sun would burn him, the ice freeze him, the devils would rage and ridicule him. And why not? For he was nothing, now, but an animated old crate of bones, a burden of garbage, a comic, foolish, futile, weak, and pompous creature—still half drunk with pride, still full of illusions, stumbling, as a billion other human beings had stumbled, through the last contortions of a precarious existence.

But he was on the way, and he had a talisman. If he kept it, nothing could touch him or impair him or cause him, in the end, to be lost in that terrible darkness which he so much feared. Because, in his heart, in the midst of all the flapping wreckage of his life, there was, now, the beginning of a love, at last, of justice.

WESTERN ADVENTURE
FROM TOR

☐	58459-7	THE BAREFOOT BRIGADE	$4.50
☐	58460-0	*Douglas Jones*	Canada $5.50
☐	58150-4	BETWEEN THE WORLDS (Snowblind Moon Part I)	$3.95
☐	58151-2	*John Byrne Cooke*	Canada $4.95
☐	58991-2	THE CAPTIVES	$4.50
☐	58992-0	*Don Wright*	Canada $5.50
☐	58548-8	CONFLICT OF INTEREST	$3.95
☐		*Donald McRae*	Canada $4.95
☐	58457-0	ELKHORN TAVERN	$4.50
☐	58458-9	*Douglas Jones*	Canada $5.50
☐	58453-8	GONE THE DREAMS AND DANCING	$3.95
☐	58454-6	*Douglas Jones*	Canada $4.95
☐	58154-7	HOOP OF THE NATION (Snowblind Moon Part III)	$3.95
☐	58155-5	*John Byrne Cooke*	Canada $4.95
☐	58152-0	THE PIPE CARRIERS (Snowblind Moon Part II)	$3.95
☐	58153-9	*John Byrne Cooke*	Canada $4.95
☐	58455-4	ROMAN	$4.95
☐	58456-2	*Douglas Jones*	Canada $5.95
☐	58463-5	WEEDY ROUGH	$4.95
☐	58464-3	*Douglas Jones*	Canada $5.95
☐	58989-0	WOODSMAN	$3.95
☐	58990-4	*Don Wright*	Canada $4.95

Buy them at your local bookstore or use this handy coupon:
Clip and mail this page with your order.

Publishers Book and Audio Mailing Service
P.O. Box 120159, Staten Island, NY 10312-0004

Please send me the book(s) I have checked above. I am enclosing $ _____
(please add $1.25 for the first book, and $.25 for each additional book to cover postage and handling.
Send check or money order only—no CODs).

Name _____
Address _____
City _____ State/Zip _____
Please allow six weeks for delivery. Prices subject to change without notice.

SKYE'S WEST
BY RICHARD S. WHEELER

The thrilling saga of a man and the vast Montana wilderness...
SKYE'S WEST
by the author of the 1989 Spur Award-Winning novel *Fool's Coach*

"Among the new wave of western writers, Richard S. Wheeler is a standout performer."
—*El Paso Herald-Post*

WESTERN DOUBLES

☐	50529-8	AVALANCHE/THE KIDNAPPING OF ROSETA		$3.50
☐	50530-1	UVALDO	Grey	Canada $4.50
☐	50522-0	BATTLE'S END/THE THREE CROSSES	Brand	$3.50
☐	50523-9			Canada $4.50
☐	50538-7	CHIP CHAMPIONS A LADY/FORGOTTEN		$3.50
☐		TREASURE	Brand	Canada $4.50
☐	50542-5	LONE WOLF OF DRYGULCH TRAIL/		$3.50
☐		MORE PRECIOUS THAN GOLD	Drago	Canada $4.50
☐	50544-1	THE LONGRIDERS/THE HARD ONE	Prescott	$3.50
☐				Canada $4.50
☐	50540-9	LOOK BEHIND EVERY HILL/ THE		$3.50
☐		BIG TROUBLE	Frazee	Canada $4.50
☐	50536-8	PROSPECTOR'S GOLD/CANYON WALLS	Grey	$3.50
☐				Canada $4.50
☐	50532-8	RED BLIZZARD/THE OLDEST MAIDEN LADY		$3.50
☐		IN NEW MEXICO	Fisher	Canada $4.50
☐	50526-3	THE RIDERS OF CARNE COVE/THE LAST		$3.50
☐		COWMAN OF LOST SQUAW VALLEY	Overholser	Canada $4.50
☐	50524-7	SHARPSHOD/THEY CALLED HIM A KILLER	Patten	$3.50
☐				Canada $4.50
☐	50534-4	THAT BLOODY BOZEMAN TRAIL/STAGECOACH		$3.50
☐		WEST!	Bonham	Canada $4.50